BRUCE LEE BOND

HIPPIE
HILL

OR

HOW I SPENT MY VACATION

MONTAG

First Montag Press E-Book and Paperback Original Edition May 2018

Montag Press
ISBN: 978-1-940233-53-6
Front cover photo © Bruce Lee Bond, 1976
Back cover photo © Denise Guelld, 1973
Jacket design & interior formatting – Niall Gray
Editor - Mara Hodges
Managing Director – Charlie Franco

A Montag Press Book
www.montagpress.com
Montag Press
1066 47th Ave. Unit #9
Oakland CA 94601 USA

Printed & Digitally Originated in the United States of America
10 9 8 7 6 5 4 3 2 1

'...your magic carpet time travel trip through all the thrills and dangers of the 1970s! I hated coming down from this book.'

— Rebecca A. Goodrich, award-winning poet and author of

Emergency Rations: How One Young Tail Gunner Survived World

War Two

'A great story about adventures and love of two teen hippies. Bruce Lee Bond turns out to be a master wordsmith.'

— Marcin Dolecki, author of *Philosopher's Crystal*

Hippie Hill Or How I Spent My Vacation by Bruce Lee Bond is a trip in the absolute best sense of the word. A pure page turner, there is simply no lulls or slowdown in Bruce Bond's prose. I was completely taken in by this amazing story of young, summer love and was left both engrossed and fascinated by a culture that has so often been glazed over by superficial tales that barely scratch the surface. But in the case of *Hippie Hill Or How I Spent My Vacation* it does far more than scratch, it takes you deep beneath that surface.

— Jonathan R. Rose, author of *Carrion*

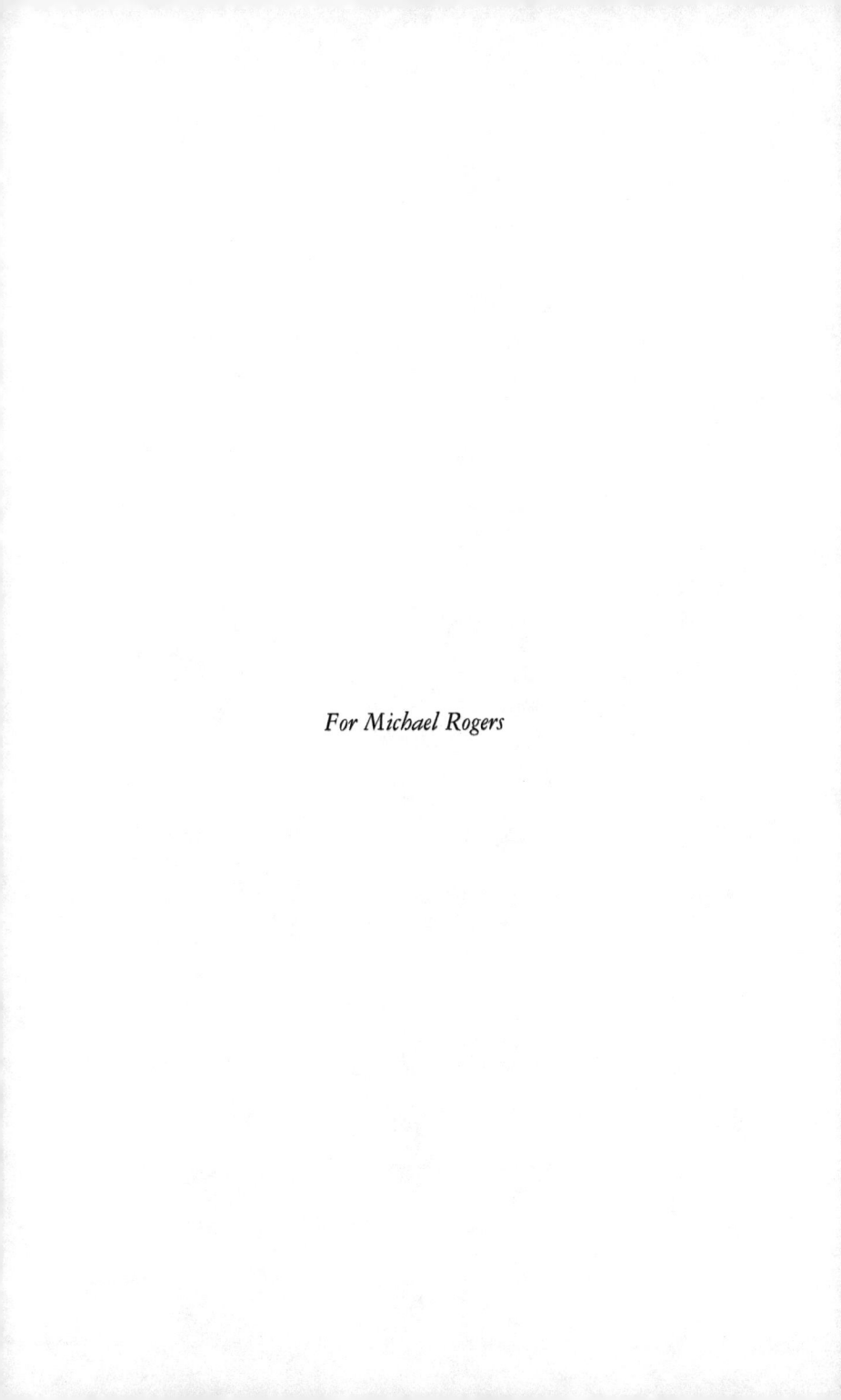

For Michael Rogers

This is a work of fiction. Any relation to persons living or dead is purely intentional.

I.

June

Mist rose from breakers where the big green island bowed to the water. Paul stared at the sea and kicked a pebble across the gravel street. There weren't many young people in Ucluelet. There weren't many people at all. His folks had dragged him north to this unpronounceable place to work on the inn they'd sunk his father's retirement into. His dad was getting edgy and hard to talk to, and his mom expected him to be around all the time — not that there was anywhere to go. Paul sighed. His seventeenth summer was turning into a total bummer.

A raven shouted at him from the twisted top of An ancient fir that along with a few misshapen cedars and hemlocks, had survived when the land had been logged. He flipped the raven his version of the bird as his thoughts returned to Susan Allen, the gorgeous redhead he'd planned to lose his virginity with in Coos Bay. She was spending the summer in Switzerland with her folks, probably drinking beer and dating some Germanic Olympian while he languished here, in purgatory.

A battered Fargo pickup, a Canadian Dodge, sputtered into town from the east and skidded to a halt at the lone stop sign. Paul sighed. He was about to toss another rock into a stagnant pool in the foundations of the old mill when he heard a girl shout, "Fuck you!"

He saw a pretty blonde about his age tugging furiously on the arm of her sweater as she tried to exit the vehicle, which was in the grasp of a big man behind the wheel of the truck.

"Hey!" Paul bolted toward them. The man turned to look at him, and the girl yanked free. "Leave her alone!" He caught a glimpse of her frightened blue eyes and hurled the rock at the cab. A loud report echoed off the façade of the town's gas station that didn't open on Sundays as a web of cracks appeared in the truck's rear window.

The big man let out a roar and threw open the driver's door.

"Oh shit!" Paul's stomach knotted and he stooped to snatch another rock as another truck appeared from the south end of town. The man cursed, slammed the door, and took off in a spray of gravel. Paul gave a shout of triumph and tossed the rock at the retreating vehicle. "Fuck you!"

He ran to the girl.

She tossed long blond hair from her face. "Thanks dude!" Paul skidded to a stop, nearly knocking her over. "Whoa." She put a palm to his chest and pressed lips to his cheek.

He panted. "Are... are you okay?"

"Yeah, thanks. What an asshole! I got a ride with him in Port Alberni and he said I reminded him of his sister. The fucker talks about how dangerous it is for a girl to hitch, and then he grabs my fuckin' boob and says he's gonna show me what it's a-boot with a real man or some hick-ass Canadian bullshit. What a fucking dick!"

"Wow, gosh... what's your name?"

"Darla. What's yours?"

"I'm Paul."

She shook hands. "Good to meet ya dude. That was killer timing." She laughed. "Karma didn't fail me again."

They wandered around the old mill talking about anything at all as Paul strove not to stare. Darla reminded him of a girl who'd showed up once with a long-haired guy in a panel truck at the motel his parents owned in the Oregon fishing town of Charleston. He'd heard a wild shriek that night and opened his window on the damp air to hear her making the most amazing sounds that seemed to go on forever. Paul had wanted to make a girl sound like that ever since.

Suddenly, Darla leapt on his back and wrapped her arms around him. It took a moment to get his balance. Her breath caressed the back of his neck and smelled good. She giggled as he fell into stride with her astride him. The salt sea breeze buffeted their faces as they made their way along a weed-choked logging flume with Paul balancing on the mossy concrete.

Darla pointed to the lighthouse perched on Amphitrite Point in the distance. "I'm living there with my dad. He's a biologist and worked at Scripps."

"What's Scripps?"

"An oceanographic institute in San Diego. Now he works for the Province. The place is totally automated, and has a two-story house with views of the ocean." She nuzzled his ear. It tickled down his neck and back up his spine. "My mom would have driven him fuckin' crazy, pining for the parties at home." She shrugged. "I'm surprised they stayed together this long. He's from Toronto, and a real Canadian in spite of living on the beach in La Jolla for all my life with us barbarians." Paul nearly lost his footing, and Darla shrieked and gripped him tighter. "Look out, don't fall!" He squeezed her thighs and she tightened her grip around his middle as they tottered along the foundations. For a moment, he was self-conscious about a zit on his cheek, but her warmth made him forget. "Watch your step!" Even commanding, her voice was a kiss.

"Scared?"

"I just don't want to slide into that fuckin' green-ass water, dude."

"Kinda slimy, huh?"

"Yuk!"

He set her down on the concrete rim but her arms continued to enfold his neck. Finally she sighed, removed her long legs with exquisite slowness, and sidled to sit beside him. Her hand slid around his leg, and he ventured an arm around her waist. She tossed back sun-bleached hair, and he studied the freckles on the bridge of her nose. Darla let out her breath. "So... what the fuck is there to do around here anyway?"

"You know as much as me. At least you get broadcasts from that lighthouse. I saw the antennas. Shit, your dad's a scientist, and you have all the technology in this part of the world. Don't you get Seattle TV?"

"Yeah, and I can sit and watch that and the waves while my ass grows bigger than that Mrs. Temple's at the store." She shook her head. "Fuck-ing bor-ing!"

"I can't imagine that."

"Hope not dude." Darla leaned back with her face to the breaking clouds and the sun illuminated her profile before the dark forest beyond. Her upturned nose was the prettiest thing he'd ever seen. "Here," she slid a warped joint out of her sweater and waved it in front of him. "I hope you're not straight." Darla snapped open a Zippo lighter and touched the joint to its flame.

"No way, I smoke grass. Where did you get that?"

"Hey, dude, you just met me and you want to know my connections?" She passed it to him and mussed his un-trimmed hair. "Acapulco gold. I brought it all the way from home."

They sat passing the joint, watching an eagle in a cedar snag. When they finished, she put out the smoldering roach and dropped it in a tin film canister. "God, it's so fuckin' old-fashioned here I can't believe it."

"I know."

"People don't know how to handle a free-spirited woman. Ever been to a commune?"

"Ah, no, but I know there's a bunch in Oregon."

"Too bad." She stared at him with those big blue eyes, and he tried not to flinch. "We should find some place we can be together." She studied his expression and responded with a grin followed by a shrug. "We're stuck here for the whole goddamn season so we might as well."

"I—"

"My dad taught me that a girl should never be distracted by boys, which is cool, and it's true, but that a girl always chooses anyway, *not* the guy. He says I never would have been born if my mother hadn't picked him, and then he sighs, and says he knows he can't really stop me, but like *please* be selective, baby. Know what I mean?"

"I... think so."

"I mean, look: you and I are here the whole fuckin' summer. You're the only guy around here who I can even relate to, and you came to the rescue like a totally skookum dude. It's all fishermen and loggers here who think women are something you buy when you go to Vancouver, or somebody to just marry, make a bunch of babies with and watch get fat." She sneered. "I got into a bar in Port Alberni today. Have you seen the separate entrances they still have for women? They don't use them anymore but they're still there, and they look at you weird when you come in too. It's like a hundred years ago. It says 'Ladies with Escorts' over one, and 'Unescorted Gentlemen' over the other. Shit! Anyway 'cause it was local and late they let me in 'cause it's the boonies and I was with a local guy, and I'm kinda cute I guess, but they'd all reach out and try to touch my ass, and then they'd act all polite when I told 'em to fuck off. Same goddamn thing over and over. Dumb shit coulda scored if he'd been cool. He was good-lookin'. I ditched him and hitched home, and then I get a ride with that asshole.

Guys like that are all the same. You're either a lady, or a whore. That *so* sucks." She sighed. "So anyway, Paul, want to get laid?"

A lump appeared in his throat. Darla's pretty mouth had a smile on the cusp of laughter. Paul stared at the curve of her cheek as he fought for a response. Her long eyelashes flicked over bright eyes that were studying him intently. The lashes seemed to ripple the air and buffet his face as if she were waving a blanket. He squeezed damp grass between his fingers and swallowed.

"Scare you?"

"No, I... *yes!*" He shook burning cheeks. "I mean... not *scared,* just *yes,* like... *okay.*"

"Okay, cool." She shook his hand and touched lips soft as butterfly wings to his own.

"You're not like any girl I ever met, Darla."

* * *

Finding a place was easier said than done. They didn't have a vehicle, and Darla let it be known that abandoned dark and damp places weren't part of her plans, and if he was serious, and of course worthy, their first project was finding a suitable space for an assignation. The gravel road toward Wreck Beach offered some hope and since it was only eleven in the morning of a long summer day, he slipped into the inn and packed a daypack with cookies, fruit and beef jerky. Paul put the Ka-Bar knife his uncle had carried as a Marine flyer in the Pacific on his belt in its stained sheath, grabbed a canteen, and they stuck out their thumbs.

A logging truck growled to a stop when the driver spied a pretty teenage girl in tight jeans and a thousand-watt smile. He was a burly guy with a brown beard and blue stocking cap who grinned hugely. Paul stared at Darla's ass stretching her Levis as she climbed in. The truck lurched forward when he had one foot on the running board and he nearly fell off before he clambered after her, staring at the smirk on the driver's face.

"Where you guys headin'?"

Darla tossed long blond hair over her shoulder, gauging the effect it had on the driver. "Wreck Beach."

"Roads are all muddy and torn up past there. Goin' berry pickin'?"

"Yeah."

"Blueberries and salmonberries are ripe. You ain't got buckets though." The man eyed Darla. "Watch out for bears and cougars. Lotsa hippies camp on the beach up there. I saw some swimmin' naked last week in that hot spell we had. They had to be Yanks. Hear a buck-naked hippie girl got chased out on the rocks by a cougar last week and had to flag down a boat. Lucky for her that they was there," the driver chortled, "lucky for the guys on the boat too."

"Um, really?

"You betcha." The man extended a hand. "Name's Burt."

"Darla, and this is Paul."

"You do that hippie thing?"

"What do you mean?"

"Like or-gees and stuff?"

She frowned. "No."

Burt turned back to the road. "Coulda fooled me, lookin' like that."

"Like what?"

Paul leaned forward. "Are you from around here?"

"Yes sir." Burt examined him. "You guys Canadian?"

Darla nodded. "I am, dual citizenship. My dad's from Toronto."

"How 'bout you?"

"I'm from Oregon."

"You eighteen yet?"

"Not 'til January."

"Gonna get drafted then."

"I'm going to college."

The driver rolled down the window and spat something brown into the wind. "That's right, all the rich ones go to college. Fellas like me wouldn't stand a rat's chance down there, and be in the jungle gettin' killed for God knows what. Fuck that."

"I've got scholarship offers. It's not a rich thing."

"Same thing. What do your folks do?"

"They bought the Benbow Inn in Ucluelet."

"The Benbow, eh? Had me a hell of a time there once after we made a bundle on a cedar sale. Got in a dust-up with some pansy manager and they called the RCMP. Landed me in jail in Victoria for a night," He snorted, "fuckin' Mounties. Took care a' three before they give me a poundin'. The foundations need fixin' on that place, and it leaks like hell in a good blow. Bet by now that whole front of the restaurant's gettin' soaked in the winter, eh?"

"The last owners fixed that, and my dad's putting on a whole new roof."

Burt grinned. "Tol' ya your parents was rich. Foundations still stink I bet."

Paul shrugged.

"Thought maybe you were hidin' here 'cause 'a that war. Hear 'bout the hard hats beatin' war protesters in New York City? Saw it on the tube. There's plenty Yanks hidin' from the draft here in B.C." Burt down-shifted, and the air brakes let out a roar as they descended a grade. "Can't blame 'em, eh?"

"In the Aquarian Age we'll make love, not war." Darla lilted.

Burt snickered. "Maybe you're the kinda girl I'm lookin' for after all."

She slid against Paul. "Just kidding dude."

* * *

They got off above a beach where driftwood shelters were visible beyond the wind-gnarled trees, and the big rig rumbled away on the gravel road. The sun was out and the sky was a welcome blue.

Darla watched the truck disappear around a bend. "I don't like that guy." She yawned and cracked her back. "So," she took his hand and glanced around, "where are we gonna do it?"

The lump was back in his throat. "I... don't know."

"Let's try that road. Down on the beach there's driftwood crash pads with freaks but it's not too private and kinda crowded, and I hate sand in my ass. Hey, look at that sign." She pointed to a sheet strung between two driftwood poles on the beach before a shelter built of drift logs. "Acid for five bucks. What a rip-off. You can get two hits for that in California." She grinned. "We got a bitchin' nude beach in La Jolla called Black's Beach where you can get a tan all-over without freezin' your ass off. I love going naked. Wish we were there."

"Freaks?"

"Yeah, you know, *stoners,* man, like not straights."

"Oh."

They followed the gravel road. Up the hill beyond some trees, an old weathered house stood on a rise looking out at the ocean with sunlight reflecting off dusty windows.

Paul pointed. "I wonder if it's occupied?"

Darla shaded her eyes. "Don't know, but it looks lots cozier than that beach. Let's check it out. I bet we can climb in a window or something." They came to a winding gravel drive to the house with grass growing on it. "Oh boy, I bet it's empty." She squeezed his butt. "We are gonna get lai-ad."

Paul fought the urge to giggle like an idiot and clamped his jaw shut.

The two-storey house had dust-filmed bay windows looking over the sea and a garage with a warped door. A faded **No Trespassing** sign was on a tree beside the driveway, which was unusual in these parts, but lots of people camped on the beach. A porch ran around the front of the house with half of it roofed and screened, and a table and chairs sat on the weathered planks. One chair was tipped over and looked like it had been for a very long time. They walked around to the side facing the hill and tried the door. It was locked.

"I'll try that window." Paul pointed to the second storey, stepped on an old wood box filled with gray logs, climbed up a post, and pushed up on the window. It was stuck. When he climbed down, Darla was nowhere to be seen.

A creaking came from the side of the house, then a banging, followed by the shattering of glass.

"Damn!"

He sprinted around the building in time to see her feet disappear in an open window, and the sun-bleached curtains parted on her smile. "Shit, I didn't mean to bust it. Come on."

He climbed up a creaking drainpipe, threw a leg over the sill, and stepped into the room. There was a neatly made bed with an old-fashioned dresser topped with a basin and pitcher, a closet with wooden hangars, and a pink overstuffed chair. The place smelled stuffy and slightly damp.

Darla was in the hall. "This place is cool. It's some old-timey house nobody's been in forever."

"Except us."

"Yeah, I fucked up that window, didn't I?"

He nodded. "Maybe I can bring some plastic and fix it."

"Yeah that sucks. Now it's too windy in there. I bet there's a room with a view. I want to see the ocean when I get laid." She flicked purple nails. "Come on."

There was a bathroom between the rooms with a white claw-foot tub and stained enamel sink. He tried the faucet but nothing came out. Two bedrooms occupied the upstairs, and the largest bed had a faded pink comforter on it. Darla bounced on it and the bed let out a squeak. She laughed and pulled her woolen sweater off over her head to sit legs-folded in a white Mexican blouse and jeans on the maroon bedspread. She tossed her sweater on a chair, grinned, patted the comforter, and a little puff of dust arose as Paul stood in the doorway.

She gave him a questioning stare and yanked off her blouse to reveal perfect breasts. "Well?"

He bit his lip and approached her. When he reached the bed Darla wrapped fingers around his belt buckle and drew him closer. They tickled as they wandered inside his jeans. She rose on her knees and fastened petal-soft lips on his. After a good two minutes, their mouths parted. Relieved laughter came from her as Darla shucked her jeans down over her hips and kicked them free. "Okay. At least you're a good kisser."

* * *

Late that afternoon she returned from peeing outside and began throwing the remnants of their food in the daypack. "I totally need a shower and dinner. Let's hit the road, toad."

Paul lay spread-eagled on the bed staring at the stained ceiling. Her scent tickled his nose. He closed his eyes and inhaled deeply. "You're a trip."

"Thanks. You're pretty cool yourself. That was fun."

"Want to do it again?"

"That'd be four times. We gotta get going. We don't want to be caught out here at dark. We got all summer remember?" She bounced on the bed and gave his penis a squeeze. "Nice dangle dude, but we gotta hitch a ride, so let's go."

"God," he sighed, "I'm so lucky."

She chuckled. "Glad you think so."

"Don't you worry about getting pregnant?"

"I'm on the Pill." She threw the strap of his daypack over her shoulder and yanked her hair out from under it. "Are you gonna fix that window?"

"I should."

"Yeah, really. I kinda screwed up somebody's hospitality. Besides, it'd be cool to come here again. We don't want to trash the place."

"I'll get some Visqueen sheeting from the inn. Dad's got rolls of it."

"Cool. So let's jam."

They froze at the roar of an engine the curve of the driveway had muffled until it was nearly to the house. The rig bumped to a stop outside, a noisy parking brake was pulled, and the engine died. Two heavy doors opened and slammed shut, and the voices of two men echoed against the front of the house.

Darla gasped. "Oh shit!"

"Oh fuck!"

He stared into sky-blue eyes as big as silver dollars and hissed, "The window!" They ran across the house to the broken window, but when they reached it, he put a hand to her chest. Her heart beat against his palm. Paul wanted to freeze the moment, just like every other moment in the last few hours. "Wait." He held a finger to his lips that smelled like her.

She squeezed his hand. "Yeah that drainpipe's loud. They'll hear us. What if they got guns?"

A thrill of fear shot through him. "Wha... why?"

"'Cause we're like burglars."

"No, we're not, we—"

"Shhhh!"

Someone jerked on the door and it rattled in its frame, followed by heavy blows.

"Fuck they don't live here... they're breaking in!"

There was a crash as the door was kicked open and Darla went out the window.

Paul sprang out after her and landed with a grunt. There was a sharp pain in his left ankle, and he sat down hard. "Ow!"

"Shhhh, shut up!" Darla yanked him to his feet and dragged him down the hill. They stumbled through mossy bark and damp leaves beneath the red trunks of cedars and night-dark hemlocks and squatted panting under the branches of a gigantic blueberry bush. A blueberry the size of a gumball bounced off Paul's head, and the sound of water came from somewhere beneath the riot of vegetation.

"Oh, shit," Paul began to take off his boot, "my ankle's fucked up."

"Don't! If it is it'll swell, and you'll never get it back on."

He nodded and swatted at the hovering black flies. Their breaths slowed as they listened for pursuit. Darla pulled devil's club thorns out of her sweater as mosquitoes made a high-pitched whine around them. She pulled a blueberry off a branch, popped it in her mouth, and swatted at the bugs. She stripped a few more berries and ate them, leaving blue stains on her hands and lips. "Well, thanks for a good balling anyway."

Paul rocked back and forth holding his ankle. "No, thank you, Darla," he said through gritted teeth, "that was better than I hoped. You're beautiful."

She giggled. "Oh, come on. I bet you say that to all the girls."

"No, really, Darla, that was like... my first."

"Really?" Her cheeks bulged and she put hands to her mouth. When she took them away her face was blue to her eyebrows.

Paul gave her a wounded look. "I... I got to third base before."

"Hey, Paul," she grabbed his hands with sticky fingers. "Oh god baby, I'm not laughing at you. I'm just jazzed I got your cherry is all. Oh wow, you were great! If I knew it was your first time I would have got it on again when you wanted to, like instantly."

"And then we woulda been naked when those guys showed up." They broke into giggling and kissed. He gritted his teeth. "My ankle hurts."

"Man, you're good too, I mean *really*. Wow... I've got a virgin to ball this summer!" She laughed. "Well, not anymore, but... this is so cool."

"We gotta get out of here. These bugs suck. Hey, didn't one of those guys sound like that Burt dude?"

She blinked. "I don't know."

A sharp crunch ended their conversation. Something big moved in the brush across the creek and they scooted deeper under the blueberry bushes. Up the hill men's voices could be heard, but they couldn't make them out.

Darla waved at the bugs and put lips to his ear. "I don't think—"

The head of a huge bear, black as night and wider than their chests, rose from a patch of salmonberries across the creek. His dark eyes glittered like polished agates as he examined them. Paul and Darla caught their breath and squeezed each other tighter. The bear stared at them for a long moment before he sank back into the foliage. Someone crashed through the bushes above them and the broad leaves of devil's club across the creek rippled as the bear made its way up the opposite side of the gulch. Its shiny black bulk was visible for a moment between two trees, and it was gone.

"Betcha anything it's that foxy hippie chick and that squirrelly kid. He won't be no problem."

"Don't know, Burt. Let's just get some beer, eh? Those guys 'ill drink it all before we get back, there ain't no cases in Ucluelet, and it's too late to make another trip half-way 'cross the fuckin' island to the liquor store."

Paul slid his uncle's Ka-Bar knife out of its sheath and ran his fingers down the flat of the blade.

"I'm tellin' ya she's worth it. You shoulda seen her. She looks like some kinda Hollywood star, Bill, just like in that porno flick George was showin' on the projector. It could even *be* her! Hell, she was talkin' 'bout free love! I betcha she's—"

"Worth what? Coulda been any long-haired punks with all these fuckin' Yank hippies up and down the beach. Ow, gaddammit! Fuck these thorns! Let's go back to the truck eh?"

Paul and Darla huddled under the blueberries swatting mosquitoes. He scowled. *Squirrelly?*

"Fuck it, you're right. Could be any of them hippies from the beach, eh?"

They sat in silence as the sounds of the men faded up the hill with an occasional, "Goddamn devil's club!"

Darla stood and kicked the damp leaves. "*See?* Redneck motherfuckers are all the same, American, Canadian, they're all a buncha fuckin' rapists. I knew that truck driver was an asshole as soon as I got in. You can't trust anybody over thirty."

"Darla, I'll fight them. They'd have to kill me first. I mean it." She hugged him.

He rubbed her shoulder and tottered on his good leg, examining their surroundings. "Let's get outta here."

She kicked at the auburn cedar duff, and a bright red centipede rippled out of it. "Yuk, these bushes suck. Let's go down to the road and get a ride."

Paul wiped his palms on filthy jeans. Darla's face was stained blue, and her complexion that had been so perfect that morning was criss-crossed with scratches and the pink eruptions of mosquito bites. Her turned-up nose had a red welt across it and her sweater was full of thorns. Her hair was a tangled golden halo, with berry splotches, a strand of spider web, leaves, and a green caterpillar. He picked off the caterpillar and laughed. "Darla, you're beautiful."

II.
The Break

They fought their way through rotten logs and the stinging branches of devil's club. Clouds of mosquitoes and black flies swarmed around their heads accompanied by occasional shrieks of misery from Darla. When they got to the road, they stuck out their thumbs and a dented Fifties panel truck ground to a stop with a howl of brakes. The long-haired couple inside were heading across the island for the ferry to Vancouver. They examined the two teens and asked how Paul and Darla had managed to get so dirty.

"We're running from fuckin' rednecks!" Darla pulled something green from her hair with a grimace. She lit a damp joint and passed it to the girl, who had huge billows of red hair and went by Sunshine. "We should be going to Vancouver too, or south or something. I'm fuckin' sick of Ucluelet. It's all drunks, rednecks and cold-ass beaches. Fuck it."

Sunshine grinned. "We're going to San Francisco. Everybody does, I mean like the whole world. It's karma."

"What is?"

"That's like fate Paul."

Paul scratched at a bite and shifted his aching leg. "I know what karma is. I mean, like what's foretold?"

Sunshine gave him a look of astonishment. "It's the Age of Aquarius, brother. It's the spirits of great seers like Crazy Horse coming back in our generation to start the new age. People like Tim Leary and Baba Ram Das, Stephen Gaskin, Indian medicine men, cool swamis, and bitchin' groups like the Grateful Dead and Jefferson Airplane all live there. There's lots of cities, but San Francisco is *The City*. It's a spiritual convergence of the higher energies in one place, like a sacred chakra of the earth or a cosmic convergence. We go back to renew our energy. It's always a good trip. This might not happen again for a thousand years so how can you miss it?"

The driver nodded and the four gold earrings in his left ear rattled. "Sunshine's an old soul who speaks the truth. You guys should come with us. You can help with gas money."

Darla chuckled. "The Summer of Love was five fuckin' years ago man. I saw a guy get stabbed at Altamont down there in sixty-nine when I was fourteen. I was sitting on top of a school bus with a Hells Angel named Big Larry, who jumped up and started screaming 'kill the nigger' and fell off . I got the fuck out of there. I'm from California, but my friend here needs to soak his foot and get it looked at... but maybe we should go south soon." She ran a hand through her tangled hair. A wad came out in her fingers. Darla made a face. "Beats the shit outta here, anyway."

The driver took the offered joint and sucked it into flame. A seed popped and showered sparks on the metal floor. "There's 'sposed to be a big gathering on the continental divide in Colorado, where the spirits of lost seers will return with the White Buffalo on the summer solstice."

Sunshine took a huge toke and nodded solemnly. "We'll all meet again. In this life or the next."

Darla took the smoldering roach and shrugged. "Yeah, maybe."

* * *

They got dropped at the lighthouse on the headland where Darla lived with her father. After a moment's hesitation Paul went in. If they were going to be around each other this summer, her father should at least know who he was even if they both looked like shit. They made up a story about being chased by crazed loggers into the bushes while walking along the road by the beach, which wasn't that far from the truth, and of course told him about the bear. After embellishments from Darla in which the bear grew to at least ten feet tall, she disappeared in the bathroom and left Paul alone with her father. The sound of water came from behind the closed door.

Mr. Argyle filled a tub with hot water from the kitchen sink, poured in Epsom salts, and had Paul soak his foot. The old lighthouse keeper's abode had heavy dark beams in the front room that looked as if they'd been scavenged from a ship. Nautical lamps and a brass clock like a ship's wheel adorned the walls with paintings of old clipper ships at sea. One had a steamer from the last century hard up on the rocks in a gale with this very lighthouse perched behind it on the headland. Mr. Argyle made tea and served Paul. He sat down and shook his head. "Well, thanks for getting her back in one piece, eh? Looks like you're a skookum fella when things get tight at least."

"Yes, sir, you're welcome."

"Darla's rather the free spirit eh?"

"Ah, yes sir."

Mr. Argyle rubbed a neat red beard going to gray and stared out the windows at the ocean. "Her mother's just the same. A California blonde who always has to make the whole world stand up and take notice." He turned to Paul with a half-grin. "Darla looks just like her mom when I met her. I was just a bit older than you are now. Pretty irresistible eh?" He shook his head. "Her mom nearly got me killed the first time we went to Tijuana. I left Toronto for school down there doing ocean research and ended up head over heels in love and getting married before I knew it. Nice climate anyway." He scratched his beard. "That was a while ago," Mr. Argyle's red eyebrows became a straight line, "just be careful, son. She's but a girl of seventeen and rather enjoys her power to provoke people. She thinks she can handle them but sometimes that can get out of hand. Doesn't help my sleep a bit. What's your age?"

"Seventeen."

"You look it. That's a bit of a relief. I took this job to get out of Southern California and show her the beauty of our own country, but it's awfully boring for a teenager in a small town I suppose. She had a lot of friends down there and loves the beach. Not much opportunity to wear a bathing suit around here and not any of those music festivals they have either. Your parents own the Benbow right, the Harts?"

"Yes."

"Where are you from?"

"Charleston, it's near Coos Bay in Oregon."

"Been there. Bet you're bored shitless too."

Paul laughed.

Mr. Argyle chuckled. "Can't blame you." He opened an ivory box on the table, took out a thick pinch of aromatic tobacco, and stuffed it in a meerschaum pipe. Mr. Argyle lit it with a blue-tipped match and puffed it into a burn. "Don't be surprised if she wants you to take off with her right out of the hat. She does it on impulse, but *don't.*"

"What?"

"She's been doing it since thirteen. She ran off to San Francisco at fourteen and ended up sick with hepatitis at some commune in Ojai. Came home yellow as a stick of butter." Mr. Argyle sighed. "She's almost eighteen and I don't see how she'll quit now. She hitchhiked to Port Alberni last week on her lonesome and didn't come back until the next morning." He shook his head. "I didn't sleep a wink. I called the RCMP, but thank goodness she showed up on her own," He rubbed his beard. "Thank God she's on the Pill. If you two decide to go somewhere for the night, make sure she knows it's proper to at least *call* me next time and let me know... please."

Paul stared into his empty cup. "Yes sir."

"You can call me Bob." Bob puffed on his pipe and sighed. "She's quite a looker, eh?"

Paul felt Bob's eyes on him. Lifting his chin was like moving a boulder, but he straightened in the chair and nodded.

"I suppose you should consider yourself lucky, son."

"That's... kind of how I feel, Mr. Argyle, um, Bob."

Bob let out his breath and stared out the windows. "I'll drive you to the Benbow. You'd better stay off that foot for a while looks to me."

* * *

Paul's mother was back from her shopping trip to Nanaimo putting groceries away in a huge kitchen the original owners must have lived in by its size. The big eight-burner gas stove with three ovens had a coffee pot perking on it, and from the smell she had something baking.

She stopped when he limped into the room and her mouth fell open. "Jesus, Paul, where have you *been?*"

"Um, me and this girl hitched to Wreck Beach and we had to hide from some loggers. I think they wanted to rape her."

"Wreck Beach? Oh my God!" She grabbed his chin and rotated his head for inspection. "You've got dirt in your hair and down your... what girl?"

He pushed her hand away. "Don't. Her name's Darla Argyle and she's living at the lighthouse. Her dad's a marine biologist."

"Oh," his mother brushed a strand of hair from her eyes and considered it, "What's she like?"

"She's nice and super pretty mom." He turned to go.

"Why are you limping?"

"Twisted my ankle. Mr. Argyle let me soak it in Epsom salts and gave me an Ace bandage."

"That was nice of him. Maybe we should go to the doctor."

"It's okay." He headed for the shower.

"Is she planning on going to college?"

"Didn't ask her."

* * *

That night at dinner Paul could only think of Darla. His father got back from Victoria late, and after finishing a plate of pot roast, potatoes, carrots and onions followed by apple pie, he pushed back from the table and burped.

"Excuse yourself, Donald."

"Right, Grace. So, Paul, keeping busy?"

"Yeah."

"Your mother says you met a girl."

"Yeah." Paul toyed with his meat and stared at the ocean.

"What's she like?"

"She's ah, she's from California. She's named Darla Argyle and her dad's a marine biologist, and she's really smart… and she's beautiful."

His father chuckled. "Good. Not a lot of 'em around here except some hippie girls that don't know what a bath is. Bet you miss Coos Bay with all those high school girls."

"We live in Charleston… and I hate high school in Coos Bay."

His mom's stare was a lead weight. "You got great scores on the SATs, honey, and you have three scholarship offers. The counselor says your tracking scores show you're a natural for Journalism and they have a wonderful department at the University in Eugene. You'll be out of there after next semester and you just have to decide where you want to go to school. All you have to do is keep up your grades, and you can go to college and not worry about the draft."

His father steepled his fingers and rubbed his nose. "I bet you miss riding dirt bikes with your friends at least."

"Yeah."

"You can live in Eugene next year at the dorms and still be able to come home for the holidays. There are lots of girls there worth meeting. When I went there, we—"

"Can I be excused?"

His father nodded. "Sure, Paul. I'm going to need your help mixing concrete in the morning."

"Why? Nobody's here."

His mother threw down her napkin. "That's a lousy attitude! For God's sake, how are we going to get guests here if things aren't *fixed?* They're planning to build a real small boat harbor soon. You know that. We have this opportunity because your father was born in Canada, and we're going to retire here, and *you're* the one who can make use of it eventually. Your brother has his own logging outfit back home and doesn't have a shred of interest. You don't want to be a logger, you don't want to go to college, and you don't want to do anything here but wander around and sleep late. Good God, we went through the Depression and the War and didn't have any of these opportunities. We're here on the ground floor and can have something that you'll take over someday if things work out." She shook her head. "We've put five year's earnings into this place, and—"

"Sorry!" Paul tossed his napkin on the table and limped up the cedar stairs to his room.

* * *

He couldn't sleep. Darla danced through his mind as he re-lived every moment again and again. He could hear her beautiful laugh, smell her, and feel her silken skin. He stared in fascination at a vision of sweat beaded across her hard belly. A stubborn erection kept him wide awake even after he'd masturbated twice. He tossed on the bed, punched his pillow, and ran through every moment of their conversation under the bushes. He felt her fierce hugs, inhaled the scent of her hair, and imagined reaching out and pulling off a caterpillar. He saw her upturned nose silhouetted against the sky, glistening with dew. Her big blue eyes were like a hot summer sky he wanted to soar in forever. She glowed like an angel. An angel come down to save *him*. Coyotes howled in the hills. He stared at the stars out the window. He growled, kicked at the covers, and punched his pillow again.

A pebble bounced off the glass with a crack. Paul sprang up, jerked open the window, and cool night air wafted across his overheated flesh.

Darla stood in the empty gravel road. She looked like a girl carved out of ivory in the moonlight, even more beautiful than in memory. She waved. "Hey, Paul, I'm goin'."

"Wha...?"

"Want to come?"

"Darla..."

"Hey, I want to hang with you, really, but I'm going to San Francisco, or Oregon, or maybe even that gathering in Colorado or somewhere else. Wherever my karma takes me. It's time, so yes or no dude. I got a ride across the island but they won't wait all night."

"Okay!"

"Shhhhh!" Her teeth flashed. "Cool, meet me by the gas station."

Paul stuffed clothes into his backpack and hurriedly threw a toothbrush and some toilet items in the pouch on its top. He strapped his sleeping bag onto the pack, got dressed, and put on the expensive hiking boots his dad had bought him for his birthday. He stuffed his swollen ankle into the left one, tied it as tight as he could, and went into his closet to dig out all the cash he had, about twenty dollars of Canadian and thirty of American money. His big Ka-Bar knife went on his belt. Paul grabbed his notebook to write something to his parents, but his mind was a blank so he stuffed it into the top of his pack. He could write on the way and drop it in a post box somewhere. He eased down the stairs and crossed the big room with its fireplace and tables. Paul unlatched the heavy oaken front door and shut it slowly behind him.

Darla stood in front of the darkened gas station with her arms out in welcome. A pickup truck was parked on the other side with its lights out, and two dark forms were in the front seats. Paul jogged toward her, ignoring the pain in his ankle. He threw his arms around her and they kissed hard. They finally pulled away to gaze into each other's eyes. He put a palm to her cheek to caress a scratch as her breasts pressed against him. Her lips were soft. She smelled like heaven.

She grabbed his hand and turned to the truck. "Throw your shit in the bed. We're on our way."

Paul threw his pack in and a girl with billows of curly blond hair riding shotgun waved as they jumped in the back. Darla pulled a dusty blanket over them, and they snuggled against the cab as the old engine sputtered to life and the truck rattled down the moonlit road across Vancouver Island.

III.
The Crossing

They bumped onto a black and white ferry at Nanaimo in the damp dawn and stood at the bow as the ship crossed the strait. A pod of orcas appeared with their dorsal fins glistening as the sun blossomed over snowcapped peaks beyond Vancouver. Darla rubbed sleep from her eyes and kissed him.

He kissed her back and gazed at the whales. "Bet my mom's shitting bricks right now."

"Think she'll call the Mounties?"

Paul shrugged.

"Maybe you should call. Tell them a story. It'll give us a day. Say we're in Port Alberni or Campbell River and will be back. We gotta get across the border before she freaks out."

Being a fugitive hadn't really entered Paul's mind. He leaned on the railing and blinked in the sunlight throbbing off white peaks in the east.

She stroked his neck. "Don't sweat it. Zillions of teenagers are on the road. We're low priority. My mom called the cops in San Diego lots of times, and they always say call back in twenty-four hours and I'm a girl. Besides, they'll be looking for you on the island, not Van. My dad won't even pay attention until another night goes by. I boogie places all the time."

"Where can we stay?"

"There's a youth hostel in Gastown in Vancouver for three bucks a night, but we should just keep going and trust our karma."

"I hope we've got enough money to get to San Francisco." Paul dug in his pocket. "I'm hungry."

"No sweat, I've got some too, and I can always get more." Darla giggled. "Watch." She sashayed toward a middle-aged couple in white straw hats at the rail. With the sea breeze and squawking of gulls Paul couldn't hear what she said, but the man reached into his back pocket and took out his wallet. Darla clasped his wife's hand, shook his, bent slightly at the knees in a brief parody of a curtsey, and bounced back across the deck giving them a dazzling smile. The couple waved back, and the man tipped his hat.

She rejoined Paul at the bow. "See?"

"Shit. What did you say?"

"That we're looking for work in Vancouver and we're broke and hungry. Oh, and I said my dad died in a car wreck last week and hinted that my drunken uncle wants to ball me and I'm going to Baptist girls' school in Oregon. They're religious folks from Texas. Nice people." She held out an American five-dollar bill.

"Wow... I thought you got a quarter or something."

"There's a Chinese dive in Gastown under a saloon where the food's good. You can get a ham and cheese omelet, potatoes, toast and coffee for two bucks Canadian. Let's go."

"Okay."

* * *

They got out on a cobblestone street. Someone was sleeping in a red phone booth under a dirty coat with his tattered boots propped against the door to hold it shut, and Paul stared until she yanked him down the sidewalk. They decided to skip the hostel, caught a cheap breakfast at the Chinese dive, and decided to head south. It wasn't noon yet.

He had a brief twinge of guilt about not calling his parents, but it was obliterated by a squeeze of Darla's hand. Hitchhiking was easy with Darla, and she let him know she felt a lot safer. People that weren't even going their way waved, and long-haired ones held their fingers in the "V" sign. His mother had been bothering him about a haircut all summer, and now he wasn't going to cut his either. Paul wished he could grow a beard, or at least some cool sideburns like the big rock stars had.

They caught a ride with two clean-cut students returning to Seattle in an International Travelall. The driver put an eight-track tape in the player under the dash, and the Grateful Dead began to shake the windows. When they reached the border at Blain, they slowed to join the line of vehicles waiting to cross into the United States beside a big white ceremonial gate. The guy driving took a campaign button from the glove box that said "Click with Dick" with President Nixon's face on it, pinned it on his cashmere sweater, and wiped his forehead.

Paul's stomach knotted when he saw an old Chevy panel truck pulled into an inspection bay. Men in blue uniforms were removing the contents and stacking them on tables. Someone was examining the underside from the look of the legs protruding from it, and the occupants stood in an office as guards patted them down. A female officer examined the copious red hair of a young woman, as if something was hidden in it.

"Hey," Paul nudged Darla, "isn't that Sunshine?"

She ran a hand down his arm. "Could be. Just maintain, man, don't freak out. That's what they're looking for. We're Americans."

"I hope our folks didn't—"

"Shhhh."

The guard asked for identification, they handed it to him, and waited for what seemed like forever as he examined it. He checked the registration on the truck, handed back everyone's I.D.s, and waved them into Washington State. Paul let out his breath.

As they rolled away the driver took off his heavy black-framed glasses and rubbed his eyes. He pulled a turtleneck dickey out of his cashmere sweater, yanked it over his head, and threw it in the back of the truck. He threw the Nixon button and heavy black glasses in the glove box and guffawed. "We did it!"

His companion shouted "Yes!" and slapped hands with the driver.

Paul glanced from one to the other. "What's so funny?"

"We got five pounds of Afghani hash under the spare tire." The driver's grin widened as he checked their expressions in the rearview mirror.

Darla shrieked, "Dudes!" and sprang over the seat between the two young men with her unencumbered breasts bobbing in the thin print blouse. She put an arm around both of them and bestowed a kiss on their cheeks. "So, guys, how 'bout a toke?"

***

They got let out on an off-ramp in Seattle with a piece of hash Darla had talked them out of. It was hot, and Darla had switched from her jeans to short cut-offs in the Travelall as the young men in the front seats tried not to stare. With her long legs, the thin Mexican blouse and her long blond hair floating in the breeze, Paul was afraid someone would run off the road looking at her before they got a ride. It was illegal to hitch on the freeway, so they were confined to the on-ramp as a procession of eyeballs passed by, all glued to Darla.

A wheezing red '40's flatbed Ford truck ground to a stop. It was driven by a man with a white beard and high sunburned forehead who had white eyebrows over twinkling blue eyes. He fought with the passenger door, beat on it until it creaked open, and they jumped in. The ashtray was full of wadded candy wrappers, the windshield was cracked, and a tattered phone cord hung from the rearview mirror with the black receiver of a telephone dangling from it that swung with the motion of the truck.

Darla slipped her legs around the rattling stick shift and shook his hand. "Thanks, Mister."

"Where are you youngsters goin'?"

"San Francisco."

"Ain't goin' that far. Portland's my destination."

"That's great. At least we can get out of fuckin' Washington."

The old man winced. "You shouldn't be usin' such language, young lady."

"Oh, sorry, really."

He fought the truck into another gear and nodded. "Kids nowadays talk that way I suppose."

"No, I'm sorry, I was just jazzed you're goin' that far."

"Jazzed? Don't see no Dorseys or Satchmos in your party. You kids musicians?"

"Huh?"

"What's in San Francisco?"

"Um... it's just the place to be."

"I worked the docks there in the Depression. Ever hear of the Longshoremen's Strike? Saw the bulls shoot down strikers in front of the Armory on Mission Street. Blood in the gutters, burnin' barricades and bodies all over the place. Terrible thing." He shook his head. "The Man won, and Joe Hill's dead. That's the truth."

"Joe who?"

"Hang on!" A boney hand shot toward the dented dashboard and seized the dangling telephone receiver. "Hello? Hello? Yes sir, you bet! I'll watch after 'em. No, they ain't goin' to hell if I got a say. What? Yes sir!" The old man wiped spittle off the telephone mouthpiece and carefully placed it on the dash.

Paul and Darla stared at each other and she covered her face. *A telephone in a truck!* The old flatbed had reached forty-five miles an hour and maintained that speed as traffic sped around them. Someone laid on their horn, and two teens in a candy apple red Dodge Challenger gave them the finger as they passed with the roar of its hemi engine.

"Go to hell, ya sinners," the old man mumbled under his breath.

It was a long ride to Portland.

*　*　*

He dropped them in downtown Portland at the bus station. "Now you kids watch your language, and... wait," The old man grabbed the dangling phone again. "Hello, yes, Lord!" He put a hand over the mouthpiece. "He calls. I gotta go." He fought the truck into gear with the useless telephone receiver cradled in the crook of his neck and waved as he clattered around a corner.

Darla giggled. "He's a trip."

"Too fucking weird. Imagine a telephone in a truck."

"That would be so cool if you could do it. Well, anyway, God told him to give us a ride." She glanced up and down the street. "It's pretty late. Want to keep hitching or find a place to crash?"

"I want to ball you."

She chuckled. "Big surprise, but we don't have money for a motel and we gotta find someplace we can crash. There's lots of bitchin' communes in Oregon so maybe we should just keep hitching. It's almost the shortest night of the year anyway." She yawned. "I need coffee. Come on."

They got coffee at the bus station, walked a few blocks on a street that fed into I-5 as it knifed south through Portland, and stuck out their thumbs. They got two short rides and soon were standing along the dark highway outside Hillsboro. Semis roared by, occasionally blowing their horns, and Paul and Darla tottered in the blasts of wind.

"Suckers would stop if I was by myself." Darla muttered.

"Sorry."

"Fuck that. Just shows they're assholes and I got you to protect me. You wouldn't believe how many jerks up and ask for a blowjob. If I was some kinda slut, I could travel free all the time."

"That sucks."

They laughed.

A white fifty-nine Chevy Impala braked, skidded to a stop, and they grabbed their packs and ran toward its triple taillights alongside the freeway. Darla leaned toward the passenger window where a thick arm rested on the door. "Hey thanks, are—"

"Jump in!" An oddly thin voice came from the big man making it.

Darla gave Paul a glance before she opened the back door. He threw his pack in first, slid in behind it, and she followed.

The two men in the front seat wore white tee-shirts over bulging waists. They had to be brothers, with their identical crew cuts and thick necks, could have been twins, and looked like Tweedledee and Tweedledum in a drawing Paul had seen in an old edition of *Alice in Wonderland*. The one riding shotgun put an arm on the red vinyl seat and leaned toward them. "Where you hippies goin'?"

"South."

"How far?"

"San Francisco."

"We're goin' to Albany."

"That's great, thanks."

The car spun its tires in a spray of gravel and clawed back onto the freeway. Paul stared at the pad of fat on the back of the driver's neck. Everything in the car smelled like grease, sweat, and cheap cologne.

The passenger, who really did look exactly like the driver, grinned. "You do them or-gees?"

"Oh shit," Darla muttered, "not again."

"Say what?"

She shook her head. "No. No orgies."

He turned to Paul. "You dodgin' the draft?"

"No, I'm seventeen."

The driver laughed. "I got a M-1 in the trunk. Ever shoot a M-1?"

"My dad has one from Korea. I've gone deer hunting with it but I'd rather take a .30-.30. An M-1's too heavy. Too powerful too."

"Good for shootin' hippies and draft dodgers."

Darla squeezed Paul's knee. He reached behind his back, adjusted the sheath of his Ka-Bar knife wedged against the seat, and unsnapped the clasp.

The driver jerked the wheel hard right and the car left the highway on the next off-ramp. He hung another right through a stop sign without slowing, and they were bumping along a narrow two-lane road between cornfields.

"Hey dude, we want *out!*" Darla's voice was high and tight and made the knot in Paul's stomach bounce in time with it.

"We'll be slowin' down directly Sweetcakes." Tweedledee said.

Tweedledum chuckled. "Yah, ya little whore."

Paul's heart thudded against his ribs as a vehicle passed going the opposite direction and Darla's frightened eyes flashed in the headlights. He could smell her fear and it filled him with rage. He squeezed the laminated leather handle of the knife.

They hung a left into a cornfield and the car bumped to a stop. Tweedledee threw it into park, and Tweedledum let out an adolescent laugh and lunged at Darla. Paul's knife flew out of the sheath and he slashed at the fat trunk of an arm reaching for Darla.

Tweedledum screamed.

Paul hit the door, ducked a blow from Tweedledee, and stabbed at the driver's arm as a huge fist came toward his face. He felt the knife hit bone and it vibrated in his grip as the man screamed in an identical note to his brother. The knife was nearly wrenched from Paul's hand as Tweedledee howled, bounced against the steering wheel and gibbered. Paul hung on to his knife, still in the big man's arm as warm blood ran over his fingers. He yanked it free, and a gout of blood hit the ceiling.

"Run!" He got out.

Darla was out the door, dragging her pack behind her. She threw it on her back, staggered into a wall of cornstalks, and turned. "Paul… get *out!*"

Paul was fighting with the handle of the other door.

"I'll kill you!" Tweedledee howled.

"I'll *kill* you!" Tweedledum seconded.

Paul dodged a flailing fist and blood spattered his face. He hit the door with his shoulder and rolled out. Paul jumped up in a cloud of dust, stumbled on his sore foot, and bolted after Darla.

"I got my M-1! You gonna die!"

"Ow! Shit, Gus, I'm bleedin' like hell!"

Paul stumbled after the sound of Darla panting through the cornstalks as wheels sprayed gravel on the road behind them, accompanied by high-pitched howling that faded with the sound of the engine.

* * *

They climbed onto a railroad track after fighting through the cornfield, brushing spider webs out of their hair. After a while they slowed to a walk. Paul's ankle was killing him. The only sound was their clopping across the wooden ties, the rasping of their breath, and the noise of the distant freeway. When they reached where the railroad tracks ran under the highway, they stopped.

She gulped air. "Think they're out cruising for us?"

"Shit no, they're at a hospital. Didn't you see all that blood? Could be cops though."

"Fuck!" Darla wiped her forehead and plopped down with a groan on the embankment. She stared at the sky and gulped air.

A giggle erupted from her chest, followed by a sob. "You were... incredible!" She ran a hand across a face shiny with sweat. "Think they'll die?"

"No," He wiped the knife on the grass, poured water from his canteen on the blade, and wiped it again before sliding it in the sheath, "God, I hope not. That makes me a murderer."

"Oh God, shit... *no!* That was self defense!"

"Think we should go to the cops?"

A semi blew its air horn above them as it pounded across the overpass. They stared at each other's pale faces and shook their heads in unison.

"Fuck it. It's their word against ours and we're runaways. They probably got a big fat cop brother or something anyway." She snorted. "Didn't those guys look like Tweedledee and Tweedledum, in Alice in Wonderland?"

He laughed. "That's exactly what I was thinking."

They broke into exhausted giggling as their sweat cooled.

Darla squeezed his shoulder. "You're a trip, man."

He sighed. "And that was a fucked-up trip."

"It's okay, baby. God, but you are so cool. You saved us from those guys. Fuck them." Darla's breath rattled as a truck's lights illuminated her. "God..." A sob welled in her chest, and he drew her into his arms.

"You're okay."

She gulped air and sat up straight. "We're not gonna let a couple retard rednecks screw up our summer. There's a really cool commune I heard about in Southern Oregon where we can hang in a place called Takilma. Everything's free and lots of people grow pot, and we can go swimming naked and drop acid." She stroked his neck with a trembling hand. "And make love."

"I've never done acid."

"You haven't? Really? It's way bitchin' man."

Paul saw tears on her cheeks in the lights of another truck and hugged her again. She sniffled and squeezed him back. He ran hands through her hair. She smelled like sweat, but it was a good smell. Darla always smelled good. He wanted to lick her all over. He took out his knife, poured water from his canteen on the blade, and wiped it in the grass.

"Here, let me wash that blood off your face." Darla poured water on her hands and wiped his cheeks with her palms.

"I guess we're outlaws now."

She made a little laugh and kissed him. "It's not so easy hitching sometimes I guess, but after the bad karma always comes the good, so we've got something really bitchin' coming. I know it." She pointed to the concrete shelf under the freeway bridge above the railroad tracks. "Let's crash there. Fuck everything. Let's get laid."

She didn't have to say it twice.

IV.
On the Road

Darla was out of sight somewhere in the trees andhad to find her. Birds sang, and a girl's laughter echoed in the forest. He quickened his pace, and a skittering of claws in the branches overhead made him glance up.

Two golden eyes stared back at him from high in the canopy of an ancient fir. He heard laughter and scanned the forest. When he glanced back up, the eyes were red as blood. Paul blinked, and they were gone.

* * *

A train pounded them awake as it rattled under the highway. The songs of birds returned. Darla curled in his arms as they spooned together under one of the bags with the other between them and cold concrete. Paul tried to stand, bumped his head on the bottom of the bridge, and stepped down the embankment to empty his bladder with a groan.

Darla's giggle made him glance over his shoulder. She was lying on her side with the bag around her chin, making little kicking motions as she worked on something under the covers.

"What's so funny?"

"You're cute, that's all."

"Oh."

She yawned. "God, I'm happy."

"Huh?"

"Here we are and we almost died but we didn't even get hurt. Life is wonderful, and all I want to do is get it on with you again and see what today brings. Life's a fucking trip. Here," she held up the sheath of his knife, "I carved my mom's phone number in it in case we ever have to get hold of each other."

He climbed back up the embankment, dropped to all fours, and crawled to the bags. Darla tossed back the top one with a flourish and he slid in beside her. She wrapped herself around him, rolled on top, and they began to rock as she pressed her lips to his ear.

She gasped. "I love balling in the morning."

* * *

They climbed on the freeway, stuck out their thumbs, and a red International pickup with bales of hay pulled over and they jumped in the back. The driver was a woman with two kids heading to Roseburg. Paul and Darla settled against the bales in a storm of straw and watched the road behind them.

"I'm glad we're in back." She said. "We need a fucking shower."

"Yeah." He pointed to a stain on the right leg of his jeans. "I got some of their blood on me."

"That's a bust." Darla examined her own legs. "We gotta wash our clothes. Got another pair?" He nodded, and she laughed. "Wow, that's really a bust... like crime and shit."

Paul stared at his pants. "Roseburg's a real redneck town. I hope we get a ride quick." When they passed through Eugene, he pointed to some distant brick buildings. "That's the university where I'm supposed to go to college."

"What are you going to study?"

"I don't know. They do this thing called tracking at my school and my counselor says Journalism, but I think my mom wants me to be a fucking lawyer. My dad says engineering, which is more realistic I guess, but I just like to read and write science fiction and ride dirt bikes." He shook his head. "I don't want to think about it." A vision of the red hair and blue eyes of Susan Allen popped into his mind. She was going to the university next year. He'd never managed to come close to scoring with her, and now he was with Darla, who was way prettier anyway. The university disappeared behind the hill, and he kissed her cheek. "Fuck it."

They rode through green mountains past gas stations, farms and ranches, and got off in Roseburg under a scorching sun beneath a rocky hill. They picked hay out of their hair and ran behind some bushes at the base of the hillside, where Paul put on his un-stained jeans.

"Hey, check it out." Darla pointed at four long-haired creatures on the cliffs as they walked back to the highway. "Goats."

"Cool."

A green and white police car pulled to a stop beside them. The cop did a double take when he examined Darla. He was a big man with sunglasses, a crew cut and a pad of fat at the base of his skull just like Tweedledee and Tweedledum. He leaned a thick red forearm on the door, spat on the hot pavement, crooked a thick finger, and motioned for them to approach.

Paul told himself the knot in his stomach was from hunger. Darla squeezed his hand, and they approached the cop. Paul took a deep breath, stiffened his resolve, and focused on her.

"Good afternoon!" the cop boomed.

"Good afternoon, sir."

"Where are you kids heading?"

"South."

"Awful hot today." The cop rubbed his head and grinned at Paul. "You'd be way cooler with a nice short haircut like mine, kid."

"Yeah, but then my neck would get all red."

The cop's cheeks bulged. "Where you kids goin'? Wolf Creek, Takilma?"

"Where?"

"Them hippie communes?"

"We didn't know about them, sir."

"Goin to Colorado to that gatherin'?"

"Where?"

"That hippie solstice celebration. Goin' to San Francisco then?"

"Um, maybe."

"Watch out for crazies." The aviator sunglasses turned to Darla. "Do your parents know you're doin' this, young lady?"

"Yes, my dad's a scientist, and is really open-minded."

The cop lowered his sunglasses to stare over the tops at her as his voice dropped. "Really?"

"Uh-huh."

"Well, mine's a logger, and he woulda tanned my sister's hide if she ever stuck out her thumb on the highway like that." The cop shook his head. "At least you got a guy to hitch with." He nodded toward Paul's knife. "That a Ka-Bar?"

"Yes sir."

"Love 'em. Had one in 'Nam. First in with the Marines in sixty-five. You're not dodgin' the draft are you?"

"No, I'm seventeen, and going to college in Eugene in the fall."

"Where did you get that?"

"My uncle was a Marine flyer in the Pacific. He got shot down twice."

"Devil dog of the air. Good for him." The big man rubbed his eyes and replaced his sunglasses. "Okay," He looked them up and down one more time, "You two be damn careful now."

"Oh, we will, sir."

"Okay, see ya." The cop twisted the air conditioning knob on his dash, rolled up the window, and took off.

"Whew," Darla let out her breath with a loud hiss, "Now I gotta pee."

"Me too."

They returned to the bushes and back to the freeway.

A multi-colored VW van stopped with four girls in it and Darla clapped her hands. "All right, good karma!" The smell of pot greeted them as the side door opened. The girl driving had long blond hair and wore a bone choker around her throat like the plains Indians. The other girls had very long hair also, wore print skirts, beads, and the two they could see were pretty. Another was under a quilt on the bunk in back with only her legs and bare feet visible. The van smelled like patchouli oil, pot, and girls.

Darla took over. "Wow, thanks so much, we just got hassled by some redneck cop."

The girl on the floor across from them, who had big dark eyes and black hair and looked like an Indian, nodded sagely. "Fuckin' pigs. Roseburg's a shitty place for freaks. After the revolution, the pigs will be gone." She leaned over a plastic bag and began to stuff red-haired Mexican pot into a blackened red stone peace pipe with a painted stem as seeds rolled across the floor. Paul watched her breasts swing in the loose cotton dress, but his stomach interrupted him when it growled. She offered Darla the pipe. "Want a toke?"

"Please." Darla crossed her legs on the padded floor. "This is righteous. Thanks again for the ride. We're coming from Canada."

The girl riding shotgun brightened. "Are you Canadian?"

"Half."

"Where are you going?"

"San Francisco."

"The City ain't what it was, sister. There's way better places to go. We had some people leave from the farm to the Gathering of the Tribes in Colorado where the good energy has moved. This guy at a commune in Drain had a dream about this spiritual convergence on the continental divide, and some awesome things coming to change the world, and it's happening. We're holding down the fort here 'cause Shauna has a warrant in Colorado and can't go." She sighed. "I sure wish we were heading to Granby."

"Where's Granby?"

"In the higher realm right now. Maybe they'll levitate the place with all the stoners there. Want some soybeans?" The Indian girl offered a paper bag of roasted and salted soybeans, and they each took a handful. Paul leaned against a pillow, hoping he didn't stink.

"I hate the City." The blonde driving said.

"You hate San Francisco?"

She scowled. "I got kidnapped by this biker gang for two goddamn weeks last summer in the oh-so wonderful Haight Ashbury. This guy told me he could get me a gig. It's fucking hard to be taken seriously if you're a girl and play electric guitar. Most assholes think you gotta have a dick or something. This one said he could introduce me to John Cipolina from Quicksilver Messenger Service, and took me to a house in Daly City. Said he was bringing in people to hear me but it was his biker friends. When I heard those choppers pull up, I knew what was happening and tried to bail out a back window but they fuckin' yanked me back in and this guy slapped me so hard I saw sparks. 'Put out or die, bitch!' this piece of shit says and shoves a gun in my ear. They hid my clothes the whole goddamn time."

"The Goddess saved you." The girl on the bunk whispered.

The Indian girl nodded. "I got a ride across the Bay at night to Alcatraz when the American Indian Movement people were holding it. That turned into a bummer too." She sighed loudly. "There were Native people from all over the place, all kinds of tribes when the occupation began, with celebrations and feasts and peyote ceremonies and I really wanted to go there. They had warriors on the guard towers with machine guns 'cause everybody thought the Feds would come at any time. It was the first place to be taken back by Native People by the words of the treaties, and we had some Miwoks whose land it was originally. I wanted to help any way I could, but by the time I got there the AIM people had left, and these two big Lakota brothers, Gary and Michael, had taken over the place. They were back from Nam, and into heroin, and they liked to keep girls who came over for slaves." She took the pipe and drew a long hit, let out the smoke, and stared out the window at the passing hills. "They fucking raped me a bunch. I didn't even know to call it rape then but that's what it was. I was fifteen and thought I was supposed to please the big Indian heroes. I was there a month before this guy Mickey from the Pit River tribe snuck me off the island." She scowled. "The brothers were too busy with some blond hippie chick to even notice. They really did a number on her. I still hear her crying in my sleep."

Shauna drove in silence and accepted the pipe from her friend. The redhead next to her held the wheel while she took a big toke. She passed it to the redhead, put her hands back on the wheel, and let out a white cloud. "After that shit in the Bay I guess I can handle anything, but I'm done with the fucking City... and men, too. I'm on Coyote Creek now living with women. Just women."

"It's beautiful." The Indian girl said. "There's so much nature, and gardens, and these old mine shafts where cold water comes out in pools and you can swim under big cedar trees and the azalea flowers make the air smell so good. We did peyote last week at the swimming hole. And it was magical. The spirits of the Takilma Indians dwell there, even if they're all wiped out." She stared out the window. "I can feel them."

"Yeah," the girl on the bed said, "and we live with righteous women only. No goddamn rapists." She rose on her elbows and stared at Darla. "You been fucking."

Darla gave her a polite smile, and the girl gave Paul a stare that he couldn't quite figure out but he smiled back. She rolled over and ignored him.

Darla took another toke and stared at Shauna, who could have been her sister. They both had the same height, eyes, and hair, but Darla's nose was way prettier in Paul's opinion. She cleared her throat. "How did you get away?"

"They went out to score dope and left me with one dumbshit. I'd hid one of their knives under the mattress and pretended I was asleep. They had guns. I wish they'd left one of those. I would have waited for the rest to come home and got 'em all I fuckin' swear. The asshole killed a bottle of Mad Dog 20-20 and came in to ball me. He dropped his pants, points at his dick and tells me to suck it... and I cut him where it *counts!*" Her mouth twisted. "I'm done with men."

Darla sat up straight. "We had something happen like that! Two big ugly rednecks tried to kidnap and rape me last night, and Paul cut them both, and we got away!" She rose on her knees. "We had to run through a cornfield and down railroad tracks and crashed under a bridge and—"

"And you can use a bath." The girl on the bunk said.

Paul felt the blood rise to his face. The idea that the girl driving was done with men obliterated any heroics Darla ascribed to him. Shauna was beautiful. It didn't make sense. He wasn't like those guys and the idea of her not ever being with a man seemed such a waste. He felt embarrassed for simply being male. It didn't feel good at all. San Francisco was starting to sound like not such a great destination either.

The girl on the bunk finally smiled. "Wanta go swimming?"

* * *

They got off the highway at Wolf Creek by an ancient white roadhouse and tavern and drove up Coyote Creek Road. The commune was far back in the hills, and they passed a half-dozen trucks and vans filled with long-haired young people who waved. They bumped across a meadow over a rutted drive and parked in front of a rambling house of sun-blasted boards that looked like it hadn't been painted in its best days. A sprinkler ticked a circular spray in a garden fenced by bent willow branches that had *god's eyes* of colorful twine wound amongst them.

Two dogs barked, and chickens clucked from a leaning coop with a purple peace sign painted on it. A naked, gray-haired, flat-breasted woman rose up amongst tomato vines with the sun-bleached hair of three little girls around her. Two young women came from the house and waved.

"Eee-yow," Shauna yelled out the window, "Happy almost solstice, sisters!"

"Welcome home," A girl with hairy legs in a Madras print skirt called. When Darla stepped out, she brightened. When Paul did her eyes narrowed.

The Indian girl smiled. "These guys escaped last night from redneck rapists. They're gonna crash here. They're cool."

The girls on the porch nodded and went inside.

They followed Shauna to a creek with a wide green pond surrounded by flat rocks. Darla had her blouse off before she got there. She kicked off her stained Converse All-Stars and stepped out of her jeans. Shauna dropped her Levis with her eyes on Darla, and the other girls yanked their dresses over their heads.

Paul tried not to stare as he doffed his clothes, dove in, and swam the length of the pond underwater. A fish darted past him into the shadow of the bank with a flash of silver as crawdads scuttled amongst the rocks. He stepped around them and came up beside Darla.

She tossed back wet hair and kissed him. "Sure beats swimmin' in Ucluelet, eh?"

"What swimming?"

The girl who'd been on the bunk was kissing Shauna, who could have been Darla's sister. Paul couldn't blame her.

V.
The City

They bathed under an outdoor shower, ate a dinner of curried vegetables and rice, and threw their bags out under the stars and a rising half-moon. The thick grass was a pleasure after the concrete of the night before.

"This is great Darla, and nobody can find us here."

A smirk spread her face under the stars. "I doubt anybody's even looking."

"Those guys had to go to a hospital and you can bet they said they were attacked, so somebody probably is."

"Ever hear that Dead song where they say: 'Let your tracks be lost in the dark and snow'? That's what's dropping out's about," Darla grinned, "and now you gotta drop out too." She giggled. "Or what it's *aboot* if you're Canadian. Turn on, tune in and drop out like Timothy Leary says. Now you can turn on and free your mind from all the bullshit." She slipped out of her clothes and slid under the covers. "We've gotta get some bags we can zip together. I saw some at Sears. A rattlesnake could crawl in these."

"They're expensive."

"So?" She yawned, and he felt her hand slip down his thigh. "You know it's bitchin' how you taught those fat rednecks a lesson. You were totally up to it when the shit hit the fan, man." She gave him a look that made the sleeping bags feel like a king's bed. "My dad calls that skookum."

"We say that where I live too. It's a Chinook Indian word. I read a lot of stuff about the Indians and did a school project on the Chinook language. They were a tribe at the mouth of the Columbia. They called all water 'chuck.' Just chuck. When white men came they said they couldn't call the ocean and fresh water the same, so the Chinook Indians said okay, and called it *salt* chuck."

Darla laughed. "Really?" She put hands behind her head and returned her gaze to the sky. "That was fuckin' scary with those dudes. It's like everything isn't the same now. A couple years ago hip people thought the new age was here. Shit, Jim Morrison and Janis Joplin and Jimi Hendrix all died at the same time. Sometimes I wonder if I will when I'm twenty-seven like they did. I hitched all over the place and ran away to the Haight Ashbury at fourteen. There's always bad shit around but nothing ever touched me. I had good karma. The Altamont festival turned into a bummer, but I left with good people for a commune and beautiful stuff happened there too. I never got raped either, but lots of my friends did." Paul felt her tighten and kissed her cheek. Darla sighed. "There's so many weird vibes now. I think it started with Altamont… or maybe with Charlie Manson."

A vision of being handcuffed in the back of a police car unraveled an unwelcome ending to his summer in Paul's mind. He was supposed to finish high school in the fall and go to college. None of it seemed real now. Darla *was.* He let out the breath he didn't know he'd been holding and ran a finger down her nose and across her lips. She kissed it. "It's the bad energy from the war I guess, and Nixon, and the draft and stuff."

She mussed his hair. "I'm glad you're with me. I like you so much."

"I really like you, Darla."

"I guess so. You want to get it on 'bout a zillion times a day." She rolled on her elbows. "Just be careful. I'm like your first lay ever and some people go nuts on the first one. I lost it to this jock in San Diego that I was ga-ga over and when I look back he wasn't worth spit. He bragged all over middle school about getting my cherry, strutting around like a fuckin' rooster and slapping hands with his buds. I had to walk to class listening to those assholes make stupid comments like I was some kinda slut or something." She snorted. "He couldn't hold it for more than three fuckin' *minutes,* and he had the teeniest pecker for such a big dude. I didn't have any idea what getting off was and wondered what all the fuss was about. Just lying under a giant motherfucker and not able to breathe? What a dick. Lucky I ran into a stoner who knew how to make a girl freak in bed. He'd go down on me for a fuckin' hour. You like to do that too." She sighed. "And now I got your cherry and you loved it. It's kinda like passing it on. Isn't that romantic?" She kissed his brow. "I've had guys follow me all over the place and fuck up what was a great time just 'cause they thought because we got it on once I was their old lady or something." She ran a hand through his hair. "I'd hate for you to go off all jealous when I'm flirting with a guy. That's how a girl gets by. It's our thing, Paul. It's karma, and it helps us both when we're together 'cause I can get shit done. It gets us things."

"How many guys have you been with?"

"You're not supposed to ask. Do I gotta teach you *everything?* Just think about how I am when I'm with you." She grabbed his hand and ran her tongue down the back of it. "Everything takes practice, although I've gotta say you surprised me. You're a natural. Getting off with you is easy and I'd say from personal experience you're hung like Jesus or something, but don't get a big fuckin' ego about it, okay?"

Paul stared at the Milky Way arcing over the dark silhouettes of trees and felt a grin spread his face. Crickets sang, and something splashed in the creek. They lay in silence as coyotes howled in the hills. Paul closed his eyes, and like a snake striking from the grass, a jolt of jealousy rippled through him toward those faceless others who'd had her first. He ground his teeth and stared at the sky.

Darla was watching him.

Jealous of what?

He was with her now and she was right. He really didn't want to know. He would take things as they came. Planning his life hadn't worked worth shit up to now, and things seemed way better when he wasn't, even with that run-in with those Tweedledee and Tweedledum assholes. Paul chuckled.

She chuckled back. "That Brenda chick sure wants to make it with me."

"Which one?"

"The one who was in the back of the van. I guess I look too much like Shauna. They're kinda together."

"Yeah I know, but you're way prettier."

"She jumped all over me just for saying 'chick.' She says it's a male superiority word and a chauvinistic something or other. She's from Boston and says we're behind the times like we're West Coast hicks or something. Then the next thing I know, she's trying to make it with me when I went out to the garden. Pretty good kisser. She wanted to go down on me right there. I mean... like she was really insistent."

He swallowed. "Well... you're a fox, Darla."

"Thanks." She ran a finger down his neck. "I told her okay, but only if you were in on it."

"Really?"

"She almost took me up on it."

A vision of being between the two girls erupted in Paul's imagination and his cock stood up and took notice.

Her fingers wrapped around it. "That always gets 'em."

"What?"

"Talk about two chicks with a guy, and *boom!*" A laugh rumbled her chest. "You'd love it dude."

"Um—"

Her laughter rippled across his throat. "I love guys. They're so predictable."

* * *

In the morning the women of Coyote Creek fed them granola, raw milk and chamomile tea, and Shauna dropped them in Wolf Creek with a kiss for Darla. They went into a café, used the graffiti-covered facilities, and stuck out their thumbs. Penny the Indian girl recommended they check out the country around Takilma in the Siskiyou Mountains. "Just get out in Cave Junction and ask any freaks you see."

Some long-haired youths stopped in a panel truck with a burlap bag of shade leaves from their pot, who were heading to San Francisco to sell it. It didn't smoke that well, but after three or four joints it was okay. They headed down highway 199 toward the coast and stopped at a natural foods store in a purple dome where Darla bought dates, nuts, dried fruit and rice, and stuffed them in her pack. Paul had a handful of Slim Jims he'd bought at the gas station in Wolf Creek. Nutrition wasn't a big priority, and he couldn't imagine where she planned to cook rice. It was more fun to make love on an empty stomach anyway. As they passed through Cave Junction, the driver pointed out the turn for Takilma, but they decided to head on to the Haight Ashbury and the fabled city of San Francisco.

They stayed that night in Humboldt County in the redwoods, where several school busses converted to live in were parked in a circle. There was a yurt pitched that had a fire burning in the middle, and people shared wine from a leather bota bag.

Two long-haired guys in their twenties were arguing about someone named Candy.

"Fuck it!" One said. He got up, shook his head and stalked out the door into the night.

The other took another swig of wine and shrugged. "I don't know."

"Don't know what?" Darla asked.

"He's all freaked out by Candy. Says it's against nature, or God, or something." The young man tugged at the semblance of a beard and scowled.

"What?"

"That Candy person. She... he... is supposed to have one of each."

Paul blinked. "Huh?"

"Like having a dick and a pussy."

"You mean... like a hermaphrodite?" Paul said.

"What's that?"

Darla blinked. "Wow. I want to see."

The guy snorted. "Get in line. Candy prefers to be called *her* anyway."

"I don't blame her, but I still want to see."

"Go for it. Her camp's up the hill."

Paul and Darla swam in the Eel River under the summer moon. They threw out their bags, made love to the songs of crickets, and lay speculating about Candy afterward.

"God Paul, I guess when someone says go fuck yourself, Candy can actually do it."

"I don't even want to think about it."

"Let's go visit."

"No."

Darla giggled herself to sleep.

***

He awoke from a dream of a girl with eyes like gems and Darla was gone. Paul got up, pissed in the bushes and yawned. He tugged on his jeans and boots as she came down the path between towering redwoods with an expression he'd never seen.

"I met Candy."

"Did—"

"She... he... let me see."

Paul swallowed. "You're shitting."

"No." Darla searched around for some remnant of the pot they'd smoked the night before and found the damp remnants of a joint on a log. "Got a match?"

Paul handed her a wooden Blue Tip match, and she struck it on her jeans and lit the roach. "What did you see?"

"Well, the dick's pretty small, but there's one there, and she's got a real pussy too. She let me touch it. All of it."

"Yuk."

"And the dick started to get hard." She giggled. "Bet I never get to do that again."

***

The next afternoon they got out at Haight and Stanyan Streets by the entrance to Golden Gate Park. Traveling was great with Darla. People took one look at her and gave them rides or invited them in. She was right about flirting too. It brought them all they needed. It would be something to have their own place with a big bed. Paul didn't think far beyond that, since every time he did, the blood seemed to rush to his cock from his brain.

Darla glanced around at the three-story Victorians, dirty streets, and walls of businesses covered with notices, posters and faded psychedelic graffiti. The Cala Market on the corner was blanketed with them. "Wow, we made it to the Haight. I ran away three times to here and always ended up somewhere else. It's kind of a dimensional doorway where you always launch into something groovy. Guess that's why I'm back again."

"Those guys on the Eel River say we're five years too late." Paul glanced at a man with his hair in tattered ropes wearing a burlap poncho and his nose wrinkled at the smell. "Your dad said you came down with hepatitis one time, in Ohio or something."

"In *Ojai.* He told you that?"

"Yeah. Where's that?"

"South." She took his hand. "Let's see what's up."

"Okay."

She pointed to the faded marquee of a movie theater. "Shit. The Straight Theater's closed." Purple letters from the last show still advertised the **GRA-----L DE-D** on it with **–OUNTR- JOE AN- THE FIS-** below that in warped red letters, and the glass cases for movie posters were broken and empty. "What a bummer. Big Brother, the Airplane, the Dead, the Youngbloods and this comedy troupe called the Congress of Wonders played there for a buck-fifty when I was fourteen and I snuck in. We sat in the balcony and the dope smoke was so fuckin' thick you could hardly see the stage. This Arab guy I was with from Oakland had... oh, never mind."

The street was filled with hip-looking people, though most were older than they'd expected. A trembling young man with ugly red sores on his face sat in a doorway with a dirty blanket over him. They gave him a wide berth. Two bikers with black leather vests and Hells Angels colors stared at Darla as they passed. A black man with a dirty red scarf on his forehead, an oily afro, and the whites of his eyes a sickly yellow leaned against the wall of a restaurant next to a sign that said **RIP-OFFS WILL BE PROSECUTED** and hissed "Kilo?" as they walked by.

Someone spewed a stream of curses from a bay window above the street and a skinny guy in a tattered denim poncho gave them the finger. The person in the window spit at him and slammed the glass with a rattle. Ragged teens panhandled every passerby and even hit them up for change. People stepped around a large dog turd in the middle of the sidewalk. From the long smear on its side, someone hadn't. A tall man with a mustache and sideburns in a wide-collared pinstriped suit stared at Darla from the door of a bar, pointed to his crotch, and patted his pocket.

"That guy's propositioning me."

"Huh?"

She squeezed his hand, "You are so fuckin' naïve, man."

"Well, I'm not a girl."

She gazed up at the ornate garrets and dormers crowning the Victorian homes to either side of them. "There's gotta be crash pads around. It would be a trip to stay in a garret. I did once and it was really cool. Check out the stained glass in that one. God, wouldn't it be cool if we were smokin' a hookah in that place and balling on a futon? We just have to find a good one where people aren't too weird, with no speed freaks or bikers."

"No, no speed freaks or bikers."

Darla shivered. "That story of Shauna's was the pits."

"So was Penny's."

Darla's mouth thinned. "All the shit I just shined-on before keeps coming back since those Tweedel-dee-dee assholes picked us up." She exhaled. "That could have been me a bunch of times. Man, I'm lucky." She gestured at two policemen coming down the block from the east. "Let's cross the street." They made it to Masonic Street where the zoo of pedestrians and hippie businesses petered out, got to the foot of Buena Vista Park on its steep hill, turned around and headed back toward Golden Gate Park.

Two guys in neon pink halter tops, red shorts and lipstick emerged from the bushes on the hill. As they passed one reached out and squeezed Paul's butt. He spun around and glared at them, and his hand went to the hilt of his knife. They waved and disappeared in an apartment building.

Darla chuckled. "Now you know how it feels, dude."

"Fuck that."

They passed a dirty storefront that had **Diggers** written in thick marker on a sheet of paper in the window and Darla yanked on his hand. "Those are the guys who give out free food. I had some cool bread they made once in gallon cans at Panhandle Park that had pot baked in it. Sometimes they give away pot and acid and stuff too."

"Let's check it out."

The place was filled with piles of dirty clothes and notes on the walls, on which half of the words seemed to be FUCK. Paul walked up to a poster. It had a wavy paisley sky drawn above a monstrous wolf-man with drool running from a fanged mouth that was crawling into a window over a naked girl on a bed, with **The Werewolf Manifesto** printed in blood-dripping letters above it. A paragraph beneath the picture called on all runaway kids to become creatures of the night, have lots of sex, and prey on the rich. A pale young man at the rear of the room gave them a crooked grin. They went back out to the street.

At the entrance of Golden Gate Park, a man stood on a box between two branching paths shouting at passersby. They stopped to listen but nothing he said made any sense. It was all about mind control and something called the Illuminati. They walked through a dank tunnel into the Park and passed bushes from which the smell of pot came mixed with those of urine and spilled wine.

"We can walk all the way to the ocean. The Family Dog Ballroom's down by Playland. It's really cool. I saw this guy Stephen Gaskin doing this telepathy thing once. Somebody threw out bag-fulls of acid and psilocybin on the stage and I grabbed two handfuls. We dropped some and went to Land's End and crawled around some bitchin' caves. I sold some too. That was a cool day."

"I never did acid."

She squeezed his hand. "Then we have to."

They came to a slope where a hundred or so people sprawled on the grass. Four black men sat on a bench at the base of the hill playing conga drums as a flute whistled, and kites bobbed overhead.

Paul squinted against a shaft of sun breaking through the clouds. "This looks like a cool place."

"This is Hippie Hill. Everybody ends up here sooner or later."

They walked toward a group of young people where a joint was going around. A pretty blond girl was talking animatedly with a guy who looked like a real Indian. He had long braids tied with red ribbons and a choker of dentalium shells around his neck that looked ancient. An older guy in his thirties with black hair, a beard and a red headband was rolling another joint. He looked up as they dropped their packs and sat down to lean on them. His eyes lingered on Paul, but he glanced at Darla with what seemed disdain. When the joint finally came around, the end was flat and soggy. Paul grimaced and passed on it, but Darla tore the wet tip off and sucked it down a good inch in a cloud of smoke.

"Hey, don't tear it up. And don't Bogart that joint, bitch."

Darla gave the man her best smile, but he sneered.

The Indian gave them both a smile and shrugged. "Seeking wisdom is an endless journey."

Paul nodded. "Where are you from?"

"South Dakota." He extended a big brown hand. "Wanbli Witco is my name. Crazy Eagle in your tongue."

Darla grinned. "Dude, you're a trip."

"I was assistant High Priest in the Native American Church. Do you know what that is?"

They shook their heads.

"We take peyote in humility, as a sacrament. Not like these people here who--"

"Bitch, give me back that joint." The man with a red head-band said.

The Indian frowned. *"Winkte."* He muttered.

"Huh?" Darla said.

Paul grabbed her hand. "Good to meet you."

They stood up, hoisted their packs, and headed down the hill.

"Wow, that guy rolling joints was uptight. I wonder what Winkte means."

She brushed hair from her eyes. "Dunno. Did you see the way that guy looked at me?"

"Yeah, I don't think he likes women. I don't think San Francisco is so great either."

"It's just one guy. There's still lots of groovy people here. We just have to find a good place to—"

Three men in black leather vests appeared on the path looking Darla up and down like they were going to drag her into the bushes on the spot. A bearded, heavy-set one with an oily vest and a Harley drive chain for a belt pointed to Paul's feet. "Nice boots. Those the only ones you got?"

"Huh?"

Darla nudged his side, "Say yes." she whispered.

"Yeah, we're hitching and broke. They're all I've got, man."

The man rubbed tattooed knuckles on his vest and nodded. "Okay."

One of his companions chuckled. "You got a hot little ass there chickee. Hope that little dude's givin' it a good poundin'. If he don't let me know."

"Um, peace, dude."

The three men laughed and continued into the park. As soon as Paul and Darla rounded a turn, they cut off the trail into a wall of rhododendrons and hunkered down in the first clearing they came to.

Paul leaned against his pack with a sigh. "Fuck this place. Let's go back to the redwoods, or back to Oregon and check out the communes."

Darla brushed hair from her eyes and peered down the trail. "Maybe you're right." The sun was getting low in the west and slanting through the tops of eucalyptus as shadows thickened around them. "We gotta find a place to crash, or we could sleep in the Park I guess."

"This place is fucking dangerous. I wish I had my .30-.30."

Darla hugged her knees and pushed eucalyptus leaves around with her toes. "Let's go back to the Haight and find a place. It's always worked before."

"Okay," he gripped the hilt of his knife, "I guess." They stepped back onto the path ready to duck in the bushes at the sight of danger. As they neared Hippie Hill, they noticed two older men in dirty denim vests following them and sped up their pace.

Two girls appeared and waved them off the trail into the shrubbery. Paul and Darla ducked in beside them, and the men strode by toward Haight Street.

The blond one sneered at the men's backs. "Those dudes suck." She grinned. "You guys need a place to crash?"

Darla gasped. "Yes!"

The red-haired one smiled. "You're safe with us, brother and sister. She's Mary Ann and I'm Squeaky. Karma brought you to us."

*　*　*

The girls took them to a white two-storey house on Waller a block up from Haight Street. "We're part of a big family," Mary Ann said, "but everybody else is at the ranch. We've got a groovy place out in the desert where you can do anything you want with no hassles and lots of psychedelics, with Owsley acid, mescaline, psilocybin…"

"And no pigs." Squeaky added.

They sat cross-legged on a scuffed hardwood floor. Mary Ann stuffed pot in the bowl of a glass bong, lit it and passed it to Darla. "You guys might fit in."

"Uh, thanks." Paul glanced around a living room spray-painted with different colors over peeling plastered walls. A big Irish setter whose coat needed brushing sprawled on a filthy couch, and **RISE** was painted in red letters on a cracked mirror over the bricked-up fireplace. Dog hair had collected at the bases of the walls and drifted in wisps when someone walked across the room.

"Yeah, too bad this shit came down. I love Sadie. She's funnier than hell. She was a titty dancer and loves to party, and Patty and Linda and Sandy are our soul sisters, and Charlie is the most aware human being on the whole fucking planet. He's how we came together, like different planets around the sun." Mary Ann gazed into space. They're awaiting liberation and we're going to help."

"It's just an illusion," Squeaky intoned, "another test on the path to enlightenment."

Darla blinked. "Saying somebody's the most aware person on the whole planet is kind of a lot. I don't turn guys into Prince Charming anymore. If they've got what I need I use it just like they do, and maybe we're friends is all. That works pretty good for me."

Squeaky got up and drifted into the kitchen.

Mary Ann shook her head. "No... like *really!* He can read your mind like right now and can let us know if you're cool from where he is."

"Those super-amazing dudes can disappoint you. He got a big dick or something?"

Mary Ann's eyes went cold. "That's not what I mean. He *is* an amazing lay, the *best,* and he does have a big dick, but he's the most incredible musician and Brian Wilson of the Beach Boys recorded him, and he just looks at you and knows *exactly* what you're thinking. He can read your mind 'cause he's sent here by God. There are old souls in the world and it's totally possible to meet a transcendental one like an Avatar, like Buddha or Jesus or something. There's as many people in the world as during all those ages living right now, so why not? We came together from forces beyond chance, heavy forces, *spiritual* forces." Mary Ann straightened and tossed a tent of blond hair from her face. "You'll know exactly what I mean, if you ever get to meet him."

Squeaky emerged from a bedroom with a red smudge between her eyes that looked like dried blood. "Mary Ann's right. We're awaiting his return." She scooted the dog off the couch, and his claws clicked across the hardwood floor as he shuffled toward the door.

Darla whispered in Paul's ear, "Be careful."

"Lie down!" Squeaky commanded. The dog gave her a sad look, groaned, and sprawled beneath the bay window with a sigh.

"I'll walk him if you want," Darla volunteered, "I love dogs."

Mary Ann shook her head. "The pigs will fuck with you if you don't take a leash. I bet you're a runaway anyway."

"How did you know?"

"That's easy sister. This is the age." Mary Ann scowled. "The fuckin' pigs are coming to a reckoning, and you don't want to be in the City when it happens. Janis Joplin, Jimi Hendrix and Jim Morrison all died after they took our man. It's not coincidence. It's their *plan*. There's going to be chaos and blood in the streets, and the niggers will rape and kill all the white women they can find. We've got a hideout in the desert where nobody will find us and it's totally bitchin'. We're collecting survival stuff and weapons, and we're gonna meet our family there."

Darla frowned. "It sounds hot."

Mary Ann ran a hand through Darla's hair. Darla stiffened as Mary Ann walked her fingers down the hollow of her back. "You should come with us, and you too Paul. We're the family of the New Age. We had a really cool old ranch in the San Fernando Valley rich Hollywood people came to. The girls are all pretty, and we got lots of dope and free stuff from these people who have mansions in the Hollywood Hills, in Laurel Canyon, Coldwater Canyon, Benedict Canyon... all these fancy places where the pigs think they're safe. I balled the assistant director from *The Trip* with Peter Fonda and he gave me a car that I gave to Charlie, but the cops took it after... anyway we're blowing this place before the landlord comes again and going to a ranch nobody can find. We stayed behind in case somebody showed who had a pot deal, but today's the deadline so that's their tough luck. Everybody shares everything where we're going and there's lots of music and we do the best acid, and when Charlie says so we have these parties where everybody gets it on. He can communicate with us from where they're keeping him through Squeaky here. She's got the Third Eye." Mary Ann patted Squeaky's leg. "He'll be free soon, and there's lots of girls where we're going," she squeezed Paul's thigh, "and we'll all lay you when you become one of the family."

"Um… how many girls?"

"About twelve, like the apostles, and just four guys so I hope you can keep up."

Darla shot Paul a sideways glance and squeezed his other knee. Paul blinked. "What?"

"Dude!"

"What?"

* * *

They slept in a big room with trash piled in the corner and a tall scuffed dresser with the drawers pulled out. A pile of half-clean clothes was on a shelf below the bay window and Paul checked out some jeans. Two pairs were a little too large in the waist, but about his length.

Darla stuffed magazines under the door to wedge it shut and put fingers to her lips. "Paul, don't you know who those chicks are talking about?"

"Who?"

"It's *Charlie Manson,* dude! *That's* the family they're talking about! That's who they *are!*" Her eyes were huge. "These bitches are crazy! They're killers!"

"Shit, but if it's that guy he's already on death row."

"It doesn't matter! They think he's Jesus or something and can come back from the dead."

They turned to the door as someone walked down the hall. Paul reached for his knife.

She exhaled. "Take the pants and leave the bloodstained ones here. It's where they belong."

"I hope somebody didn't have the crabs."

"Yuk."

Paul vigorously shook out the two pairs of jeans, put one in his pack and the other on a chair for the morning. He wadded up the bloodstained ones and threw them onto the pile in the corner.

They made love with their bags on the floor but stopped at every sound from the house. He kept his knife within reach as Darla bounced on top of him until his tailbone felt flat. When they finished she let out a shuddering breath, pulled damp hair from her mouth, and pressed soft lips to his ear. "Let's go north."

"Good idea. Where?"

"Takilma. Things were pointing us there. We should have gone with the flow in the first place." Darla sighed. "This place is fucking dead and the energy is bad. I'm never coming back to the Haight again."

"What if the cops in Oregon are looking for us?"

"How? Those fat fucks you cut didn't know our names."

"I don't mean that. I'm from Charleston, and my parents must have called the Oregon cops by now."

She slapped at a flea and grimaced. "We're supposed to go there. That's what karma was trying to tell us. Trust me."

He studied her lips and let out his breath. "Okay."

* * *

Paul jerked awake from a vision of a girl's pale face with bright green eyes, wishing he'd stayed asleep long enough to kiss her.

Squeaky and Mary Ann made a breakfast of sausage, potatoes and eggs while extolling the wonders of their new age family. When they were done cooking, the girls threw the dirty pans into an overflowing trash barrel in a backyard dotted with dog turds. Two big gray rats jumped out of the barrel and disappeared under the house. "We're not taking this material shit," Squeaky explained. "There's plenty where we're going."

Mary Ann laughed. "Maybe we should torch the place. That'd freak the fuckers out."

Squeaky shook her head. "Then they'll be after us. We can't catch heat after—"

"Shhhh." Mary Ann threw a finger to her lips and turned to Paul and Darla. "You guys want to go with us? We got a ride. There's nothing waiting but love."

Darla forced a smile. "Thanks for your hospitality but we're going to Oregon."

"What's in Oregon?"

"What's in Death Valley?"

"Freedom, love, and enlightenment sister, and you'll be with real people when the shit comes down."

"Okay, but no thanks. Peace."

* * *

As they headed down Fulton toward Nineteenth Avenue and the Golden Gate Bridge, Darla shot him a look of disgust. "God, Paul, you are such a fuckin' sucker when there's girls with some bullshit story."

"What do you mean?"

"Those chicks had a black aura. I knew it instantly that they were talking about Charlie Manson. Why did I have to even *tell* you? Shit, you are such an amateur, it's like… like I've got to protect you from bad shit that you don't even notice." She squeezed his butt. "But I love you for it too."

Paul swallowed. "I… I love you too, Darla."

She groaned. "Not like we're crazy in love like Romeo and Juliet or something. I mean you're supposed to try and love everybody, and you're pretty cool, and you're my friend

and stuff, and you're good company and you're a bitchin' lay."
She grinned. "If you weren't I wouldn't be around, but just
don't trip-out on it okay?"

"What do you think would have happened if we went with
them?"

"You think they were just gonna ball you? They're kinda cute
but did you get any good vibes? Their vibes were fucking *black.*" Darla stuck out her thumb as they reached Fulton Street. "Didn't you hear
how they kept saying 'Charlie-Charlie-Charlie' like little robots?" She
kicked a can into the street. "That Squeaky chick has fuckin' zombie
eyes. I bet that dot on her head was somebody's blood."

"That was weird."

"We don't want to meet any of his friends either. They think
he's God or something. Who knows what they could do to us?" Her
face darkened. "I bet they wanted to use me as a present for some
weird guy. 'Here, Son of Charlie or whoever-the-fuck-you-are, here's
some nice blond beach pussy from San Diego you can rape and kill
when you're done.' Maybe they were gonna sacrifice me, or you,
or both of us. I heard they put peoples' skulls on sticks in Death
Valley. I had a girlfriend from high school who ran away a couple of
years ago, Connie. They found her staked out on the ground dead
in Angeles National Forest with pentagrams carved in her. I always
wondered if it was the Manson family. Anyway, fuck them. I've met
people like that before and they're insane. They kidnap girls all the
time. Remember what Shauna said? There's all kinds of assholes in
the world and you gotta have your antennas out. Look at me. I'm
a girl, and I've been all over and survived. Get in touch with your
karma, Paul. Harness your spiritual power. Use your telepathy or
something." She sighed. "You totally need to do some psychedelics
with me so you're more aware. We gotta fix that." She kicked her
pack. "Stupid cunts. Let's get outta this town."

VI.
North

They got six rides and had only made the eighty miles to Cloverdale by late afternoon. The highway shrank to a comfortable two lanes, which was good for hitching. As they stood in the cicada-buzzing heat under the shade of ancient oaks, Darla announced they were going to the coast. "There's way more hip people there." She wiped her brow. "It's lots cooler too."

Paul would go wherever she wanted. He hadn't called his parents, and his mom must be making life hell for his dad by now. A twinge of guilt rippled through him at the thought. What did Mr. Argyle think of Darla running off with him? The guy obviously knew Paul was balling his daughter but he didn't seem to care. No, that wasn't quite right. Bob knew he couldn't do much about it and must have decided Paul was better than most. Actually that was pretty cool. Somebody would always be with Darla. She was way too cute and too hip. Even other girls had tried to take her away from him but she'd avoided it and warned him about those psycho Manson chicks. She'd been around and she was smart. Someday, if he had a daughter, would he be able to handle one like Darla? What about those girls on Coyote Creek who were living without men? What if his daughter ended up like them?

Shit. Don't they ever want a dick?

A big brown 50's Chevy pickup with a visor over the window, a toolbox behind the cab and running boards with red jerry cans mounted on them rumbled to a stop and the driver waved them in. They threw their packs in the back, and Darla put herself in the middle and thanked the driver.

"Where you guys headed?" The driver was in his twenties with a thin dark beard and greasy ball cap. He sat with the truck idling, staring at Darla.

"Mendocino."

"Lots of people camping there." He lit up a joint and yanked the truck into gear.

Oaks and pines began to yield to the dark towers of redwoods as they followed the Navarro River west. As they neared the coast, the steep green slopes exploded in a riot of yellow scotch broom framing the blue vastness of the Pacific Ocean. They passed through Albion and crossed a bridge over a dark green river. A sign on the bridge said **Big River,** but it wasn't. A whitewashed line of nineteenth century buildings on the opposite bluff announced the old logging town of Mendocino. They thanked their ride, slung their packs, and wandered into the picture book village.

They bought food at a market and decided to eat watching the ocean. An ancient green bronze bench with grey redwood slats sat amongst grass and sedges but someone was on it, so they plopped down in the grass. Yellow gorse and scotch broom crowned bluffs across the river. Screeching gulls and a cream and brown osprey wheeled overhead. The smell of driftwood fires rose from the beach below by an emerald cove where the mouth of the river met the sea as fishing boats bobbed on the ocean beyond rocks crowned with seabirds. Paul cut pieces of Tillamook cheese with his knife and tore off chunks from a twenty-nine cent loaf of sourdough bread. He took a bite and pulled out his notebook to pen a long-overdue letter to his parents.

Darla reached under her loose blouse and produced a pint of Wild Turkey whiskey. "Want a hit?"

He slapped the notebook on his leg. "Wha... where the fuck did you get that?"

"I took it while that zitty guy at the counter was watching the chick with the fishnet top and big tits." She pulled off the cap and took a swallow. 'Eyow... that's *strong!*" She wiped her mouth and examined the label. "One-hundred and one proof. How do people drink this shit?"

"Shit, Darla, you could have got us busted for shoplifting."

"He was a wimp. If he'd tried, I would have made him sorry."

"Then where would we go? He would have called the cops, and we would have got busted, and that would be the end of everything. That's not cool."

She passed him the bottle. Paul turned it over in his hand and examined the label. "Do you want any or not?"

Paul took a belt and his face scrunched up. Darla laughed. He shoved the notebook back in his pack. "We can't be shoplifting." He said in a hoarse voice. "That's fucked-up. I'm paranoid enough 'cause we're runaways."

Darla gazed out to sea. The breeze played with a strand of her hair as her breasts rose and fell with her breathing. He studied her throat and bit his lip as she continued to ignore him. Paul dug his heels in the grass, unscrewed the cap on the bottle, and took another sip.

"Then don't drink it."

He put the cap back and shoved the bottle between her legs. "We... we can't be stealing, Darla. What if you get caught? Then we're fucked. I don't have the money to get you out of jail even if we weren't runaways." He gazed at the ocean. "I just care about you is all. Shit."

She leaned on her elbows and stared at him. Her eyes were bluer than blue in the sunshine. Her lips were shell pink and he wanted to kiss them badly. She sighed and sat up. "Yeah, you're right. I just wanted to have a drink with you and was kinda careless I guess. We never did it before... I mean drink whiskey together."

He took her hand and they headed to the beach.

They sat on a drift log beside a campfire. People were cooking marshmallows on green sticks, and a girl with a ring in her nose squeezed one between two graham crackers and handed it to Paul. The half-burned marshmallow oozed over the slab of milk chocolate onto his fingers and he almost dropped it. He blew on it, took a small bite, and handed the dripping remainder to Darla, who inserted the entire thing into her mouth. Her cheeks bulged and she moaned, fanned her mouth, gasped, and licked her fingers. Someone played conga drums around a big fire toward the water, and somebody rolled joints as the sun set in the ocean like a crimson jewel.

Darla took his hand and they moved away from the fire, where she pulled out the whiskey. Paul checked to make sure their packs were unmolested as her hand slid down his pants. "I'm horny." Her breath bounced in his ear and she kissed him until they began to lose their balance. "Where are we gonna crash?"

"I don't know. I wish we had a van or something."

They spread their bags behind a half-built shelter of drift logs, made love, and fell asleep after finishing the whiskey.

He was hiding with Darla under the bushes. Someone approached. Darla trembled beside him. Paul was angry, angry that she was afraid. The footsteps stopped, and a form stood before their refuge beyond the leaves. Paul sprang up, ready to fight for his lady love. He tore the thin shroud of branches away to reveal the most beautiful woman he'd ever seen. Her eyes were golden jewels like the sun. Then she was gone, leaving only a luminous smile that faded in the mists.

They awoke in the chill mists of the Pacific with headaches, dying of thirst.

* * *

They ordered an expensive but meager breakfast at a little restaurant in an old Victorian home, where they were grudgingly allowed to use the bathroom. They went in together and tried to wash up as well as they could. The ancient faucet whistled when it was turned on and the toilet nearly plugged. They began to make love again standing in the narrow space with Darla's back against the wall. Her shoulder split a poster from the Family Dog Ballroom in San Francisco, and someone banged on the door.

"Just a minute!" She pulled up her pants, wrapped a bar of soap in a paper towel to stuff in her pocket, and they returned to their blueberry muffins and cold coffee. They gazed at the ocean and each other while drinking all the coffee they could get the waitress to refill. Darla stuck a handful of jam packets in her pockets before they paid the scowling woman at the cash register, and they walked out to Highway One to stick out their thumbs. The air had the smell of the sea. There wasn't much traffic, and they sat on their packs and yawned.

Paul spotted a piece of cardboard. "We should make a sign."

"Why? Nobody can read it. You ever read any of those stupid cardboard signs people hold up?"

"I was thinking we could make one that says Yukon, or Alaska or something. Something that gets peoples' attention."

She ran a finger across the back of his hand. "I think that last guy who gave us a ride was a creep. I'm glad you were with me."

"That guy?"

She nodded. "Yeah, from the way he looked at me. When you're with another guy somebody like that will be cool, but when you're alone…"

"It must be scary sometimes, being a girl."

"Dude you got no idea. I caught a ride from Santa Monica to Ventura once and this guy drove me up in the hills. He said he recorded with Joanie Mitchell, and it was a nice neighborhood around Malibu and he seemed okay. He invited me to smoke some grass, so I went into this place with him." She kicked a pebble across the road.

"What... happened?"

She bit her lip.

"Did... he rape you?"

"Almost! The house looked like he was just crashing there, or he broke in or something, and there was this mattress with blood on it. He wouldn't let me go back to his car. I was fucking scared. He kept asking me all this weird sick shit, and tried—" she swallowed, "I had to suck his dick just to get out of there."

"Why didn't you just run?"

Her eyes flashed. "I guess I could have, maybe I should have, but he was big, and he had a big fucking pit bulldog and I didn't know where the fuck I was." She tossed hair from her eyes. "I was *scared,* man. He gave me a ride to Ventura afterwards, and I had to sit and listen to his fucking life story." She spat into the black-berry vines alongside the road. "I couldn't get the taste of his cum out of my mouth. I woke up the next day and still could taste it. I'd like to go back there someday, and when he opens the door..." she made a gun with her fingers, "*bang!*" Darla ran a hand through her hair, yanked on a tangle, and snarled. "But it probably wasn't his house anyway."

"I'd never let that happen to you."

She squeezed his hand. "I know."

A black and white highway patrol car slowed to have a look at them. They stared back, holding hands. The cop began to stop, when Darla crushed Paul's hand in her own and unleashed a thousand-watt smile. The cop grinned, tipped his hat, and sped off.

"Whew, I used up every fuckin' bit of energy for that one."

Paul let out his breath and kissed her.

A Volkswagen microbus pulled up with swirls of color across it and plastic pot leaves hanging from the rearview mirror. The driver was way-old, perhaps sixty, with a mass of beard and graying hair under a battered straw hat. The woman riding shotgun was old too, and wore a purple beaded headband over long black hair streaked with gray. As the doors opened, Paul and Darla inhaled the welcome smell of pot.

Darla called, "Where you guys goin'?"

"Oregon!"

"Cool, where?"

"Takilma."

"Good karma!" She bounced into the van and held a hand out to Paul.

* * *

They stopped at the Russian Gulch campground to use the showers for fifty cents. Paul and Darla crowded into one, finished what they'd started in the bathroom of the restaurant, and used her new soap and some shampoo. They climbed in the van with big smiles and wet hair, passed through Fort Bragg, and rode smoking homemade hash from a big black block that their hosts Moses and Destiny put in a resin-stained burlwood pipe that was carved like the head of a gnarly-looking dwarf. Darla pointed at a place called Benbow Inn along the Eel River.

Paul thought of his parents and shrugged. This was his life now.

VII.
The Party

They headed inland up the Smith River into Oregon and coastal redwoods were replaced by sugar pines and Douglas fir. Red-barked madrone wound their sinuous branches over water pouring from rocky terrain as the country opened into a high valley ringed by rugged peaks. They reached the little town of Cave Junction and gassed up.

Moses headed down Rockydale Road toward a cluster of snow-flecked peaks. Run-down ranches spread on either side of them with pastures full of skinny horses whose un-groomed tails swatted flies. Logged over clear-cuts and the pale scars of old mines dotted the surrounding slopes. Scruffy youths drove by in beat-up trucks or walked along the road and waved. A stout man in a new Ford pickup with a red ball cap passed with a scowl. A long-haired couple with three dogs flashed them the peace sign before disappearing into the trees.

Darla grinned. "This place looks cool."

Moses nodded. "There's lots of communes and places up the east fork of the Illinois: Sun Star, the Barn, the Meadows. My Vet's benefits go a long way here and buy lots of pot. You could come with us but we're doin' a hash deal and the people we're gonna see are kinda paranoid. They do too much speed."

"That's okay. Can you buy food in Takilma?"

"Not much, but people have lots of gardens. Some of the carnivores raise animals and hunt deer, and there's a natural food store in—" Someone was on the side of the road with his thumb out, and Moses pulled over.

The hitchhiker jumped in. "Hey, babe." The young man staring at Darla had one blue eye and one brown. He reminded Paul of husky dogs he'd seen as he held out a dirty hand. "I'm Rainbow Bob."

Her nose crinkled. "Rainbow, uh... is that like, 'cause of your eyes?"

"Yeah. I'm one in a million." His grin exposed a missing incisor. "You're a fox. Want to come to my camp and do acid?"

"Not right now."

Bob showed more missing teeth as he shouted to Moses. "Let me off by Hope Mountain." He turned back to Darla. "There's some bitchin' places to stay up by the gypsy camp and the Queen a' Bronze. It's a old mine with tunnels and ghosts and stuff. People seen flying saucers too. Fauna saw one last year when she was on 'shrooms. It's a trip up there with tons of parties. Wanta be my old lady?"

"No thanks," she pointed to Paul, "I'm with him."

Bob turned to Paul for the first time. "What's your name, man?"

"Paul."

"Wanta buy some acid?"

"Not right now."

"Ain't no better. It's orange sunshine, real Owsley acid from Berkeley. None of that speedy shit."

"Maybe later."

"Okay, cool. Lemme know."

They rounded a white false-front store from the previous century where people and dogs lounged around its whitewashed windows. A fine black horse that was far better groomed than the humans stood tied to a hitching post with a rifle in a beaded scabbard hanging from its saddle. Rainbow Bob jumped out and made a "V" with his fingers, "Peace!" He trundled up a dirt track heading toward the mountain across the road.

Moses snorted. "Buncha speed freaks at the gypsy camp. Not a good place for ladies. Where do you guys want out?"

Darla glanced at the store. "Here, I guess."

Destiny handed them a piece of homemade hashish. They thanked her, got out with their packs, and approached the store. A tall young man with long blond braids and a battered black cowboy hat emerged with a paper sack in his arms, unbuckled the saddlebags on the beautiful black horse, and proceeded to stuff bags of rice and beans in them. The long barrel of a pistol protruded from the holster on his hip over faded jeans. He looked up, saw Darla, and showed a good set of teeth before nodding at Paul over her shoulder.

She returned his smile. "Hi, where's a good place to crash?"

"You guys just get here?"

They nodded.

"People crash in the Meadows. Lots of transients there." He glanced at the half-dozen scruffy guys lounging around the front of the store who were watching Darla. The man removed his hat and ran a hand over blond braids, pulled the hat down on his brow, and stared at Paul. "There's people you guys should stay away from."

"Like who?"

"Keep away from the gypsy camp and watch out for the Muslims up the east fork past Black Michael's." His right hand ran across the butt of his six-gun, and he spat on the gravel. "Fucking Abdullah. He puts chicks in these fucking bags made of sheets and says he has the right to four of them as wives. Nothing wrong with having a few ladies, but one of them stands guard at the bathhouse with a shotgun while they bathe. That's *communal* property. I helped build it myself. He beat the shit out of a chick who wanted to split a couple of weeks ago, and me and Fauna had to hide her. Just a little runaway from Seattle with two black eyes, scared as hell." He spat on the ground again. "We might have to clean the whole bunch of 'em out but Abdullah's the real problem. Cut off a snake's head and the rest 'ill scatter," He swung a leg over his horse and leaned on the pommel, "and don't get high with Dolly Dagger. She's totally nuts since her baby got burnt-up in a fire at the Meadows last year. She'll cut your throat while you're sleeping or while you're on acid thinkin' the whole world's lovey-dovey, or start throwing knives at you for no reason at all. Watch yourselves. You guys are young. There's lots of good people around here but not everybody, and it's probably a good idea to stay off Hope Mountain unless you know people there and you're armed."

"Where do you live?"

He grinned. "Hope Mountain."

"What's your name, dude?"

"Mel." Mel tipped his hat and cantered his horse across the pavement toward the dirt road up Hope Mountain.

Paul watched Darla, who was watching Mel, and wished he had a horse, a six-gun and longer hair.

She turned to one of the guys lounging around the store. "Where's the Meadows?"

A man with matted hair pointed to a gap in a ridge across the river. "Over there. You gotta cross by the Barn where the bath house is. You'll see people with towels just ask 'em 'bout the ford." He looked her up and down and exposed a gap in his yellow teeth. "Got any grass?"

"No, I was gonna ask you."

"Bummer." He spat in the dust, lit a hand-rolled cigarette from a yellow can of Top Tobacco, and began playing a corroded harmonica that looked like it had been run over at least once.

They shouldered their packs and walked up Takilma Road. People passed them in battered trucks and vans. The girls smiled at Paul as much as the guys smiled at Darla. One with long black hair, blue eyes and a world-class tan sat bare-breasted on bales of hay in the back of a 40's Chevy flatbed scratching the head of a big black dog.

A couple in a pickup truck stopped and asked if they needed a ride before they'd stuck out their thumbs.

Darla nodded. "We're looking for a place to crash. We just came down from Canada."

"Canada, cool, I'm Susan." The girl driving said from beneath a tent of wavy auburn hair.

The guy riding shotgun motioned them into the back. "You can stay at our place."

Darla squeezed Paul's arm. "This place is full of hip people."

"Yeah. I wonder what that gypsy camp's about?"

Darla laughed. "Maybe that Abdullah guy's there with his harem."

"No. Mel said he's up past Black Michael's, wherever that is."

"Who knows?"

* * *

They awoke to Susan singing as she bustled about a cluttered corner serving as a kitchen in a little house built of scavenged lumber. The intriguing scent of coffee wafted on the clean morning air. Paul kissed Darla and inhaled her scent. It was even better. She giggled and sprang up naked to dash through the dappled shade of a sycamore tree to the outhouse. He yawned.

"What do you take in your coffee?"

"Uh, cream, thanks."

"Here." Susan handed him a rough purple mug with the face of a gnome on it. "Where in Canada are you guys from?"

"That's where we've been this summer. I'm from Charleston, near Coos Bay. Darla's from San Diego but she's half Canadian."

"Oh." Susan tossed hair from her face and sat cross-legged on the floor. "There's a peyote party at the Big Tree swimming hole. Weasel's back from Arizona and he's throwing a potlatch."

"Huh?"

"You know, like a big giveaway."

"Oh."

"He always comes back with lots of trade goods like turquoise and silver and mescal and Mexican coffee, and pot and peyote of course, and then he gets everybody high for a couple of days. It's a blast. Then after the party he goes around to everybody's place and does deals while they're all mellow." Susan shook her head. "He's a real Jew about it, not that I mean that's bad, I mean he *is* Jewish, but shit, so am I."

"Oh."

"Ever do peyote?"

"No."

"Oh-my-Ghod. It's the key to the Aquarian age! He gets it from an Indian medicine man in Arizona, at least that's what he says." Susan grinned. "He's got some killer connections anyway."

Darla returned from the outhouse and slipped her legs into her jeans. She pulled her blouse over her head, accepted a mug of coffee from Susan, and stirred two heaping spoonfuls of thick brown sugar into it.

"I'd recommend not eating breakfast if you're gonna do peyote. You'll just puke."

Darla's eyes widened. "Peyote?"

Susan and Paul nodded.

"Right on!"

* * *

The Big Tree swimming hole was a natural amphitheater of rock where the east fork of the Illinois River poured down from the Siskiyou Mountains amongst towering trunks of incense cedars.

Flat rocks made perfect places to dive into the deep green water or lie in the sun and fifty people had already collected there in anticipation of Weasel's peyote potlatch. At the top of the swimming hole by a little waterfall, a tall wiry guy with a long dark ponytail and beard stood in jeans embroidered with Indian beadwork over a big black kettle like a witches' cauldron. The military tattoos on his arms rippled as he stirred with a yew wood ladle and occasionally scooped water from the torrent coming over the rocks to pour into the kettle. Two naked teenage girls painted with Indian designs and feathers in their hair fed the fire as the bubbling black liquid gave off a strange, dark scent that wafted over the breath of the river.

Weasel lifted a ladle for one of the girls to sniff. She grinned, scooped some up in a dented enamel coffee cup, and held it up in a shaft of sunlight coming through the trees. She put it to her lips, took a sip, grimaced, and took a big gulp. A loud belch echoed off the rocks. She wiped her face and nodded.

"Come on, children," Weasel shouted, "party's on!"

Paul and Darla joined the others lining up along a narrow stone ledge to the cauldron. They returned to the rock they'd chosen beside the pool and blew on their mugs to cool the tea. Darla took a sip, and her face scrunched up.

Paul tried it and gagged. "Fuck!" The black potion seemed to curl in his stomach like a snake. He put a hand to his mouth and burped.

"I've done it before." Darla adjusted the expression on her face and took another sip. "It's worth it."

"This is the worst-tasting shit I ever—"

"Yeah, but it's the best high. It's like there's somebody who *lives* in it almost, a really happy dude who's eternal and totally cosmic."

"That sounds weird."

"You'll see. Indians call him Mescalito. Did you ever read Carlos Castaneda? Mescalito likes to play practical jokes and stuff like with your soul but it's okay. It's all lessons from the other side and you're in the realm of the spirit. It's a privilege. I did it in Ojai with this shaman dude that came up from the desert who knew all that stuff, and he didn't even try to lay me. If you're humble you won't puke either. You just can't let your ego get in the way. He taught me that and it really works." She squeezed his thigh. "And it's totally transcendental to make love on. You totally merge your souls 'cause it's telepathy to the max."

A shiver rippled up Paul's back. The sun had worked its way over the tops of the trees and warmed the rock they sat on. The warmth felt good, but the shivering remained.

Darla took off her blouse, stood up, and stepped out of her jeans. She was shivering too. She wrapped her arms around herself and ran her hands down her sides. Her stomach trembled, and sunlight played in the translucent trail of downy hair running down from her navel. She *glowed*. Darla ran hands through her hair and held out her arms to the sun. "Better to be naked."

One couple had thrown out a blanket on the rocks and grappled in an embrace. Paul couldn't tell where one person began and the other ended. "Shit... this is a trip." His head bobbed as he took in his surroundings. Things kept changing when he tried to focus on them and the roar of the river sounded like a million voices. He heard a beautiful voice singing and could almost make out the words. The red bark of cedars above them began to pulse as their trunks swayed, and a huge blue dragonfly hovering over his head roared like a bomber. He stared into its multi-faceted eyes and it gave him a rainbow wink.

Darla sat cross-legged rocking with the roar of the dragonfly and the river. Her skin gave off a damp perfume in the sun that melded perfectly with that of the pink azalea blossoms around the swimming hole. The blossoms began to beat like big bright hearts, and the freckles across the bridge of Darla's nose danced and changed places. Watching them made Paul dizzy, and he laughed. She laughed back. Her teeth were translucent. He could see her tongue behind them. Her lips pursed for a kiss and he leaned toward her, but they seemed to walk across her face. When he finally found them, they were indescribably soft. The river pounded the rock they sat upon, and it quivered like jelly.

Someone appeared with a big black coffee pot of the tea and refilled their mug as girls' laughter rippled across the water like the voices of angels.

Darla spread their clothes out under them, grabbed him, and he was inside her without knowing how it happened as they rocked with each thrust and the river roared in their veins. Paul wondered if they were going to fall in the water and laughed. She rolled on top of him and bounced like a luminous being come down from the sun. The trees swayed to their rhythm and became great glowing red candles around the altar where they lay. Darla's eyes were blue diamonds that held the vastness of space within them.

A ball of light grew in their middles to erupt simultaneously in an endless orgasm. They bucked and heaved, and Darla made little sounds that fluttered away in the perfumed air like butterflies as their souls drifted like flower petals over the water.

She croaked like a frog, collapsed on top of him, burped, and began to puke.

Darla pulled hair away from her face. "Yuk!"

They plunged in the water and she was a golden being in a green world. Clouds of bubbles streamed from her mouth as her hair billowed around her like white wings.

Fish clustered under an overhanging bank and Paul swam toward them. A huge steelhead shot away like a silver missile into a mossy pile of logs, eliciting bursts of bubbles from Paul and Darla that billowed around their heads. They came to the realization they had to breathe and shot to the surface holding hands.

Her eyes were gems. Her lips were so red he thought for a moment she was bleeding. Her skin was flushed the color of the azalea blossoms and her freckles danced. "How do you like it?"

"This is incredible!" His whole being was a gigantic smile. "We should stay here forever."

"Yeah. That was the best fuck in the world, wasn't it?"

"Let's do some more."

"Peyote, or get it on?"

"Both."

VIII.
Fauna

The party lasted three days. Sometimes they separated but always found each other in the friendly dark like two halves of a single being coming together. A jovial presence seemed to be watching them and playing gentle tricks as if they were children on a wondrous adventure. Darla kept saying they were in the presence of Mescalito. Paul could only smile and nod, which was easier than speaking. Whoever or whatever he was, or whatever they should call him, his presence was there.

On the third day they met a girl named Fauna who lived on Hope Mountain. Even when she wasn't naked at the swimming hole, Fauna only wore knee-high moccasins and a tiny fringed leather loin covering held up by a leather belt and Concho buckle. She had a worn .45 Colt Peacemaker in an old holster on her left hip, a belt-full of shiny copper cartridges, and a big hunting knife. Fauna had long blond braids, piercing blue eyes and a tan that glowed like the coat of a palomino against her sun-bleached mane. Paul liked her enthusiastic moaning the second night as she went at it with some guy, while he and Darla did the same.

In the morning they sat with Fauna drinking coffee by a fire. "I got room in my tree house if you need a place to crash."

"Cool." Paul got out.

Fauna corralled a ride, and they rode away from the Big Tree swimming hole singing the refrain from *Come Together* by the Youngbloods in the back of a pickup to the road up Hope Mountain. She led them up a rutted track for a good mile and turned off to the right toward a forested gulch. Soon there was only a meager trail. Paul was amazed at the swiftness of Fauna's stride and found himself straining to keep up. He'd never seen a girl move that fast. Darla puffed along behind them with sweat pasting her hair to her forehead. He grinned, waited up for her, and squeezed her hand. Darla gulped air and nodded.

"I live up there," Fauna motioned toward a ridge, "the gypsy camp's there." She pointed to the left. "More and more of those fuckers are showing up from some rat-hole in the Bay. They're speed freaks who do crystal meth and they drink the water from the Queen of Bronze. It makes 'em crazy. I tell everybody I meet not to drink it but they're usually just checkin' out my tits and they don't pay attention." She shook her head. "Half the world has 'em and dudes still go all fuckin' weird." She wrinkled her nose. "Never met one of those fuckers from the gypsy camp who didn't stink." She spat on the forest floor. "Wouldn't fuck 'em if my life depended on it."

"What's the Queen of Bronze?"

"An old mine. There's a story that when the ore ran out the owners herded all the Chinese workers into a tunnel and blew it up so they didn't have to pay 'em. They say their ghosts haunt the mountain, and that's the UFOs people see at night." She shrugged. "I saw one last year. It was all round and luminous and floated straight up from a pond. Tripped me out! I don't know what it was but the water from that mine's full of arsenic, I know that. That's enough to make you crazy without any ghosts, plus all that speed and other shit they do."

She patted her revolver. "They raped some runaway last spring and kept her prisoner for two weeks. Some punks were camping nearby and heard her crying but didn't' do nothing about it; they just told somebody down at the clinic after a couple days. I went up there by myself and faced the motherfuckers down, took her over to Mel's, and got her a ride to Florence. She was like fourteen." She sneered in the direction of the camp. "Me and Mel been talking about cleaning 'em out for a long time but where do you put the goddamn bodies? It's like if we used the mine shaft we'd be doin' the same evil shit that place is famous for and that's totally bad karma. We could end up just as crazy as they are, or cursed, or something... maybe possessed even." She scowled. "I've got my own spirit helper." She gazed up the mountain. "Anyway, this is one pussy they'd have to kill to get into." Fauna patted her pistol. "After I take at least six of 'em with me and whoever I get with my knife."

Darla let out her breath. "Is that the Mel who has the six-gun and braids and the pretty black horse?"

Fauna nodded. "He's my best neighbor. His horse is named Lightning." She grinned. "He's hung like a horse too."

"You're pretty fuckin' awesome, Fauna."

"You guys hungry? I've got some venison cooling in the creek. A young doe. Got it two days ago and it's nice and tender. I just got food stamps too, so there's lots of stuff to eat."

"I'm starving." Paul eyed Fauna's .45. "Did you kill her with that six-gun?"

"With my bow. I love stalking. I've been right on top of those guys at the gypsy camp and they didn't even know it. I let the doe's twin sister go so the karma's good, and I did a ceremony for her spirit of course. Hunting on peyote is supposed to be kinda a sin 'cause it's so fuckin' easy, but I made sure things were tight between our spirits, and I really did need the meat."

"How long have you been living here?"

"Kinda forever, but since last year I guess."

Paul glanced at the peaks. They were on the north side of the mountain. The shade was welcome this time of year but it would be cold in the winter. "Does it snow?"

"Shit yes. I cut a lot of wood and trade pot for the rest. I have a nice pot patch. Everybody who isn't a slob grows their own. You have to watch out for rip-offs though, and you really have to watch it after you kill a deer. Their momma will go after your pot and waste it for revenge. The old does keep track of their families. Even grandkids. The bucks don't. They're just out to fight and get laid. I used to hang guts in the trees around my pot to scare the deer, but then I had to deal with a bear family. The cubs are cute. I tracked 'em all over the mountain, but I'd never shoot 'em unless they start something." She shrugged. "There's always friends' places to crash in the winter if the snow's too deep to get home. Last New Years Eve David and Judy threw a clear light acid party down by the river and people stayed for days." Fauna grinned. "That was some world-class trippin'. Some of us even jumped in the river where the current wasn't too strong, but fuck, it was *cold,* acid or no acid."

Darla shivered. "Sounds trippy all right."

"Yeah. This Jesus freak named John tripped out on the Bible *way* too much. He had a staph infection on his left hand, and you know how in the Bible it says 'If the hand offends thee smite it off, if the eye offends thee pluck it out'?"

Darla gasped. "Oh shit, did—"

"Yeah. He went and smote it off with an axe. *Whack!* That kind of fucked up the party, and of course him." Fauna ground her teeth. "Shit, that still freaks me out. I'm left-handed."

"What happened to him?"

"Funky Egg Robert tied a tourniquet on his wrist. Man that was a lot of blood, and they drove him to Cave Junction to the fire station. After that I don't know. I hear he went to Alaska. Somebody dried his hand and has it at their cabin at Sunny Ridge over on Althouse Creek. Pretty freaky. Weasel offered them a quarter pound of pot if he can use it next Halloween."

They reached a narrow shack built of ancient gray boards between the trunks of six young madrones about eight feet off the ground. A stairway of two notched logs with cedar steps led up to the door, and a god's eye of colored twine hung in the plastic window. Fauna twisted the valve on a big propane bottle under the tree house and a hissing began in the copper tube. "I'll make coffee." She pointed to a creek bubbling amongst rocks down to the right, "The meat's wrapped in Visqueen under the green serpentine rock by the plank for crossing. Bring a hindquarter. We can roast the hindquarter in the Dutch oven and have some fried with eggs in the morning."

A hollowness in Paul's stomach awoke, and he bounded down the hill with a grin. "I love venison."

Darla followed Fauna into the tree house while Paul wrestled the meat out of the cold water. He smelled the musk of deer and the hair rose on the back of his neck. Paul imagined the deer's spirit watching him. What did Fauna mean about hunting on peyote being a sin? He envisioned being so close to the spirit of the deer it couldn't get away and being able to reel it in with a filament of his will. He'd never thought of hunting like that before, but after three days with peyote it made all the sense in the world.

As he turned over the green rock, he glanced toward where the gypsy camp lay and the Queen of Bronze mine. Paul imagined a horde of creatures like orcs in The Lord of the Rings that he'd read three times, sitting around a fire gloating over a young girl who was bound to a stake as they prepared to devour her. He saw himself slaying them and rescuing her to stand holding her in his arms amongst the ugly dead creatures before carrying her to a well- deserved union in a bed.

A wisp of cloud curled along the ridge like a ghost, and the dark forest seemed to shrug in the shadows as his ears strained for sounds. He wanted a gun.

* * *

The smell of meat cooking was pleasant torture as they waited with appetites whetted by wine from a green gallon jug of Gallo Vin Rosé Fauna had bought in Cave Junction for eighty-nine cents.

They demolished the haunch of venison along with potatoes, carrots and onions cooked in the Dutch oven over a cast iron burner. Afterward Paul sat snuggled under a Pendleton blanket on Fauna's bed between her and Darla smoking immature pot buds from a bamboo bong watching the play of light on the walls from the kerosene lanterns. The slide down from the peyote adventure was pure contentment. He gazed at the barrel of Fauna's .45 protruding from the holster where it hung from a hook above her bed. The copper cartridges had a warm red glow in the slots of the belt and throbbed in the flickering light. He rubbed his eyes and yawned.

The girls yawned.

Darla reached across him and lifted a blue stone pendant on a leather thong Fauna wore around her neck from between her breasts. "Where did you get this?"

"It's a present from somebody I met."

"A guy?"

"Nope. My spirit helper."

Paul rolled onto an elbow and examined the tiny figure of a woman with feet like a predatory bird holding strange symbols in either hand with an owl on either side of her. "What is it?"

"An ancient goddess. One of her relatives gave it to me."

"A relative of a goddess?"

"Yeah, kinda."

Darla stretched, and her toes came out from under the blanket. "That was one of the best trips ever."

Fauna nodded. "Peyote was gracious with lots of good vibes. Bet some really high babies got conceived at that party who'll grow to be enlightened beings. People will be there until Weasel's stash runs out." She yawned again. "I wonder who got pregnant this time."

Darla giggled. "There sure was a lot of balling." She rolled on her elbows. "This was Paul's very first trip."

"Really?" Fauna chuckled, "You got the best possible start, man. You've been blessed."

Paul stared at the gray boards overhead. "Where does this lumber come from?"

"From old homesteads and mines and shacks in the hills. There's timbers in stacks they never even used and old railroad ties that kept really well 'cause of the creosote. You have to watch for snakes and black widows when you're going through a pile, and these little brown spiders that can kill your ass with one bite, and yellowjacket nests too, but there's lots of free shit for the taking."

"You can just take it?"

"This is Josephine County, the most un-employed place in America. It's a perfect hideout for freaks. There's refugees from every place where heavy shit came down in the Sixties."

"Cool."

Fauna nodded. "It's almost perfect, and the money people spend at the stores in town is really appreciated no matter what rednecks say. Shit, people like David down the hill made big bucks dealing acid in Berkeley. Him and Judy throw killer parties and there's people like Weasel and Gus who came here to buy cheap land. Money goes way farther in this corner of the world 'cause it's so depressed, and there's tons of spiritual energy from the Indians, and killer swimming holes... and room to live."

Darla closed her eyes and sunk deeper into the pillows. "I love it here Paul. We could build a house before winter and stay."

He wrapped an arm around her.

Fauna's fingers danced across their chests. "You guys are cool. I can show you all kinds of incredible shit around here."

"I don't know about right *here.*" Paul muttered, "I kinda don't like the sound of that gypsy camp, or that mine either. I don't know how you do it, I mean being a chick here."

Darla snuggled in the crook of his arm. "Takes a tough lady like Fauna to live on Hope Mountain I guess."

"I scare the shit out of lots of people but I only like guys with balls anyway." She snorted. "Big ones."

Paul wrapped his other arm around Fauna's hard shoulders and she draped an arm across his chest, cupped Darla's breast in her hand, and pressed her cheek to his. "That's stupid, Fauna. Why in hell would anybody be freaked out by you?"

Fauna's breath rolled across his cheek. "Only wimps and bad guys."

* * *

Paul awoke with the welcome smell of coffee along with venison and eggs frying and an overwhelming need to void his bowels.

Fauna wore a rough cotton poncho over her bronze physique in the morning chill. She pointed with the plastic spatula in her hand. "Shitter's over there. Paper's by the door. Bring the roll back when you're done or the critters 'ill chew it up." Paul sprang from the covers shivering and followed her directions. "Use my flip-flops." She nodded at a worn pair near the door swaddled in duct tape.

Paul made a dash for a pit in the ground that had a box with a hole over it beneath a triangular shelter of scavenged planks. He broke a spider web when he sat down and ran hands through his hair. When he climbed back to the tree house, the girls were talking. He stopped halfway up the ladder to listen.

"Think we should check out the Meadows?"

"There's lots better places. Up by the Oregon Caves there's this old claim called China Gardens that's really cool except they're all vegetarians there and some of the men are pussies, and there's Browntown on Althouse Creek. The old bunkhouses are still up and people live in 'em but there's a lot of drunks and some of them do speed. I knocked a guy's tooth out there last year who tried to jump on me when I crashed in the loft. Sunny Ridge is close by and it's better, and out on the Illinois River in the gorge on Klondike Creek and the Foster Claim are some totally cool people growing mass pot." She shrugged. "And there's mines and caves around here that go on forever. Lots of 'em have water you can use for irrigation. They say the Oregon Caves come out down by the Marble Mountain Wilderness in California and that's how Indians and outlaws used to escape in the old days. You should try doing acid in one of those, if you've got the balls." She laughed. "There's a party at the Foster Claim this weekend too. My friend Donny grows dope and mines gold there. You guys oughta come."

Darla giggled. "This is the coolest place on earth."

"Not everybody is. There's those sleezeball speed freaks at the Gypsy Camp and that asshole Abdullah up the river. There's redneck vigilantes that sometimes shoot at people too. Some guys formed a protection group called the Takilma Rifles and they have a bunker up the river by Black Michael's place, but all they do is walk around with their guns and brag at parties." Fauna snorted. "It's just another bullshit way of getting laid if you ask me. I could sneak up on any of 'em and take 'em out easy if it came to it."

"Where are you from anyway?"

"Doesn't matter. The bullshit world where I grew up doesn't count. My past is over. I'm who I am now. You learn on acid that all is illusion and that all temporal attachment is bullshit anyway. Everything passes. *Everything.* I probably shouldn't be repelled by the petty stuff either, that's what the enlightened people say like Tibetan Llamas and swamis and shit. Ever read the *Psychedelic Experience?* I used to carry it with me everywhere. It's really hard to give up all physical attachments and find illumination though. I still believe in turn on, tune in and drop out, but some things you just have to stand for. That's what you call a paradox I guess. I love going against some of these suckers who think they're so bad like those motherfuckers at the gypsy camp. When I'm high I've got all of nature with me. I've learned that being alone in the woods on psychedelics is the best high of all. I found an ally here on this mountain, my personal spirit helper. Anyway your soul is a mirror of nature when it's clean and you become invisible. The

Lakota call that part of the soul *sicum.* It even beats fucking... at least with some people."

"How did you get here?"

"Hitched, Darla. Same as you. I had to cut the shit outta a guy near Redding once."

Darla ran a hand through her hair. "So did we up by Hillsboro and Paul fought them off. I've been filling Paul in on the shit girls have to deal with when they hitchhike and he got a lesson pretty quick."

"Yeah. A couple of years ago I got picked up by a guy who drove me to his friend's and they tried to rape me."

"Did you get away?"

"With the help of the Goddess." Fauna stared into the trees, "She made me promise to take care of business myself the next time and I did, and I really haven't been afraid of anything since."

"Who? Her?"

Fauna fingered the amulet hanging from her neck. "I'll tell you about her sooner or later although you won't believe it. I've taken care of shit myself since then."

"How did you haul your stuff up here?"

"I carried it. I borrow Mel's horse sometimes too."

Paul finished climbing the ladder and stepped in the door. Sunlight spilling through the plastic windows lit the girls up in a nimbus of gold like two blond angels. It was unbelievable he was here. Finishing high school in Coos Bay seemed like a life on another planet: a dead world to which he could never return. He was adrift on a current that was taking him where it may and he couldn't imagine not letting it. It was karma.

"You hungry, Paul?"

He hugged them both. "Famished."

IX.
The Neighbors

Darla promised to buy groceries, so they left their packs at Fauna's and headed to Cave Junction. "This beats the shit out of San Francisco." She pronounced as they walked amongst Douglas firs, red-barked madrones, and past ancient stumps of logging from a century before.

"Yeah, but there's some weird-ass people around." Paul glanced toward the unseen gypsy camp and the mysterious mine. "I want a gun."

"That's kind of a good idea."

"I'm glad you're not one of those veggie chicks who freaks out on guns."

She squeezed his hand. "I'm one of those survivor chicks who hangs out with good-looking studs like you. After those Tweedledee-Tweedledum whoever-the-fuck-they-were creeps, I'd like to have a gun. I've got a switchblade knife a guy gave me in my pack somewhere but I don't even know where it is. There's some fucked-up people around." She sighed, "I guess that's how it is anywhere."

"I guess. Those guys at the gypsy camp sound really bad."

"Yeah but Fauna's so cool. She's beautiful and trips around like a fucking goddess in that little loincloth and moccasins and dares any wimp to mess with her. That takes balls." She shook her head. "I don't know how she does it with those assholes living on the same mountain."

"She said something about having an ally."

"Yeah, a chick." Darla stopped at a little creek running from the heights above and bent down where it purled over mossy rocks to drink.

Paul grabbed her arm. "That's coming from the other side of the gulch where that mine is."

"Think its poison?"

"I don't know. How does it look?"

"Like water."

"Does it smell funny?"

Darla scooped up some in her hand, sniffed, and tasted it. "I don't know." She let it run through her fingers to the forest floor.

"Better wait 'til we're down the mountain."

"I'm fucking thirsty."

As they continued down the hill, a distant shouting could be heard in the gulch from where the creek came. Maniacal laughter followed, and a high-pitched howl. They quickened their pace.

They hit the rutted road, reached the valley floor and eventually came upon a white ranch house that had a screened porch with people crowding it. The walls beside the door were plastered with notes and somewhere inside a baby cried. A woman's voice called out someone's name and a very pregnant girl about their age levered herself out of a wicker chair and shuffled inside. Paul and Darla drifted toward the house, where a warped plank hung over the door with **TAKILMA FREE CLINIC** painted on it.

"Oh, cool," Darla said, "I need more BCs. Come on."

Inside at a battered desk sat a dark-haired, large-breasted young woman in a Madras print dress surrounded by three benches with people on them. A child's shriek came from the room beyond.

"Hold him still please."

"He's never had a shot before."

"How long has it been like this?"

"Almost a week. We couldn't get a ride over Tennessee Gap."

"There, all done. Give him one of these four times a day and get some acidophilus in him. This is strong stuff and it's going to tear up his guts for a while."

"We don't have any money Jim."

"No surprise. Just get some yogurt with your food stamps. That should do it. Judy makes good stuff from her goats down by Four Corners and does trades."

"Okay."

Darla sashayed up to the girl behind the desk. "Can I score some BCs?"

The girl glanced up. "We've got to get some information and you'll have to wait your turn." She brushed one of her dark braids off the ledger before her and gave them a look of exhaustion. "We got a shitload of people today. There's staph infections going around with the swimming holes warming up and all these chicks having babies."

"This is really cool, I mean like to have a real clinic and all."

"So many people caught the clap around here last year the county authorities were going to start busting a few characters. They did it with this guy Barry, one of the River Rats, and put him in Josephine County Hospital for five days under quarantine. The dumb ass was *proud* of spreading the fucking clap." The girl scowled. "Just what the rednecks need to hear to think we've all got our heads up our asses. What a dick."

"That's disgusting. How did he get chicks to ball him?"

"Honey, if you can't get laid around here you're dead or you ain't tryin'. Guy goes to a party and catches some little chick coming down off a trip or drunk and even somebody like him can score. She'll not even remember who she fucked the next day, and in a couple of days she's got the clap." She shook her head, "What's your name?"

"Darla."

"Last name?"

"Uh, Jones."

"Okay Jones, you're on the list. It's gonna be a while." The girl's voice dropped. "Just between you and me, how old are you really?"

"Seventeen."

"Runaway?"

Darla nodded.

"I was too. Watch out for Sheriff's deputies if they show up with more than one car. That's when they do sweeps. It doesn't happen often but sometimes somebody's parents get them to come through. You should have seen this place a couple of years ago. Some heiress chick was hiding out up at Sun Star and her parents had a huge reward out for her. They swept up about a dozen runaways but she booked it over the mountains to Happy Camp with some guy named Brother Bob and I hear they went to Alaska. She wrote some people a letter and said they were living in the wilderness and she was pregnant, and that he changed his name to Papa Pilgrim and had three wives. Guess they're still there. There's some punch in the cooler if you get thirsty. No acid in it today I hope."

"Somebody put acid in it?"

"Last year. It sure freaked out a couple kids. Doc Jim had to give them baby doses of Thorazine." The girl shook her head again. "Couple dumbasses from the gypsy camp thought they were funny or something." She scowled at the mountain from which they'd come.

"Shit."

"Are you guys staying on Hope Mountain?"

"We just spent the night after the party at the Big Tree swimming hole."

"Who with?"

"Fauna."

The girl smiled. "Fauna's cool, and so is Mel, but watch out for the fuckers from the gypsy camp. There's some shitty stuff been going on up there for years."

"Yeah, we know."

"Not half of it lady."

They found seats on the porch between a hairy little guy in a tattered burlap poncho with a yew wood staff and a very pregnant girl with auburn hair, blue eyes and a dusting of freckles across her nose. She looked about fifteen and had her blouse pulled up over the protuberance of her belly that she was rubbing.

The hairy guy's weathered face split a grin, and he held out a callused hand to Darla. "You guys runaways?"

Paul scowled. "Jesus fuck."

Darla's nose twitched at his smell. "We're free." She turned toward the girl. "When are you due?"

"Any day." Dappled sunlight played on the girl's fair complexion as a kick shoved the skin next to her navel out an inch. She grunted.

"What do you think it is, boy or girl?"

"Kicks like a dude, that's for sure, but I want a girl. I think it is... a *she,* I mean."

"I'm Darla, and this is Paul."

"I'm Sunshine."

Another Sunshine. Paul smiled. "You sure are." He reached toward her stomach. "Can I...?"

"Sure." Sunshine pulled her blouse up and guided his hand to her belly. Paul spread his fingers over it and his eyes widened. "Never felt a baby before?" He shook his head. She guided his hand to one of her swollen breasts and his mouth fell open. She moved his hand back to her stomach. "I don't even know where the guy who gave me this is, but I'm with aware people now."

"Where... where are you from?"

"Illinois, and now I'm in the Illinois Valley." Sunshine sighed. "I balled two guys before I left Chicago and one on the way. I *think* I know who the daddy is, but it could be wishful thinking I suppose. I'll see who she looks like soon anyway."

"How old are you?"

"Fourteen."

"Shit."

She laughed. "That's what everybody says. I'm just glad they have this clinic. If I had to go to Grants Pass they'd haul me off to Chicago. Fuck that. I'm never going back."

"Where do you live?"

"China Gardens. Starr got this beautiful teepee all ready for me with a willow rocker that hangs from the poles that was blessed by a real Medicine Man. He did a ceremony for the whole space and burned sage and cleansed it with prayers for the baby. He's a carnivore, and we're vegetarians, but he's really aware. And Lisa made this beautiful baby blanket on her loom with the four directions in the four sacred colors and has been burning sage in the teepee every day. I'm staying here in Takilma until the baby comes and then I'm going back."

"What are you going to name her?"

"Starlight Meadow I think. She'll be a Gemini if it's soon, or a Cancer if it's next week but I can't think of anything that's enlightening that has to do with crabs. It depends, something special could happen at the birth and I want to be open to it."

"What if it's a boy?"

Sunshine shook her head. "It's a girl."

"Oh."

"Ha," the hairy guy in a burlap poncho said, "if it's a boy, name him Dick."

Sunshine frowned. "It's not a boy, and I hear *you* got the crabs."

* * *

After an hour and a half Darla got her birth control pills. Doc Jim, a rail-thin blond guy with gentle hands and kind eyes, gave her a gynecological exam and pronounced her supremely healthy. He followed with a short lecture on staying that way along with an admonition to keep away from several local men by name, including the guy on the porch in the poncho, who he called Sean.

She thanked him, dug into the right front pocket of her jeans, and put a five-dollar bill in a gallon jug half full of money on the table beside the water cooler. Paul's eyes widened. They left the clinic with best wishes to Sunshine and headed toward the pavement to hitchhike into town.

* * *

They got dropped off in front of the Sentry Market in Cave Junction. "After we buy some stuff here I'm gonna find someone to score some wine, or maybe even a bottle of whiskey at the liquor store." Darla announced.

"That was a lot of money you left at the clinic."

"So? You have to give to the good."

"How much more do you have?"

She shrugged. "Enough. Trust in karma."

"I guess."

"Let's get something to eat."

"Okay."

They headed into a bakery and coffee shop next to the Sentry Market with a sign advertising hamburgers for twenty-five cents, sat on stools at the empty counter, and ordered cheeseburgers and coffee. The guy at the grill in a white cap and apron gave them a suspicious look, but Darla coaxed a smile out of him with one of her own.

Paul slid a discarded newspaper over. "Check this out. Somebody got shot over pot. It says at Browntown over on Althouse Creek."

She leaned over. "Bummer. Did they die?"

"No, but he got really hurt and busted for being a runaway. It says he was from Anaheim and he's in critical condition at the hospital in Grants Pass."

The man behind the counter was staring at a long-haired boy and a girl with a woven shoulder bag who were examining the bags of day-old donuts on top of the display case.

Paul whispered, "I bet they're looking for me here in Oregon. If something like that happened and the cops ever checked us out, even as witnesses—"

She squeezed his knee. "Don't freak out. We've got high energy. Look how we got away from those two assholes up by Salem." She gave him a smile that made the whole world brighter. "I feel so much closer to you after that peyote trip. It's telepathy. I read about it in the Kama Sutra. When you come together for a really long time it's called a 'High Union' and you share your spirits after that. You become spiritually linked through sex." She kissed his cheek. "Guess we gotta get laid a lot more."

"What's the Kama Sutra?"

"An ancient text on sex from India."

"I should read it." He ran a hand from her knee up her thigh and pressed his fingers between her legs.

Darla scrunched down on the stool and grinned. "You looked so cute when you were holding Sunshine's boob. Like a little boy."

"Huh?"

"Never felt a pregnant girl's tit before?"

"No."

"My girlfriend Abigail got pregnant in—"

The door banged open with a rattle of glass, accompanied by a shout from the proprietor. "Goddamn it! Come back here you fucking punks!"

The couple who had been examining the day-old donuts were running across the parking lot with a brown paper bag stuffed halfway into the girl's woven satchel. In three bounds the man from the bakery caught up with her. The girl shrieked as he gave her long red hair a savage yank that landed her on the pavement and day-old donuts spread in a fan across the blacktop. One rolled all the way to the street.

The boy skidded to a stop and turned. "Let her go!"

"Fuck you! Police! Thieves!"

Two muscular young men in dirty work shirts, denims and red suspenders sprinted from a yellow Chevy pickup and lunged at the boy, seized each of his arms, and lifted him off the ground.

The baker let out a barking laugh. "Where you goin' *now*, hippie?" He rolled up his sleeves, wound up, and punched the trembling youth in the stomach. The boy folded around the man's fist with a gagging sound accompanied by a sob from the girl on the pavement, who sat amongst wads of her hair holding her head.

"You're goin' to jail, hippies!" One of the loggers barked.

"Thanks Jess. I owe ya. Come by for free donuts and coffee anytime. You too Bill."

A crowd had collected in front of the Sentry Market, where a stout man in slacks and a tie stood before the big glass doors with arms folded. Two young men in white aprons had joined the two loggers and stood grim-faced over the teens on the pavement.

A green Sheriff's car pulled into the lot with its red light flashing, and a fat khaki-clad cop emerged in a white cowboy hat and aviator sunglasses. He chuckled as he bent the young man over the hood of his car and handcuffed him. Paul and Darla watched the proceedings from the door of the bakery as their hamburgers sizzled on the grill behind them.

The baker returned and they sat down. Suddenly, he made a slicing gesture with his hand. "That's *it!* No more hippies the rest of the goddamn summer! You're all a buncha fuckin' thieves!"

Darla responded in her best little girl's voice. "We weren't doing anything sir, we just wanted some ham—"

The man grabbed the receiver of a telephone. "Get out! Before I have the cops bust you too!"

Paul grabbed her hand. "Come on."

"And you'll pay for the hamburgers and coffee!"

"Can we have them to go, then?"

"Get *out!*"

"What...?" Paul began.

Darla tossed a dollar down. "We're sorry sir!"

The man wiped his hands as if cleaning their spore from them and reached under the counter. Paul's stomach jumped at a vision of him pulling a gun, but he took out a ready-made sign with **NO HIPPIES ALLOWED** on it. He strode to the door, hung the sign, yanked the door open with a rattle, and thrust his finger at the parking lot.

They stood in the lot wondering where to go. The young man was still face down on the hood of the sheriff's car and moaned as the big cop twisted his arm. The cop noticed them staring, lowered his sunglasses, and fixed Paul and Darla in a hard stare.

Darla tugged on Paul's hand. "Let's get out of here."

As they headed for the market across the street, Paul locked eyes with the frightened girl in the back of the police car with tears glistening on her cheeks as the car door closed.

X.

Deeper

They went in a market across the street with a hand-lettered sign beside the door saying **WATCH YOUR KARMA.** Under it was *HAVE A NICE DAY* in a cursive feminine scrawl. The girl at the checkout counter's body looked interesting through her loose Madras print blouse. She wore a beaded headband around long blond hair as she stood on the platform behind the cash register smiling within a nimbus of patchouli oil. "Welcome, brother and sister. Remember your karma here. This store's good people. Not corporate pigs."

Darla sashayed up. "I love your headband. Is that your sign?"

She nodded. "Yeah, Lisa from China Gardens made it."

"Is she the one who made the blanket for Sunshine's baby?"

"Yeah," the girl extended a hand, "Virgo." She pointed to her headband. "See the Greek chick on it? I'm Megan."

"Darla, and this is Paul."

Paul dragged his eyes from her tits and shook Megan's ring-covered hand.

"Where you guys staying?"

"Around. We stayed with Fauna last night. We just got down from Canada."

"Canada? Cool. My boyfriend Dale went there to get away from the draft." Megan frowned. "I hope he got across the border."

"Lotsa guys doing that." Darla glanced around the cluttered store. "This place sure has better vibes than across the street."

"Yeah. Fuckin' Sentry Market gets all the rednecks and straights. The cool people shop here."

Darla rolled her eyes. "I see why. We went into the bake shop in their parking lot, and this guy and girl tried to scam a couple donuts. The baker chased them out and some loggers caught the dude... and they just *held* him while the guy punched the shit out of him, and they *laughed*. Then the baker guy wouldn't give us the cheeseburgers we ordered and made us pay for them. He said he was gonna have the cop bust us if we didn't."

"Yeah," Paul nodded, "what an asshole."

Megan sighed. "Shit happens. There's fuckers around who'd like to kill you for no reason at all, but the pure of spirit can still triumph."

They nodded solemnly.

"You guys runaways?"

They nodded.

"Join the club. I've been 'round here a year and a half and I'm still not eighteen. There's so many cool people in these mountains it's easy to get by." She grinned, "It feels like a lifetime already. It's a trip."

Paul inhaled the scent of patchouli oil. "How do you... you know, how do you work a straight job with paychecks, and taxes and all? Can't they catch you like that?"

"At first it was cash under the counter but now I'm on the payroll for real. I'd be fucked if I was using my own I.D. although the people here wouldn't snitch me off. I got a driver's license that says I'm nineteen and I can get food stamps. I live at Sunny Ridge where we all pool our money for shopping trips. People trust their brothers and sisters who go to town and get what they agreed on so they don't even have to come in except once in a while. You can do acid and peyote, and garden and swim, and grow pot and make love. We put our money in the communal kitty and everybody gets by. It's the way of the new age."

"That's trusting."

Darla brightened. "Do you know anybody who could get us I.D.?"

"Yeah, we could really use it."

"Sure, maybe. Do you know Weasel?"

"We were at his peyote party at the Big Tree swimming hole. It was bitchin'."

"Got anything to trade?"

Paul shrugged. "Not much."

Megan grinned at Darla. "Sure you do, I mean she does." The girls laughed.

Paul glanced from one to the other.

There was a rattle of valves and a squeak of brakes outside as an engine wheezed to a stop before a half-dozen long-haired youths piled into the store.

"Yeah, but how good is it?" Darla went on. "Could it fool the Man?"

"Check it out." Megan tossed a pink paper Oregon driver's license on the counter. "I've been checked half-a-dozen times and never been busted and I skipped out on probation in Reno." She shrugged. "Weasel's pretty good, I mean balling him isn't a bummer or anything. He's got a nice dangle and he never gave anybody the clap far as I know, and he's not violent or anything. You use BCs?"

Darla nodded.

"You guys engaged or something?"

Darla shrugged. "No, we're just hanging out."

Paul's chest tightened.

"Check it out." Megan glanced at Paul. "She'll be doing you a favor man. She's still your lady, just don't be too attached. You can't tie down a free spirit. It's the New Age and people got to handle it."

The store grew loud with the six people from the truck all talking at once. A tall dark-haired man with braids in a hempen poncho grinned, leaned over the counter, and stroked Megan's hair "Hey, Megan."

"Hi, David." Megan purred. "See ya 'round, Darla and Paul. Peace. Stay high."

Paul stumbled against a rack of potato chips, and Darla took his hand and kissed his cheek.

* * *

She got someone to buy a bottle of Wild Turkey at the state liquor store next door and they caught a ride back to Takilma. They got off with a big bag of groceries and the whiskey across from the old store and headed past the clinic up Hope Mountain to Fauna's tree house. Crows shouted at them from the trees and mourning doves warbled in more pleasant tones as they entered the forest's shade. Something small, fast and gray ran across the road ahead and ducked into the blue-tinged leaves of manzanita. Darla was spending money she'd never mentioned she had but it made things a lot easier. They'd double-bagged the groceries but the paper was starting to tear, and Paul cursed as they hit the trail to Fauna's.

The sounds of footsteps and harsh voices came from up the trail. Paul and Darla slipped under a thick canopy of hazels downhill, climbed over the big roots of a maple tree, and huddled amongst mossy rocks in the shade.

"Yeah, that fucker sure freaked out when you showed him the business end of your shotgun!"

Darla winced at the booming voice that seemed right on top of them.

"*Better* have. Motherfuckers think they can get over on me. I'll fuck him up."

"Let's find a party."

Paul peered through the hazel leaves at the two men on the trail. A big man with a curly black beard and a dirty leather cowboy hat cradled a pump shotgun not fifteen feet away. He spit a brown glob of tobacco and showed yellow teeth. "And a couple'a more runaways. That fuckin' chick Mushroom took off with my pipe. If I ever catch her ass—"

A flash of his companion's tattooed arm was visible. "She didn't even say nothin' when I put it in her ass."

"Bitch probably don't know the difference anyway."

"Ha. She was scared shitless."

The men roared with laughter.

Darla's eyes were huge. Paul hugged her.

Suddenly a spray of urine spattered off the leaves overhead accompanied by the sound of a shotgun jacking a shell into the chamber. Paul put a hand to Darla's lips as a big red centipede undulated across a mossy rock in front of them, driven from its lair by piss. He brushed the creature into a crevice.

"See that squirrel?"

"Where Dave?"

"Little fucker in the fir, right... *there!*"

Claws skittered on bark above them accompanied by the angry scolding of a big gray squirrel as it rounded the trunk of a Douglas fir to put the tree between itself and the men on the trail.

"Missed my shot."

"Fuck it, let's go."

"Yeah, not a lot of meat 'less you kill a bunch."

"Not like that fat 'ol Labrador."

Hoarse laughter followed. "That was pretty good eatin' for a dog."

"Did you hear that chick calling it last night? She put up a sign at the store."

"Woof. Maybe we can invite her up for a look-see and some leftovers."

"There's some good eatin'."

The men on the trail roared again as the sound of their foot-steps faded down the hill. Paul crawled to the edge of the trail and peered down it, then clambered back for the groceries.

Darla climbed onto the path. "I hope Fauna's home. She's got a gun."

"I want a gun!"

"Let's get off this mountain. There's other places to stay."

"We'll need protection anywhere." The grocery bag tore fur-ther and he shifted it in his grip. "I don't know how we'd hitch-hike with a gun though."

She squeezed his hand. "I'll buy one if Fauna knows some-body. You can put a six-gun like hers in your pack."

"Then why can't you buy I.D. from Weasel?"

"I can, silly."

"Then how come...?"

"We were just talking." She laughed. "I'm going to ball somebody for it." Squirrels scolded them from the trees as they climbed the hill. "Did you believe that?"

"I—"

She giggled. "We were just fucking with you."

"Why?"

"I don't know. Just girl talk I guess."

"Oh."

***

Fauna wasn't home so Darla set about preparing a meal and Paul filled two water jugs at the creek. He glanced in the direction of the mysterious gypsy camp as he struggled up the hill, still wish-ing he had his .30-.30 back in Charleston. He imagined those ugly thugs with gaps in their teeth coming through the woods and dropping them with two quick shots. He was better with a gun than they were. He'd bet on it. He'd dropped a deer on the

run with one shot at a hundred yards once and those guys sounded like idiots. Paul imagined them trying to rape Darla and him
shooting the big guy's balls off.

Darla had bought four pounds of chuck steak for a buck
and cooked it in a cast iron fry pan with barbecue sauce. By the
time Fauna returned at dusk, Paul's stomach was growling. They
uncorked the whiskey and toasted the meal of meat and a green
salad. After the dishes were done they sat smoking pot by the
light of kerosene lamps.

Fauna yawned. "That Gypsy Dave guy is a fuckin' rip-off and
rapist," she spun the cylinder on her Colt, "and a goddamn coward
too. It's past time to get them off the mountain." Fauna gazed into
the distance. "Some people just don't deserve freedom is all."

"Why don't you move?"

"Why? I found something here and I'm not walking out
on it. There's a spirit that dwells here, and something, I mean
somebody, that knows who I am. That sounds weird, I know, but
there's a goddess dwelling here. Anyway I built this place myself
and have friends all over Takilma, and I got a pot patch that's not
ready 'til fall. They know if they ever ripped me off I'd go ballistic
and come for them swear to God. Those guys aren't worth shit,
so why should I leave this whole mountain to them? Besides, Mel
lives here too. I'd be betraying him by splitting."

"Won't there be more of them?"

"Not if we burn their shit down. But we don't want to start
a forest fire right now so me and Mel are waiting 'til it rains. Then
we're gonna torch their camp so they don't come back, even if we
have to waste some of them doing it."

"Wow." Darla yawned as she put away the dishes. "You're a
trip. Is it true Weasel can get I.D.?"

"Weasel can score anything."

"Paul thought I was gonna ball Weasel for some I.D. just 'cause
this chick Megan at the store said I had something I can trade for it."

The girls laughed.

"Yeah, well, you said you were screwing with me. It wasn't like I was freaking out on my own or something."

"You know I just ball who I want. I can talk guys into lots of shit but my ass isn't for trade."

Fauna nodded. "Yeah, that's kinda whorin' it." She scratched under an arm and gazed out the plastic window. "I did ball a guy once to get a boyfriend out of jail though."

Paul studied her in the yellow lamplight. "That's... that's something he probably appreciated I guess."

"Fuckin' *aye* he did. We got the hell out of Arizona after that guy put up bail so I guess he lost his money too. Five hundred bucks. That makes me a spendy piece of ass I guess."

They laughed.

Fauna climbed into the loft. "Night."

"Night."

* * *

Paul stared at the roof and tried to remember where he was. He reached out and ran a palm across the rise of Darla's breast and down her stomach. She moaned in her sleep.

A girl's voice had awoken him. Paul slid out from under the blanket and sat beside Darla, beautiful in the moonlight coming through the window. He pulled the blanket over her, kissed her cheek and went to the door, opening it on a luminous swath of the forest floor glowing between the shadows of trees. He climbed down the ladder and stepped on the soft litter of fir needles and leaves.

A voice floated through the forest. He couldn't make out words but it came from up the creek. Paul began to climb the hill and broke into a loping stride that grew longer with each step until he was bounding like a deer. He threw out his arms and began to glide between the steps until he rose off the ground on a billow of air. He exhaled and gained speed. He took another breath, dipped toward the ground, and rose again as he let it out. The air flowing up the mountain was his own breath that carried him deeper into the forest.

The gulch widened to a meadow and the creek into a pond fed by a luminous waterfall flowing from a cleft in the mountain. Tall cattails glowed like phosphorescent candles in the moon-light. The cry of a loon pierced the night, and a beating of wings erupted in the dark branches overhead. A huge bird sat a few feet away on water still as a mirror holding up the sky. Paul stood on a flat rock amongst the cattails, listening for that lovely voice. There was only the purling of the waterfall, the cry of a loon and the wind in the trees.

He wrapped arms around himself and shivered. "What am I doing?"

Distant laughter echoed in the night.

The waterfall glowed like molten silver as it poured from a cleft in the mountain. The duck-thing circled the pond, leaving a luminous wake. It was huge, far larger than any duck he'd ever seen, if it *was* a duck. It wasn't a goose. Its neck was too short.

A serpentine rock shining in moonlight, just the right size for throwing, lay in the outlet of the pond. He stooped, and his fingers closed around it.

The bird circled and came toward him until it was ten feet away. Paul cocked his arm with the stone in his fist as it watched him with eyes like glowing amber beads. The beating of wings overhead grew louder, and he felt teeth in his lower lip as he slung the stone with a grunt.

There was a thud, and the bird rolled over in the water.

Crows exploded from the trees in a cacophony of cawing and mud squished between his toes as he waded toward the duck-thing and seized it by the neck. It was heavier than he'd imagined and very warm.

"Wow."

Droplets of water ran from its feathers and its legs trembled and stretched. A broken sound came from its chest.

"Shit." The bird made a guttural quack, and he dropped it in the water with a splash. The wings in the trees beat wildly as a gust of wind came across the water that nearly knocked him down.

His head spun and he closed his eyes. The beating of wings overhead died away, and silence fell on the pond until only the sound of the waterfall remained. He opened them.

Two red ones stared back at him from a pale face as bright as the moon. A woman stood before him with hair so black it swallowed the moonlight as it draped her ivory white body. The sweetest scent enfolded her, and a nimbus of warmth beat upon his face. Her pale fingers traced a smear of blood on her throat and full lips curled in an expression that made him feel low and mean. After an eternity, it was broken by a smile.

"Oh God," he blurted, "I'm sorry!"

"There is something you must do."

"What?"

"You will be with three. But first you must be with me."

Their lips touched and he inhaled the breath of the night.

XI.
The Swimming Hole

"Paul!" Darla shook him. "Wake up!"

He slapped her hand away and rolled on his side. Fir needles scratched his cheek and Paul rubbed his nose. He sat up and moaned.

"What the fuck were you doing? Sleepwalking?"

"God," Fauna said, "We thought you were gone."

"Or the guys at the gypsy camp got you or something."

Sunlight slanted through the treetops. Paul slapped an insect off his leg and stared at their concerned faces.

Darla shook her head. "Dude you're a trip. Too much good lovin' drive you crazy or something?" She pointed to the dried mud on his penis and the girls howled with laughter. "Like... *look* at you!"

"Where did you go swimming?"

They pulled him to his feet. Paul opened his mouth but nothing came out.

"You look stoned. Did you do acid or something?"

"You need a shower. How did you get so dirty?"

"I don't know."

Darla gave him an unreadable expression and he put a palm to her cheek. "I'm okay. I had the most incredible dream though."

"Like what?"

"Like I heard a girl in the woods and went looking." He rubbed his face and dried mud flecked off in his hands. Paul pointed an unsteady finger up the gulch. "Is there a pond up there?"

Fauna nodded. "Yeah but it's like an hour's hike. It's got cattails and tall trees all around it and a little waterfall at the top that comes out of a cliff. Great place to go swimming. It's really pretty with green water and there's lots of game that comes to it. That's where I saw the UFO, and something else."

"I was there."

"You climbed the mountain naked, at night?"

"I don't know. It felt like I flew."

Darla's eyes widened. "Whoa."

Fauna looked him up and down. "That's a long-ass way to go at night, barefoot and all. How did you get back?"

"I don't know."

Darla made a nervous laugh. "Wow, shit."

Fauna gazed up the gulch. "Guess the mountain's done it again. There's been people seen heavy shit around here for hundreds of years and now you're one looks like." She hugged him. "Some stuff you just gotta accept."

Darla gazed into the treetops with unfocused eyes, ran a hand across her face, and shook her head. "I think maybe you're both tripping too much about spirits and shit."

"You're the one that said there's a guy called Mescalito in peyote." Paul gazed up the gulch. "I met a woman."

The girls fell silent.

Fauna stared up the gulch and let out her breath.

Paul brushed mud out of his pubic hair, cracked his neck and brushed hair from his eyes. "I met someone. Really."

Darla shifted from one foot to the other. "Like who?"

"I don't know, but she was really old, and really beautiful, and she had something important for me to do, and she was there because of you guys. I know that."

Fauna yanked Darla's hand so hard she stumbled. "I believe him. I had a vision in the same place last year around the solstice. Things wake up in midsummer. There's a spirit there and that's where the UFOs come from I swear to God. I think they're not from outer space at all. They're from right *here,* and you'd better believe it. It counters the bad energy from the gypsy camp and it's way-older like Indian medicine, except she—"

Paul gasped. "She? You know who she is?"

"Not really but she's here. There's a male spirit in peyote and this one's female but way different. She rescued me when I was hitchhiking and guided me when I thought I was gonna die a couple times, and she's been with guys at night but they can't remember afterward. That's how she gets by."

"That's what they call a succubus."

"Did she fuck you?"

Darla shook her head. "This is weird."

"I'm really hungry." Paul sighed and stumbled down to the creek to wash off the mud.

* * *

After a breakfast of deer meat and eggs Paul had three helpings of and a long drawn-out discussion of reincarnation, Indian shamans, mystical signs, UFOs, haunted mines, astrology, vegetarianism, demonic possession and the Book of Revelations, they decided to go swimming. They burned through three pots of coffee and several joints as the day grew hotter. Fauna grabbed a tattered blanket and some towels, threw them in a bag made of loosely woven hemp with a bottle of coconut oil, and they headed to the big swimming hole. They hiked down the mountain as grasshoppers exploded like popcorn from the grass and cicadas roared like broken wires in the trees. They were glistening with sweat when they reached the flats.

They passed a tall Indian wearing a bone choker who was sprawled unconscious beside the road with his long black braids at right angles. A freckle-faced girl sat beside him in a madras print skirt with her knees under her chin and waved as they passed.

Fauna chuckled. "That's White Fox, with his old lady Karen waiting for him to wake up."

"Weird." Darla said. "Is he okay?"

"Just passed out drunk. Karen does whatever he says. That's one way to get into Indians I guess. What a wuss. I wouldn't follow some drunkass dude anywhere, no matter who he was. Let alone fuck him. I've had some bitchin' Indian dudes, but he ain't one of 'em."

Fauna led them onto the rocky floodplain of the Illinois River past ramshackle shacks. Two young men sat on the sagging porch of one of them staring at the two girls while passing a bottle of wine. "These guys are the River Rats. You can build here for free 'cause nobody owns the land."

"Yeah," Paul said, "'cause all this shit will wash away. It's on a floodplain."

Fauna shrugged. "All things pass. Some things just last longer than others."

They came to a line of willows with the sound of voices beyond, stepped through a screen of leaves, and came upon a hundred or so people sprawled naked on blankets or swimming in the river. Pot smoke filled the air as naked children laughed and chased each other across the pebbly beach. An immensely pregnant girl with a bone-deep tan shouted at a tow-headed youngster who'd stuffed sand in the mouth of a squalling baby. Three more young men were passing a jug of wine and staring hard at Darla and Fauna as two bronzed bodies humped enthusiastically in the meager shade of a stunted viney maple.

"My kind of beach." Darla yanked off her blouse, stepped out of her cutoffs, tossed her clothes to Paul, and dashed toward the water.

Fauna spread the blanket on a vacant patch of sand. "Leave your shit here when you swim. It's cool."

Paul shucked his jeans and wadded them up around his knife. "You sure?"

"Yeah. People will see rip-offs so they won't chance it. The only time people get ripped off here is when it gets dark or if there's a party. It's only noon so it's cool." She stepped out of her fringed leather shorts and ceremoniously wrapped her gun belt around her holstered pistol before she put it under a towel. Fauna waved at two tan young women sprawled on a sun-bleached Pendleton blanket. "Can you watch our shit?"

One girl rocked her head back from the wide barrel of a bamboo bong and released a funnel of smoke. "Sure."

"Thanks, Jane." Fauna dashed to the river, dove in, crossed the swimming hole, and returned dripping to plop down on the blanket as Darla sat down with a spray of droplets on Paul's other side.

The crowd on the beach was almost all girls. "Where's the guys?"

"Workin' their patches. They'll show up with beer after it gets too hot." Fauna waved at a balding black man sitting with a skinny tattooed blonde drinking from a leather bota bag of wine. "You gotta meet these guys." She grabbed Paul's hand, they moved over to the blanket next to the couple, and the man passed them the wine bag.

Paul held out a hand. "I'm Paul."

"Michael, people call me Black Michael, as opposed to Mountain Michael or Medic Michael, or all the other Michaels." He grinned. "I'm the easiest to spot."

"I'm Danielle." The skinny girl held out a ring-covered hand to Paul, then turned to Black Michael, who was leaning on his elbows with a frown, and rubbed his arm. "It's okay baby."

"It is not okay."

Paul blinked, wondering what invisible boundary he'd crossed.

Michael held up a palm. "Hey, it's not you. I'm just pissed off at that fuck Abdullah."

"It's not your fault baby."

"I brought him here." Michael grabbed a rock and squeezed it until his knuckles paled. He sighed and put it down. "It's on my karma. He was a fucking junkie pimp and now he's doing the same thing without the needle. He's just using that religion shit to control those naïve white chicks. He's doing speed too." He ran a hand over a high forehead and exhaled through a wispy beard. "It's bullshit."

Danielle rubbed Michael's sinewy shoulder with a scar running down it. "You were just doing the righteous thing and he took advantage of it. You wanted to help him get his shit together is all."

Michael glanced at Paul. "I promised his mama in Compton 'cause his brother was a buddy of mine in the Army who got killed in sixty-seven in Nam."

"He just drained your energy, baby."

"Fuckin' aye."

Fauna returned from the river and plopped down beside them. "Yeah Michael, nobody blames you."

He turned to Paul. "I've got a lot of brothers and sisters here I brought this shit on. He's fucking dangerous." Sand ran between Michael's fingers from a closed fist. "And that insane shit with the bath house has gotta stop. We built that place when he wasn't even around. If that fucker *ever* comes near my—"

"Baby, calm down, please."

Paul passed the bota bag and Michael took a pull of wine. "And fucking Christine. She calls herself Fatima now and stands guard in a veil at the bath house while those Muslim chicks are showering. They're not even real Muslims. I bet they couldn't tell a surah from something out of Poor Richard's Almanac. The dumb bitch used to give blowjobs right here at the swimming hole and now she's in a fucking *burkah!* It's fucking schizophrenic." He rose and dusted sand off his calves. "Anyway it's nice meeting you guys. Sorry I'm being so un-cool, but if you're smart you'll stay away from Abdullah and the goddamn Muslims."

Paul forced a smile. "Good to meet you man."

"Yeah, peace." Darla rose and went to the water.

Michael and Danielle rolled up their blanket and headed toward the road with his rant carrying across the beach. "I'm taking a motherfucking shower, and if those assholes are at the bath house—"

"Baby it's cool."

Paul watched them disappear in the trees. "What's a burkah?"

Fauna snorted. "A fuckin' tent he makes his women wear. I heard Abdullah was called Snake or some shit in Portland. He's still a pimp in his head and thinks he can have a harem and snatch chicks off the beach for slaves. Black Michael's righteous people and every time he hears about some other thing the asshole did he feels responsible because he brought him down here and thought he could mellow him out. You can't blame him."

Paul gazed over the naked girls on the beach and tried to imagine them covered in tablecloths. He put hands to his face to stifle a snort. He noticed that the girl smoking the bong was staring at his cock and caught her eye. She grinned, and the dream from the night before rose into memory for a fleeting moment, of a glowing white body astride him with eyes like stars. He felt his blood rise in response and made for the water.

Darla was at the far end of the swimming hole with some guy. Paul felt a surge of jealousy as he plunged into the river and streaked across the hole underwater. There was an eruption of bubbles as a girl dove in from the other side and a pale face passed him surrounded by a weightless mass of auburn hair. She brushed his thigh as she swam by, and he turned to watch her undulate across the sandy bottom like a pale vision. He couldn't go home. He couldn't imagine Charleston being home anymore. Captain John's Motel, high school, and prison all seemed the same to him now.

As he rose toward the surface there was a flash and the blood red eyes of his dream apparition stared at him. Paul's mouth opened in surprise, he swallowed water and came up coughing. He blew it from his nose and treaded water in the middle of the swimming hole as the world collapsed. His control... his *mind,* were washing away in a tide that had begun with the peyote and had become a cascade with the dream of the night before.

Am I crazy?

A naked girl with long red hair stood on the beach with eyes closed and arms spread to the sun. She could be having the same kind of experience right now. He scanned the faces around him. Many were high and somewhere else. Paul let out his breath. If he was crazy, at least he had company.

He followed Darla to the beach and flopped on the towel beside Fauna.

"God," Darla examined her legs, "I have got to get tanner. I used to be like you Fauna, when I lived in San Diego."

The crowd had grown with the heat of the day. The couple beneath the viney maple were still fucking. Paul had to give them an "A." He turned to Darla. "These guys got a head start. We were in British Columbia where it's too cold to get a tan."

Fauna yawned. "Hang around. You'll look the same." She rolled on her elbows. "You should see this little guy who comes down from O'Brien. Girls call him donkey dick."

Darla rolled her eyes. "Really?"

Fauna laughed. "Yeah, he's not much to look at and dumb as a rock, but he's got a dangle like an extra arm or something. That thing looks dangerous."

"Some of the dumbest dudes get hung with the biggest ones. Don't that suck?"

"Uh-huh. Jane says he doesn't even know how to use it and gets off in two minutes. What a waste. Guys that do know how get some great reputations though. Sometimes girls will bring their friends to them 'cause they're having a hard time." Fauna grinned. "That's called a charity fuck."

Darla chuckled. "Hey Paul, want to give a charity fuck? After you make somebody else come maybe you'll quit worrying about me." She burst into laughter. "Hey Fauna, want some charity?"

Fauna reached over and squeezed Paul's cock. "I know he ranks with the good ones. You guys were going at it forever last night, but I'm not hurting for charity right now."

Darla did the same from the other side. Paul sucked in his breath. "Cut it out." He rolled on his stomach.

"Don't be shy."

"God, Fauna, this place is better than Black's Beach. There's no straights on the cliffs with binoculars."

"Yeah, but there's guys like Abdullah around. Christine used to be here all the time." Fauna dug her toes in the sand. "I saw her getting it on here in front of everybody last summer with Weasel and now she's calling herself Fatima. It's gotta be hot as shit in those stupid robes."

Darla made a face. "That's crazy. Why in the fuck would somebody want to wear a veil?" She blew hair from her eyes and struck a pose as she gazed into the bright blue sky.

"Search me, sister. I love my skin. Other people seem to like it too."

"You're beautiful Fauna. I'm gonna be as tan as you by the end of summer."

"There's lots of places to swim in these mountains. I bet there's a couple thousand people at swimming holes right this minute." Fauna arose and bounded to the water like a bronze goddess.

Darla ran a hand down Paul's back. "Roll over, rover."

Paul eased around, pulled his wadded-up shorts under his head for a pillow, and squeezed his eyes shut against the glare. Darla slid up beside him on her elbows. Her skin was warm from the sun and she smelled good.

"I'm not doing it in public."

"Not yet, but we could do some showing off if you wanted. We could make a movie even. Want to do a porno flick? I got invited to do one once but I turned it down. They'd pay us in L.A."

"No."

A shadow fell across them and they gazed up at a tiny blue-eyed girl with bobbed blond hair. If it wasn't for her breasts, she could have passed for a child.

"Here," Darla patted the spot beside her, "We got room."

The girl nodded and folded effortlessly into the lotus position on the blanket.

"I'm Darla," she said, "and this is Paul."

"Hi," the girl extended a hand, "I'm Cindy."

"Where are you from?"

"Saint Paul in Minnesota." She glanced down the river. "Did you see any cops at the store?"

They shook their heads.

"Good, 'cause they're looking for me."

"There's lots of runaways around. Don't sweat it."

"No, they're looking for me." Cindy ran a hand through her hair and frowned. "Do you guys have a place I can crash?"

Darla nodded. "We're staying on Hope Mountain. Why do you think the cops are looking for you, I mean more than anybody else?"

"There's a reward."

Paul scanned the paths coming from the road and sunk lower on the towel.

"Oh."

"I'm supposed to be in Munich."

"In Germany?"

Cindy nodded. "At the Olympics. I'm on the gymnastics team. At least I'm 'posed to be. I had to get away from my coach and my fucking parents pushed me all the time like it was their lives and not mine, and they didn't believe anything that was going on, so I headed for somewhere people are supposed to be aware." She sighed. "Know what I mean?"

"Wow, shit, you're an Olympic gymnast?"

"Uh-huh." Cindy put her hands behind her on the blanket, cocked her hips, and put her legs around her head with her knees next to her ears. She crossed her ankles behind her neck and rose off the blanket on her palms as they stared, as did everyone else on the beach who'd noticed. Cindy uncrossed her ankles and returned to the lotus position in a twinkling.

"Wowie-zowie." Darla got out.

Paul gasped. "I believe you."

"Yeah." Cindy cracked her back. "You guys got something to eat?"

* * *

Each time Paul looked away his eyes returned to Cindy.

An *Olympic Gymnast.*

Fauna had brought rice cakes and deer jerky, and the girls on the next blanket shared their wine. Cindy ate anything she was given, drank the wine and grew talkative in the heat. They swam, laughed, and rubbed coconut oil onto each other from a brown bottle with occasional glances in the direction of the road. Paul did Cindy's back. Darla and Fauna did too. They all had to touch her and couldn't believe how hard her muscles were, like iron under her smooth skin. She rippled like water but was tough as whipcord. Paul fought getting aroused again and had to lie on his stomach. Darla and Fauna exchanged glances and laughed. Cindy gave him the cutest smile, which didn't help much.

* * *

They were dozing in the late afternoon sun when something flew out of the bushes and landed on Fauna's chest with a hollow *thunk* and a bright splash of blood.

"Goddamn it!" Fauna knocked the floppy-eared head of a goat off with a scowl and sprang to her feet with the barrel of her Peacemaker glinting in the sun.

Cindy yelped and scrambled behind Paul as blood ran down Fauna's stomach and legs.

Fauna glared at the willows behind them with an expression like gunfire.

XII.
Moving

"Fauna, mellow out. It's me."

"Motherfucker!"

The tall man with blond braids and black cowboy hat that they'd met at the store strode out of the bushes with a cross painted on his bare chest in blood. "We're barbecuing a goat at the Barn. Want to come?"

"Fuck!" Fauna's lip curled in a sneer as she flicked blood from her breasts. "You fuckin' dick. You're lucky I didn't shoot you."

People were picking up their blankets and moving away. Cindy looked like she was about to cry. Paul grabbed her hand, Darla grabbed the other, and Cindy contracted between them with her knees under her chin looking the size of a toy poodle. Darla whispered something in her ear.

"Sorry, ladies." Mel tipped his hat to the girls and turned to Fauna. "Thanks for not tryin' to shoot me babe. Hate to draw on you."

"You're fuckin' crazy." Fauna slid her .45 back in the holster with a growl, stuck it under her tall moccasins on the blanket, and dashed to the water. She dove in and reappeared at the far side tossing back golden hair in a spray of droplets giving Mel the finger.

Mel tipped his hat. "You're Fauna's new buds, Paul and Dar-la, right?"

"Yeah." Darla nodded.

Mel examined the girl between them. "Who's this?"

"Cindy. She's with us."

"How the fuck old are you?"

Cindy scowled. "Sixteen."

"Really?"

"Yes, really, I'm just small."

"Wow."

Fauna burst out of the water, grabbed her shorts, and proceeded to slide them up her legs. She plopped down on the blanket and began to lace her moccasins. "I've been telling these guys how cool you are and then you throw a goat's head at me."

"Hey, didn't hurt."

"Did too." Fauna rubbed her chest and took in Cindy's expression. "Let's go home guys. Cindy, you can stay with us."

"Okay."

* * *

They had stewed rice, carrots, lentils and onions with deer meat for dinner and washed it down with herbal tea sitting on logs around the campfire. Fauna broke out some wine and rolled joints on a dented enameled tray with a picture of Lawrence Welk and the Lemon Sisters on it.

Darla passed the big green bottle to Cindy. "How did you get to Oregon?"

"I got a ride to Portland with this guy who wanted me to be his old lady in some apartment when we got there, and just cook and shit, and of course fuck him all the time." She shook her head. "I went to a natural food store down the block and caught a ride with some people to the Country Faire in Veneta but I left all my stuff at his place. I met some people at the Faire from Takilma but

I didn't want to stay with them after I got a ride here 'cause they were smelly and gross. So here I am."

"What kind of reward do they have for you?"

Cindy examined Darla for an instant. "Fifty thousand."

"Shit."

"Wow."

"Unreal."

Fauna laughed. "Lucky you're with people that material shit doesn't work on. I wouldn't turn you in if my life depended on it 'cause of the karma." The sound of hooves approaching made her yank out her pistol and she stared into the falling dusk.

Mel emerged from the shadows on his black horse, tipped his hat, and dismounted. "Evenin', ladies." He gave Paul a nod.

Fauna holstered her gun, crossed her arms, and scowled. "You come to apologize for that dumb-ass goat shit?"

"Not really."

Fauna strode toward him with fists balled, but upon reaching him, they grappled in a passionate embrace. She broke away breathing hard, brushed hair from her eyes, and announced she was going to Mel's for the night. "Here," She unbuckled her gun belt and handed it to Paul, "I'll leave this in case guys from the gypsy camp show up or anybody else who sucks. Keep it clean. If we hear shots we'll come running."

Mel mounted his horse and Fauna swung up behind him. She wrapped arms around his waist and laughed. "And don't go sleepwalking with my gun. I don't want it all muddy." They waved and cantered away in the dusk.

Paul took the gun out of the holster, examined it, slid it back in, and poked the fire with a stick. "I thought she was pissed off at him."

Darla shrugged. "They're kinda made for each other I guess."

"I guess so. They were hot."

Cindy giggled.

Paul and Darla slept in Fauna's bed. Cindy slept on the floor feigning sleep as they made love until there was only the sound of night birds and wind in the trees. Long after the girls were asleep, Paul lay staring at the ceiling listening for that seductive voice from the forest again. The woman's eyes seemed to watch him wherever he went, sometimes from the face of a wolf or a great black bird in his imagination. The tree house rocked gently as the madrones shifted in a breeze. Fauna's pistol swung softly from a hook overhead. His fingers ran over the notches carved in the grip.

Were they from people Fauna killed?

He'd never felt so vulnerable, but it wasn't to people, it was to someone or something who could see him in dreams, who could read his mind yet couldn't even be real. How did he protect himself from *that?*

Something had changed forever, beginning with the peyote trip.

So am I crazy?

He had to keep it together for Darla and Cindy to protect them. Paul closed his eyes.

* * *

They sat up to a howl.

Someone crashed down the hill from the direction of the gypsy camp breaking branches, snapping twigs and loosening rocks that rolled downhill sounding like an army. Paul yanked Fauna's .45 out of the holster in the dark and rolled to his feet. Cindy jumped on the bed with Darla and they hugged each other.

"What?" Darla began.

"Shhhh!" Paul stroked her neck and peered out the window. Moonlight slanted through the trees but the plastic made clear vision impossible. He crawled over to the door with the old Peacemaker in his hand and opened it a crack.

"Help!" came from directly below him.

He jerked back and almost shot the face staring up at him. It was a blond-bearded young man in a down winter jacket. The man shivered and shifted from one foot to the other.

Paul swallowed. "What... what do you want?"

"They want to kill me! There's sparkling spiders in the mine and the rascals want to bury me there! They have an altar and they're going to cut my head off!"

"What the fuck?"

The stranger grabbed the rungs of the ladder and began to climb.

"Get out of here!" Paul cocked the gun with the muzzle a foot from the man's face, hoping he wouldn't try to grab it.

The stranger blinked, gave Paul a vacant grin, and began to dig in a pocket of his filthy down jacket. "I have some acid—"

"I don't give a shit, and keep your hand out of your pocket! Go away!"

There was a moment of silence as the man hung onto the ladder with a vacant expression.

Paul swallowed. If the guy was crazy, none of what he'd said might make a difference. He'd keep coming and Paul might actually have to shoot him. He let out his breath as the crazy man slowly descended to the forest floor, looked back up the hill in the direction from which he came, and shrugged. "Maybe the spirits have gone to sleep. There's dead Chinese that can fly at night. Did you hear them in the woods? There's a witch that leads them. You can hear her laughing." He held up two fingers in a "V" and walked away into the night. "Peace!"

Paul cradled the six-gun and watched the madman disappear in the forest.

Darla's hand was on his shoulder. "Baby, I'm so glad you're here."

They climbed onto Fauna's bed, where Cindy huddled in the corner against the wall. "Can I sleep with you guys?"

"Sure."

Cindy unwound like a coiled spring and wrapped trembling limbs around him. Paul pulled her perfect body closer but his ears were straining, listening to the night.

* * *

He arose before dawn and headed to where Fauna said the Queen of Bronze mine was and reached the diggings in twenty minutes. Piles of timbers and heaps of tailings made a pale slash across a bench carved into the mountain that vegetation hadn't reclaimed in a century. A stream of water flowed from the dark mineshaft that was discolored even in the first gray light. Paul stared down the mouth of a tunnel waiting for some nightmare to appear as the day grew brighter and night retreated into the bowels of the mountain. When the sun crept over the ridge, the water flowing from the mine was red as blood. He sat for a while on an ancient tailing pile, watching sunlight touch the distant peaks. A pileated woodpecker rattled the trunk of a dead Douglas fir with his bright red head a blur. Squirrels scolded. He inhaled the solitude and said a little prayer to whatever forces ruled these mountains. Paul hoped they weren't bad.

He returned and woke the girls. They wanted to leave but had to wait for Fauna. Cindy looked so young it probably wasn't a good idea to take her with them, but there was such a thing as doing the right thing, and leaving her on Hope Mountain was simply out of the question.

* * *

Fauna returned at noon. She had abrasions on her knees and elbows, bruises on her thighs, and flopped on her bed with a groan. When they told her about the strange visitor of the night before, she laughed. "That's Jason. He's insane. He wears winter shit all summer and spouts total bullshit. I saw him in the sauna at the bath house wearing a down jacket. He stinks."

"I *guess.*" Darla said. "He scared the shit out of us. He's lucky Paul didn't shoot him."

"Yeah." Fauna yawned. "The Rascals are back at the gypsy camp."

Paul took the joint from his lips. "That's what he said but I thought it was babbling. He was yelling about the rascals and that they were gonna cut his head off, and all this bullshit about spiders or something."

Darla nodded. "And flying Chinese, and a witch."

Fauna rolled on the bunk. "Yeah, the Queen of Bronze is supposed to be haunted by the Chinese workers who were herded into a tunnel the owners blew up on them so they didn't have to be paid. I don't know if that story's true or not. The Rascals are a biker gang from down around Sacramento. Just a bunch of punks." She spun the cylinder of her .45. "Me and Mel could take 'em out in a heartbeat." A chuckle rippled her lips. "That man is *awesome.*" Fauna cracked her neck and sat up. "You guys could go to Selma. I've got friends that got turned onto this old goat dairy, eighty acres, and they need somebody to hold onto it and help with their pot." She glanced at Cindy. "Mel says you should get off this mountain quick and not tell anybody about the reward. You oughta be safe over there."

Paul rubbed his chin. "How do we get there?"

"See Gus at Four Corners. Look for the truck that says 'Freewheelin' Franklin's Sanitone Service' on it. He's got a pot gig going at the goat dairy and the people who've been staying there are kinda breaking up so he's gonna need some help. Just tell him the truth, and that you're my friends. He's good people. I'll write a note." Fauna grabbed a dog-eared notebook and scribbled in it. She tore off the page, tossed it to Darla, rubbed her face and yawned. "I'm gonna crash."

* * *

They hiked down the mountain unmolested. The clinic at the base was crowded. As they passed, Cindy walked on the outside with Paul and Darla between her and the people on the porch. When they got to Takilma Road a half-dozen guys lounging in front of the old store stared at them. Everyone they didn't know looked suspicious.

They stuck out their thumbs, got a ride within three minutes, and reached the junction called Four Corners, where a sprawling ranch house sat under big oaks. Parked in the yard was a truck with the hood up. **Freewheelin' Franklin's Sanitone Service** was painted on a big white tank on its back.

As they walked up the driveway a huge brindle pit bull let out a bellow and charged from under the shade of a weeping willow. Cindy yelped and ducked behind Paul, and both girls dug their fingers into his arms as he unsheathed his knife. The dog stopped ten feet away, baring fangs in a huge block of a head and looking like a frog with a bad attitude.

"Smaug! Shut the fuck up!" A skinny balding man with a drooping Fu Manchu mustache and a cigarette between his lips shouted from the porch as he cradled an old double-barreled shotgun. He looked them over and waved at the dog. "Get your ass back here! Ya dumb shit!"

The dog returned wagging a stump of tail. The man bent over, scratched him at the base of it, and pointed to a plastic kennel sitting at the end of the porch. Smaug went in, turned around twice, and sat down with his head on his paws watching the newcomers.

Paul waved. "Are you Gus?"

Gus nodded.

"Fauna said you needed somebody to help with some pot in Selma."

"She did, huh?"

Darla gave him her best smile. "Yeah, she wrote a note. We've been staying with her but Hope Mountain is kinda weird."

Gus's laugh exposed a missing incisor. "Fuckin' aye it's weird. What's your trip?"

"Huh?"

"You runaways?"

Paul shuffled on the gravel driveway. Darla and Cindy blinked.

"Ha," Gus waved them into the house, "Come on."

The living room looked more like a campsite than a home. Two couches with tired Mexican blankets draped over them flanked a cold stone fireplace full of cigarette butts and ashes. A young woman with long brown hair was cooking in the cluttered kitchen and nodded as they came in.

"Coffee, Joyce!" Gus commanded.

Joyce brushed hair from her eyes and examined the three newcomers. "You want cream and sugar?"

Darla nodded. "Yes, both, thank you."

"Sit down." Gus waved to a table covered by magazines and a dented trash can lid full of immature marijuana buds. They did, and he proceeded to roll a joint. "So, you guys want to stay at the goat dairy?"

Darla shrugged. "We'd like to see it, I guess."

"Are you cool?"

"Yes." Cindy said.

Gus eyed her critically. "What the fuck are you, thirteen?"

"Sixteen."

"You sure?"

"Yes, I'm *sure*. I'm just small. Bet I can arm wrestle you, man."

Gus burst into laughter.

"She looks really young 'cause she's a gymnast."

"Oh," Gus's eyebrows narrowed, "really?"

Cindy stood, walked to the center of the room, and flipped onto her hands with her feet arrow-straight pointing at the ceiling. She did three pushups like that with her back ruler-straight, sprang backwards onto her feet with a flourish of her hands, and bowed.

"Holy fuckin' shit." Gus pulled at his moustache and nodded approval. He turned to Paul. "What I mean is: if you're cool you'll help out with the project there, make some money, and keep your mouths shut even if you get busted for something else like bein' runaways."

"You mean your pot patch."

"That's *patches*. There's some serious money involved, and… I don't know. Every fuckin' time you go to town some cop is gonna check her." He motioned to Cindy. "She looks like a little kid, back-flips or no."

"I'll stay up there then."

Darla gave Gus a hopeful smile. "Can't Weasel get fake I.D.?"

Gus leaned back in his chair and struck a wooden match along the thigh of his jeans. He puffed the big yellow joint he'd rolled into a burn and nodded. "Yeah, so can I."

She clapped her hands. "Oh cool. We all need it."

"Yeah, so if you guys stay up there and I pay you, say, twenty-five bucks a week apiece, and get you I.D. too, you'll help out, shut up and hang for a while? Like until harvest time? You'll get a share of the profits that way too."

Darla sat up straight. "We promise."

Paul glanced from Darla to Cindy. He accepted the joint after she took a hit and passed it.

Gus played with his moustache as he examined them. "The guys I got up there now in a school bus are fighting all the time. It sucks 'cause Rayella's really responsible. She's a hardcore country chick and I like her. Don't know why they're even together. She's a goddamn fox but Danny's more into boys I think."

"We're just into each other." Darla volunteered.

Gus exhaled smoke. "Okay. We'll try it."

* * *

They rode through Cave Junction that afternoon on the bench seat of Gus's big old truck with a septic tank on the back proclaiming **Freewheelin' Franklin's Sanitone Service.** He stopped at the Sentry Market and admonished Cindy to stay in the cab. She slid down in the seat, and Paul and Darla accompanied Gus into the store. He bought three bags of groceries and they rode out of town with them balanced on their laps. Cindy sat scrunched next to Gus with the big gearshift rattling between her legs. His hand lingered over her thigh every time he shifted.

As they approached the rusted cone of a lumber mill's slash burner in the tiny town of Kerby, Gus pointed out a gap in the ridge to the west beyond the broad green pastures of a ranch. "That's Tennessee Gap. The Gunslingers live back there on Sebastopol Creek. Good people. They were in the White Panthers in Detroit until the cops killed or busted everybody who didn't get out of there. There's a cool old guy has some claims back there on Josephine Creek who gave them their claims, Bob Cutler. It's a good place to hide, but the fuckin' ground's too goddamn rocky for growin' dope."

"What's the White Panthers?"

"Some guys in Detroit like the Weathermen, but more into guns than bombs. They weren't black so they called themselves the White Panthers."

"What did they do?"

"Don't matter. Their day's done. They're all in the joint, dead, or hiding out like the gunslingers."

They crossed a cultivated flat with a big sign saying SWEET CRON FOR SALE.

Gus chuckled. "That's the Sauers' place. They been here for a hundred years and do that so people think they're hicks." He turned right on a dirt road. "This place we're going to belongs to the Mayor of Grants Pass. He's just glad somebody's keeping it from getting trashed. He's been out once in the last three years and never asks questions. If he ever shows up, say you're watching the place for Gus. We got water all set up for irrigation and some killer red-hair Oaxacan growin' on the hill." Gus slowed to cross a creek running across the road and a half-dozen deer bounded up the slope. "Lota deer on Reeves Creek." He turned to Paul. "You use a gun?"

"Sure, I hunted deer on the coast. Elk too."

"Good. You can get red meat and watch my shit. There's a .30-.30 at the place you can use and you can do all the huntin' and patrolling you want. I need eyes."

XIII.
The Goat Dairy

Gus turned up a rutted fire road and a two-story farmhouse of unpainted wood with tar paper nailed to its cedar shake roof appeared. An ancient barn sat behind it of weathered planks and half-collapsed logs. Gus pulled under huge old oaks into the yard and killed the engine. Behind the house was a cinderblock shed and pens that had once been used to milk goats. One had been converted into a chicken coop and a few red hens scratched in the dirt. A big sable German shepherd barked once and was joined by a spotted furry mongrel with tail wagging. An old red school bus sat under the oaks with a wisp of smoke coming from a tin smokestack poking through its roof. As the truck bumped to a stop, a willowy young woman with long brown hair and huge green eyes appeared in the door of the bus. She waved and disappeared inside.

"That's Rayella." Gus led them up the creaking boards of the porch past a swing hung from rusty chains, into the house, and past a battered wood stove. They followed Gus up narrow stairs to a second storey with two rooms under a low ceiling. "I brought up the mattresses a couple months ago and you guys got bags. There's extra blankets around here somewhere. Come on." They followed him down to a kitchen, where a blue enameled Charter Oak wood stove sat next to a wood box across from warped cabinets and a sink.

Gus opened the door to a low shed added onto the kitchen. "Here's the swamp cooler." A box draped in burlap hung from wires in the dark recesses of the shed with a damp hole in the floor below it. "You pour cold water from the creek on it. The evaporation keep stuff good for a few days. You gotta haul water but there's plenty of five-gallon jugs around."

Paul inhaled the smell of mildew and scanned Darla and Cindy's faces.

Rayella was in the yard on her knees scratching the furry mongrel. She stood up as they stepped off the porch and Paul marveled at her height. She had high cheekbones and full lips and looked like a model even in a ragged blouse and jeans.

"Where's Danny?" Gus asked.

Rayella shrugged. "Search me. Ah don' give a damn."

"You guys still fighting?"

"We just don' got a lot in common." Rayella's drawl was thick as honey on a warm biscuit. She tossed back a curtain of hair and extended a hand to Paul. "Howdy."

"Hi," Darla said, "I'm Darla, this is Paul, and this is Cindy."

"Ah'm Rai-el-ah."

Darla laughed. "Where are you from?"

"South Carolina."

Paul grinned. "Did your daddy want a Ray?"

"You got it."

They put away the groceries while Gus and Rayella had a conversation in the bus. When Gus returned he had an old Marlin .30-.30 in his hands. "Here," he handed it to Paul along with two boxes of ammunition, "Danny'll be pissed but I'm letting you have it. The fucker never took care of it anyway. He's leaving and I don't want him taking it with him."

Paul pointed the barrel away from everyone and opened the action for inspection. He held it up to the light coming in through the plastic-covered window and squinted down the barrel. "Needs cleaning."

"No doubt. Danny don't know shit about guns and he don't care to learn. There's cleaning stuff around here he never used. He did kill a deer with it after about five shots but he fucked up a lot of the meat."

"And Ah cleaned it."

Gus motioned to the hillside. "Come on." He led them past an ancient hand-dug well filled with trash down to a meadow where a creek widened in a hole dug in the clay bottom. "Here's where you get water. Like I said, you gotta haul it. I bought PVC to run a gravity line from upstream and if Danny wasn't so fuckin' lazy it would be at the house. You can do it." They crossed the creek to a meadow where a dappled horse grazed on tufts of grass. "That's Rayella's horse. She'll probably let you ride her."

Cindy brightened. "All right!"

Gus scratched the head of the big German shepherd who'd joined them. "Watch for snakes." He said over his shoulder, and they began to climb the opposite hillside. They ducked under bushes on a trail that avoided open places and came out on a long terrace of well-worked soil on the hill with logs holding it up. Empty fertilizer bags lay under the shade of the manzanitas and a faucet was mounted on the end of some black PVC pipe from up the gulch that ended in the crotch of a little scrub oak with a green garden hose coiled below it. Two dozen of the most beautiful chest-high marijuana plants Paul had ever seen filled the terrace.

Darla ran a hand across one of the buds coming into flower, rubbed her fingers together, and smelled them. "Wow."

"Water in the evening or early in the morning. By the time the shade's gone the ground should be dry enough planes can't spot it if you keep leaves and stuff over it. Don't wear any bright shit, and *never* stand around in the open." Gus picked a big shade leaf off one of the plants, sniffed it, and handed it to Cindy. He bent down to scratch the dog, who was avoiding the plants. "Bozo here is okay around the patch, but that dumb dog Spyro of Rayella's never comes up here. Chuck a rock at him if he tries. When the leaves start to curl on the ends, trim the big ones. It gives more sun to the buds." He grinned. "You can smoke all the leaves you want. Keep putting forest shit around the plants to camouflage them, and remember to cover the holes where the ground gets wet. There's six of these patches, so it takes a while. I'll show you the rest." He paused. "Oh, and if you ever hear a helicopter, get the hell under cover, and *don't* fuckin' shoot at it, okay?"

"Okay."

"Some fucking idiot did last month on the Applegate and brought the heat down like gangbusters. Two families got busted." Gus stroked his mustache and scowled. "Don't fuck with the helicopters. We're the Viet Cong, and they're the gunships. Just keep your heads down and remember you're here until harvest."

"Okay."

* * *

Gus left after they'd become familiarized with their duties, promising to return and pay them in a week. Darla and Cindy set to work arranging things in the kitchen and sweeping up with a butchered straw broom. Paul sat in the porch swing cleaning the gun with stuff Rayella brought from the bus and Bozo sat down with a loud doggie sigh.

Rayella plopped down beside him with a battered Martin guitar, strummed a couple chords and tossed hair from her face. "Where y'all from?"

"I'm from near Coos Bay, but me and Darla met in Ucluelet."

She kicked the swing into motion. "Where the hell is Uke... Uke...?"

"It's on Vancouver Island, in Canada. Both our parents are doing stuff there for the summer but she's from San Diego. We took off for San Francisco but when we got there it sucked."

"Fuck the City. There's way better places to be. Where's Cindy from?"

"Minnesota. She's an Olympic gymnast. She supposed to be in Germany right now in the Olympics."

"No shit. She do look damn buff. How old are y'all?"

"Me and Darla are seventeen, Cindy's sixteen."

"Ah'm nineteen but nobody's give me shit for a long time anyway 'cause Ah'm tall. Cindy's sixteen?"

"Yeah. What's Danny like?"

"He's okay an' all. He's kinda artistic. When the tags run out on the bus he painted on new ones so we don't get stopped. He used to do signs in Portland." She yawned. "Mighty tired of his shit though."

"That's what Gus said. Where is he?"

"Hell if Ah know. He went with a guy from Thompson Creek somewhere, over to Waldo Road or somethin'." Rayella shrugged. "He'll be back."

"Where did you meet?"

"At the Rainbow Gatherin' in Colorado. We were helpin' dig wells and do trails and ended up together after a mushroom trip." She shook her head and a curtain of hair caressed the strings of her guitar. "Still ain't sure how. We went to Portland but Ah don't like his friends there. Ah heard about this neck a' the woods at the Gatherin' from some people from O'Brien and we headed on down." Rayella kicked the swing into motion. "Reminds me of where Ah'm from, kinda, not the country so much but the country people. Ain't so damn humid either."

"Is that his bus?"

"It's mine. Got it from a guy from upstate New York wanted to marry me. Paid him three hundred bucks from my modelin' money. He had it since Woodstock. It costs too damn much in gas and fixin' though. He was my photographer in Manhattan when I was modelin' last winter and we took off together. Tol' me he loved me. Fella was good-lookin' too, and smart, and a damn good lay when he wasn't whinin' 'bout his art and all. Them New Englanders think they're so fuckin' sensitive and act like us southern folk are all stupid or somethin'. Ah got tired of it. We were at a commune in New Hampshire where they were all like that and it bored the shit outta me. He wanted me to go to Toronto with him but he was so damn possessive. He was from some rich ol' Conneticut family and talkin' about maybe I could be in the bloodline an' all like Ah oughta be grateful to be Barbie to his Ken. Don't trust borders much anyway. I got in a bit a' shit in New York and didn't want to try it, 'case there was some kinda warrant out for me. Ah don't do jail."

He gazed at her profile against the sunlit trees. "You do look like a model."

"Ah was, but Ah do not like New York City. Ah'm from the country, and 'cept for all the relatives that wanta jump yer bones it's a damn sight better place to be. Punched out a couple a' cousins growin' up." Rayella strummed her guitar and sighed. "Wish Danny had more gumption. Ah do more work on the pot than he does and he's always whinin' about something or other. Ah get up first, feed the critters, fix breakfast and he jus' lays around and talks about what a fuckin' artist he is, and how people oughta be and all like he can fix the world talkin'. Drives me crazy but Ah'm stickin' around for my share come harvest time." She yawned. "Wanta beer? Got some in the cooler in the bus."

"Sure, yeah."

Rayella returned with two Blitz beers, expertly punched two holes in one with her sheath knife, and handed it to Paul. He waited until she'd opened hers and they drank rocking in the swing. She took the rifle from his lap, held it up, and peered down the barrel. "First time it's been really clean since we got here. Ah jus' went over it quick 'cause we had to butcher the deer. He didn't do shit on that either." She handed it back. "Gotta tell y'all 'bout Danny. He's maybe gonna try an' suck your dick so don' freak out."

"Huh?"

"That's kinda why we been fightin'. All his friends are like that. Ah mean Ah don't mind, they were all over the place when Ah was modlin', but he kept on wantin' to fuck me in the ass. Says it's good as the other way and he wanted me to stick stuff up his like a banana and all. Wouldn't let him after just once. Fuck that. That goddamn *hurts!*" Rayella shook her head and gazed at Bozo, who returned the concerned expression. She stretched her long limbs and chuckled. "His friends in Portland like to watch each other shit on a plate they put on their chests."

"Say what?"

She giggled. "What'd you take Paul, me, or a big 'ol turd on your chest?"

He sat speechless as they rocked on the porch. After a while he reached out and ran fingers up her thigh. Rayella smiled, extended a leg and flexed her toes. "Oh, man, I don't even know what to say to that. You're fucking beautiful Rayella. Shit, you're a fox."

"Thanks. Been wonderin'."

* * *

There was a hindquarter of deer in the swamp cooler that was beginning to go green. Paul cut off the slimy surface, washed it in the creek, and they tried to cook it in the old stove that evening. The wood supply was mostly pieces of boards from outbuildings or oak that was old and damp, and after an hour trying to heat the oven to a reasonable temperature, they moved it to the propane oven in Rayella's bus.

The bus had most of the seats removed with one left behind the driver's seat and a long counter on the right side with cabinets and a sink. The propane range and a small wood stove were on the same side with a couch on the left. There was a table screwed into the wall of the bus below the windows with one of the old bus seats on each side of it. A wooden partition separated a queen size bed in back with closet space and shelves.

An old Homelite chainsaw sat on the back porch of the house along with a dull splitting maul and an ax that had seen little care. Paul volunteered to cut wood in the morning. "Is there a saw file around here?"

"Yeah, a couple in the barn. Danny don't do firewood too good."

"That's for sure." He mopped up juice from the meat with a slice of bread. "That was near past prime but it cooked up nice and tender."

Cindy was separating hers into slivers with her fingers and eating the pieces slowly. "I never had deer before. It's good."

Darla sloshed a gallon jug of wine. "I hope we get back to the store before all the good stuff's gone."

"Y'all are a relief around here. Ah don't like drivin' the bus to town by myself, but if y'all chip in on gas we can go to the store anytime."

"Cool."

Rayella took a container of black pepper from the spice rack above the stove and shook the peppercorns out on a piece of newspaper, then pulled out a small plastic bag with several pills in it. "Been savin' this."

"What is it?"

"Back east they call 'em soapers. They're Quaaludes.""

Darla sat up. "Fuckin' aye! I love ludes."

Paul examined the pale yellow pills with 714 stamped on them. "What are they good for?"

Darla grinned. "Orgies, man."

Cindy's eyes widened.

"Oh."

"Here," Rayella gave two to each of them and they washed them down with wine. "Now we jus' kick back until they come on."

Paul sat next to Darla on the couch and rubbed her back. Rayella sat beside them with the lamp light glowing through the tent of her hair.

As Paul waited to feel something, he let out a nervous laugh. "Man, Danny's crazy."

"Yeah," Cindy said, "you're really pretty Rayella, and I love the way you talk."

Rayella struck a big Blue Tip match on the side of the wood stove and puffed a pipe into a burn. She inhaled deeply and spoke in a cloud of smoke. "Y'all are really an Olympic gymnast?"

Darla took the pipe, "Sure as shit she is. You should see her do stuff. Cindy, do that thing behind your head."

Cindy put her feet behind her neck and became a human pretzel.

"Damn," Rayella muttered, "Ah thought Ah was flexible. Betcha boys go cuckoo for that." She tried to put a leg behind her neck, and with a grunt of effort did with her face almost to the floor and a groan of pain. As she levered her ankle back over her head, her foot hit the neck of her guitar against the wall, it gave out a twang, and she grabbed it as it tipped over. "No way Ah'm gonna try that again. Now my head's spinnin'."

Darla was watching Paul, who was watching Cindy and Rayella. "Hey Rayella, Paul says Danny fucked you in the ass."

"Damn!" Rayella punched Paul's arm. "You gone and *tol'* her that?"

"I—"

"Just *once* Darla, fuck that."

Cindy made a face.

Paul laughed. "That's missing the target by a couple inches."

Darla squeezed Rayella's toes. "Paul's been staring at you since we got here, at least when he's not staring at Cindy."

Cindy giggled.

"Ah appreciate it after the last couple a'months."

"He's always sweating I'm going to lay some other guy." Darla shot Paul a grin. "I bet you've been bored stiff living here."

Rayella sighed. "Ah do miss gettin' around. Ain't too much into celibacy."

Cindy nodded. "I've been around too."

Darla's hand slid over Paul's fly. "Hum," she pursed her lips, "thought so."

"Cut it out."

Cindy's cheeks dimpled.

The girls' gazes were a hot bath and Paul's limbs began to tingle. He stared at the ceiling and squeezed his eyes shut. The face from his dream smiled back and he opened them quickly.

"Fuck it, I have gotta show you guys this." Darla began popping the buttons on Paul's Levi's and he grabbed her hand.

Rayella giggled. "Don' be shy, fella. Darla been talkin' you up jus' like you been tellin' stuff on me."

The roof of the bus began to rotate like the spinning cylinder at an amusement park where the floor drops out and you find yourself stuck to the walls. Paul's limbs felt rubbery and full of ginger ale. From the expression on Cindy's face, she was feeling the same thing. He dug teeth in his lip and let Darla finish opening his pants. It seemed a part of him hovered on the ceiling watching the goings-on in the flickering light of the kerosene lamp. A ripple of laughter echoed in his memory. He closed his eyes and two huge red ones stared back at him as in the dream on Hope Mountain. He opened them quickly.

Am I crazy?

If this was crazy, maybe he should go along for the ride.

With a final tug, Darla freed his cock and waved it in a tumescent salute at the other girls. Paul stared at their wide eyes.

Rayella's hair tickled his stomach. "That's a big'n."

Cindy giggled "Wow."

The girls shucked their clothes and they moved to the bed. Cindy sprang on him with a laugh and his hands closed on the hard cheeks of her ass. She grinned fiercely and their lips locked. He rolled her over and ran his mouth down silken skin over her hard belly down between her legs, licking and teasing as she bucked and squealed. Her back arched on the mattress as Darla and Rayella shouted encouragement. Rayella slapped his ass.

He marveled at Cindy's tightness as she began to grind. He rolled her on top and she bounced enthusiastically. Paul reached out to stroke Rayella's cheek and she put his fingers in her mouth. He slid them out to run them across soft lips and down her long body between her legs, and Rayella rose on her knees with a melodious sigh.

Darla blew in his ear. "Here's your super-duper cerharity fuck." She melted into Rayella with a long kiss as their bodies undulated above him and Cindy in the moonlight slanting through the windows like reeds around the luminous pond of his dreams.

XIV.
Workin' Daze

"Y'all ever gonna wake up?" Rayella stirred Krusteaz pancake mix in a chipped earthenware bowl as the gray light of dawn silhouetted her legs through her thin cotton skirt. A bowl full of fresh eggs sat on the narrow counter and the welcome smell of coffee filled the bus.

Paul ran a hand down the hollow of Darla's back. She stretched and yawned. Cindy was curled in a fetal ball on her other side and he reached across Darla to squeeze the hard cheek of her ass. "Goddamn."

"Guess so fella. You can strut around like the cock a' the walk later but it's time to water the crop. We didn't do it last night and it's gonna be hot soon so we gotta hustle."

"Oh… shit."

"Yep, we're jus' niggers on Mr. Gus's farm. Hope y'all got some energy left for workin' after all that bangin'."

Paul staggered outside crushing oak leaves under bare feet and pissed an arc in the cool morning air. Bozo chewed on a deer bone Rayella had tossed him and stopped to watch Paul's performance with interest before returning to the task between his paws. Rayella went to the chicken coop and Paul followed as she shooed a squawking bantam hen off a dozen eggs. Four big brown ones stood out amongst the small green ones of the bantie hen.

Rayella tossed hair over her shoulder. "Love them banties. When Ah got here there wasn't no chickens 'cept an ol' bantie hen and three of her young what was livin' in the trees. Critters ate all the others, but banties act like grouse and make do. They moved right back in when Ah cleaned out the coop. Got them New Hampshires for layin' big ol' brown eggs and the banties do the sittin' if you wanta hatch 'em. They'll go off in the woods like grouse and come back with a dozen chicks. They're *survivors*." She handed him an empty coffee can. "Fetch me some o' that scratch in the barn will ya?"

Paul found the feed sacks in a fifty-five gallon drum in the storeroom with a rock on top of the lid to keep rodents out. He filled the can and returned.

"Thanks." She tossed the scratch out and chickens exploded across the pen. "Them banties are kinda like us: hidin' in the trees and waitin' for the turn of the age and all."

"Do you think the age of Aquarius is coming?"

She shrugged. "Astrology don' mean shit to me. People ain't never gonna change."

Paul wondered again if she was really sixteen. She looked like a baby although she sure hadn't acted like one. As he inhaled the smell of coffee and pancakes, the scent of the girls erupted in the back of his nose from the night before and he was aroused.

Not now.

"Shit!" Darla threw her arms out and flopped on the mattress. "I don't *want* to get *up!*"

"Come on." Cindy sprang up as if lifted by strings and stood beside Rayella. "Need some help?"

Rayella slapped her butt. "Y'all better put on some clothes or Paul there's gonna have a tough time gettin' his pants on, honey."

"Oh."

He sighed. "God, I love you all. Really."

Rayella flipped a pancake. "We all love ya too Paul."

* * *

The yawning troop reached the first patch forty-five minutes later
with a stop for Cindy to hug the horse.

Rayella pointed up the little valley. "There's a pond up the
creek feedin' the hose, but it's getting' low and it's only July."

Paul leaned the .30-.30 in the crotch of a tree. "Then we
should dig it out deeper."

"That'd be good." Rayella filled the depressions at the bases
of each plant with the hose until they overflowed. She worked
across the terrace and returned to do it again after the water disappeared into the thirsty ground. "Y'all need to get some leaves
and bark to put around the plants so the wet spots don't show."

They scooped up forest litter from under the trees and
tucked it around the base of each plant. Rayella shut off the water
and they moved up the hill to the next patch. When they reached
the fourth terrace, the sound of an airplane came over the ridge.

"Git down!"

Paul slid into the shade under blue manzanita leaves, squatted with the gun across his knees, and the girls joined him. The
aircraft was coming from the high country in the east where
rocky peaks thrust their heads against the blue sky and was flying
straight overhead.

A white and green Cessna appeared not five hundred feet
above them and did a circle of the little valley where the old goat
dairy was the only homestead as they huddled under the bushes.

Rayella hissed at Bozo and the dog wandered over to join
them. She scratched him between the ears. "That there's the Man
sure as shit, lookin' for pot."

Paul peered through the leaves. "How do you know it's not
the Forest Service or a private plane?"

"'Cause Ah been to their airstrip by O'Brien. Went there
with Sheree from Takilma to check it out and flirt with the deputies. She's got a sugar daddy in the cop shop who talks a blue

streak in bed. You can find out some good stuff if you dress right and you don' even have to lay 'em. Ah got clothes from modelin' in New York and them suckers puff up like a bantie rooster and squawk like hell to impress ya. Ah wrote down the tail numbers of all their planes and that there's one of 'em sure as shootin'."

"Cool," Darla said, "like spying."

"Yep."

The plane headed west toward the highway, and they crawled out from the brush.

"Eek!" Cindy shot into the patch, almost trampling one of the pot plants. She pointed at the bushes. "Snake!"

A loud buzzing erupted near where Cindy had been sitting.

"Rattler!" Rayella shouted.

Darla seized a stick, held it in front of her, and approached the snake.

Cindy stood behind Paul with her nails digging into his arm.

Paul laughed. "They're good to eat. Squash its head Darla. I'll show you how."

"Yuk." Cindy said.

Darla stopped six feet away. "You do it."

"Okay."

Paul found a stouter branch and approached the rattler that was coiled in a shady pocket beneath a manzanita. He held the stick out, waved it in front of the snake, and after some prodding, the rattler struck. Paul yanked the stick away and swung it after the snake had extended in its strike and the creature's body vibrated with the blow. He hit it again, and the snake's body writhed and coiled around its flattened head. Paul pinned the crushed head with the stick, picked the snake up, and stretched it out in his hands. "Man, this is like four foot something."

Rayella laughed. "Good work. Danny woulda been tryin' to shoot it or run off squeelin' and leave me to deal with the fucker." She glanced at Cindy on the opposite side of the patch, who was peering through the leaves of a pot plant. "Girl, your eyes are big as chicken eggs. Swear to God."

"That's scary!"

"They're good eating," Paul volunteered, "and the easiest things to clean in the world."

Darla ran a finger down the serpent's back. "Can you make me a belt out of the skin?"

"If I mount it on a real belt. Otherwise it'll fall apart." Paul cut off the head and buried it, slit the snake along the belly with his Ka Bar knife, pulled the entrails out with one yank, and tossed the pink gut sack into the bushes. "That'll keep the deer away."

Rayella grinned. "Glad you're here, although that could bring a bear 'round." She squinted at the sun coming over the ridge.

"A bear won't touch a rattler's head."

"Let's take that to the ice chest in my bus." She nodded at the other girls. "Come on, it's gettin' hot. Two patches to go."

* * *

When they returned Rayella fetched some grain from the barn and called to her Appaloosa gelding Storm. She shook the bucket, whistled, and the horse trotted up from the meadow with head held high to stick his nose in the bucket as Darla and Cindy stroked his neck.

Paul rolled off the skin of the rattler, cut it into sections, and split the ribs so that it would lay flat in a pan. He planned to cook it for lunch and give Darla and Cindy a taste of snake. Cindy had a look of trepidation on her face as she watched Rayella dredge it in flour and melt Crisco in a cast iron pan. "Don' be so scared girl. People been doin' this forever. You know what they say: tastes like chicken."

Paul thought of Rayella the night before as she sat astride him making love to Darla. He'd stared between Darla's legs as their graceful bodies melded in the moonlight and for a moment saw the woman he'd seen in his dream. If he was crazy, it sure was a fun kind. All the things he'd seen in magazines and on TV about free love were nothing like this and he could understand the stories of men who'd had multiple wives. What had begun with Darla's choosing him as a lover one afternoon in Ucluelet had snowballed into the time of his life, and he wasn't going to throw the brakes on now. He couldn't see going home at all... *ever.* They should go swimming and have sex in the afternoon. That was a plan.

The rattle of a truck broke his reverie. Rayella turned the sizzling pieces of snake in the cast iron fry pan, sighed, and walked to the door of the bus with the spatula in her hand. Cindy faded into the shadows of the barn behind Storm, and Darla stood with an arm around the horse's neck.

"It's Danny."

A blue '48 Studebaker pickup pulled into the yard on tall tires and wheezed to a stop. The guy driving was a dark young man about their age or a little older with a wispy beard and long wavy hair worn in a red headband. A handsome young man with a halo of curly blond hair sat beside him staring at the newcomers. He stepped out of the truck with eyes fixed on Rayella.

"Hey, 'Ella."

"Hey. Where you been?"

"Cruisin'." Danny stared at Paul. "Who's this?"

"This here's Paul, and that's Darla, and Cindy's hidin' her cute little ass in the barn, looks like."

Cindy appeared at that juncture. "Hi."

Danny and the driver gave her wide-eyed stares.

"She's sixteen, fellas, really."

"Okay."

The driver ground the starter of the truck and yelled over the noise of the engine. "See ya Dan!"

Danny stood watching as the truck climbed out of the yard onto the fire road and disappeared in the trees. He wiped his hands on his jeans, put hands on his hips and glanced around. "You water the pot?"

"Shit, yes. What the fuck you think we been doin'? You ain't been around for two days. If it was up to you them plants would be all shriveled and dead. These guys are here to help. Gus brought 'em."

Danny stared at Cindy, glanced at Darla, and turned to Paul. "Anyway, good to meet you." He extended a hand and Paul shook. His grip was soft. Danny stepped into the bus and Rayella followed.

Darla put a hand on Paul's arm when he began to follow. "Wait."

"What the fuck is that?" Came from within.

"It's rattlesnake, Danny. Paul kilt it."

"Ugh! That's fucked up! Get it out of here!"

"To hell with that. It's lunch. People been eatin' rattler forever. You oughta try some."

"Not in a million years. That's fucking *sick!* Where's my gun?"

"Ain't your gun, it's Gus's. He says Paul's got it now."

"What?"

"Ain't your gun."

"I killed a deer with it!"

"And Ah cleaned and butchered it and it was a gut-shot mess and you didn't even clean the fuckin' gun. You seen them rust spots on the barrel? My daddy woulda tanned your hide for takin' care of a gun like that. He said a gun is the next best thing to a wife, and sometimes better."

"Was that before or after he fucked you?"

The sound of breaking glass preceded a gargling scream. Danny staggered out the door of the bus and fell headfirst on the ground, holding his face. Wine stained his plaid shirt purple and he had green glass in his hair. "You cunt!" He rose to his knees, and when he took his hands away from his face, there was blood on them. "My eyes!" He howled.

Darla squeezed Paul's hand. Cindy appeared and grabbed his other one as they stood watching Danny writhe in the leaves and sob.

Rayella appeared and leaned against the folding bus door with her arms crossed. "That's it, motherfucker."

Paul split a smile.

Rayella's big green eyes flashed and her mouth had the sexiest sneer he'd ever seen.

Danny staggered to his feet, wiped blood from his forehead, and spat a pink glob on the leaves. "You fucking cunt!" He balled his fists and started toward the bus but Paul stepped in front of him. There was no way Danny was going to hurt Rayella. Paul looked Danny up and down and felt a malicious grin spread his cheeks.

Danny swiped at the blood on his face. "Fuck you all!" He stalked up the driveway onto the fire road, waggled his middle finger at the old bus, and spat, "Bitch!" Paul followed to make sure he was leaving. Danny turned to look back once, gave him the finger and was gone.

Rayella brushed hair from her eyes. "Thanks Paul, you're a Skookum guy. Shit... Ah gotta clean up this fuckin' mess 'afore we eat."

Cindy laughed. "I'll help."

IV.
Paul's Pride

Everything Paul wanted was here. The old house was dank and oppressive and they remained in Rayella's bus making her bed creak long into the night and filling it with laughter. He was protector of all he surveyed now with three lovers, a territory, a purpose and a gun. He didn't question the vagaries of fate when they ran so much in his direction.

That evening they watered the pot. "It's good and done now." Rayella announced. "We can skip tomorrow so poor 'ol Darla don't have ta scream 'bout gettin' up early and can go swimmin' at the big hole in Takilma."

In the morning they bathed in the creek. Cindy was first out of the bus and out of the water. She ran to the barn, got a hackamore on Storm, and was riding around the meadow bareback in cutoff jeans. Darla sat on a rock beside the water brushing her hair. Rayella suggested they go to the store in Selma with the bus before they hit the swimming hole, and went up the hill to secure things for the trip. Paul lingered with Darla in a scented nimbus from the pink azalea blossoms crawling over the rocks, utterly content to watch Darla stroking her hair.

"Baby, you got it so fucking good." Darla yawned, gazing at Cindy as she circled the meadow.

"I know." He checked the rifle that he'd lain on a log. He wasn't going anywhere without it.

"Aren't you glad you took off with me?"

"I'm glad we went to Wreck Beach in the first place."

She yawned again. "Yeah. I just wanted to get laid but it sure changed somebody's life, as in *yours*, so I guess I'm responsible." She shook her head. "What a trip." Sunlight glistened in her hair as she tugged on the brush and snarled. "I have got to get some conditioner!"

"I'm glad you did." Paul studied her against a sunny palette of nature full of greens, golds and browns. Light reflected off the water of the creek and did a dappled dance on her skin. He wanted to freeze the image in his mind and carry it with him forever. He cracked his back. "Let's do peyote."

"It's easier to drop acid, or mescaline, or 'shrooms. There's not all that puking."

"Okay. Acid then."

"We have to score from somebody we trust. Lots of speed in some of the shit going around."

"Fauna oughta know."

"Yeah."

"Darla?"

"Hum?"

"You know when you said you loved me but that you're supposed to try and love everybody, but not to trip out on it, and that you shouldn't get too attached 'cause it's a bummer, and that you won't reach enlightenment or something?"

She rested her chin on her knees, kneaded moss with her toes, and gazed at him with big blue eyes. "Uh-huh."

"Am I like every other guy to you? I mean if we were apart, would you be just as happy if you were hanging out with somebody else and laying them?"

"I'm with you, aren't I?"

"Yeah, but would you miss me?"

She squeezed his knee and laughed. "Shit yes. People aren't supposed to be possessive if they're going to reach enlightenment and all that shit, but I love you." Darla ran hands through her hair and gazed at Cindy jumping Storm over a log at the end of the meadow. She shook her head. "Okay I admit it, I'm attached. But what if I was balling another guy in front of you like you've been doing with Rayella and Cindy in front of me? You and Cindy were totally into it on the floor for what... a fucking hour?"

He put a hand to his face. "Well, you started it. Besides I laid you too and you got off, and you sure liked making it with Rayella. It's not like you were just sitting there waiting your turn or something."

Darla giggled. "That girl can kiss."

"And lots of other things." They sat for a while alternating between adolescent grins and hints of something greater. Paul splashed his feet in the creek and stared at the ripples. "I don't know, it's kinda not the same. I don't know how I'd handle it if you were balling another guy in front of me."

"Tell me about it. Guys are always that way. I think women are the only sane bisexuals, at least in my experience."

"How much have you had?"

Her mouth twisted. "We weren't going to do that."

"Yeah but—"

"Don't start." She stood up and brushed bits of moss from her legs. "I'm not going to fuck some guy in front of you just to prove a point if that's what you're freaking on. I'm not out to push your buttons and have everything go to shit Paul. I know guys, and you're fucking lucky I *have* been with a few. I know how to treat my man and I admit that you're my man now so let's go with it. You're special, okay? We're together and I love you, and I feel safe with you, and it's been pretty excellent so far and I'm not jealous of Cindy or Rayella. They're like sisters to me, which is fucking amazing if you knew me up to now. I'm a pretty competitive chick." She turned that smile on him he wanted to frame. "I know who you love."

Paul's expression wandered into unfamiliar territory. The staccato rapping of a pileated woodpecker rescued him and he turned to gaze at the trees. "If somebody ever tries to hurt you, like those guys at the gypsy camp, or those bikers in San Francisco, or... or... *anybody,* I'll kill 'em."

"Okay."

* * *

The bus didn't want to start and Paul removed the filthy air filter. Rayella turned the key, and the engine gasped when it was allowed to breathe and rattled to life. "You've got to get a new one as soon as we get to town. The dust 'ill fuck up your engine."

Rayella chained her dog Spyro in front of the barn, left him food and water, and ordered Bozo into the bus. They drove toward Selma and passed Lake Selmac, where a small resort stood. A scattering of tourists was on the beach and out on the water in rented pink plastic paddle boats.

They made it to the highway and turned into the parking lot of the Selma store with dishes rattling in the cabinets. Several tables surrounded by rough-cut seats of cedar logs sat before an ice cream parlor next door to the store. Rayella yanked on the handle of the door, and the dog made a dash for the shade of the trees to flop between the roots of an oak with his tongue lolling.

"Ice cream. My treat." Darla said.

The girls got triple ice cream cones, Paul got a double, and they sat in the shade on the cedar seats. As he licked his cone Paul found himself getting more pleasure watching the girls eat theirs. Ice cream began to run down his hand and he ran his tongue up the cone. "Hey Rayella, how come you call your dog Spyro?"

"'Cause Ah had a Baptist grandma who used to tell me Ah'd get spirochetes from hippies, present company included."

A yellow one-ton van with a roof rack filled with chainsaws and gas cans pulled in next to Rayella's bus, and eight young men in dusty grey work shirts, denim pants and red suspenders got out. The loggers grinned at the three girls as half the crew filed into the ice cream parlor, and the other half walked to the store.

"Somebody's gonna mess with us." Rayella said, "Their noses are twitchin'. See the way that one's lookin' at Cindy? We better get goin'."

Darla frowned. "Fuck it. I can handle 'em. I'm gonna finish my ice cream right here." She ran her tongue along the side of her waffle cone in an effort to stay ahead of its melting.

Pink ice cream dripped over Cindy's fist as she reflected a logger's gaze. "That guy with the red hair looks like my boyfriend in Minnesota."

"He sees you watchin' him hon. Be careful, you're gonna start somethin' even givin' him that much, Ah swear."

The red-haired logger emerged from the ice cream parlor. He smiled at Rayella and Darla but his eyes fastened on Cindy. "You guys live around here?"

"We're traveling," Darla spoke up, "on our way to Crescent City."

A tall man with a mustache and sunken cheeks joined the redheaded guy, who was still staring at Cindy. "Watch out, Pete, that's jailbait for sure."

"I'm sixteen."

The two loggers glanced at each other, and the tall one smirked. "Looks thirteen to me." He fixed eyes on Paul. "What are you doin' with an underage girl, hippie?" He tossed his ice cream cone in a trash can, hooked thumbs in his pants, and his eyebrows formed a straight line as he laid a hard stare on Cindy. "Where's your daddy?"

"That's none of your fuckin' business."

"Whoa." The tall man was joined by three more of his crew and his gaze returned to Paul. "You askin' for some kinda statutory rape beef?"

Paul twirled the waffle cone in one hand and the other drifted to the hilt of his knife beneath the table. Darla reached under the table and dug her fingers around his kneecap. He flinched.

Rayella rose to her full six feet, wiped ice cream from her hands, and unleashed a scathing glare. "He's her *brother*, and we don't take kindly to nobody saying such terrible things. Her daddy just come back from Viet Nam with one arm and signed her out of school today in Roseburg so she could see her momma. Goddamn. Y'all oughta be ashamed."

One of the loggers elbowed the one who'd made the comment and the redheaded one stared down at his dusty caulk boots, avoiding Rayella's eyes.

Another of the crew with a quart of beer in each hand joined them. "You chicks do or-gees?"

"Shut up." The redhead snapped.

An older man appeared from the store with a case of beer over his shoulder and waved the crew toward their truck. "Okay, children, say goodbye to the ladies and get in the crummy."

"Sorry." The redheaded guy muttered. The crew piled in, the rig backed out into the lot, and they headed toward Cave Junction with everyone staring at the girls.

Paul finished his cone. "Wow, that was really cool, Rayella."

Darla nodded. "It was bitchin'."

"Little ol' fashioned scoldin' works on them fellas most of the time." Rayella waggled a finger at Cindy. "Anybody else asks, he's your *brother*, got it?"

"Okay."

"You jus' can't go 'roun' actin' like you're gettin' it on with him, or *anybody*. Hell, I'm the only one over eighteen here, and

I sure don' want somethin' hung on me for rapin' y'all." She laughed. "You gotta remember that."

Cindy sprang out of the log seat with a scowl and kicked a cloud of dirt toward the trees. "Fuck it! That guy pissed me off! A million guys who're way better than him were after me in high school, and wanting my autograph and everything after the National Championships. They all wanted to go out with me. I was fucking famous last spring and in the papers all over Minnesota, and the New York Times too."

"Yep, and now you're a fuckin' fugitive. Who knows who's heard about Cindy Swift hereabouts? Y'all gotta 'member your parents got a big 'ol reward out for ya and Paul and Darla are runaways too, and your name and face in the papers don't help none." Rayella squeezed Cindy's hand. "You gotta use your head, honey."

"Okay, whatever. I'm just tired of everybody treating me like a kid. I worked my ass off, and I can't even talk about it 'cause I'm a bust for the rest of you." Cindy scowled at the conical rise of Eight Dollar Mountain in the west. "Sometimes I want to go back but it's too late for the Olympics. I fucked that up, and my coach is a dick, and everybody there will know what he did if I tell them why I split..." Her eyes brimmed, and she wiped her face. "I can't even joke like everybody else, 'cause they think I'm a kid, and somebody can go to jail just 'cause they're getting it on with me even if it's my decision, and if I just smile at a guy, shit happens like *that*. It sucks. I'm not a kid! It's like this shitty pressure on me, you know?"

Paul hadn't ever considered what Cindy was dealing with. All he'd ever thought of in regard to her was how cute she was, how she could do things with her body nobody else could, and how amazing she was to make love to. His returning to Charleston and high school in Coos Bay would hardly make a ripple compared to Cindy's situation. She'd given up her chance for glory on the world stage, and here she was sharing a bed with him and the girls. It made him feel selfish and kind of stupid. He put an arm around her. "You can joke with us."

Darla kissed her cheek. "We love you."

"Me too, hon, but please jus' don't get nobody busted. Ah look shitty in one of them jail jumpsuits. Don't go with my hair."

Cindy stifled a laugh and swiped at her eyes. "Let's go swimming."

* * *

Cindy waited in the bus while they shopped at the store. Paul found an air filter and opened the hood to install it as the girls moaned about the heat. Darla found two pot growers who'd come out from the Kalmiopsis Wilderness for supplies, got them to buy wine and beer, and they carried it to the bus for her. Donny was huge, with curly blond hair, a scruffy beard and a battered cowboy hat. He had thick tattooed arms with a globe and anchor on the right one under the letters USMC, and had a .45 automatic in an ancient scuffed holster on his hip. His friend was equally hairy though not as big and went by Hubcap. Bozo barked once when they climbed in the bus before wagging his tail in recognition and they smoked some pot with Paul and the girls.

Donny pulled a big gold nugget out of his torn jeans, passed it around, and invited them to his mining claim. "This is about four ounces, maybe a hundred and fifty bucks." His eyes roved over the girls. "There's a big party at the Foster claim this weekend. You guys oughta come."

Darla bounced the heavy nugget in her palm. "That's the place Fauna told us about."

Donny laughed. "Ha, Fauna. You guys ever get her to talk?" "Huh?"

"Fauna. She don't talk. I've known her a couple of years and I can't remember her sayin' shit."

Darla shrugged. "She talked all the time when we were staying at her place."

"Really? I never heard one word from the chick. All she does is cruise around Hope Mountain and Takilma lookin' like sun-tanned sex on a shingle with them knee-high moccasins and that Peacemaker. A friend of mine laid her and he told me she never said a word the whole time."

Hubcap grinned. "I'd like to make her talk."

Donny snorted. "You'd like to make her squawk."

Darla grabbed the smoldering joint. "She talks."

Donny glanced out the window. "Shit, there's a fuckin' trooper checkin' the bus in the parking lot. Guess it's time we head back out the river." He stood, ducked his head under the low roof, and tipped his hat to Paul. "Nice gig you got here."

As Hubcap bent to pick up his hat, he whispered in Paul's ear. "Which one of these chicks are you doing?"

Paul blinked in the nimbus of beer, cigarette and pot breath as his gaze skipped from Darla, to Rayella, and to Cindy. "Ah... all of them."

"No *shit!*" Hubcap punched his arm. "You're the man!" He placed his cowboy hat on his head, adjusted his gun belt, and gave Paul a thumbs-up and a toothy grin as he left.

Paul watched the two growers jump in a near-new Dodge Powerwagon painted camouflage brown and green with a gun rack in the back window that held an AR-15 and a pump shotgun as they took their leave with a spray of gravel and accelerated into the mountains. "Nice truck."

"Yep," Rayella said, "Donny bought it with pot money last fall."

Cindy let out her breath. "He's big."

"Watch out girl, he was lookin' at you like you was a it-ty-bitty morsel."

Cindy grinned. "I'm more than a fucking morsel. I could handle that."

Paul laughed. "She's a six-course dinner."

Rayella started the bus and they pulled out.

Darla jumped in the seat behind her and leaned over her shoulder. "Do you know Fauna?"

"The tall blonde with braids who wears a six-gun that they were talkin' about?"

"She's our friend."

"Seen her at the swimmin' hole."

"You'll like her."

"Ah like any girl who packs a pistol and runs around half-naked in the woods. Teaches rednecks a lesson 'bout women's rights and all."

Paul leaned back in the seat with an arm around Cindy and she folded her legs and tucked herself into his side. He kissed her forehead and stroked her hair. He was really stoned from Donny's pot and the whites of Cindy's eyes were red. It would be a great thing to grow a whole bunch of his own and buy a Powerwagon. On second thought he'd want something bigger that he could get a whole bunch of girls in.

XVI.
Diggin' In

They drove as close as they could to the big swimming hole and parked the bus. People were coming out of the communal bath house, and a very pregnant girl was drying her hair on the porch. Rayella locked the door of the bus with a padlock and they headed to the river. She spread a big Mexican blanket out, and Paul lay amongst the three girls in overwhelming contentment. In his seventeenth summer life had reached its cusp. He didn't question it. He just wanted it to last.

Fauna and Mel appeared. "Why don't you come up to our place tonight? Mel killed a deer and we can have a feast."

"Okay," Darla said, "Rayella can park at the end of the road."

Rayella tossed a curtain of hair away from her legs and stared at her toes. "Ah don't know. No offence, but it sounds like you got some fucked-up neighbors up there and nobody's back at the goat dairy. Hope Gus don't come up and find us gone."

Fauna shrugged. "Gus is in the Bay doing an acid deal. There's a meadow where you can park and nobody'll fuck with your bus. Not with me and Mel around. If they do, we'll get 'em."

"They'd better not." Paul added.

Darla yawned. "We were thinking of doing acid."

Fauna stepped into her shorts and buckled her gun belt. "Perfect. I got a shitload. Weasel fronted it to me yesterday and I sold a bunch at the swimming hole and the Barn. I made his share already so the rest is mine."

"Bitchin'."

They piled in the bus and drove past the clinic. Doc Jim waved from the yard.

Mel squeezed Rayella's shoulder. "Stop."

Jim came to the door of the bus, spied Cindy and shook his head. "I thought so. The cops were here showing me a picture of a runaway named Cindy who's supposed to be in the Olympics or something. Somebody's got a big reward for you and I wouldn't put it past some of the characters around here to try and collect. They were just at the store in a patrol car and an unmarked one with guys in suits. They're headed to the swimming hole now. They even went up to the gypsy camp, and those guys scattered." He chuckled. "Maybe they'll get the hell out of here now."

"We can hope. How close did they come to my place?"

"Don't know Mel, I've never been there."

Rayella scowled. "Shit."

Cindy sat on a seat against the window with her hands around her legs.

Darla kneaded her shoulders. "It's cool baby. You're with us and we love you."

Doc Jim gave them an expression befitting a doctor who spent his days taking care of people for next to nothing and sighed. "They're done up there unless somebody sends them back. Don't show yourselves in public today and keep off the road. Where are you guys staying?"

"On Reeves Creek."

"That's far enough." Jim eyed Cindy. "How old are you?"

"Sixteen."

"Really?"

"Yes!"

* * *

Rayella drove as far as the road allowed and they hung on as dishes rattled and things fell from their places. She turned around at the last possible opportunity and parked in the flattest spot beside a little meadow.

"Good driving." Mel waved at the hillside, "We're going to my place."

Rayella frowned. "People from that gypsy camp might try somethin' even with the dog in the bus. Darla said they eat dogs." She shook her head. "I'm comin' back after dark." She let the dog out to do his business, left him some water, and grabbed a .22 rifle and her guitar. She secured the rear door from inside, snapped the padlock on the front door, and they started up the trail with her glancing nervously back at the bus.

The girls hustled to keep up with Mel and Fauna, who reminded Paul of a deer with her bounding strides. Fauna and Mel had six-guns, Paul had the .30-.30 and Rayella had her .22. as they scanned their surroundings with the natural paranoia of animals. Not in fear, but with a bone-deep caution that felt right.

Paul noticed new bruises on Fauna's thighs and his mind began to wander. Making love to her seemed ordained, although Mel looked pretty possessive. It didn't go with Fauna's unattached philosophy, but when she was with Mel it didn't seem to apply. It could wait until karma dictated. He had his own girls to take care of.

My harem.

He laughed and Darla slapped his ass. She could read his mind.

Where the trail to Fauna's camp began, they took the left fork lined with hoof prints and horse droppings and headed toward a ridge that pointed north like a compass needle.

Mel's camp was mostly paddock for his horse with a corral, a stall, a shed for hay and a tiny house built against the mossy cliff.

In front was a big fire pit with sections of logs for seats. About five cords of firewood was stacked in a neat pile. Mel broke off to tend to his horse and Fauna led them into the house built of scavenged lumber with three windows and a planter holding scrawny sun-starved pot plants. It reminded Paul of a hobbit house from the Tolkien books.

"It looks small, but wait." Fauna said.

The front room had a table with a wooden bench along the outer wall. In the back was the entrance of a mine. The ten-foot-wide tunnel mouth contained Mel's bed and had shelves carved into the ochre stone of the hillside. He'd constructed a rear wall of old timbers with an iron-bound door in it that looked like some dungeon in the Middle Ages. The rusting rails of ore cart tracks led under the door, and boards were lain over them to make the floor even. Trunks, boxes and duffle bags were stacked against the walls and kerosene lamps hung from hooks driven into the timbers shoring the ceiling. Fauna lit four lamps and the place filled with a yellow glow.

Paul slung his rifle on a peg. "Wow. How far does the mine go?"

"Who knows? Fuckin' far," Fauna shoved kindling in the wood stove, "but the lower tunnel's flooded. It makes a great cooler for meat and the water's good. Not like the Queen o' Bronze's water that makes you crazy."

Darla sat on the bench against the windows and wiped her palms on her jeans. "What a trip."

Fauna held up a plastic five-gallon jug and pointed to the mine. "Can somebody get some water?"

Mel came in, hung up his black cowboy hat, and unlocked an ancient padlock on the heavy door to the mine. He swung it open, clicked on a big nine-volt flashlight, and handed the jug to Paul. "Follow me."

Darla jumped up. "I want to go."

"Me too!" Cindy shouted.

"Shit, guess Ah'm comin'."

Twenty feet in the tunnel narrowed where an ore cart sat loaded with rocks. Old tools leaned against the wall on the right collected during Mel's explorations, and several boxes were stacked and padlocked in an alcove to the left. One looked new and was labeled **EXPLOSIVES**.

Paul laughed. "Dynamite."

"Yeah, for blasting wells and shit. I'll show you how. You met Chuck yet?"

"No."

Chuck's the best. People call him Reverend Boom-Boom. He can blast a perfectly round shaft straight down for like thirty feet. Ever see those old round wells?"

"Sure."

"It wasn't just digging. You do a shaped charge and it's a piece o' cake. The old timers did it like that. Dynamite's great trade material too."

Cindy ran a hand over the box. "I want to blow something up."

Laughter echoed in the tunnel.

She put hands on her hips. "No, really. That'd be cool."

Mel grinned. "Maybe I'll let you level the gypsy camp when the time comes."

"Really? That'd be super cool."

Rayella patted the box. "Damn. We could blast a new well at the goat dairy."

"I'll do it." Paul volunteered.

Mel scratched a blond wisp of beard. "Got anything to trade?"

Rayella put a hand to her chin in imitation. "Well, you don't look like you're tryin' to trade for a piece a'tail so how 'bout some pot?"

"I got plenty. Any tools, or guns?"

"We'll figure somethin'."

Mel turned his flashlight down the tunnel and they followed him to where it split into a shaft sloping up to the left and one down to the right. On the right the floor grew wet within a few feet. "Watch your footing. You gotta straddle the water."

They followed him down the right shaft with their legs spread and feet on either side of the stream. The ore cart tracks disappeared beneath the water and the ceiling got lower until it brushed the tops of their heads. The walls of the tunnel grew damp and the air chill as the sounds of water echoed in darkness. The tunnel opened into a black void and Mel stopped at a rocky berm. He stepped up on it, grabbed a rope tied to an ancient hexagonal iron bar driven into the rock, and pulled a plastic bag full of meat out of a dark pool in a separate hole. "You can fill the jug in the big one. The water's fine."

Paul pressed the jug under the surface and bubbles echoed in the tunnel as the jug filled.

Suddenly the light went out.

"Eek!" Cindy yelped.

"Goddamn!"

Darla grabbed Paul and they nearly slid off the muddy berm. He let go of the jug.

"Ha," Mel switched the light back on, "pretty dark huh?"

Darla gasped. "I *guess!*"

Paul dropped to one knee in the cold water and grabbed the jug before it disappeared.

"There's all kinds of tunnels in these hills. People been disappearing for years around here since the gold rush and lots are in the mines. There was a snitch last year out on the river who disappeared. You can bet he's in some shaft. Bet I know where too."

"Like the story about the Chinese workers and the Queen of Bronze?"

"Exactly Darla."

"God," Cindy said, "I hope there's no dead people in this water."
Mel chuckled. "Gives it flavor."

* * *

After a meal of fried deer backstrap and onions, Mel broke out a
bottle of homemade liquor. "Old Bob Cutler made this on Josephine Creek. He won't trade. It was a present. That's an honor."
He popped the cork from an old Wild Turkey bottle and poured
some of the near-clear stuff into a shot glass for each of them. Mel
held his up in the last red light coming through the windows
and gazed over the dark treetops and peaks beyond as the smoke
of a campfire made a black column against the crimson sky. "To
eternal freedom."

"Ack!" Cindy croaked.

"Wow!" Darla got out.

"Damn," Rayella shook her head, "jus' like the moonshine
where Ah'm from. Might even be better. Gotta meet this fella."

"He'll ask you to stay when he gets a look at you. Bob was
born north of Yellowstone and homesteaded in Alaska. He's got
eleven claims on this stuff that he says is from the core of the
earth, these nickel iron nuggets that look like they came from a
meteor. He named it Josephinite. It's the only place in the world
where you can find it and he's getting a hundred and twenty-five
bucks an ounce for it."

"What? That's three times gold. The only place in the world?"

"So far Paul. Bob says it's the most common thing in the
world too."

"Say what?"

"He says it's from the core of the world. The weight and
mass of the earth is two-thirds nickel iron, but Josephine Creek
is the only place that it came to the surface." Mel laughed. "That's a
true prospector. Get a hundred twenty-five bucks an ounce for the
most common thing in the whole planet."

Paul wiped his mouth as the liquor lit a fire in his stomach. "Where are you from Mel?"

"Detroit. Ever hear of the White Panthers? After the riots and the revolutionary shit went to hell, some of us got out of there before they killed us too. Most of my bros are over Tennessee Gap on Sebastopol Creek but there's no good ground for growing pot." He ran a hand down the barrel of his shotgun. "I like it here where I can have a patch or two in the woods. Even if some of the neighbors need changing."

Fauna laughed. "There's a total pussy shortage over there. Mel would die." She poured everyone another shot. "Ready for some acid?"

Rayella ran a hand down the barrel of her .22. "Hope nobody's fuckin' with my bus. Hate to have to walk down there on acid to crash, and find some fuckers broke into it."

"It's cool. Your dog's in the bus and they'll know you're with me and Mel and they'll leave your shit alone. They won't fuck with us Rayella. You won't sleep anyway if you do acid."

"Hey Paul," Mel nodded toward the .30-.30, "you good with that Marlin?"

"Sure. It's like the one I learned to hunt with."

"If things get shitty with the gypsy camp, or that fucker Abdullah, I'll be counting on people like you so don't be surprised if somebody shows up at the goat dairy with the call sometime."

"No problem Mel."

"You might have to drop things and come running."

"Okay."

"Thanks."

Fauna scowled. "That guy Abdullah says he's Muslim so he can have a pussy stash and call 'em wives, then he puts 'em in bags so nobody can see 'em. What a dick."

"He's got a few dudes camping with him doing the same."

"Sure. When some fucker says you can have four female slaves for wives and beat the shit out of them, you'll find assholes who want to do the same. They better not try and enslave anybody I know."

"They got Christine. It's their religion."

"Fuck 'em."

Cindy finished her second shot of moonshine, scrunched up her face and belched. "Are we gonna do acid?"

With her leg around the bench Cindy's thigh looked like it was going to bust out of her jeans and Mel squeezed it. "If she's doin' it we'd be wimps not to join her. Who'd let this little girl drop acid alone?"

"I am *not* a little girl, dude."

"Okay."

"I'm just small."

"Baby, people just say that 'cause you're so damn cute."

"You're only fourteen months older than me Darla. I'll be seventeen soon."

"You're in the best shape of anybody here anyway."

"I'd better be."

Mel filled the bowl of a peace pipe and solemnly offered it to the four directions of the compass. He struck a Blue Tip match on the cast iron stove, puffed the pipe to a burn, and offered it to Cindy. She took a big hit and held it while the pipe went around until her face grew red. Mel grinned. "So, you're an Olympic gymnast for real?"

"You bet she is." Paul said. "She's the buffest person I ever met and can do shit you won't believe."

Darla massaged his neck. "It's true."

Fauna exhaled a cloud. "Bet I can beat you in a race through the woods though."

Cindy's face arced toward scarlet. She finally let out the smoke and coughed. Rayella poured a cup of water from the jug, passed it to her, and she took a big gulp. "Maybe so. Just 'cause I'm good at some things doesn't mean I'm good at everything. I worked my ass off in gymnastics but I couldn't beat a sprinter or marathoner. It's different muscles, but I bet you can't do this..." Cindy did the behind-the-neck thing with her legs, balanced on the narrow bench on her hands, and lifted herself in the air.

Mel whistled. "So you dropped out even though you were going to the Olympics." He ran a hand down a blond braid and stared at the sky. "'Let your tracks be lost in the dark and snow' like the Dead say. I don't exist to the Man anymore and that's the way I like it. Better to be a ghost and be free."

"Ah love the Dead. Rather disappear in the woods with hoods than be on a magazine cover anyway, though the money's nice. But we can make good money in the pot business and it's only gonna get better, and I can lay who Ah want instead of some perfumed cocksucker in New York who treats me like a fuckin' Barbie for sale."

"Shit yes. Pot's the future."

Cindy cracked her back. "I'd rather be with you guys than go back to the shit I went through. Fuck the Olympics."

"Y'all fellas better live up to this lady's expectations so she sticks around."

"Hey," Paul said, "what's the trip with deer around here? I noticed the big bucks have these fucking red eyes in the headlights. It's not like on the coast or anywhere I've ever been."

Fauna laughed. "The spirits are strong in these mountains. You met one so maybe you should ask." She grabbed a beaded deerskin pouch off the shelf and shook a pile of purple disks in her palm. "Time for a trip." Fauna filled an earthenware cup with cold water from the bowels of the mountain and passed it to Cindy.

Cindy held out her hand. Fauna dropped a purple disk in it. Cindy tossed it in her mouth, washed it down, burped and glanced around. "You guys gonna let the little girl do acid alone?"

Darla tossed one in her mouth. "Fuck no."

Fauna grinned like the Cheshire Cat. "Maybe you'll see your lady again Paul. She must have plans for you. We've got her in common."

"What do you mean?"

"She'll let you know."

Paul turned over the purple tablet in his palm. Something in his head seemed to implode before he even put it in his mouth.

He shivered and put it on his tongue.

"I love acid." Fauna said.

Darla leaned toward her. "We met Donny and Hubcap from out on the river. They said you never talk."

Mel grunted. "She picks her people."

"Some people I never talk to, even some of the hip ones. If you don't have telepathy fuck it. I never even talked to Mel 'til after I'd laid him a couple of times."

"That's true."

Fauna's stomach rippled in the lamplight. "It's like hunting when you're on psychedelics; you don't have to talk to the deer to *talk* to it and you ask its spirit to allow you to take it. Sometimes you just meet it and leave, even touch it. Deer live in silence, and it's done in *silence.* Your soul does the talking. If you open your mouth you break the spell."

"You're a spiritual warrior." Darla shifted on her seat. "Shit... I'm coming on."

"Ah bet all the telepathy you get from some guys is they wanta jump your bones. You're pretty hot girl."

"You got that right. I mean about people wanting to jump my bones just 'cause I'm comfortable in my own skin, but that's life."

"Um," Mel shrugged, "maybe running around pretty much naked has something to do with it?"

Rayella laughed. "She does have a nice bod."

Cindy nodded. "Your legs are beautiful."

Paul grinned. "And they see her gun."

Mel rubbed Fauna's shoulder. "She's badass with her bow too. Girls oughta know how to use weapons."

"And my knife."

Mel's shoulders trembled in the yellow lamplight. "Let's get a fire going before we're too high."

XVII.
Trippin'

While Paul was building the fire, a piece of wood began to throb in his hands. He clutched the red limb of madrone and tried to focus in the puddle of light from a kerosene lantern. Mel splashed something on the pile of wood and it exploded like the sun. The stick bucked in Paul's hands. It became a snake and he tossed it at the flames to hang suspended in the air against the wall of brightness bouncing off his retinas.

People were around the fire. He tried to make out Darla. His eyes went from face to face as each in turn became Darla and changed again.

"I'm here baby."

Her voice was all around him and he turned in a circle. Something moved amongst the rippling trunks of trees and skittered into the branches leaving a luminous trail of laughter. Paul stared at the sky. The stars pinwheeled and he whirled with them.

Hands went around his waist. Darla's breath buffeted his cheek. "Don't get lost." She took his hand and a shock ran through him as her fingers melted into his own. She led him to a seat by the fire and pushed down on his shoulders with damp palms. He tried to sit up but as his breath flowed out of him, he felt as if he were getting shorter, collapsing like an accordion until he wasn't any bigger than a mouse. Paul gazed up at the giants around him.

"Sit up." She pulled him erect and he gasped. "Baby, you are *so* high."

A leather bota bag appeared. He followed the hand that held it and saw Fauna. Red firelight played on her smooth bronze skin as her blond braids danced. She wore war paint over cheekbones of molten metal. He reached out to cup her breast and ran fingers around a nipple. Her teeth flashed, and she was the Cheshire Cat.

He blinked in recognition. He'd known it all along. She'd been in a tree gazing down at him since he was a kid, hiding in the branches when he'd gone into the forest to play and ducking out with a barely-seen flash of tail in the woods to disappear at the roar of his motorcycle as it spit mud on the trails. He thought of Tweedledee and Tweedledum and wished he'd had Fauna with him. She would have shot them from the trees and made love to him afterward.

Had that happened?

Darla held the bag to his mouth. He tasted purple as wine ran down his throat and let out a long "Ahhhh!" Someone laughed.

Cindy pulsed and shifted on the other side of the fire like a coiled spring. Mel was between her and Rayella and they were kissing. Sap popped in the fire and a shower of sparks made a geyser to the stars.

People rocked on their seats making sounds of wonder. The fire was a glowing river and Paul fought the urge to jump in. He held onto Darla and Fauna's thighs and they squeezed his hands between their legs. His fingers became roots, growing longer as their bodies seized him. He was the tissue connecting them and began to stretch like taffy between their bodies. He was nearly blind, with only the pulse of their blood to feel his way. He was a corpuscle, an egg, moving toward a long-awaited blossoming. The thought he might be tossed out on a girl's next period erupted like a slap across the face, and hysterical laughter erupted from his chest.

"Fuck, I'm high." Darla said.

"Me too." He got out.

"Owsley purple saucers." Fauna said.

"Night," Cindy shouted, *"Night!"*

"Y'all lookin' real trippy over there. Everybody okay?"

A gunshot split the sky and everyone hit the ground.

Paul peered through a swirling cloud of dust, looked for blood, and saw it everywhere. "What the fuck!?"

Mel stood up and dusted off his pants. "It's the motherfuckers at the gypsy camp."

"Is somebody *shot?*" Darla's voice quavered with the paranoia that had replaced her sense of wonder.

Mel shook his head. "Don't freak. It was down the ridge. Fuckers are drunk and shooting in the air again."

Rayella growled. "Dumbasses."

Everyone climbed back on their seats. Cindy looked terrified and Rayella wrapped an arm around her.

Darla began to roll a joint but her shaking hands tore it in two and marijuana floated to the ground. "Shit."

Mel took the broken joint and stuffed it in his peace pipe. "Gotta get centered." He stood up straight, held it to the four directions, lit it, and passed it around.

Paul had to piss. He went to the edge of the terrace and launched a luminous stream in the dark as a night bird's cry rang through the forest like a string of bells. He thought of the woman with no name, remembered her eyes, and called out silently.

Okay I'm crazy. Fuck it. We all are.

The Milky Way arced over the treetops with a hissing sound as a breeze buffeted him. Paul rocked back and forth, awaiting her presence. He felt her: a memory as big as the sky that fought to rise above the dark ocean where she hid from sight. Suddenly she was there beside him with eyes like stars.

He gasped.

It was Fauna. "Didn't mean to scare you."

He let out his breath. "I thought—"

"The lady."

"Who?"

She took his hand. "Come on."

She led him to a vale where moonlight pulsed in the leaves of viney maple and made phosphorescent candles in the tops of this-tles. The smell of herbs was a three-dimensional map of his sur-roundings and bark rippled on trees as their roots made the ground dance. Fauna was a graceful deer in her element, loping through the dark forest to a cedar log. Beyond it trees danced in the red light of a fire. Fauna held a hand out palm down, and they dropped to their bellies to peer under the bent trunk of the fallen tree.

A leaning shack stood beside two poorly pitched tents where a fire illuminated beer cans strewn across the ground and a dirty mat-tress on which five figures sat. The barrel of a pump shotgun glinted red between the knees of the one drinking from a bottle that glowed like blood as he tipped it to his face. The voice of his companion was a brutal croak that hurt Paul's ears. It felt like the bones of his skull were grinding together, and he shook his head like a dog.

Fauna's hand was on his shoulder. He knew what she was feeling, what she was thinking, yet he couldn't understand the words of those below. Her Colt Peacemaker was in her hand. He kissed her cheek and her fingers caressed his ribs like the keys of a piano. He reached out to her throat and felt blood pounding under his fingers. They lay for a long time until the noises beyond formed words.

"Yah, fuck, bitch needs learnin'. I'm gonna go down to the river, shoot that nigger calls himself Black Michael and bring his little whore up here for us to party down."

"I hear she's pregnant with his baby."

"I'll cut it out when we're done and we can toss her ass in the Queen a' Bronze. Don't need no zebra babies."

There was harsh laughter, followed by a brief tussle over the bottle.

"We oughta raid their patches."

"Which?"

"That Mel guy," The one who'd spoken glanced over his shoulder at the forest, "and that blond bitch who thinks she's so tough."

"You wanna take out Fauna?"

"Let's grab her ass. Why let a nice piece'a ass run around this mountain and not use it?"

"She's good with a gun."

"And a bow."

There was silence.

"And a knife. Sneaky too."

"Gotta wait 'til fall when the pot's ready anyway."

"Yeah."

"There's a party at the Barn."

"We gotta get some money man."

"Gypsy Dave, you goin' to the City?"

"Fuck that. I got a crystal connection in Grants Pass. They got a warrant for me in California from that fucked deal in Berkeley, remember?"

"I want some speed."

"I wanna fuck a bitch."

"I wish that chick Mushroom would come back."

"The way you beat her ass I don't think so."

"That fuckin' Fauna got her gone I know it. She ran over to her camp and the bitch was standin' there with her fuckin' gun when we went over." Dave snarled. "She woulda shot me too."

"Think she fucked the chick?"

"You mean sloppy seconds?"

"Tenths!"

The men's laughter reminded Paul of the orcs from the Lord of the Rings books.

The hammer on Fauna's pistol rolled back with a click. She *glowed.* He wished he'd brought the .30-.30 but couldn't remember how he'd got here in the first place, or even where he was. He ran his fingers up the hollow of her back to the nape of her neck and she rippled under his palm. He closed his eyes and saw the Cheshire Cat grinning down at the little men around the fire. When he opened them, he saw a pale form watching from the trees on the other side of the camp. Red eyes flashed and it was gone.

They crawled backward and returned to Mel's camp like the breeze.

* * *

They heard singing and followed Rayella's voice, but the singing stopped before they reached Mel's. When they climbed out of the vale, a figure stood at the edge of the landing outlined by the fire.

"Where did you guys go?" Darla hugged him hard.

His mouth found her throat and he felt blood pulsing beneath his lips. For a moment he had the greatest urge to bite. He didn't need to say anything. He couldn't speak anyway.

She pushed away and held him at arm's length. "Where did you go?"

Mel hugged Fauna. "I said you guys were stalking the gypsy camp."

Fauna nuzzled his shoulder. "Yeah."

"God, Paul, I was scared."

"Did you miss me?"

"Don't start."

Cindy lay wrapped in a blanket on the ground. Rayella was nowhere to be seen.

"Where's Rayella? We heard her singing."

"Singing?" Darla glanced around. "She went to the bus."

"By herself?"

"Yeah. What did you see?"

"An ugly bunch of losers that were drinking and talking about raping and killing people."

"That's fucked-up."

"Yeah." They rocked together coming down from the acid as a chill took hold. "Fauna's right about cleaning them out. It's necessary."

"Let's go crash in the bus."

"Okay."

They roused Cindy and he retrieved the .30-.30.

The woods were loud with their senses still raw from LSD as the moon illuminated the forest floor between the shadows of trees. Paul carried the rifle over his shoulder and listened to the breathing of his lovers. Fauna was right about cleaning out the gypsy camp. She was a goddess of the forest and was always right.

He saw golden eyes staring down from a tree and froze in his tracks.

"The Cheshire Cat!" Cindy shouted.

"Yeah!"

Their grins floated into the trees, leaving only their teeth and the flash of their eyes.

XVIII.
Serious Stuff

Paul awoke as the engine rumbled to life. Cindy moaned. He peeled a leg off her, staggered to his feet, and headed for the door to piss.

Rayella was behind the wheel of the bus ready to go. "Gotta get back to the goat dairy so Gus don't throw a goddamn fit. We gotta water the pot. The chickens need feedin' and waterin' too."

"Hold on." He reached the door and she threw it open with the lever on the dash. Paul stepped into the damp grass and launched a stream into hazel bushes. The big German shepherd dashed out of the bus behind him, and Bozo sidled up to the bushes to cock a leg in mutual duty. Paul locked eyes with the dog and laughed.

He climbed back in, Rayella slammed the door and put the bus in gear. She cut the wheel hard to the right and the school bus lurched backward. The rear wheels reached the edge of the road and tree branches slapped the windows.

Darla and Cindy sat up sleepy and confused.

Paul staggered on the tipping floor. "Shit, hold it, let me guide you." Rayella nodded, and he jumped out to stand naked and shout directions until the bus was turned around. He jumped in and they rocked and rattled down the dirt road as three people struggled to dress.

***

Twenty minutes later Rayella pulled into a gas station in Cave Junction. "Everybody puttin' in?"

"I'll get it. Fill 'er up." Darla said as she and Cindy made a dash for the restroom. They tugged on the locked door and walked back to the office to get the key.

"It's a goddamn nickel higher than Grants Pass." Rayella stared at the price of $.34.9 on the pumps and leaned out the window. "Fill 'er up Ah guess."

The attendant yanked his eyes away from the door of the restroom and nodded. The big tank on the bus held sixty gallons. Paul stared as the pump registered fifty gallons and continued to climb until nineteen dollars and forty-four cents was rung up. "That's a shitload of money." He counted out four dollars from his pocket.

"Tol' y'all, this thing's thirsty."

Darla appeared in the doorway. "Don't worry I've got it." She went into the station and stood at the cash register as Cindy got on the bus.

Darla was smiling and talking to the attendant, who had a grin a mile wide as she leaned over the counter beside the cash register in a loose men's shirt that was half-open and tied at the waist. She reached into her jeans and handed a credit card to the attendant. He ran the card on a metal imprinter, handed her a receipt, and she got back in the bus. Darla wadded up the receipt, tossed it out the window, and plopped down behind Rayella. "Let's go."

Rayella tossed her hair and slammed the door. "Thanks."

Paul blinked. "You never said you had a credit card."

"So?"

"Whose is it? Is it stolen?"

"It's my mom's."

"Won't she—"

"Don't worry." She kissed him. "Let's get breakfast."

They stopped at the New Café at the end of town, where Paul ordered biscuits and gravy with two eggs for sixty-nine cents. The girls got pancakes with strawberries and whipped cream and the waitress brought a thermal pot of coffee. They emptied it and she brought another as they sat blinking in the morning light.

A bottle rocket shrieked across the road and exploded. It was almost the Fourth of July. Paul glanced over Cindy's shoulder at a phone booth in the parking lot. He fingered the change in his pocket. He ought to call his parents and let them know he was alive at least. His mother was probably making life hell for his dad, and the work on the inn probably had stopped. Were they still in Canada?

He could see his mom throwing in the towel and dragging his dad back to Charleston and he was the cause of it all. His older brother Dan, who was a logger, always said Paul was a worthless dreamer and would probably hold it against him until the day he died. Paul imagined his sneering face from beneath a yellow hard-hat as he sat behind the wheel of his new Ford pickup.

Cindy dropped something down the oversize man's shirt she'd tied across her stomach in imitation of Darla. She swore, opened it to pull a chunk of ham off a perfect young breast, and gave him a wink. Paul stared at the shiny spot on her skin and forgot about calling.

* * *

The bus bumped into the goat dairy's yard and they piled out. Paul stood under the rustling trees and stretched. Bozo brushed against his leg. The dog turned in a circle, stared at the barn, let out a low growl, and put his ears back. Bozo approached the barn door and sat down to gaze at Paul with ears flattened.

Rayella cracked her back. She was so slim it seemed she had extra vertebrae. She rubbed her long neck and glanced around.

"Where's Spyro?" She stared at the corner of the barn where she'd tied her dog and whistled. "Where's Spyro, Bozo?"

Bozo's tail fell between his legs and his tall ears went flat against his head. The big sable shepherd made a keening noise.

"That's weird," Cindy said, "I hope the horse is here." She whistled, and an answering neigh came from the meadow as Rayella followed Spyro's chain into the barn.

"No!"

Cindy sunk fingers in his arm and Paul headed for the barn. Darla fiddled with her hair and bit her lip.

Rayella reappeared with high cheekbones sharpened by the sunken cast of her face. Paul was stunned how someone so beautiful could change. Her green eyes blinked rapidly and welled with tears. "Somebody kilt my dog!"

Paul and Darla ran toward the barn. Cindy scrambled into the bus.

Spyro lay before the feed trough with his head a fan of brains and blood. Yellowjackets fed on the contents of the dog's skull, buzzing past them as they commuted between the windfall and their nest.

"Oh!" Darla swiped at one and dashed into the yard.

Rayella leaned against the wall of the barn with her arms crossed over her chest.

Paul let out his breath. "I'll bury him."

"You'll jus' get stung. Wait 'till dark." She turned toward the door and stepped out of the barn with a sob.

Paul took her in his arms and she bawled into his shoulder. They rocked together as yellowjackets droned past them and his shirt grew wet. He brushed her hair away from her face and kissed her forehead.

Her upper lip trembled. "He was a good dog." She swiped at her nose.

"We'll find out who did it."

"Oh shit!" She pushed away and stared at the wall of the barn as if she could see the hillside beyond. "What about the pot!"

He dashed to the bus. The door was shut and he banged on it. Cindy opened it slowly and sat down on the couch beside Darla as Rayella followed him into the bus. Storm neighed from the yard and circled the bus. The Appaloosa's skin quivered as he pranced, snorted, and shook his head at the smell of death.

"We've got to check the patches." Paul said.

Rayella sat on the couch beside Cindy and Darla. "We're fucked if the crop's gone."

Darla stared at her feet. "What will Gus do?"

"Don' know but it ain't nice."

Cindy drew her knees under her chin. "I'm scared."

"I'm fucking tired from being up all night on acid." Paul checked the magazine on the rifle and placed extra shells on the table. "But let's act like it's still there and we got to water like normal, okay? We just have to be ready to get into it with somebody if it comes to it."

"What about the dog?"

"Gotta wait 'til them fuckin' yellowjackets go to bed 'less'n y'all wantin' to get stung, honey."

Darla kissed Rayella on the lips and stroked her hair. "I'm so sorry."

Rayella hugged her. "Could be Danny."

"What?"

"Wouldn't put it past him."

"That's fucked."

Paul jacked a round into the chamber of the rifle and lowered the hammer to half-cock. "Would he go after the pot?"

"It ain't ready for harvest but he don't care Ah bet. He just wants to get back at me for takin' up with y'all and might tear it up outta spite. He's jealous even if he'd rather be suckin' a dick."

Bozo leaned into the open door of the bus with ears down wagging his tail hopefully.

"Come in dog." Rayella let out a little laugh that deteriorated to a sob. "You didn't do nothin' honey. Sure wish you could talk an' tell us who did this." The German shepherd stepped shyly into the bus, put his chin in her lap, and she scratched his big head fiercely. "Good dog."

Paul sighed. "Who's going with me?"

Cindy bit her lip and scanned the hills. "We need more guns."

"Ah got one." Rayella picked up her .22.

"Bet you're good with that."

"You bet I am."

"Let's go."

Nobody wanted to stay with the bus, so Rayella locked it and they headed across the meadow to the patches. They marched up the hill with Paul in the lead and Rayella bringing up the rear. Darla looked determined. Cindy looked resigned. Rayella looked ready to kill. Paul wished Fauna was with them but brushed off the thought. She had her own wars but making love to her was something that had to happen sooner or later.

He stooped as they reached the narrow trail through the blue leaves of manzanita. Paul imagined going down in a blaze of glory giving his life to protect the women. He imagined Darla crying over him as he lay dying. The last thing he would ever see would be her beautiful face streaked with tears against a blue sky. His eyes went out of focus as he wondered what last words he should say.

What if it's the law?

The vision switched to his parents being notified by uniformed Sheriffs with headlines screaming of his demise. He thought of Susan Allen, who he'd expected would be his first conquest, reading of his violent death in the Siskiyou Mountains with only some fat lawman to deliver an uncaring epitaph. That would totally suck.

Paul brushed branches out of the way and stepped onto the first terrace. Bright green pot leaves fluttered in the breeze. The plants were obviously thirsty but there.

He let out his breath. "It's okay!"

The girls filed out of the bushes and Rayella leaned her .22 against the crotch of the little oak where the hose was coiled. "It's gotta be Danny. He's gettin' back at me Ah swear." She wiped her hands on her jeans. "Y'all don't mind if Ah shoot him if it comes to it do ya?" They shook their heads. "Okay then, let's get to work." Rayella approached the second biggest plant in the patch and examined it. "Shit." She grabbed the top and bent it over. "Shit." She repeated before she grabbed the thick trunk and ripped it out of the ground with its roots clutching a ball of dirt.

Darla's mouth fell open. "What are you doing?"

"It's a male. We gotta pull it 'fore the girls go seedy. People are doin' that now so the buds get bigger."

"Wow." Paul stared at the empty spot in the terrace and shook his head. "What a waste of space."

"Tell me 'bout it. Fella named Big out on the river says you can sex 'em before they get in the ground but I don' know how. Sure would be nice, wouldn't it?"

* * *

Paul and Rayella buried the dog that night. Darla and Cindy expressed a passionate lack of interest and stayed in the bus. When they tamped down the hole Rayella said a prayer. Her voice floated on the night air like an angel with words inherited from generations of southern Christians. When they reached the yard, they held each other for a while in the darkness before stepping into the bus to sleep for twelve hours.

XIX.
Reverend Boom-Boom

They fell back into a routine of watering and fertilizing in the cool hours of evening, trimming shade leaves that turned brown, and tearing the occasional male from its place amongst the females before the flowers burst and loaded female buds with pollen. The water was getting low in the hole and they'd have to deepen it soon. Paul got the saw running and cut up a dead oak and two madrones for firewood and a cedar for kindling. He split it with the maul, and the girls helped haul it to the yard and stack it next to the house.

As the days went by the mystery of the dead dog became another facet of their lives: something to remember, but not give much energy to. If it wasn't Danny it could have been a random redneck, or even somebody like the scum from the gypsy camp living in the woods that they didn't know about. They didn't even know who lived over the next ridge, or if anybody did at all.

Trucks occasionally drove up the fire road and often slowed to check the place out. A couple men in a new yellow Dodge pickup stopped and stared at three pretty teenage girls in the company of a single boy. They cruised by twice more that week. Cindy began taking the .22 in a stained buckskin scabbard that she found in the barn when she went to ride Storm. Darla bemoaned the lack of a proper swimming hole as the water got lower and was bored.

One day a beat-up half-ton 1950 Chevy rattled into the yard and stopped. A tall blond man with scruffy hair, a wisp of beard and a high sunburned forehead stepped out. He fell to his knees to pet Bozo, whose tail lashed the air in greeting. "Hal-lo!"

Rayella was on the porch swing with her guitar, Paul and Darla were cooling off in the creek and Cindy was riding Storm but everyone heard the truck and came to the yard.

"Hey. I'm Chuck." He extended a hand to Paul, who'd slung the .30-.30. "Gus sent me with your money and he wants me to take a look at your water."

"Huh?"

"Your water. It's getting low."

"Yeah."

Chuck grinned. "I can fix that. You like dynamite?"

"Yeah... sure."

"Good. They don't call me Reverend Boom-Boom for nothin'. Wanta smoke some hash?"

Darla bounced on her heels. "Yes please."

Chuck sat on the ground in the oak leaves and they joined him. He lit a meerschaum pipe carved like a wolf's head, passed it, and began to count out the money, splitting a hundred dollars between them. Cindy's eyes lit up and she stuffed hers in her pocket. Darla slid hers in her pants and Rayella took hers to the bus. Paul stuffed his in his jeans and passed the pipe.

"Gonna blast out that waterhole up the gulch." Chuck began, "Oughta last the summer if I make enough of a hole."

Darla pushed leaves around with her bare feet. "Won't somebody hear it?"

"You can't tell where dynamite's comin' from. Maybe a hundred eighty degrees but that's all. It's not a sharp crack, just a flat boom. I used to blow downed planes in 'Nam that they didn't want the gooks to get. We'd land with a helicopter and you had to get the fuck in and out of there pronto. Seen enough green tracer for a couple a' lifetimes." Chuck grinned. "It's like smoking Park Lanes. It's a habit you can bring home later."

"What's Park Lanes?"

"They're machine-rolled joints in 'Nam. They're packaged like cigarettes in a nice little pack with a trippy label. I was bringin' some back but the fuckin' C.O. had them all collected before we got discharged."

"That's cool."

Darla's eyes lit up. "Can you make us a swimming hole?"

"Sure. Why not?"

"Oh wow," Darla smiled, "That's bitchin'."

"But you gotta do some shovelin' to earn it. Come on."

* * *

Chuck took a half-dozen pink sticks of dynamite out of his truck, spools of green and yellow blasting cord taped with shiny silver blasting caps, and a fist-sized battery. They got shovels from the barn and a tool Chuck called a hoedad that had sat unused since they'd got there. He said it was for planting trees. "Best tool in the world for chopping a hole." Chuck had three pot grows of his own in the vicinity, along with agreements with half-a-dozen other growers to do things like maintain their wells and had sales networks in San Francisco and Portland. Paul listened intently, trying to absorb all he could of the older man's wisdom imparted from the lofty age of twenty-four.

Chuck brought an empty gallon can with him. When they reached the waterhole for the pot, he removed the line and funnel, told Paul to dig down until he hit a hard bottom, and then hack out a hole the size of the can. Chuck set to work cutting the can in two with his sheath knife and punched holes in each end.

Paul stepped into the foot of water left in the hole and his worn sneakers squeaked in mud as he began to dig. When he had removed a few inches of silt, he hit harder ground and stabbed at it with the point of the shovel.

"Here," Chuck waved Paul out of the hole, stepped into the water, and swung the hoedad, splattering mud across Cindy.

"Eek!"

Chuck laughed. When he'd deepened the hole, he cut a stick of dynamite in two with his knife, inserted a blasting cap in the end, and fed the wires through the can. He stepped into the water and placed the half-can with the top up and the wires coming out of it into the hole he'd chopped out and stomped it tight. He scraped all the loose muck he could on top of the can and stomped it again, then lifted a big rock from the hillside and placed it on top of that. Chuck got out of the hole and ran the wires out toward the trees.

The girls dashed behind a clump of viney maples and Paul stepped behind the trunk of a Douglas fir. Chuck took another spool from his pocket, twisted the ends together with the blasting wire, and backed up. He unwound it sixty feet to a big rock and knelt behind it.

"Watch out!" Chuck touched the wires to the poles of the battery.

"That's—" Paul began.

There was a *WHUMP!*

Water and gravel geysered up and the rock Chuck had put on top cartwheeled twenty feet into the air to land downhill in the creek with a splash.

"Look out!"

A brown water column rose like a genie summoned from the bowels of the earth before it bent toward the girls crouching behind the screen of viney maple. Mud and gravel slashed across the leaves, accompanied by three high-pitched screams.

Chuck and Paul burst into laughter.

"We're fuckin' *soaked!*" Rayella howled.

Chuck chortled. "Good. Now you ladies can dig without worrying 'bout gettin' dirty."

***

After they'd finished blasting and digging, the girls went to the creek near the house to wash up. Chuck checked the patches with Paul and pronounced them satisfactory. By the time they returned to the meadow, Paul's pants felt glued to his legs. He stepped out of them, rinsed off in the creek, and returned to the yard. Chuck was standing with mud smeared across his high forehead next to the bus, gazing at the girls as they changed clothes. He saw Paul and cleared his throat. "Who needs I.D?"

Darla waved. "We do! Are you gonna make us a swimming hole too?"

"Damn." Chuck laughed, "This lady wants me to get her a new name, *and* make her a swimmin' pool. I already brought your money and cleaned out your irrigation system."

"Gus said he could get us I.D." Paul said.

"Yeah, but he won't."

"Why?"

"Then you can boogie outta here whenever you want." Chuck grinned, "He's got you for slaves. No I.D. no split and Gus needs the labor. You're runaways and he's got a good thing goin'. Would you give up that if you were him?"

Paul shrugged. "Yeah, I would."

"That's cool. You're young. Tell you what: I'm going to Eugene tomorrow and a friend of mine there makes the best I.D. in the Northwest. He's kept a lot of brothers and sisters out of jail. Sean's the guy who printed *Prairie Fire.*"

"What's that?"

"The Weathermen's handbook."

"Gus mentioned them, and Mel too. What's the Weatherman?"

"The *Weathermen,* they're the dudes who blew up the draft offices in Chicago and fight the pigs and shit. There's riots downtown Portland and Eugene right now and he's busy as shit making fake I.D. He's got sheets of that pink paper they print the Oregon driver's licenses on, with the same watermarks and font types and everything. Give me your stats and how old you want to be, and I'll have him do one for each of you. There's three, right?"

"Yeah,"

"No problem. It'll cost twenty apiece though."

"Shit." With their new-found wealth, Paul had been planning a trip to town. He knew the girls were too.

"You can pay me next week after Gus pays you again, but don't tell Gus I scored it, okay?"

"Let me ask." Paul motioned to Darla, who had moved to the porch swing. "Chuck can get us I.D. for twenty apiece."

"All right!"

"He says we can pay him next week."

Rayella put down her guitar. "Y'all get me one too, that says Ah'm twenty-one?"

Darla walked over to Chuck, hooked an arm through his, and turned him around. "Let's talk, Mr. Boom-Boom." She maneuvered the big man on her arm toward his truck, where they spoke in hushed tones. Rayella and Cindy joined Paul, and Darla returned with a grin on her face. "I'm going somewhere with Chuck." She glanced at Paul and gave him a hug. "Don't worry baby, I'm not gonna ball him." She kissed him. "See ya in a few." Darla bounced over to Chuck's truck and waved. Chuck waved and they pulled onto the fire road and were gone.

"What the fuck?"

"Girl's got her shit together." Rayella squeezed his hand. "Don' get jealous."

Cindy squeezed Paul's butt. "Let's make Darla jealous when she gets back."

"How we gonna do that?"

"She knows we're balling him so I guess we really can't."

Rayella squeezed the other cheek of his butt. "Not by layin' him, though I ain't rulin' it out or nothin'."

"We could wear him out at least."

"And scratch his back up."

They awaited a smile from Paul but it didn't come.

Rayella made a theatrical sigh and punched him in the shoulder. "Dammit, quit lookin' so worried."

Paul stared at the empty road.

"Paul don't like her runnin' off like that."

"I just... I wonder what's going on, is all."

"Mellow out hon. She's got somethin' cookin'."

"Yeah, but what?"

"Gotta be good." Rayella stretched and rubbed her eyes. "Hope he's gonna blow out that swimmin' hole. It'll take a while to settle out and I wanta go swimmin'."

"I'll do it if he gives me the dynamite. I wish we'd got some from Mel. We were so high everybody forgot to ask."

"Probably woulda blowed ourselves up we was so stoned."

Cindy clapped her hands. "That'll be cool. Can I set some off?"

"Sure, I guess."

"Anybody want lunch?"

* * *

The afternoon went by at glacial speed. Darla hadn't returned by dark. Paul didn't even want sex in case Darla showed up while he was engaged with Rayella or Cindy, or both. After sitting with them on the swing singing songs to the accompaniment of Rayella's guitar, he got up the third time they began *Come Together* by the Youngbloods and wandered down to the meadow. He almost fell in the creek while crossing it in the fading light. Storm was a dark mass that snorted at his approach. The sound of the horse tearing at a tuft of grass seemed loud now that day was gone. Paul sat in the grass as a night bird called from the hillside.

You're a pussy!

He tossed a rock and some animal skittered in the leaves.

You are!

The possibility she was balling somebody to get something even when she said she wouldn't made his stomach churn. She had the right. What if she was? Was he going to leave? Last night he'd forgotten Darla completely until he'd felt her eyes on him and Cindy and he'd ignored it as he shoved Cindy's body across the bed with his thrusts while Cindy made the cutest sounds. Darla was beautiful and could have anybody, so did he think it would always be a one-way thing?

"Shit." Paul sat for an hour until he jumped up at the sound of a truck and almost fell in the creek crossing it.

When he got back to the yard, Chuck's truck was parked next to the bus. Paul let out his breath and steeled himself to act nonchalant. He could hear laughter inside and banged on the door. Rayella sprang into sight, yanked the lever and the door folded open. Paul stepped into the bus expecting to see Chuck.

"Baby!" Darla embraced him.

He inhaled testing for the smell of sex but it was the same sweet Darla that greeted him as far as he could tell.

"We got a truck, and I got the I.D. covered too."

"Huh?"

Her mouth rose at the corners. "You didn't think I laid him for it?"

"I—"

She burst into laughter and was joined by Rayella and Cindy. "Dude, you're like purple."

"How did you get his truck?"

"I bought it. I gave him three hundred dollars for it and the I.D. He's getting one for Rayella that says she's twenty-one too. He says the valves suck and it's gonna blow up sooner or later, and it eats oil, but we still—"

"Three hundred dollars?"

She nodded. "Yeah, we went to the bank in Cave Junction but I had to go to a branch in Grants Pass and he had to go to Waldo Road, and I had to drop him off in O'Brien and he had to take his shit out of course. He gave me some tools to work on it and said check the oil every day, and I drove back in the dark. That Reeves Creek Road is scary in the dark."

"Thanks, y'all, for the new I.D."

"Cool! Thanks, Darla."

"Three hundred dollars?"

"Yeah, from my mom's account. It's cool."

"But… how come you're not afraid that the cops will find out?"

"Because she won't tell them. Don't freak out. She won't tell my dad either, so your parents won't know."

"Oh." Paul sat on the couch with Darla beside him.

Rayella handed him the pipe and a can of Blitz Beer.

Cindy bounced up and down on her seat by the table and jumped on his lap. "I want to go to town."

"Hell yeah. Now we can go places without my bus."

Darla laughed. "And use the showers at the campground on the highway."

Cindy's laugh joined hers. "That's so groovy. Darla I love you."

Paul sighed. "But why do you need fake I.D., if your mom knows where you are?"

She blew in his ear. "For us, baby."

XX.
Complications

"Let's go to town."

Cindy jumped in the narrow cab of the truck and Darla handed the key to Paul. He hung the .30-.30 in the warped gun rack across the back window and got in with a truck full of girls and a rifle. Cindy being the shortest sat next to him and wrapped her legs around the rattling stick shift. He rested his hand on her warm thigh between shifts as the flash of fireworks erupted over Lake Selmac to the north in a Fourth of July celebration.

"I wish we could get in a bar." Darla lamented.

"How old did you tell Chuck to make us?"

"I'm twenty-one, you're nineteen and Cindy's eighteen."

"You mean, you and Rayella can get in a bar and I can't?"

"We're *girls*, Paul. Guys will believe almost anything if you have something to make them, but you're both too young-look-ing. Besides, you'd probably get in a fight when somebody hits on me and blow everything."

"Ah get in anyway. When you're tall men don't bitch, they buy ya drinks." Rayella's voice was flat as she stared out the window.

Paul glanced at her leaning against the door. "What's the matter?"

"Thinkin' 'bout my dog."

"That was a bummer."

Darla squeezed Rayella's knee. "There's always shitty people around. Stay high."

Cindy squirmed as he shifted and settled her legs around the stick. "If I shot a bad guy, you think I'd get off for being a minor?"

Paul stared at the road. "That's a good question."

Darla studied the silhouettes of horses as they rolled by a pasture. "You should be glad you're not eighteen Paul." She chuckled. "You'd be a criminal for fucking me and Cindy."

He was silent as they bounced over the road. The engine rattled as he released the gas pedal when they topped a rise.

Darla put a foot on the dash. "That's so stupid. God, *everybody* gets it on and the Man wants to slam you for doing somebody who's almost your own age. We gotta remember to check the oil every time we stop 'cause the engine's pretty wasted. There's a gallon can in the back but we should get more."

Paul mulled the twin revelations of the credit card and Darla's use of a bank account, along with her carefree attitude about a lot of other things. Darla had a pipeline to money. She was a rich girl. A very pretty rich girl, which explained a lot. Her mom was in on her travels too. Everything was play for Darla because she had an out, maybe even a get-out-of-jail-free card. She was used to getting her way and had initiated that first night with the other girls but probably hadn't realized how much he'd love it. He thought of the look in her eyes last night while he'd been with Cindy and Cindy had made the most amazing noises as she dug her fingers in his back. He couldn't have watched another guy with Darla like that in a million years.

Darla stared at him over the top of Cindy's head.

"Watch the turn!" Rayella shouted.

He jerked the big wheel to the right just before they ran off the road and the girls shrieked. "Sorry."

"Don't wreck my truck Paul!"

Paul stared out the window.
Her truck.

* * *

They stopped in the tiny town of Kirby at a little Mexican restaurant. There was only one couple there but a stout black-haired woman showed them to a table as if the place were packed. She hurried back to the kitchen and a pretty girl appeared with menus as the couple got up to go.

"Hey." The girl said. She may well have been the woman's daughter but with the miracle of youth and metabolism, they differed by eighty pounds. She brushed back her hair, gave Paul the wink of an almond-shaped eye, and he winked back. The screech of cables and whine of saws came from the sawmill a hundred yards away as the door opened and closed behind the departing customers. "Don't worry. We'll stay open for you. Hungry?"

They nodded.

"Ah want a beer."

"Sure."

"You got Dos Equis?"

"Of course," the waitress glanced around, "anybody else?"

Darla grinned. "How 'bout a pitcher of Blitz and three glasses?"

"Sure." The waitress walked over to the **OPEN** sign in the window, turned it off, locked the door, and smiled. "Coming right up."

They ordered combination plates and the waitress brought the pitcher and poured a glass for each of them. She popped the cap on the bottle of Dos Equis and poured it in a frosty glass for Rayella, put chips and salsa in the middle of the table, and disappeared into the kitchen as the sound of firecrackers erupted outside.

Rayella raised her glass. "To us."

Cindy drained hers and poured another.

Darla scooped salsa with a chip and washed it down with beer. "This place is cool."

"Yeah, and we don't even have our I.D.s yet."

"Shhhh. Yours wouldn't work anyway. They're being cool so don't blow it." Darla poured more beer.

Cindy wore an Olympic halo of happiness, Darla looked like a Southern California beach goddess, and Rayella leaned back in her chair with the catlike grace of a born model. Paul wanted them all as soon as they got home.

Darla chuckled. "Did you see the waitress watching Paul?"

"Huh?"

Rayella nodded. "Yeah, when a guy's gettin' it good, other girls know. That's what my momma always called intuition. Girls *know.*"

Cindy swallowed a mouthful of chips. "It's telepathy."

"There's other kinds of telepathy too, like with Fauna." Paul said.

Rayella ran fingers across the back of his hand. "You and Fauna have telepathy?"

"When we checked out the gypsy camp we sure did. She's like a spirit in the forest, and when I slept between Darla and Fauna a couple weeks ago is when I had this dream that started something. It was at the same place where she saw the UFO. I still don't know how I got way up that mountain at night and back naked."

Darla put her glass down and leaned on her elbows. "You didn't. It was a dream. How did that start it? *I* started it. I got your cherry, and I started it with Rayella and Cindy too. Your dream didn't have shit to do with it."

"But that's when it was, I mean... when she told me it would happen with three girls before anything did."

"Who?"

"The woman in my dream. She said something about having part of me in each of you and Fauna and that was why she came. And I don't mean sex 'cause I never balled Fauna. It was 'cause of both of your powers that I met her, not mine. That wasn't something you planned." He ran a hand across his face. "I think I was just channeling it... channeling *her*, and if I thought it was me it would go away. Maybe that's the ego thing people talk about. Maybe like girls have something that guys can't know unless there's more than one of them... I mean girls. She said there would be three." He gazed into each of their eyes. "And here you are."

"You didn't fuck Fauna?"

"No. When could I and you wouldn't have known it?"

"But you want to."

Paul tried to hide his smile and failed. "That's beside the point. It was telepathy. She promised me three lovers, I mean the woman in my dream did, and it happened."

Rayella burped. "Like some kinda prophecy?"

"Yeah. It was like déjà vu or something I guess. I'm starting to understand what everything's about with psychedelics and the Age of Aquarius, although I still can't stand that astrology shit. I mean when me and Darla met I had no idea—"

"He was a virgin."

The girls laughed and the food came.

* * *

After another pitcher of beer, they pooled the twelve dollars for dinner and drinks, Darla left a three-dollar tip, and they crammed into the cramped old truck in the glow of the waitress's smile.

"What time is it?" Paul asked.

"Don't know. Nobody's got a watch."

He got out, stepped on the porch of the restaurant, and peered in the window at the pink neon Budweiser clock on the wall. "It's eight-thirty. What time does the store close?"

"Sentry Market's open 'till nine but they're closed tomorrow on the Fourth."

Cindy bounced around the gear shift. "I want to shoot off fireworks."

They drove to Cave Junction with the six-volt headlights brightening every time he stepped on the gas and dimming when he let off and piled into the Sentry Market. Clean-cut young men in white aprons shadowed them as they shopped, and a lady had to unlock the doors, as they were the last to leave. They put the groceries in the back of the truck along with a gallon of cheap paraffin motor oil. Paul popped the hood and checked the oil in the light of the store, emptied the half-full gallon can of oil Chuck had left in back into the engine with a funnel, and wiped it with a rag wedged beside the battery. He slammed the hood, wiped his hands, and opened the door to get in as the whistle of a bottle rocket echoed from somewhere.

The roar of a chainsaw made him glance across the street.

A muscular blond man with a crew cut stood in front of the Rusty Spur Saloon beside a yellow Dodge pickup hefting the biggest chainsaw Paul had ever seen. The man squeezed the trigger and the saw screamed. His huge biceps flexed as he held the saw up in the light of the saloon's sign, let out a howl, and charged into the bar with the saw.

Rayella grabbed the door handle. "Goddamn! Lookit that fucker!"

Darla pressed her nose to the back window. "What's that guy doing?"

One of the clerks who'd been shadowing them in the market was standing beside the market's door smoking a cigarette. "That's Terry Cox! He's nuts! He's gonna cut somebody in two if they don't watch out!"

Darla and Cindy hugged each other. Paul put a hand to the rifle in the rack.

"Somebody's gotta call the cops!" The clerk banged on the locked door of the store.

Two men hurtled out of the Rusty Spur Saloon and dashed down the street in different directions. There was a scream from the bar and a window exploded as a body crashed through it onto the sidewalk. A purple neon sign advertising Miller High Life sparked and popped as it joined the glass shards hitting the concrete and landed beside the man in a heap as a pool of blood spread around his head in a glistening halo that reflected the streetlights.

"Holy shit!" Paul yanked the .30-.30 off the rack and jacked a shell into the chamber.

Darla grabbed his arm. *"Don't!* Let's get out of here! Don't do anything!"

"What if that guy comes out and tries to… and what about that guy on the sidewalk? He could be bleeding to death."

"The store guy called the cops! We're witnesses! We gotta split!"

They jumped in the truck and turned toward the highway running through town just as the big blond man came out of the bar with the chainsaw. He tossed it in the back of the Dodge, jumped in and took off diagonally across the street with a squeal of tires. The Dodge's headlights blinded Paul as he bumped down out of the parking lot into the road and the much faster truck bored down on them. The girls screamed as the Dodge fishtailed around the rattling old Chevy like it was standing still and they watched its tail lights disappear heading south with not a cop in sight.

"Fuck!" Paul glanced over his shoulder at the man in front of the bar. Now that the big man was gone, several people were around him and he was sitting up. "Who the fuck is that guy?"

"The clerk said Terry-something or other."

"Shit."

"Damn," Rayella said, "Ah heard a' him from Gus. He likes to shoot people's animals for fun and gets away with rapin' hippie chicks and even locals whose parents are so scared a' him they don't call the cops. Hear he raids people's pot too. Gus says he's into needles and stuff." She hit the dash. "Maybe he's the one kilt my dog!"

Cindy gasped. "That's one of the guys I saw on the fire road! He's got the weirdest eyes I ever saw. They're all empty like there's nobody there at all." She shivered. "Like there's no soul. He was with two other guys and they were watching me when I was riding Storm. They know where we live!"

Paul let out his breath as they left the lights of Cave Junction. "I can't wait for that I.D. If he gets in our faces when I've got I.D. I can do something about it."

Darla grabbed his arm. "Don't try and be a fucking hero. You're a bust for all of us if you do and that guy's really dangerous. What do you want to bet he's killed people? I don't want you to be in some stupid shootout and see you dead."

"Yeah, honey, 'let your tracks be lost in the dark and snow' 'member?"

Cindy squeezed Rayella's hand. "But we could shoot him at the goat dairy, right?"

Rayella brush hair from her eyes. "That ol' well's pretty deep I guess."

* * *

When they returned to the homestead Darla grabbed her sleeping bag out of the bus and walked into the house.

Paul stood in the yard watching a match flare in the window and the glow of a lamp before he followed her upstairs. "What's going on?"

"I'm sleeping here tonight. You can if you want, or stay with Cindy and Rayella. It doesn't matter."

"You've got to be kidding. Let me get my stuff."

When he went into the bus Rayella was rolling a joint and Cindy was on the bed. "Excuse me." He said. Cindy lifted her bottom up for him to slide his sleeping bag out from under her and he couldn't resist a squeeze.

Rayella smiled. "Better get after her, cowboy."

Paul stopped with the bag in his hands, not sure what was going on.

"Hurry up Paul, she's actin' like she's boltin'." Rayella gave him a peck on the cheek and shoved him out the door of the bus.

Darla was lying on her bag with her chin on crossed arms. There wasn't a fire downstairs and the house was drafty. He threw his bag over her. She rolled over, sat up and pulled her blouse over her head. Paul let out his breath and relaxed. Sex would make things better but he still didn't know what was happening or why she was acting like this. Maybe her period? He shucked his pants and slid in beside her.

She rose on an elbow and stared at him. He gave her a smile but she didn't return it. He ran a hand down her cheek, across her neck and cupped her breast in his hand. Darla ignored it.

His penis tugged furtively for attention but retreated. He couldn't do a thing with her looking at him like that. "Wha... what's the matter?"

"What are we gonna do?"

"What do you mean?"

"I don't want to be stuck here."

"But we promised Gus."

"So? He'll get somebody to watch his shit. Who knows what we'll get out of it anyway. Maybe you should just stay with Cindy and Rayella and I'll go find something else."

It was a knife in his chest. Paul fought to swallow the lump in his throat. *"No!"* He grabbed her shoulders and stared into her eyes. "No way! I love you! What are you talking about?"

"Then will you go with me?"

"Of course."

"Okay."

Her mouth took an eon to reach his lips. When it did her kiss was everything. Everything that mattered. Darla threw back the covers and her breath tickled his stomach. She'd grabbed him from the edge of a precipice and yanked him back.

She glanced up through a tent of golden hair. "Just checking."

XXI.
Gravity

Sunshine spilled through the window. Paul reached for Darla but she was already up. He inhaled the scent of her overlaying the faint smell of mildew from the house and stumbled downstairs into the yard. Smoke came from the chimney of the bus, so Rayella and Cindy were up. He scratched his hairless chest and yawned.

Darla's truck was gone.

Paul sprinted toward the bus and banged on the door.

"Hol' yer horses!" Rayella glided to the handle of the door and yanked it open.

He sprang in and almost hit his head on the low ceiling. "Where's Darla?"

Rayella yawned. "Jeez Paul, said she was goin' to visit a friend and for you to quit bitchin' 'bout it when you got up. Want some coffee?" She poured a cup, stirred in cream and handed it to him. "Don' freak out. She was happy this mornin' but she's kinda bored. Darla ain't a country girl, she a socialite from San Diego." She sat at the table and he sat across from her. "She jus' wanted y'all to herself for a change with the way you been goin' at Cindy the last couple a' nights—"

"I guess I was spending a lot of time with Cindy."

"Ah *guess.*" She gazed over the rim of her mug. "She's sore. You got to learn some consideration, thumpin' away at her like brer rabbit or somethin'. She may be tough but she's still a it-ty-bitty girl."

"Why didn't she say something?"

Rayella gave him the same look his English teacher did in Coos Bay when he'd said something incredibly stupid. "'Cause she's sixteen and just wants to please Ah suppose."

"Where is she?"

"Ridin' Storm. Spends more time with her than I do lately."

"Oh."

There was the sound of a truck on the road and they glanced out the windows. A moss-green Forest Service rig slowed at the head of the drive, sat idling and turned into the yard.

Rayella scowled. "Shit."

Paul examined the driver and relaxed. "It's Chuck."

Chuck waved as he parked the ex-Forest Service truck and got out. "You guys up?"

Paul stepped out of the bus.

"I promised her I'd blow out that swimmin' hole so here I am." Chuck shook his head. "That Darla's one persistent chick. I was going to my patch on Sucker Creek but she stopped by my place this morning and talked me into coming here first."

"She... really?"

"Yeah. Hey, I got something for you." Chuck pulled three driver's licenses out of his pocket and handed one to Paul.

Rayella came running from the bus. Chuck handed one to her.

Cindy appeared leading the horse up the hill. Chuck waved her new license at her. She took it and hugged him. "Thanks!" She grinned. "Now we can get food stamps."

Paul examined the new license with the name James T. Stevens on it. He was now nineteen and was from Gresham up near Portland.

"Memorize that. Darla's name is Susan Stevens. No relation 'less you want her to be, although if she was my sister I'd have a hard time not goin' for it." Chuck pulled three blue cards out of his other pocket. "I got social security cards. Sean gave me a deal so they're on me. And... oh," he pulled out another card from his shirt pocket, "here's a draft card now that you're nineteen." He grinned. "You're 4-F for schizophrenia."

Rayella laughed. "Hey Paul, say thank you to Reverend Boom-Boom. Now you can play crazy if the cops fuck with you."

"Yeah thanks."

Chuck yanked a canvas tarp off a box in the bed of his truck and lifted out a handful of pink sticks along with taped packages of blasting caps and electric cord. "Darla paid me to leave you some dynamite but you gotta be careful as hell." He ran a hand across a sunburned forehead. "Guess my new booby trap has gotta wait 'til tomorrow."

"Booby trap?"

Chuck nodded. "Some fuckers ripped off my prize Indicas from my patch on Sucker Creek. I'm gonna sting 'em good if they ever come back."

"What's Indica?"

"Most pot's Sativa, like Mexican red hair. This shit's from Afghanistan. *Skunk weed*. Its way tastier and stonier and it give you lots more weight per plant too but you can smell it a half mile away on a hot afternoon. Those plants were huge and stony as shit. All females too. Mr. Big out on the river showed me how to sex 'em in a greenhouse." Chuck scowled. "Seven prize ladies smack in the middle of my patch. Someday that's all people 'ill grow but right now it's hard as hell to get the seeds. Somebody snuck in and took 'em and it's gotta be another grower. I pollinated one and the seeds were worth their weight in gold and now it won't ever mature. The motherfucker thinks he's smart. He was wearing moccasins and I couldn't track him too far." Chuck slapped the hood of his truck. *"Revenge!* I'm gonna build a booby trap with rock salt that'll sting him good if he comes back."

"Wow, uh, did Darla say anything?"

"'Bout what?"

"I don't know. About me I guess."

"Nope, 'cept to give you this dynamite she bought. Then she went to Takilma."

"Oh."

* * *

He stashed the dynamite in the barn and went to work with Chuck on the swimming hole while Rayella and Cindy tended the pot. After four blasts interspersed with countless shovelfuls of mud and gravel, they enlarged the hole to the point where water came to Chuck's chest for twenty feet along the length of the creek and a dozen feet across.

Chuck stepped out of the hole with his cutoffs stuck to him and his ragged sneakers squeaking. "Looks good. Oughta fill up by morning."

Paul took off his jeans and wrung them out. "Darla's gonna be happy."

Chuck grinned. "That little beach babe has this poor nigger doin' her dirty work for a smile and a peck on the cheek. She's probably at the swimming hole in Takilma right now layin' in the sun with every guy in a mile tryin' to get next to her." Chuck held a hand over his brow and squinted in the glare. "Is she as good as she looks?"

Paul took in Chuck's grin and grinned back. "Better. Best I ever had, and she gets it on with me and the other girls too... like all of us together."

Chuck's high forehead twitched in sunburned envy. "She *was* talkin' about you actually."

"She was?"

"Yeah."

"Like what?"

"Hey," Rayella and Cindy appeared to inspect the new swimming hole. "Wanta beer?" Rayella handed a cold quart bottle to each of them.

"Right on!" Chuck tipped an imaginary hat and twisted off the top of the bottle. "Thank you kindly, ma'am."

Paul poured the cold beer down his throat. He still wanted to know what Darla had said.

Rayella patted his ass. "Y'all did good."

Cindy stared at the water. "How long does it take to clear up?"

"Overnight."

"That's gonna be so cool. Now we can swim anytime."

Paul walked to the clean water upstream, took off his shorts and sneakers, and lay in the creek. He washed the remnants of mud out of his hair and returned. "Hey Chuck, can I catch a ride with you into town?"

"Sure."

Paul hustled up the hill to change his clothes.

* * *

Chuck dropped him in Cave Junction at the Tastee Freeze. Darla had told Chuck that Paul was her man, which was enough. Paul ordered a cheeseburger and fries and sat under an awning sipping Pepsi and examining his new I.D. Trucks driven by long-haired youths passed by loaded with fertilizer, coils of PVC pipe, tools and building materials. Everybody was growing pot in the only gold rush the country hereabouts had seen the last one and the timber boom after WWII. He spotted a blonde who must have been six-foot-three as she strode out of the liquor store in cutoff jeans and his mouth fell open.

Imagine balling that.

If little Cindy could take what he had, how would that goddess with legs up to here take it? Paul sucked his drink dry with a rattle and began to rise, when a wadded-up bag bounced off the back of his head followed by loud laughter.

"Get a haircut, hippie!" Three youths about his age sat at the next table. The biggest one rubbed his crew cut for emphasis and grinned.

"Yeah. We don't need no hippies eating here."

That pit-of-the-stomach feeling was back. Paul tried to steady his breathing. They were alone under the awning of the Tastee Freeze. It was three against one. Even if he won the fight there was nothing but bad in store from the cops and locals.

"I'm no hippie. My family's loggers in Coos Bay. I've been workin' a contract on the Coquille and haven't had time to get to the barber, but if you fellas wanta make something out of it, I'll start with the big dude."

They were silent until the big one finally spoke. "Sorry man, we thought you were one of those trash fuckers hidin' in the bushes. I apologize." He stepped forward and offered a hand.

Paul took it ready for some trick, but they shook and the three walked to their pickup. He exhaled and headed for the Caves Highway to hitchhike.

It felt good to be alone. He'd been with Darla constantly since they'd met, even when they were hanging with Fauna or making love with Rayella and Cindy. Still, he wanted to find her. He could say he'd come to Takilma to hang out and swim, and then just run into her on the beach or something.

The thought of her with another guy swept the last vestige of the blond Amazon from his mind and he ground his teeth.

Don't start. Darla's voice echoed in his brain. He wasn't doing very well with this "don't be attached" thing everybody was preaching. It was like astrology: something people talked about that never meant much in real life. How could you *not* be attached if you loved somebody? He walked to the edge of town and stuck out his thumb on the Caves Highway. A green sheriff's car slowed to look at him and Paul smiled as he fingered the new I.D. in his pocket.

A familiar VW van appeared and Moses pulled over. "Hey Paul, how's life treatin' ya?"

"Hey, Moses." Paul jumped in beside him. "It's Jim Stevens now."

"Say what?"

"I got new I.D." Paul flashed the driver's license.

"Looks like the gods been kind pilgrim. Goin' to Takilma?" Moses fought the rattling stick shift into gear.

"Yeah."

"Where's your girlfriend?"

"Dunno. Probably at the swimming hole."

"Pretty low stress."

"Huh?"

"Your life. This ain't shit. I fought in Europe with the 101st when I was your age. Ever hear of Dachau?"

"No."

"It was a concentration camp we liberated. I saw people blown to bits before that and a guy roasted alive trying to bail out of a tank but I never want to see shit like that again. So now I'm retired where people think the world is gonna be a better place and love will rule." He shook his head. "Maybe. Maybe not. Personally I doubt it, but it's a hell of a lot better than what I saw at your age. When I go to the VFW in Grants Pass they call me Hippie Moses and laugh, but guys whose kids have run off and dropped out always come up to me and ask what it's about around here."

"What do you tell them?"

"I say it's hard to explain unless they drop acid."

They laughed.

Moses slowed for a teenage couple down the road and leaned out the window. "Where you guys goin'?"

"Is Takilma this way?"

"Yep."

The couple got in the back of the van. The girl was small-boned and pretty with long brown hair, freckles and big hazel eyes framed by long lashes. She looked about sixteen and had an innocent smile that made Paul want to kiss her. Her boyfriend looked even younger.

"Do you guys know where there's a place to crash maybe?"

Paul leaned over the seat. "You can try the Meadows but stay away from Hope Mountain," he said with authority, "and look out for Abdullah and the Muslims unless you want them to put you in a veil, and the guys from the gypsy camp are really bad, and Dolly Dagger throws knives, but most people are really aware and cool. Check out Sun Star commune maybe."

The youngsters nodded solemnly.

* * *

He checked for her truck each time a rig passed them and got out at the bath house. Moses had volunteered to introduce the newcomers to people at a commune and continued up the valley. The sun was getting low but he headed for the river hoping Darla might still be there.

Paul stopped at the sight of a woman in a head-to-toe veil standing on the porch of the bath house with a shotgun doing her best to look menacing as three girls' voices blended with the sounds of running water from within. All he could see were her bright blue eyes and what appeared to be a bruise around the left one.

He examined the double-barreled shotgun in her hands. "Hi." He ventured.

"No men allowed!"

"Yeah, um, okay. What's your name?"

"Fatima."

Black Michael and Fauna's mention of Fatima brought him to a stop. He gave her a tentative smile. "Didn't you used to be called Christine?"

The girl's eyes narrowed. "I should not even speak to you. That's an infidel name from a lesser prophet. There is but one final messenger, peace be upon his name."

"Isn't it hotter than hell under that stuff? What's it made of?"

She exhaled, the silky material covering her face bulged, and Paul examined the redness in her left eye.

"I heard you're a fox under there."

"That's none of your business."

"If I wanted to use the bath house, would you shoot me?"

"Yes."

"Really?"

"Yes!"

"I don't need to wash up anyway. I'm going to the swimming hole."

"There's wickedness there, and sorrow and disease. You should listen to Abdullah and the teachings of the Prophet. Worthy things will come to you and you will have wives to comfort you who do not whore themselves with other men but serve you faithfully."

"I've got girls now. Would he beat you if you took that shit off?"

"He would do the will of Allah. I would only submit."

"Did somebody hit you?"

"I—"

"Didn't you used to hang out at the swimming hole? I mean… like even get it on there?"

The barrel of the shotgun rose toward him.

Paul glanced at the twin holes in the end and held up his hands. "Hey, I—"

"That was another life. A time of sin. I'm a vessel for Allah's love now and an instrument of his will."

He wanted to say "And Abdullah's dick" but thought the better of it. Instead he approached the steps of the bath house and sat on them with his back to her as she stood above him.

"What are you doing?"

"Just wondering. I won't try and go in. Where are you from?"

"The past is past."

"Yeah, but everybody's from somewhere."

"Southern California."

"I'm from Oregon on the coast and I ran away." Paul stared out at the river. "I guess everybody's got a reason for what they do."

He heard her feet on the steps, and a silken robe brushed his shoulder as Fatima/Christine sat down beside him with the shotgun between her knees. "I ran away too, from Burbank. My dad works for Disney."

"Cool."

"Not really. There's fucked-up people down there and famous people are the worst. They get away with all kinds of shit. A fucking studio guy raped me when I was thirteen and the fucker's rich."

Paul examined her hand resting on her knee and fought an urge to touch it. He could just make out the shape of her right breast under the cloth and wondered if she were naked under there. "Why do you want to be a Muslim?"

She was silent for a while. Paul stifled a yawn. "For truth, something to believe beyond the flesh that betrays you and dies. I had a girlfriend who was murdered in Hollywood. I just got high after that and I was fucking guys just to be popular." She shook her head. "It doesn't work. They shit on you just like where I came from and I don't want to go to hell."

"I don't shit on girls." He felt her stiffen. "I mean I'm not hitting on you or anything, but I'm living with three girls right now and we get it on and I love them all. Really."

"Maybe you should meet Abdullah. Allah allows you four wives who will stay with you in the afterlife."

"Yeah but marriage is different. Do you have to do what he tells you?"

"Of course. It is written."

"Did he give you that black eye?"

She drew her knees up under her chin. "I must learn to submit to Allah's will. You should learn the five pillars of Islam and you too might be fit to teach your women through example."

"I don't know if I'm ready for that. I don't even know if I *want* them to do what I tell them. Sometimes they know shit I don't and they're right. If they just did what I tell them, how would I learn what they know that I don't?"

"You haven't become a man yet and haven't studied the word of Allah. You're a child and a fornicator."

"Well... what if God's a She?"

"That's blasphemy."

The door of the bath house opened a crack, a girl peered out and slammed it shut upon eyeing Paul.

"Okay, peace. That's not for me right now but thanks... and I wouldn't hit you even if I was a Muslim." Paul got up and headed toward the swimming hole with his spine tickling as he imagined a shotgun blast to the small of his back.

"You will discover salvation or be damned. Listen to the teaching of the Prophet and be saved!" Fatima shouted. "Peace be upon you!"

"Yeah. Peace."

* * *

A couple dozen people were lingering at the swimming hole in the late sun but no Darla. Paul decided to hang out since it was the best place to meet people. Darla still might show up, and he would check Fauna's place next. He dove in, swam the length of the big hole, returned to the beach, and sat on a rock to dry.

Black Michael and Danielle were on a blanket with their bota bag of wine. They waved Paul over and offered him a drink.

"I just walked by the bath house. This chick was there in a veil with a shotgun just like you said. She said she'd shoot me if I tried to come in," Paul shook his head, "I think she meant it."

Michael scowled. "Motherfucking Abdullah."

"Babe, don't get excited."

"Sorry."

"I got her to talk to me. She's from Burbank." Paul imag-ined Fatima under her veil naked on the beach and wished he'd met her as Christine then. He accepted another sip from the bota bag and rubbed his eyes. "Have you guys seen my old lady, or Fauna?"

"Fauna's probably at her patch," Black Michael said, "or wandering around in the woods with her pistol looking for trouble."

"Or with Mel." Danielle added.

Paul shoved pebbles around with his toes. "She tries to stay out of trouble."

"Dressed like that? I mean, not dressed?"

"She's *Fauna,* Michael."

"I'm looking for Darla anyway. The girl who was with me when we met."

Michael rubbed his eyes. "Which one? What does she look like again?"

"Really pretty, long blond hair, blue eyes and freckles with a turned-up nose."

"Only seen ten of 'em today."

"Michael…"

"Well? That's just what Christine looks like under that fucking burka for what it's worth." Michael grinned. "I remem-ber her man."

"She's driving an old brown Chevy truck with a loud engine."

Danielle sat up. "I saw her. She's your old lady, right?"

"Yeah, kinda."

"She was going up Hope Mountain this morning when I stopped at the store, with a couple guys that looked like they were from the gypsy camp."

"What?"

"Yeah, I wondered how they could pick up on anybody that good-looking." Danielle's mouth tightened. "Kinda freaked me out."

Paul grabbed his pants. "Thanks."

* * *

When he got to the road he broke into a jog. The shadows of evening already cloaked the north face of Hope Mountain. He put his hands on his knees, caught his breath and fondled the knife at his belt. A vision of Darla held hostage at the gypsy camp came to him, and his breath rattled his chest. He had to find Fauna or Mel.

"Shit."

Maybe that hadn't been Darla at all.

Maybe she'd given a ride to a couple friends of Mel's or something.

What do White Panthers look like?

She could be with Fauna right now talking about how possessive he was. She could be back at the goat dairy wondering where he was. She could be fucking some guy that he'd never even heard of and ready to ask him what right he had to complain.

The road up the mountain was dark under the trees. A poorwill fluttered down from the branches and landed on a rodent as it crossed a patch of gravel. The mouse let out a tiny shriek, and the bird returned to the trees with a liquid cry of triumph. He came to the clearing where Rayella had parked the bus and the shape of an old Chevy pickup loomed against the dark forest.

Darla's truck.

Paul went by instinct up the path. He gazed up the draw above Fauna's and wondered how he'd ever climbed to that pond at night, or if he had. Maybe it was just some crazy dream from the peyote. Maybe he was as crazy as that nut job Jason. Maybe he'd drunk some of that bad water and didn't even know it.

Coyotes howled up the gulch and he shivered.

He caught a faint glow from Fauna's tree house and made the last hundred yards in a trot. When he was within fifty feet, someone blew the lamps out and the place fell into darkness. "Hey Fauna it's me."

"Paul?"

"Yes."

"Shit." There was the click of a hammer being lowered, the scraping of a match, and a lamp flared back to life. Another lamp blossomed at the other end of the tree house and the door opened on a dim shape. "What the fuck are you doing here?"

"Is Darla here?"

"No."

"Is she at Mel's?"

"No. He went to Sebastopol Creek."

He climbed up the ladder. Fauna hugged him and flinched when he touched her right arm. "Her truck's parked down the hill."

"Are you sure?"

"Yeah. Danielle said she saw her driving up here with a couple guys."

"Black Michael's Danielle?"

"Yeah, she said they looked like somebody from the gypsy camp."

Fauna covered the beginning of a laugh and put her other hand to his chest. "Sit down." As she pushed him onto a stool, he noticed a deep cut in her right forearm and a trail of blood across the plank floor. "What truck?"

"What happened to your arm? She... she bought a Chevy from Chuck the other day, an old brown one. It's parked at the end of the road."

Fauna sat on the floor cross-legged and he slid off the seat to sit across from her. She ran a hand down a blond braid with blood on it. "Why the fuck would Darla hang out with those assholes from the gypsy camp?"

"I don't know." He pointed to her arm. "What happened?"

"There's a lot of old Chevys around here." She ignored his question, lit a pipe and passed it to him. "I was up watering today and snuck by the gypsy camp to see what was up. There wasn't anybody there."

"Really?"

"Yeah. I don't know where they are." She dabbed at her arm with a wet cloth, stood up and wrung it out over a bowl of bloody water. "I would have torched it right then but it's too dry and it could start a forest fire and bring all kinds of shit down. We have to wait 'til fall."

"You're hurt."

She flashed a smile. "Yeah."

"What happened?"

"I dropped mescaline and climbed the mountain before dawn. This meteor came down over the peaks all orange and green, and then I saw the aurora in the north like a green rainbow. That's like once in a decade around here and never in the summer, so something special is going on. It was so beautiful, like I was rising into the lights out of my body and I didn't ever want to come back. I wanted to... to give something back is all."

"Like blood?"

"What else do I have? I'm just on loan from the universe anyway." She sighed. "Now I gotta stitch it up." She reached for a thin sewing needle bent in a curve threaded with dental floss. She grabbed the rag, used it to lift the globe of the kerosene lamp, and held the needle over the flame. Fauna put the lamp chimney back and lay her arm on the table. The gash was cherry red in the lamplight and deep. Paul could see the grain of the muscle. She slid the needle into her skin, tied a tiny knot, and cut it with her knife. Fauna cinched the wound at one end and hissed.

The sliced muscle reminded him of when he'd butchered deer, but this was *Fauna* and she was alive. Paul bit his lip. He'd been on a wild goose chase and now it was night. "She's gonna think I'm an idiot. I don't even have a ride home." Fauna made another stitch and he rubbed his eyes. "I hope she's not broke down somewhere."

"Attachment karma's got you good." Fauna hissed again and ground her teeth.

"Why?"

"That's Mel's friends' truck from California. They went over Tennessee Gap in the other one and left that one here."

"Say what?"

"And one of them is a blond California chick who looks a lot like Darla. Those surfer chicks all look like Darla and Danielle's only seen her once."

Paul slapped the floor and groaned.

"Rumors sprout here like mushrooms in the fall. Everybody has a story and Danielle just wanted to be part of yours. It's the wheel of gossip, man. It's the endless mandala of illusion, of bullshit. That's what attachment does to you. You just go around and around on the great mandala 'til you die." Her bloodstained fingers glided over the back of his hand. "You're really in love with her aren't you?"

Paul stared at the crimson scar on her arm and counted the stitches. *Nine.* He let out his breath.

"Think she'll worry about you not coming back?"

"I don't know. Maybe. Doesn't that hurt?"

"Sure. You can crash here. It's too dark to hike down and hitch. You'd never get to the goat dairy this time of night and you'll just get stuck in Cave Junction with the rednecks." Fauna held a clean cloth to her arm, blotted the blood and examined her handiwork. She took a bottle of Wild Turkey down from the shelf, splashed some on the cut and hissed through her teeth. She put two beige coffee mugs taken from a café in town on the floor between her legs, poured in two fingers' worth of whiskey into each and held hers up. "I need a drink... and somebody to drink with."

Paul toasted his foolishness. The whiskey went down in three swallows to form a warm pool in his stomach. He began to speak but thought better of it. He could never have done that: stitched himself up while carrying on a conversation. He gazed at the half-smile on Fauna's lips and squeezed his eyes shut.

When he opened them Fauna's lips were on his own.

XXII.
War

An owl hooted in the trees and their bodies grappled as dampness filled the bed. Fauna flinched when he grabbed her wounded arm and when she put weight on it, and it began to bleed. She sprang up, added more gauze and adhesive tape, and returned to the bed. Fauna: wild girl of the mountains, daughter of a Goddess he'd met in a dream, a succubus, or what he wasn't sure. After a very long time they fell into an exhausted sleep. Safe in the space they'd carved through the exertion of their bodies.

Paul dreamt and this time flew easily. He arrived at the moonlit pond and called out to one who dwelt there.

She answered with a smile and took his hand.

* * *

It rained. They awoke shivering and made love under the covers. When they finished Paul noticed a large blood stain on the mattress. He slid down from the loft with a spinning head to get more bandages for Fauna and nearly fainted when his feet hit the floor.

"You need to eat but there's something we have to do first." Fauna built a fire in the stove, made coffee on the propane burner, and they sat gazing at each other cradling their cups. The coffee warmed the void in Paul's middle. A pot of peyote tea was beginning to boil and the smell made the hair on the back of Paul's neck dance.

She stroked her purple yew wood bow and yawned. "It's raining. The Goddess brought you here. I thought me and Mel would do this but she told me to wait for you." She hung the bow and buckskin quiver up, poured half a steaming mug of the black potion for each of them, and they downed them in unison. Fauna belched and wiped her mouth. "That's enough. All things in balance."

Rain pattered on the roof and the air smelled green. Fauna knelt and reached under the bed, pulled out an iron-bound chest, and forced a key into the old brass lock. The lock yielded after some twisting and she lifted the lid.

An old Winchester pump shotgun with a short barrel lay amongst boxes of ammunition in the yellow lamplight and she handed it to Paul. He spied the base of a shell in the long tubular magazine, pumped the action, and a red buckshot shell bounced on the floor. He scooped it up, closed the bolt on another, checked the safety, and thumbed the shell back in the tubular magazine.

"Watch out for the big fucker, Gypsy Dave." Fauna filled two quart bottles with white gas. She took a burlap bag from under the sink, cut off two pieces, rolled them between her hands, and inserted them into the mouths of the bottles. She handed one to Paul, then put big wooden matches into two screw-top plastic containers and gave him one. Fauna stepped into her jeans, laced her moccasins up over them, pulled a khaki shirt on, and tied a brown scarf over her hair. Paul had never seen her so dressed. She chuckled at his expression as she climbed down the ladder.

Their dilated eyes devoured every trace of light as a soft glow rose from the ground. Deer burst from brush and bounded up the hill, leaving phosphorescent trails and wisps of musk in the damp air. When they reached Mel's, they gazed into the gulch that had throbbed with life when they'd stalked the gypsy camp on acid. They headed into the luminous forest, crossed a creek he didn't remember, and reached the cedar log.

Remnants of a fire glowed in a stone-lined pit before the dilapidated shack. One of the tents stood. The other had collapsed in the rain. Fauna's breath made a cloud in the first light as moisture beaded her cheeks and glistened on her eyelashes.

"Terror."

He nodded.

"The trail is on the downhill side. If they run, shoot over their heads."

He nodded again.

"If they *run*. If they fight…" She crushed his fingers in her own.

A molten stream connected them as if their arteries had linked.

Something in him reached out toward the shack but retracted in revulsion.

"Four of them."

"Yeah."

"You burn the tent. I'll take the shack. Fire over their heads after I light the roof." She glided to his right and disappeared amongst the dark trunks of trees.

Paul went to the left. The door of the shack faced him and he kept the tent between it and himself. He took a position behind a tree within an easy toss of the bottle and took out a match. He'd have to use a thumbnail to light it. Everything else was damp.

There was a rattle as Fauna's bottle landed on the roof of the shack, followed by a *WHUMP* and an orange explosion blinded him for a moment and bounced off the back of his eyes. Paul lit his bottle, rolled it into the tent, and it lit up like a Chinese lantern.

Two men staggered out of the shack with a shotgun and a .22. The big man with a black beard who'd exited first swung the shotgun at the forest and roared as he held a hand to his eyes against the glare. Paul took a breath, leveled the shotgun at Gypsy Dave, and held it with the trigger slick with rain. A skinny guy

with gaps in his teeth covered in prison tattoos followed and another barefoot in ragged jeans. The roof and back wall of the shack
were alight as the men staggered between it and the blazing tent.

"Where are they?!"

"Back there!"

Gypsy Dave pumped a round into the chamber of his shotgun and bellowed, "I'm—!"

Paul's shotgun bucked against his shoulder, the roof exploded in a cloud of splinters, and all four men dropped to the ground.
He fought a laugh as the one with the .22 scuttled like a crab back
and forth between the shack and the blazing tent with his eyes
rolling in his head as if he was having a fit.

"We're surrounded!"

Gypsy Dave fired blindly into the trees and the denizens
of the gypsy camp sprang up and fled down the mountain. The
guy with prison tattoos crashed into the one with the .22. They
went down with a yelp, scrambled to their feet, and fled howling. Paul let loose a load of buckshot over their heads and the
tattooed guy screamed as fir needles showered on him. The shack
creaked as something collapsed and there was a loud *pop* as a
round of ammunition went off. Paul ducked and scanned the
trees for Fauna.

She was beside him.

"Shit!"

Fauna put a hand on his shoulder. Her laughter was soft but
it made him feel like a fool. "Good thing I'm not a bad guy."

"How the fuck did you get here?"

She shrugged.

"Think that Dave guy will come back?"

Her teeth flashed red in the flames. "He thinks he's a tough
guy, so if he does…" She kissed his cheek. "That was fun. Now the
whole mountain belongs to me and Mel."

How had she snuck up on him?

Fauna was his ally and a lover, but the whole idea that she could was just wrong.

She slid arms around his neck. "It's 'cause our souls are one Paul. You felt no threat because I was yourself."

"You know what I'm thinking."

"Of course. You have to have permission from the soul of the prey. It's a mirror of your own. We're born like a still pond that reflects the whole universe. The Lakota call it *sicum,* one of the four parts of the soul. I learned that from a medicine man I met in the mountains. You were open to me like that, like prey, but I'd never kill you. Besides, the Goddess picked you and who am I to question that." She kissed him. "We'll make love and go hunting."

"We just did."

A round went off in the burning shack and they ducked.

* * *

The sky dawned bright blue and they had a huge breakfast. He cleaned and dried the shotgun and she put it in the chest. They ate venison, potatoes, toast and eggs with appetites whetted by love and war and drank two pots of coffee.

Fauna stood by the window inspecting the wound on her arm.

Paul drained another cup of coffee and sighed. "I couldn't even see the sights on that gun. They were dancing and melting all over the place."

"That's called the wave structure of external unity in *The Psychedelic Experience.* I read it a bunch of times when I was like fourteen and dropping acid but I got too high and the pages melted."

"How old are you?"

"Does it matter?"

"No, I guess."

"Eighteen." She went back to examining her arm. "This is gonna scar. Think I'll get a tattoo of a medicine wheel. I can use the scar for a horizontal spoke and do eagle feathers on either side.

I'll go to Lyle Tuttle's parlor in San Francisco this fall when I go down to sell pot. Jane got an awesome butterfly over her tit there." She smiled, "Mel's gonna be so jazzed from us burning out the gypsy camp he probably won't even care I laid you."

Paul put down his cup.

She grinned. "Not that I'm gonna tell him. At least right away."

He refilled the mug and took another sip.

"You gonna tell Darla?"

Paul shrugged. "I guess." He grinned, "She'll probably want to get it on with both of us."

"That'll work." Fauna climbed down the ladder and squatted to pee.

The sound of a helicopter pounding over the ridge made Paul spring out of his chair and glance out the door.

Fauna yelled, "Hey!"

Gray smoke cloaked the trees over the gypsy camp. A white and red helicopter hovered above it, but it was the sounds from down the hill that made his heart leap in his throat.

Sirens.

Paul shook his head like a dog as if he could adjust his hearing. Those guys at the gypsy camp wouldn't call the cops; it would mean their arrests, but voices came from the forest. Voices that could mean only one thing.

"Cops!" Fauna shouted.

He climbed down from the treehouse. "What's going on?"

"I don't know."

A jolt of fear shot through him. Paul wondered if he was going to see Darla again as the sounds of vehicles grew closer. Down the gulch crows shouted in their wooden voices and took flight in alarm.

She climbed up the ladder. "I'd better get some clothes on for the Man."

Two sheriff's deputies wearing green body armor toting M16s and an older cop with a black shotgun appeared puffing up the trail as the helicopter followed their progress overhead. The loud *thok-thok* made the whole forest seem to retract on itself. The cops with assault rifles moved to either side and aimed at the treehouse and the older one cupped his hands around his mouth. "Attention! Come out with your hands up!"

Fauna had on her hempen poncho. Paul counted two fillings in her open mouth and for the first time saw fear in her eyes. He felt a burning in his middle he hoped wouldn't precede a loosening of his bowels.

She put her hands out the door with her fingers spread wide. "Hey don't shoot! What's the matter?" The men seemed to relax a bit at the sound of a female voice and lowered their weapons slightly. "We're coming out!" Fauna's muscular arms trembled as she climbed down the ladder and Paul followed. They stood in the yard hands raised as the three cops outfitted for war approached.

"Anybody inside?" The man with the shotgun asked.

Fauna shook her head and nodded in recognition to the stocky deputy on the right.

"Do you live here?"

"Yeah."

He glanced at Paul. "How 'bout you?"

The instant that it took to find words seemed an eternity. "No sir, just… visiting."

"You have identification?"

"Up there."

The old cop rested the black shotgun in the cradle of an arm and glanced at the man Fauna had nodded to. "They say anything about a girl?"

"That's Fauna sir," the deputy answered, "she lives here. Don't know who the kid is."

"Hi Chuck."

"Hey Fauna."

The leader turned to Paul. "Do either of you know the people at that place they call the gypsy camp?"

"Gypsy Dave." Fauna scowled, "He's fuckin' trash. They're rip-offs, and I know they raped a chick 'cause I helped her get the hell outta there. That's all."

The man gave her a grim smile. "More than you know. Do you guys know Moses or Rainbow Bob?"

"Yeah, sure."

"They're dead. Those guys at the gypsy camp killed them last night on Rockydale Road. Shot 'em in the back when they stopped to piss on a ride from Cave Junction and took their beer."

"What?"

"Somebody ran to the clinic and told 'em about it and somebody actually had the good sense to call us." The cop ran a hand over his face. "Nobody believed it until we found their heads."

"What?"

"Do you know why they'd do something like that?"

"Fuck no!"

The older cop gazed around the forest and stroked his shotgun. "I can't believe you actually live up here by yourself, a girl that looks like you a goddamn stone's throw away from those maniacs. You're damn lucky you didn't end up like that... or worse."

"She packs a .45." Chuck volunteered.

"Where is it?"

Fauna motioned with her chin. "In my house."

The man's grey brows crinkled over tired hazel eyes as he managed a half-smile. "Keep it close. You need it." The other cops had their weapons at rest and were gazing at Fauna, having forgotten Paul entirely. The head cop hooked his thumbs in his belt. "How many hippies live up here?"

"You mean freaks? We don't like the word hippies. You mean besides those fucks at the gypsy camp? Just me and Mel, at least permanently."

"Okay freaks then. That's the one called Hope Mountain Mel?"
She nodded.

"Where is he?"

"Over Tennessee Gap."

"Those guys." The old cop shook his head. "That's one heavy crowd. The last of the White Panthers from Detroit. Even the FBI's paranoid going there. They call those guys the Gunslingers right? Quite a bunch, but there's no good soil for growing pot over there."

"They're mining gold."

"And Josephinite." Paul added.

The old cop's smile softened. "Any more girls around here like you?"

Fauna shook her head.

"Well it's nice to meet you in the flesh. I thought some of the stuff I've heard about you was bullshit but I have to say you fit the description to a 'T.'" He looked her up and down. "Did you get dressed for us after you heard the sirens?"

"Yeah."

The cop chuckled. "You guys lucked out being this close to those scumbags. There's gonna be a hell of a lot of law all over this whole fucking mountain for a few days, so please don't get crazy, and tell Mel to do the same. We're not looking for pot and we'd really appreciate your cooperation." He rubbed his chin. "Do you know any last names of those people?"

"No. Gypsy Dave's the only one I even know the first of. We don't socialize."

"Well, we got the four that did it and we've got a witness. The guy who ran to the clinic. They burned their camp to hide the evidence and were running off the mountain when we caught 'em coming down the road just like fish in a barrel. They gave us some bullshit story about somebody else burning the place." He squinted at Fauna. "Can't understand you kids nowadays. It used to be all peace and love, and now..." He gave them a weak salute, waved to his deputies, and they turned to go. "Let us know pronto if you see any of their friends up here. It could save somebody's life. Please."

"Sure, of course."

He looked Fauna up and down one last time, acknowledged Paul and ran a hand across his forehead. "Keep your heads on a swivel kids."

"You too, officer."

"So long, Fauna." The deputy said.

"So long Chuck."

The cops disappeared down the trail as smoke drifted from the ridge where the gypsy camp had been in a pale shroud with the ghosts of trees the only witnesses to their morning of mayhem.

A wet croak rattled Fauna's chest. "Moses!"

Paul wiped a tear from her cheek as a tangle of emotions seethed within him seeking a place to land. Fauna sobbed and squeezed him until the air left his lungs. He squeezed her back.

"Ow!" She rubbed her arm.

"Sorry."

She cried quietly in his arms and stared at the smoke.

He stroked her neck. "I've got to get home."

She ground her feet in the leaves. "We shoulda killed 'em.".

"Then we'd be fucked. They're caught and we're free. Shit, the cops didn't even check my I.D. We lucked out Fauna." She shivered, and Paul lightened his grip as if he were holding a snowflake that might melt in an instant. "Are you gonna be all right?"

"Shit yeah. We cleaned out the gypsy camp. I can handle cops." She chuckled. "Big grows pot on Chuck's parents' land out the river road. That's where he bred his polypoid Oaxacan plants." Something between a laugh and a sob rippled her throat and she swallowed hard. "Hope they never figure it was us who blew 'em outta here though. God, I'd love to tell Chuck someday." Fauna swiped at her eyes. She held her arm out before her and ran fingers over the wound. "I'd better go to the clinic. I'm so stupid. No wonder people like me don't live long."

"No you're not. You're smart and will live a long time and you're the bravest chick I ever knew. Really."

She dug her chin in his shoulder. "Those motherfuckin' cowards! Moses and Bob were just hitching and they shot 'em in the back. Moses didn't even own a gun and they shot 'em for their fucking beer!" She pushed away. "Go home to your girls. Me and Mel gotta stash some shit if cops are gonna be around." She gazed at the smoke-shrouded trees. "I wish we'd killed 'em."

XXIII.
Passage

His mind boiled like a pot of peyote tea on the way down the mountain seething with thoughts and feelings half-seen that rose like dragons from the mist. He thought of his parents hearing of him connected to the horrors of the night before and of getting busted. He thought of the power of Fauna and her passion, of a spirit who seemed to be there with them that had taken him as a lover in dreams and the incredible rush he'd felt when they brought terror to the gypsy camp. He thought of her sneaking up on him like a ghost of the forest and wondered if she would tell Mel that they'd been lovers and if he'd be pissed off. Burning down the gypsy camp hadn't been his usual Fourth of July.

He hoped Darla was waiting. He snapped the towel Fauna had given him for the bath house at a wild rose, and pink petals exploded across the trail.

Darla. He'd been searching for Darla. It seemed a million years ago but it was yesterday. She must be with Rayella and Cindy. He drifted into the memory of the three of them together, grew aroused, and stumbled in the damp leaves.

There were two green jeeps, two sheriff's cars, a trooper car, two unmarked ones, and an ugly black armored van in the meadow where Rayella had parked her bus and Paul had discovered the old pickup he thought was Darla's. The pickup was there hemmed-in by the law. The red and white helicopter sat in a clearing up the hill. Half a dozen cops glanced up as he emerged from the forest and put hands to their weapons. One was the deputy Chuck. He waved at Paul and told the others to stand down. A black German shepherd barked from the back of a car and Paul felt stares on the back of his neck as he headed down the trail. Did they think he was like one of the guys who'd murdered Moses and Rainbow Bob?

It was long past time to call his parents but what would he say? Maybe he and Darla should just take her truck and leave, or they could all take the bus and go somewhere together. Anywhere. There was no reason to part with Cindy and Rayella. They could be together forever. Summer was waning fast, and there were jobs picking fruit up in Hood River. With three girls it would be an adventure wherever he went.

He bathed at the bath house with the soap and shampoo Fauna had pressed into his hands, scrubbing her scent off him and missing it as soon as it was gone. There weren't any girls with veils and guns around but there was a fat chick who gave him a look of lust and a skinny guy with his hair tangled in ropes and some kind of lesion on his ass. Paul hurriedly washed and dried on the porch.

He went to the road and stuck out his thumb. Two cars passed he was sure would have picked him up yesterday, but their passengers gave him suspicious stares.

He got a ride on Rockydale Road with a couple of long-haired locals. The driver slowed to point out where Moses and Rainbow Bob had been shot. Yellow police tape was strung along a section of the east fork of the Illinois River and a single sheriff's car was parked by a little bridge where the road crossed a creek. "Julie Tilton found Rainbow Bob's head where it washed up behind her house." The guy volunteered, who also was named Bob.

"She totally freaked out and had to pull all her plants." He shook his head. "Bummer."

"Fuckin' assholes at the gypsy camp." His passenger grumbled, "Somebody should'a cleaned them out a long time ago."

Paul stared at the receding cop car. "Yeah."

"There's gonna be tons of heat now. I hear they're bringing cops from California to raid people's crops."

"That's fucked-up."

"Did you hear about that hitchhiker they caught in Gasquet on the California border who had human fingers in his pocket? I mean not like his own. He was eating them for snacks and was headed to the gypsy camp."

"That's gotta be bullshit."

"Swear to God. It's in the paper."

The driver shook his head. "Fucking place is turning into a Mecca for psychos."

Paul got out in Cave Junction with his thoughts racing. He bought a quart of orange juice at Hammer's Market and walked to the north end of town to hitch. Vehicles passed by with their occupants staring at him but no one pulled over to give him a ride. Did they think he was some kind of killer?

No! I burned the motherfuckers out!

He had to get back to Darla. What was she doing? Maybe she hadn't even come back. If she'd balled somebody else, he didn't even care. There were much heavier things to deal with now. At least he didn't smell like Fauna. Darla and Fauna made great friends and he didn't want to ruin it. The only way he wanted to come between them was when they were in a bed together. They should have been together already. That at least could be a welcome outcome from his trip to Hope Mountain.

He took a big gulp of orange juice as a yellow Dodge Power-wagon heading north slowed. The big blond guy with a crew cut driving gave him the finger. Paul gave it back. The truck braked on the shoulder with a hiss of gravel, hung a "U," and pulled up into the parking lot of the gas station. The door flew open and the big man leapt out.

"Hey punk-ass hippie, you got problems?"

"No." Paul recognized Terry Cox, who'd torn up the Rusty Spur Saloon with a chainsaw. His two passengers stood behind him grinning in anticipation. Paul let out his breath. "You flipped me off first man."

"Because you're a fuckin' pussy. You take it in the ass, pussy?"

"No."

"Betcha do." Terry was even bigger in the daylight with arms the size of Paul's thighs. His pale blue eyes looked empty, as if there was nothing behind them.

Everything that had happened in the last twenty-four hours swirled inside Paul. He gazed into the empty eyes of Terry, saw the face of Gypsy Dave backlit by flames, and ground his teeth. "Fuck you."

The fist came in slow motion. Paul dodged to the left, slapped it away, and landed a haymaker left of his own on the side of Terry's head with a meaty whack. His knuckles stung.

Terry went "Wuff!" and swung again. Paul ducked.

Paul landed a flurry of blows that felt like hitting a rock sheathed in meat. Except for a momentary hesitation as each blow landed, Terry gave no indication they were making any difference at all. Terry grunted. He lunged forward to wrap his arms around Paul and began to reel him in like a rat in the coils of a snake. Paul somehow slipped out of Terry's grasp and closed his hands on the giant's throat. Paul's knee came up once, twice, three times in Terry's crotch and he squeezed his muscular throat with all his might. They went down hard with Paul on top and he heard the big man's head hit the blacktop as Terry's pale eyes stared without emotion.

Blows rained on Paul's back and a fist glanced off his cheek, and his head rocked from the impact as Terry's companions seized his arms and wrenched him off.

Terry stumbled to his feet with a hand to his throat and the other to the back of his head that came away bloody. Pink spittle dribbled from an insane grin. "Now... you gonna *die!*"

With a surge of adrenalin, Paul shook off the grip of the men holding him just as Terry's hands reached his throat and they went down on the pavement. Paul felt his shirt and jeans tearing on the blacktop as he fought for his life. Terry pinned one of his arms and rolled on top of him. Paul grabbed Terry's crotch, squeezed, and with strength he didn't know he had, lifted the big man off him by the balls. Terry loosened his grip on Paul's throat and Paul wrenched the hand off and punched frantically at Terry's face, throat and stomach until his hand hurt. Terry snorted and landed a single blow in Paul's side that drove the air from his lungs. Terry's hands found his throat again.

Paul shoved a hand in Terry's face. Terry bit his thumb. Paul stabbed an index finger in the big man's eye as Terry's teeth began to grind and Terry released his thumb but choked him harder. Sparks flashed in Paul's eyes as he felt his life draining away. He pounded on the massive creature choking the life from him as each blow grew weaker.

"Break it up!"

Terry let go of his throat.

Paul struggled to his feet gagging as a cop stepped between them with his club in hand.

Paul tried to speak but could only croak.

The cop jabbed him in the ribs with the club. "Break it up!"

Paul rasped "What the fuck are you doing? You think I stopped a truck with three guys in it?"

"It's okay officer Queen, just teachin' the hippie a lesson."

The cop looked Paul up and down and smirked. "You look like shit, hippie."

Paul's mouth began to form the words *fuck you* but stopped. He wanted to beat the shit out of the cop with his own club. He wanted to choke the shit out of him. He wanted to kill him. Paul wobbled on his feet. His throat burned as he pointed a shaking finger. "He attacked me!"

The cop turned to Terry and his companions. "Is that what happened?"

The three shook their heads. Terry grinned and wiped away a rope of bloody snot running down his chin. "No, sir."

"It's their word against yours." The cop slid his nightstick back in his belt. "Guess it's over anyway."

"Thanks officer Queen." Terry and his buddies jumped in the truck and slammed the doors. He gave Paul the finger and grinned as the engine roared to life. "You gonna end up just like that fuckin' dog!" Laughter mixed with the squeal of tires as they pulled onto the highway.

The cop turned to his car. "You better watch your queer ass around here buddy."

"They stopped to beat me up! Why didn't you arrest them?"

Officer Queen turned around. "You wanta whine about it like a little long-haired bitch do ya? Let me see your I.D.!"

As he fished in his pocket, Paul glanced at the knees of his jeans. Bloody flesh glistened like raspberry jam through the holes. His elbows and shoulders were similarly raw as the adrenaline of the fight subsided to be replaced by pain. He handed the man his new license with a bloody thumbprint on it.

"You're nineteen, huh? Oughta be in the army. Got a draft card?"

Paul fished it out and handed it to him.

"4-F huh? Another bitch from the booby hatch. You heading back to Gresham?"

"Uh, yeah, eventually."

"Don't take too long. We don't need your kind around here." A smirk twisted the man's thin face beneath aviator sunglasses. "You know those gypsy guys?"

"Who?"

"Them be-headers?"

"No."

"You fuckers all look the same to me. A bunch of crazy 4-F motherfuckers comin' here from all over. Get goin'!" The cop threw his license and draft cards on the blacktop. Paul picked them up as Officer Queen got in his green sheriff's car and drove away.

Paul rocked on his feet as his wounds stung and his throat burned. The right side of his face was swelling and his left side where Terry had landed his one good punch ached like a rib was broken.

* * *

He got a ride in a dented Studebaker pickup from a redheaded girl named Chris who knew Gus and volunteered to take him to the goat dairy.

"Ohmygod… that was Terry Cox! He kills peoples' dogs! That fucker robs people and rapes girls. People say him and a guy from Kerby killed a whole family over by Copper and got away with it. You're fucking lucky to be alive."

Paul groaned and sipped his warm orange juice. It burned going down and one of his teeth felt loose.

"Did you hear about Moses and Rainbow Bob?"

He managed a grunt.

"You gotta get some antibiotics for staph 'cause there's lots going around. You got enough abrasions to kill your ass if you catch it."

Paul leaned on the rattling door. "Fuckin' shit."

"Don't go to the big swimming hole in Takilma. People pee in the water upstream. Don't go swimming at all. You got to boil water sterile to wash your wounds and keep 'em clean and get some antibiotics at the clinic."

"Yeah." He slumped against the door and closed his eyes.

After a long while she killed the engine and he opened his

eyes to see Rayella's bus and Darla's truck parked under the trees. A twinge of pain shot up his neck as he opened the door.

The girls appeared with towels draped around their shoulders and wet hair from the new swimming hole. Rayella lowered the .30-.30 when she saw who it was.

"Hey," Chris waved, "I got your friend and he's fucked up. Terry Cox attacked him when he was hitching."

Darla dropped her towel and bolted to him. She began to throw arms around him, but when she saw his wounds she shrieked.

They helped him into the bus and to the bed. Rayella undid his belt and tugged on his jeans. "Sit up." He did with a groan and she peeled off his shirt. Cindy heated water on the propane stove to clean his abrasions as Darla kissed his cheek and made sounds of comfort in his ear. He kissed her back and her eyes brimmed with tears, the most beautiful eyes he'd ever seen.

Chris accepted a smoldering pipe from Cindy and sat on the couch. "He was standing at the north end of Cave Junction lookin' like he got run over."

"Thank you, thank you, for bringing him home!"

"It was Terry Cox." Paul muttered.

Cindy dabbed at his knee with a washcloth and he hissed.

"Where were you last night? I came home from the Foster Claim and they said you went looking for me." Darla's eyes were big with concern. It felt good.

"I got stuck after dark on Hope Mountain. Somebody told me you went up there and there was a truck just like yours, and…" Paul closed his eyes, "and me and Fauna burned down the gypsy camp."

Cindy looked up. "What?"

Rayella blinked. "Wow."

He lay back and stared at the ceiling. "Did you hear what happened?"

"They killed Moses and Rainbow Bob!" Chris blurted before he could get it out.

The girls fell silent, then began talking all at once.

Paul held up his hands as Cindy began working on his elbows. He grimaced as she dabbed his bitten thumb with hydrogen peroxide and his breath whistled through his teeth. "We didn't know that. They killed Moses and Rainbow Bob and cut their heads off but we had no idea. *Ow!* Jesus fuckin' *Christ!*" He gulped air, "It rained and Fauna wanted to get rid of them when we wouldn't start a fire so we snuck up on them and burned their camp and chased them down the mountain. You should have heard those assholes screaming. That big fucker Gypsy Dave was a pussy. I bet he pissed his pants."

"It rained?" Chris asked, "It didn't rain in Takilma."

"It rained on Hope Mountain."

Cindy went to work on his right shoulder. Paul bit his lip and sighed. He'd forgotten how pretty she was. "We didn't know they killed those guys but in the morning the cops came up like gangbusters 'cause somebody saw it and we found out they got them when they were running down the hill... from us." He flinched as she moved to his other shoulder. "The cops thought they burned the place to hide the evidence and didn't even check our I.D.s."

Rayella swept back her hair. "Damn Paul, you fought *murderers!*"

"And won." Darla added.

Chris nodded. "You and Fauna are heroes."

Darla squeezed his thigh. "Baby you're so brave. God, I could feel the evil vibes from those guys every time we went up that mountain."

"There's like an army of cops checking things out with helicopters and jeeps. Fauna and Mel are busy camouflaging their patches but the cops said they didn't even care about the pot...

at least for now." Paul shook his head. "I wish we'd done it a day sooner and Moses and Rainbow Bob would be alive. Moses saw all this shit in World War Two and he ended up getting shot and beheaded in fucking Takilma Oregon the fucking counterculture utopia. Fauna's really pissed off we didn't kill 'em. She was ready to do it and cried like hell when she heard about Moses."

"Fauna cried?"

"I didn't know Fauna ever cries."

"She cried. It's fucking chaos over there. I hope those guys don't get busted."

Rayella put a hand on his chest. "You're gonna have to stay out of swimmin' holes for a long time, maybe all summer. Y'all got seven open wounds and there's lotsa staph goin' 'round."

"That's what I told him." Chris sat on the bed and grabbed his hand. "God dude, you're incredible. You dusted the bad guys. Wait 'til I tell people in Takilma what you did."

"Actually it was Fauna... I mean it was her plan and it worked but I had the shotgun."

Rayella got up to make coffee. "Chris, please don' say shit about them burnin' them fuckers out right now. There's bad energy come down an' we gotta watch out it don't touch us."

Cindy frowned. "Does that Terry guy know where you live? He was on our road. You think he'll remember?"

Paul closed his eyes. A vision of his bedroom full of model motorcycles and posters beside rain-smeared windows overlooking the little fishing port of Charleston flashed across his eyes. He saw the red comforter his mom had bought him when he was ten with the old-time trains on it and wanted to crawl under it and sleep. Here he was surrounded by girls and he couldn't even cuddle one. Every angle of his body had a wound on it. He wanted tomato soup and a grilled cheese sandwich. He wanted to curl up and sleep forever.

Darla smiled. "Guess you gotta get laid on your back for a while. Those scrapes gotta heal."

"I love you." He swiped his eyes with the back of a hand. "I was looking for you."

"Sure was. Took off like a dog on your scent honey."

Darla licked her lips. "I know. I love you too. Forever baby."

"We all love ya Paul."

Cindy planted a kiss on his cheek. "Yeah."

He sat up. "Terry's the one who killed your dog Rayella. He said so when he took off and he said I was gonna end up the same, so he knows where we are."

Rayella's green eyes widened. "Goddamn." She ran a hand down the barrel of the .30-.30 and stared out the window. "Goddamn."

XXIV.
Back in the Bushes

An ancient green army Powerwagon broke the morning calm and ground to a halt under the trees with Gus behind the wheel. His pit bull Smaug leapt from the back, immediately made for Bozo, and Gus screamed at him to stop. The dog gave him a look of disappointment, scraped a few leaves with his hind legs in disdain, and pissed on a tree trunk.

Paul's wounds were beginning to scab, leaving pink spots on the bed where they'd drained. He ached all over. The girls had awoken before him to water the crop and had returned to nurture him. In his troubled sleep he'd imagined their voices were angels. Rayella clucked as she changed the bedclothes and stuffed the stained sheets in a laundry bag for a trip to town. She'd fried up some of the prolific bantie chickens for him, and there was a constant bowl of cold fried chicken on hand with a towel over it to keep the flies off, which was the best part of being bedridden. That girl could cook.

Gus had their pay but wanted to inspect the crop. He returned in an hour and came into the bus to look at Paul. "Man you are fucked up. Better get some antibiotics from the clinic."

Paul sipped coffee. "Darla got some."

"Lucky you got this posse'a chicks to do your grunt work for a couple'a weeks."

"I'll be okay soon."

"The scabs will open if you do shit. Better to hangout for a while. You deserve some R and R brother." Gus stared at Darla through the window. "Damn she's cute."

Paul gazed at his lady love in the yard as Cindy poured him another cup and began to massage his neck. He sighed, closed his eyes, and leaned into her small strong hands.

"The cops are bringing up extra spotter planes." Gus leaned out to check on Smaug, who was tied to the trunk of the oak. "Shit's gotta tighten up. They're on Slate Creek right now doin' a sweep and sooner or later they'll hit Selma. Probably in the next couple'a days." He began to roll a joint. "I heard about you and Fauna takin' down the gypsy camp. It's all over the valley. People are wonderin' if you two are gonna get together now, sayin' you're bad to the bone and made for each other." He chuckled. "Mel's sick of hearing it but respects you. You should lay low here so the cops don't find you." He handed the joint to Paul, struck a big wooden match, and held it as Paul inhaled.

"Sounds like redhaired Chris been talking."

Gus nodded. "That's pretty Skookum shit dustin' them motherfuckers even if you didn't know they offed Moses and Bob. Think you can handle rip-offs?"

"That's part of the job."

Gus nodded. "If this place gets raided I don't exist, right?"

"Of course, man."

"If the shit does come down, let your tracks be lost brother. Head up the fire road to the Thompson Creek drainage and when you get down to Thompson Creek Road, take a right over the mountains and you'll come out on Caves Highway. Maybe head for China Gardens. They're all vegies and pacifists and nobody oughta look there and that way you can avoid the pavement. Even better you could head over the back way from Takilma to Happy Camp. I know people on the Hupa Reservation. There isn't shit for law there and I know for a fact the guns for the Alcatraz occupation came from there on the Grateful Dead's dime. There's other places too. I hear Mel's thinking about takin' up ol' Bob Cutler on some claims on Josephine Creek, so you might consider going over Tennessee Gap for a while if this place gets raided. You could build a cabin on one of Bob's claims or hang with the Gunslingers. I'll put in a word." Gus glanced around. "They'll appreciate you bringin' your friends here too."

Paul stared at the twenty-five dollars on the table. It wasn't much for the work let alone the risk. He hadn't taken it seriously when it started as if it was a gift or something, but somebody could actually get killed around here. Somebody *had*. "We need more money. Things are getting heavy."

To Paul's surprise that elicited a grin. Gus stroked his drooping mustache. "Yeah you're right." He reached in his pocket and threw four more tens on the table. "Everybody gets a ten-buck raise and Paul gets a badass bonus." He handed him two twenties. "You make a pretty good outlaw man. Just don't let Fauna get you into any more shootouts. Pussy can make you wanta go out in a blaze of glory but I need your ass around here."

"Cool." Cindy's fingers went up a gear as she kneaded Paul's shoulders.

Paul glanced at the fifty extra bucks. "Thanks."

"Just stick around."

"Okay."

Gus shook hands and left.

* * *

The girls took care of the crop and in three days he was going crazy. On the third day they returned to the bus after a swim and took turns riding him as he lay on the bed, then left to swim again. Afterward the inactivity was worse than ever as he lay staring at the ceiling. He wandered around the place as he healed, fed the horse, dog and chickens, and bathed his wounds with water that had been boiled sterile. The girls took turns dabbing his abrasions with washcloths and made cute comments as they did the rest of him. He felt like a lapdog that had been salvaged after being run over.

After four days he went with Darla to the Selma store and felt a knot in his stomach when a yellow Dodge pickup appeared on the highway. His hand drifted to the rifle in the rack. What would happen if he had to use it? He would if it came to it. When they got back to the old goat dairy he was bored in minutes.

Time crawled.

Once he could wear something over his itching knees and shoulders, he began helping again on the crop with his thumb bandaged wearing gloves. By the fifth day he felt nearly normal. On the sixth he arose in the dark, grabbed the .30-.30, and headed out. He tied Bozo at the barn hoping to surprise a deer in the first light. A successful hunt would revive him. The dog gave him a mournful look and Paul apologized, but bringing home some meat would make him stop feeling like some useless pet or a damn gigolo.

Mist rose from the meadow as he scanned the tree line. A cloud of breath wreathed Storm at the far end. The horse snorted once in surprise as Paul stepped softly through the damp grass, climbed past the patches, and reached the ridge top in twenty minutes. He stared into a brush-choked gulch on the other side and rested on a boulder at the top of the ridge. The rising sun set the rocky top of Little Grayback Mountain aglow in the east as he stretched on the rock and yawned. His abrasions stung, but the coolness and solitude were a needed tonic.

Paul sat up with a start as a helicopter ripped the morning air when it rose over a hill to the south. He slid off the boulder into the unfamiliar gulch and continued to slide in the loose soil under a screen of manzanita cursing at the dust he kicked up. The helicopter cruised along the ridge top coming straight toward him. Paul crawled down a game trail into thicker cover and stopped in a fold of the hillside under a tangle of branches. He squatted with the rifle across his knees and leaned against the cool stone.

A big buck deer sat with legs folded some ten feet away with his antlers blending into the branches around him. His tawny coat matched the ocher soil of the hillside as his dark eyes stared at Paul and Paul stared back. They sat there in silence as the helicopter thudded overhead and his finger caressed the trigger of a rifle that grew heavier and heavier. The eyes of the deer were an abyss that deepened the longer he stared.

They remained there long after the helicopter's noise faded. Sunlight glowed on the slopes and the perfume of herbs filled the warming air.

Time stopped. When the sound of a pileated woodpecker banging on a snag brought him back with a jolt, he edged out of the hole and climbed the ridge with the deer's eyes upon him. Paul reached the top and stood on an outcropping of serpentine stone. He spread arms to the sun and laughed.

* * *

He descended to the highest terrace, leaned the rifle in the crotch of a madrone, and began to water the thriving plants. He trimmed leaves that were turning brown, working his way down from one patch to the next as the sun lit the little valley and the air warmed. Birds sang in two-part harmony as squirrels chattered in oaks claiming the best trees. Work was a relief and the solitude was even better. He thought of the being dwelling behind the deer's dark eyes and was grateful to be alive and alone. This experience was his own. Something he wouldn't. That he *couldn't* share.

His wounds itched fiercely and he fought the urge to scratch. He'd avoided catching a staph infection and now all he had to do was make sure he didn't tear off the scabs. The girls had gone twice to the big swimming hole in Takilma while he'd recuperated. He imagined the attention they generated. Darla said people were calling him a hero. He wanted to be with them the next time, risky or not. Paul closed his eyes and soaked up the sun as a goshawk called from a cedar snag. That interlude with the buck was something, a clear reminder of that different, more *real* world. The world people like Fauna lived in. He could share his experience with the deer with Fauna. The feeling he needed both the knowledge carried by being utterly alone and with the company of women spun within him as the two opposites sought some kind of balance. He wondered if they ever would.

While he watered the third patch, he heard footsteps through the leaves on the hillside. Paul turned off the water as Darla stepped out of the shade.

She tossed hair from her eyes. "Need some help?"

"Sure."

They worked in silence as the day brightened. Paul gazed at her with the sun in her hair. Darla: the girl who'd jumped on his back in Ucluelet, loved him in an abandoned house by the sea, and snatched him away from all he knew in the seventeenth summer of his life.

She smiled back.

He began to think about her having his baby and what their child would look like. Words like *forever* came into his mind. He shook his head to clear the thought but it came back stronger. She glanced up and the freckles on the bridge of her nose twitched as Paul said he loved her without words. He imagined his eyes were the buck's speaking from an ancient fold of the mountains in a voice as old as time while gazing in approval at the lineage that would issue from their union.

He was about to tell her about the deer when the sound of vehicles broke their peace. He could make out three as they approached the old homestead. He heard the door of the school bus open and imagined Rayella stepping out.

Car doors slammed and Paul stiffened as the tone of a voice told him in no uncertain terms that it was the law. Rayella spoke but he couldn't make out the words and a man's voice spoke again.

Paul heard him say Cindy.

They knew!

"Oh… fuck!"

Darla gasped. They ducked under the bushes and watched four cops jump the creek and cross the meadow. Rayella and Cindy were caught and at the mercy of the law.

The *thok-thok* of the helicopter returned. Darla let out a moan as their world scattered to the winds and they crouched under the blue leaves of manzanita. Was he going back to Charleston or jail?

Was Darla going away forever?

Paul grabbed Darla's hand and they sprinted up the canyon.

* * *

They passed the waterhole Chuck had blasted and clambered and crawled through thickets along the creek. Yellowjackets screamed past their heads as they brushed spider webs off their faces. Deer burst from the brush and bounded away with a black and white flash of tails. The sound of the helicopter thumped overhead twice and they huddled under bushes until it faded. He stumbled upon a rattlesnake and slung it buzzing into the brush with the barrel of the rifle. Darla paused for a moment, wiped her face, and hurried on beside him.

Two hours later they came upon a fire road and stopped by a culvert. The dirt road looked like paradise after fighting their way through vines and brambles but it offered the threat of being spotted from the air, a vehicle or someone on foot. They hunkered under the cover of hazel bushes and tried to collect their thoughts.

Darla's cheeks were scratched and red, her forehead was beaded with sweat, and she had leaves in her hair.

He laughed.

She swiped hair off a damp cheek and snarled. "What the fuck's so funny?"

"Remember when we first got together?"

Darla's cheeks bulged before she began to shake with laughter and put hands to her mouth. "It was just some redneck loggers then. Now we got a whole fuckin' army after us." She caught her breath, "Guess we stepped up." She kicked at a rock and coughed. "God I'm thirsty."

"Not what we expected when we headed for Frisco huh?"

"What's gonna happen to Rayella and Cindy?"

"Cindy's going back to Minnesota. It's too late for the Olympics and she's probably in a world of shit. It could be for the reward that those guys showed up for all I know. Maybe they don't even know about us. I don't know about Rayella. She's a good talker and she's legal age. I hope she's not going to jail." He tore off the branch of a viney maple and yanked at the green strip of bark holding it to the trunk. Two of his best friends in the world were just *gone,* half the lovers he'd had in his whole life, and there was nothing in the world he could do about it. "What about your truck?"

"The pink slip's in the glove box but my name's not on it. Chuck never put his name on it either. He uses fake I.D. anyway so I don't know how they'll connect it to me. I'll leave it if I have to." She wiped her palms on her jeans. "So do we follow the road?"

"I don't know. They can spot us from the air if we do."

"Yeah but we're way up here now. Wherever that is." She glanced up the road to where it topped a saddle in the ridge and disappeared over the other side. "I wonder where this goes?"

"Over to Thompson Creek."

"What's there?"

"Thompson Creek."

She began to laugh, but it came out a croak.

"Gus said we can take it to the Caves Highway and go to China Gardens."

"If we can get my truck, you mean. I'm not hiking."

"We can try after dark."

"You think we can walk on the road?"

"We'll duck out if we hear trucks or planes."

"What if they've got dogs? Do you think they're even searching? I mean, they got the pot obviously," Darla glanced down the canyon, "and Rayella and Cindy. God I love those guys."

"Probably not, I mean they're probably not still searching. I didn't hear any dogs and Rayella and Cindy wouldn't say shit." He shook his head. "This sucks!"

"Let's go back after dark. I've got the keys to the truck in my pocket and I'm fucking dying of thirst. Maybe we can just get our shit and go and we can hide out at Fauna's or something."

"I don't think Hope Mountain's a good idea, or Takilma either. That's where the heat is."

"I went up to Sunny Ridge on Althouse Creek and saw Sunshine with Lisa from China Gardens. She had her baby girl and invited us up there to stay in her teepee. Maybe we're supposed to go there."

"I guess that's as good a plan as any." Paul put an arm around her and flinched as her hand contacted the abrasion on his shoulder.

"Sorry baby." She stood up and swiped at the dust on her face. "I'm glad we're together anyway."

He rose to his feet. "And back in the bushes."

"I guess we haven't come that far at all."

"Nope." He closed his eyes and saw those of the deer. They were replaced by the blood red eyes of the woman beside the pond, then the golden ones of the Cheshire Cat gazing down from the forest of his dreams. "But it's a zillion miles."

* * *

They hiked down the road in the late afternoon heat stopping to drink at every trickle of water. Once they heard a vehicle and scampered into the brush. It was a green sheriff's jeep with two deputies in it. The jeep climbed to the saddle above them where the deputies glassed both sides with binoculars and returned. Paul and Darla sat for another fifteen minutes after they left and continued down. When they neared their erstwhile home, they observed from cover on the hill above. A single jeep was parked in the yard. Hours passed as they leaned against a boulder in whispered conversation.

Darla endured the wait without complaint except for the occasional mention of water. They had nothing to do and kept moving with the shade. She made patterns in the gravel with the heels of her sneakers and yawned. "How's your scabs?"

"Still there." He ran a hand down the barrel of the .30.30. He wasn't going to shoot it out with cops, but the rifle had become a part of him that he didn't want to give up either. "Think Gus got busted?"

"I don't know. How else would they know about this place?"

"Gus would never tell. Lots of people came up that road. Maybe it was for Cindy, or maybe that fucking Terry guy told them. She said she saw him on the road, remember?"

"Well, if Gus got busted I guess you can keep the gun."

"Why?"

"His old lady Joyce said he skipped parole in California. She said he stole a new rig to get home from Berkeley last week and that he drove it into a mine shaft and blew up the tunnel. If he's busted he's probably going down for a while."

"Oh." Paul closed his eyes and the buck was there staring back at him. "When I was hiding from that helicopter, I—"

"What?"

"I was with this great big buck under the bushes and we just hung out. He was the biggest deer I've ever seen, like something out of... I don't know, I never thought of shooting him. It was like a visitation or something."

"Maybe it was a spirit. I guess if you killed him you would have been all bloody and had to haul him back, and we would have been cutting him up when the Man came and we would have got busted."

"Yeah, we would have been at the goat dairy and busted for poaching and been fucked."

"So maybe he showed up to keep you from coming back, like a messenger."

"Yeah. Like a guardian spirit or something."

She yawned. "Fauna has a guardian too. She says a goddess gave her that pendant. Oh, she told Mel she laid you." The waxing shadows of night made Darla's face a mask in the dusk and he couldn't read her expression. She chuckled. "Paul, Fauna told me she laid you days ago."

"Oh."

Her fingers wound in his and she raised their hands to stare over the knuckles. "And I laid Mel. It was kind of a trade Fauna set up to balance out the karma so he wouldn't be pissed."

"Oh."

"She kinda built it up for me so I had to try him. We thought it was the right thing to do." Darla shrugged. "Seemed fair. It's kinda funny you were always freaking out about me going off and you were the one that did it although that's what guys do, but we have a lot more serious shit to deal with. You were just acting like a guy and I did the same 'cause I'm a free soul too, so does it matter?"

He leaned against the lichen on the side of the boulder and stared at the sky as the silhouette of a whippoorwill bounced past a rising Venus and glided over the homestead in the soft air. "No, I mean yes but not really. I've had it my way a lot I guess."

"Sure have. Know what?"

"What?"

"You're way better. Maybe 'cause of love." She chuckled. "We always seem to come back together, and in this world that's pretty amazing."

"Yeah, we do."

"We could stay at my mom's in San Diego if we have to. She'll even give me one of her cars I bet. You'd dig Black's Beach and we can cruise in a convertible."

The sound of an engine ended their conversation and they rose to peer down at the yard. The jeep was pulling out on the fire road and they ducked as headlights flashed through the trees. The jeep disappeared down the road and the night grew darker.

Darla began to rise, but he grabbed her arm and pulled her back down. "Wait."

Sure enough, the jeep returned, pulled down into the yard and stopped. A spotlight flashed on the old house, across Darla's truck, the bus and both ends of the barn. The jeep sat idling for a while and left again.

"Think they're really gone?"

"Let's wait a little longer."

After a half hour they clambered down the hill. Bozo greeted them joyfully and tugged at his chain, where he was tied to a tree. Paul released him and Darla got a flashlight from her truck. The bus was locked, but she was slim enough for Paul to boost her through the driver's side window after yanking on the glass.

"What a fucking mess! They trashed everything!" Her voice echoed from inside the bus as she fumbled with something until she let out a long gasp. "Oh God that's good!"

Darla handed an open quart of beer out the window. Paul had a hard time not drinking it all at once. She opened the back door and he jumped in the bus. They stuffed bread and cheese in their mouths, gathered their things, and threw their packs out the back. She tossed a bag of dog food out and they climbed down and shut the door. Darla dropped the tailgate of the old Chevy and Bozo jumped in without urging.

Storm snorted from the meadow and Darla sighed. "We can't do shit about the horse. Bye-bye goat dairy. Let's get truckin'."

XXV.
Sucker Creek

The road over the mountains would have been bad enough in daylight. Every time they came to a fork, they stopped with the six-volt headlights illuminating twenty yards ahead and discussed which way to go. Paul had to get out and guide her four times where the road's shoulder sloughed into a canyon.

At the forth washout Darla fought with the old manual transmission, popped the clutch, punched the steering wheel and screamed. They switched drivers and soon his arms were in spasms as he held the big wheel steady. The road narrowed further, and Paul squeezed the wheel and stared straight ahead. Darla yelped as they teetered along a cliff. There was nowhere to turn around, and he couldn't back up. "Shit, I hope this doesn't just end."

She slugged his arm. "Don't *say* that!"

They descended on a gravel road and turned right toward the Caves Highway. After more dark miles, they hit pavement and turned left toward the Oregon Caves and the road to Sucker Creek. The night was black and moonless and the Milky Way arced over the dark bulk of peaks and the tops of trees. They had to stop three times for herds of deer with their eyes glowing in the headlights. The does' eyes were green. The bucks' eyes went from yellow to orange and all the way to fiery red for the big ones. He thought of the buck in the bushes and saw those eyes blazing red like the woman who haunted his dreams. These mountains were a magical place.

"Why do deer's eyes do that here? I've seen deer eyes in the headlights all my life and they're always green."

"Fuck if I know. I hope the cops aren't looking for this truck."

"Everybody around here has one. I thought this one was parked on Hope Mountain last week and you were up at Mel's."

She squeezed his knee. "Yeah and it got you laid, and you cleaned out the gypsy camp with Fauna and now you're a big hero from following your dick."

He laughed. They'd been with other lovers but it hadn't ended anything. They had each other even if they were two fugitives on a dark night. "I love you more than ever."

Darla put a foot on the metal dash and stared through the two-piece windshield. Paul gazed at her profile as a passing vehicle illuminated the cab. Her hair went white for a moment before the shadows swallowed her. He put fingers to her lips and she kissed his fingertip. He massaged her neck and removed his hand to shift.

She yawned. "It was pretty amazing with Rayella and Cindy. I mean the whole trip. It was a cool friendship and we weren't jealous of each other at all. I've been competitive with other girls my whole life but it was like having two sisters. I never had a sister. I've never been in that space before. It's the only time I ever did that, I mean with three other people, and I know it was for you." She paused as the old engine rattled and settled back into tune. "But I guess people usually end up as couples in the end."

"Thanks for snatching me from a boring summer. Thanks for the whole thing. Even the scary parts."

She chuckled. "I'm the seducer."

"You sure are."

"God Paul, I hope Rayella isn't going to jail. She's the only one over eighteen."

"Me too."

She dug her fingers in his thigh. "You're a good man."

"Thanks."

"I'm happy with you. Right here. Right now."

Paul pushed the lump in his throat down and downshifted as the road returned to gravel.

She laughed. "At least for now."

"Afraid of commitment or something?"

"Dude, that's what girls say."

"I know."

"Okay I'm happy for real. I'm not looking for anybody else. If we can get out of here and get our shit together who knows? Good things happen and our karma's still pretty clean I hope."

The engine grew louder. Paul pulled over and grabbed the flashlight, the can of oil and a funnel and opened the hood. He emptied the oil into the engine, slammed the hood, threw the can in the bed, and jumped in. "That's the last. We need more."

"Let's just get to China Gardens." She rubbed his thigh. "I don't want this to be our last night together."

He kissed her. "Every night could be our last." He ground the starter and the engine rumbled to life. Soon the road forked with a sign for the Oregon Caves on the left and a gravel road to the right.

Darla directed him onto the gravel one. "I came up here after I ran into Sunshine at Sunny Ridge and we went swimming but the water's pretty cold. The swimming hole in Takilma is a bummer with all the cops. I think they keep going there just to stare at naked chicks." She leaned forward and peered into the yellow cone of light ahead. "Keep an eye out for... there."

Two old trucks were parked on the shoulder of the road. Paul squeezed behind them and killed the engine. The sounds of water came from below wafted on a cool breeze. Bozo bounced out of the truck bed, trotted to a trail that descended into darkness, wagged his tail and looked at them expectantly.

"He knows this place."

"Yeah." He grabbed the packs and Darla locked the truck. "Should I bring the gun?"

"That might freak them out. They're all peace and love veggies here so stash it behind the seat."

"Time for astrology shit. I hope they aren't always eating lentils. I hate lentils."

"You never even asked me my sign."

"Nope."

"It's Virgo."

He laughed. "I was the virgin."

Darla led the way down. The flashlight was none too bright and they stumbled over roots and when a switchback pivoted around a rock. The ground grew damp and the sound of the creek grew louder. Dogs barked at Bozo's arrival somewhere below and their voices echoed off trees. A sliver of moon had risen reflecting off the creek's water, gravel bars, and mounds of rock piled up by long-ago Chinese labor. He could make out a fenced garden, outbuildings and the conical shape of a teepee in the glow of kerosene lamps from the windows of a building. A trapezoid of yellow light spread its illumination across a plank porch as a door opened to illuminate a chopping block and child's tricycle.

"Yo!" came from a silhouette in the doorway.

"Hey, it's Darla and Paul."

"Welcome."

A bare-chested young man with a halo of frizzy hair and jeans barely held up by slim hips stood on the porch with a bamboo bong in his hand. "Want a toke?"

"Darla!" A girl's voice called.

A woodstove gave out a sigh as the logs within shifted, and a plume of red sparks rattled up the stovepipe and over the roof. Paul helped Darla take off her pack, shucked out of his own, and leaned them against the wall.

Refuge.

A much slimmer Sunshine hugged them both. "Meet Summer." She held up an infant that opened big brown eyes and made sucking motions. Sunshine put her to a swollen breast and Summer latched on. "I named her Summer 'cause she came at noon on the hottest day of the year. I sleep in the house at night. You guys can sleep in the teepee but be careful. I found a scorpion on the liner and I can't have the baby sleeping there."

Darla made a face. "Yuck."

"Thanks."

"Oh Paul, this is Rick O'Shay and Laura."

The frizzy-haired guy waved them to the couch. He picked up a half-gallon wine bottle from the table, offered it to Paul, sat back down, and ran his free hand down Laura's thigh. "We got tons of room. This is the emptiest the place has been all summer. Everybody's freakin' out since those killings in Takilma and people have moved out to their patches so they don't get seen coming and going and are doing the guerrilla thing. Clint almost drowned crossing the creek yesterday from his patch, 'cause he thought the Man might be watching his regular ford."

Laura played with the buttons of Rick's Levis. "And Chuck's still freaking over the rip-offs who stole his seven Indica plants. He think's it's Red Hawk."

Rick shook his head. "It wasn't Red Hawk. Chuck thinks that just because they wore moccasins like Red Hawk."

Paul took a gulp of wine and passed it to Darla. His head spun with exhaustion and her head wobbled on her shoulders. "Is that where Chuck's patch is?"

Rick nodded. "He's got that place wired like Vietnam with tripwires and shit." He shook his head. "Bad karma. I don't like it at all. We got enough heat around here and there ain't even anything growing on this side of the creek."

"It must have been a trip when they were mining here."

"Yeah, with about a zillion Chinese. Think of all the rice that got ate on this creek a hundred years ago. We could live for another hundred years on it. I found nine opium bottles in an old trash heap and traded 'em to Chuck for some gree-gree."

"Gree-gree?"

"Yeah, it's a potion he makes for parties. It's peyote and hashish in pure grain alcohol with some other shit he says is secret. Sure puts you on your ass."

"Does anybody mine gold?"

"Gold Dollar Dave does up the creek. Him and Martha are working the old Gold Dollar claim and live in the cabin. It's about the oldest cabin in this part of the world. He's found some big nuggets."

"I'd like to live in that cabin."

"You always say that Laura but you don't want to walk that far." Rick turned to Paul. "It's from eighteen fifty-two and made out of big old logs. Oughta last another hundred-twenty years I bet."

Sunshine burped Summer and returned her to her breast to nurse. The wine, the hard day, and the sound of the baby suckling were making Paul's eyes close. He rubbed them, but they felt glued shut.

"Wanta crash?"

Paul glanced at Darla, who was fast asleep on the couch, and nodded. Rick lit a kerosene storm lantern and handed it to Paul and he managed to shake her awake. She mumbled and sat up.

Paul nodded. "Thanks a lot."

"No problemo. You got a gun?"

"I left it in the truck so you guys wouldn't freak out."

"Oughta get it in the morning."

* * *

He rose through a leaden shroud of sleep to stare past a bundle of teepee poles at a blue sky between smoke flaps. The sounds of the creek melded with the songs of birds as the shadows of leaves dappled the cone of canvas overhead and danced when a breeze caught them. An empty crib of bent red willow branches hung from the poles and swung gently to the shifting of the teepee. He yawned, spooned against Darla's warm ass, inhaled the scent of her hair and kissed the nape of her neck as she made lovely sounds in the cradle of his arms.

Paul climbed off the bed, threw open the door flap of the teepee, and walked out with the creek's breath caressing his skin. He pissed in the grass and fought the urge to scratch a scab on his shoulder.

Over in the garden Laura's back was a warm bronze amongst hues of green. She brushed back long dark hair, put down a trowel, and waved.

He yawned again and waved back.

They hadn't planned anything beyond escaping and had been far too exhausted to think when they'd fallen asleep. Paul stretched and cracked his back. A baby squealed from the far side of the garden and he spotted Sunshine's auburn hair beyond a pea trellis.

What now?

Going with the flow had been all there was while things were great, when pretty girls were popping out of the woodwork and Gus was giving them money. Now, they had to have a plan. He hadn't planned anything since meeting Darla. He'd just let things happen. If they managed to stay here, or somewhere else, what would happen when winter came? How would they get by?

Sunshine approached with Summer in her arms. "Hungry?"

Paul nodded.

"There's some oatmeal and tea in the house and some good bread Laura baked and honey."

"Thanks." Paul retrieved the rifle from the truck, returned to the teepee, slid under the blankets beside Darla, and buried his face in her hair. No matter what happened, no matter how long he lived, he'd always know her scent. He closed his eyes and drifted to a luminous world where something scampered and grinned from the trees.

* * *

A breeze off a field of flowers caressed his skin as it rose and fell with the breath of someone kneeling over him. A red sun rose in the distance and an endless plane of flowers unfurled their blossoms across the sky. Soft laughter rippled the air around him as soft lips found his own. Darla's blue eyes were staring into his own, became golden like the Cheshire Cat's, and grew the color of blood as he entered her. They shuddered as their union grew until every cell of their bodies merged in endless orgasm and they cried out with all their beings for time to stop.

Something erupted inside her in a flash of light and a sun blossomed in the darkness of her womb.

XXVI.
Bad Boys and Booby Traps

"Yo!"

The afternoon sun cast a silhouette on the teepee's canvas of a tall figure holding a rifle with a curved magazine.

Paul grabbed the .30-.30 with a jolt of fear that subsided as he recognized the voice. "Hey Chuck."

Darla sat on the edge of the bed eyes wide. He ran a hand down the hollow of her back and the tension bled out of her muscles. She produced a string of yawns, opened her mouth to speak and another yawn came out.

"You guys gonna sleep all day?"

"What time is it?"

"Shit man, it's afternoon."

"We had kind of a hard day."

"I heard."

Darla rubbed her eyes. "How?"

"Gus got busted and Joyce asked me to check on his shit. I went over, cased the goat dairy, and you guys were cleared out with the patches all torn up. Things majorly suck in the whole valley. What happened to Rayella and Cindy?"

"They're gone." Darla threw a blanket over her shoulders. "Come in."

Chuck bent his tall frame through the door of the teepee, placed a Mini 14 Carbine on the carpet, and folded his long legs as he sat down.

Paul rubbed his eyes. "We don't know what happened to them. We went over the back way last night after hiding all day in the woods and never saw 'em again after the cops came."

Chuck thumbed hashish into a red stone pipe and lit it with a Zippo lighter. He puffed a thick white cloud and passed it to Darla. "You can bet when they heard about the reward for that gymnast you won't be seeing her cute ass anymore." He pulled a twig from the laces of his moccasins. "Things are fucked-up. They didn't get any of my patches though. At least not yet."

"That's cool."

Chuck's dour expression morphed to a sunburned grin. "Brother, I love what you and Fauna did to those assholes at the gypsy camp. Too bad you didn't finish the fuckers off. What's with the scabs?"

"I got in a fight hitchhiking with this big redneck logger Terry."

"Terry Cox?"

Paul nodded.

"That motherfucker's an animal. You shoulda killed him too. He shoots up acid and coke and goes on rampages and nobody stops him. I know this chick who got raped by him whose dad's a logger. The old man's been here all his life, shit, he was a god-damn Marine and he's still afraid to call him out." Chuck shook his head. "I'd kill the guy if he hurt me or mine if it took forever." He laughed. "Brother, you got nine lives if you're still walkin'. He's gotta outweigh you by eighty pounds." Chuck gazed at shadows dancing on the teepee canvas and shook his head. "What are you guys gonna do?"

"We don't know."

Darla passed the pipe. "Maybe go to Arizona or Canada."

"How will you get across the border?"

"It's easy."

Chuck turned to Paul. "Might as well relax here. You never know about tomorrow. Hey Paul, wanta see one of my patches?"

"Sure."

Darla yawned for the hundredth time and flopped on the bed. "You go. I'm not doing shit today."

Chuck's eyes lingered between her legs before he levered his gaze back to Paul. "I could use some help. My patch across the creek is pretty well done 'til harvest but I lost a good partner to the law on another yesterday. Wanta see my bomb?"

Paul felt the laugh boiling up before it reached his mouth. "Sure."

If he was going to be an outlaw, he might as well learn what it was like to go all the way.

* * *

After wolfing a few slices of homemade bread and honey washed down with herbal tea, Paul was ready for the hike to Chuck's patch.

"I drive in off a fire road from Althouse Creek. There's a whole wide bench with good exposure, a couple square miles. Only me and Clint are usin' it." Chuck led him across Sucker Creek on the slippery rocks by hanging onto a rusting cable strung from the trees. "Nobody tries this in the winter!" He shouted over the roar of the creek.

"I see why!" Paul shouted back as he balanced on the slippery rocks with the rifle in one hand.

They hiked up a steep slope, crossed an old clear-cut peppered with twenty-year-old firs and broad-leafed trees and hiked toward a ridge. The drone of an airplane sent them into the bushes and they sat smoking hash and drinking from Chuck's canteen as it flew over.

Chuck got up when it passed. "Me and Clint are growin' some killer sensi bud. Clint back-crossed Big's polyploid Oaxacan Sativa with Afghani Indica. It's got pretty pink-hair buds and it kicks everybody's ass."

"Sensi?"

"Sensimilla. Seedless pot. Monster bucks."

"Oh."

"People in L.A. pay six bills a pound for it."

Paul's mouth dropped open and he swatted at a fly that sought to investigate. "Six hundred bucks?"

"Yeah, the very best seeded stuff only goes for one-fifty, maybe two."

"Six hundred bucks. What a trip."

"We better shut up and listen. We're gettin' close." Chuck motioned Paul to his right and circled in the trees on the left.

Paul did on the right. What would he do if they ran into the law? It depended on what the law did he supposed. He didn't live around here. He didn't live *anywhere,* and he could just sneak off with Darla.

What if they start shooting?

If someone were going to shoot him, he'd have to stop them even if it meant shooting them. He guessed he *would* shoot, which would be fucked. If it were that asshole cop named Queen, who wasn't worth spit, he'd probably enjoy it. Then he'd really be an outlaw. He tried to imagine people calling him a killer. He saw Susan Allen, his erstwhile dream girl, watching some cop on TV announcing that he'd been caught and charged with murder.

To hell with it. They'd never catch him alive.

"Shhhhh!" Chuck held a finger to his lips and motioned toward some bright green seven-foot pot plants in the clearing beyond. He pointed to a log that had a light switch nailed to it before he bent down and flipped it. "That disarms the bomb. Otherwise, you hit a trip wire... and *boom!*"

"Oh." Paul saw a battery and more wires under the log. "Did you do this by yourself?"

"Michael helped me wire it for fun. We were both in Nam."

"Which Michael?"

"The one who was in the Green Berets." Chuck stood up. "There's two live tripwires of monofilament fishing line and about twenty fake ones to scare the shit outta rip-offs if they come back." He pointed to a sign in the middle of the patch: **If You Can Read This You're To Close! This Patch is Mined, Motherfucker!** "Don't hit *any* of the wires."

"Okay. You left out the second 'o' in too."

"So the fuck what?" Chuck laughed. "They can fix it after they get wasted."

The plants were thicker and greener than those Paul and the girls tended, being better fertilized in richer ground. They were all females and loaded with pink and white flowers. A camouflage tarp was on the other side of the patch draped from the trees over a hibachi barbecue, a pup tent and two folding chairs.

Chuck lifted a small fir tree out of a log frame over what Paul thought was solid ground to reveal a flash of sky reflected in water filling a circular well. "See how round the shaft is? Shaped charges. I love dynamite." He grinned. "We hit water ten feet down and it rose right to the top. Just six half-sticks of rock powder and a lotta diggin'."

"Cool."

"Watch out! That's a live wire. We'd be fucked if I didn't disarm the bomb." Chuck pointed to a head-high cedar stump in the middle of the patch. "It's there under the bark: a gallon jug of rock salt with a half-stick in it." He chuckled. "*Boom!*" That'll sting the shit outta 'em. Maybe even blind 'em."

"Shit."

"If that rip-off comes back, he'll be hurtin' I'll tell ya that." Chuck pointed to an empty patch of ground where seven hacked-off stalks about two inches in diameter protruded from the earth. "See those? Those were the only pure Indicas I had and the motherfucker took 'em."

"What if somebody else sets the bomb off, or a deer?"

"Naw," Chuck shook his head, "I bought panther piss from Idaho and put it on the trees to keep deer away and I don't use fish fertilizer so the bears don't come in here. Ain't nobody 'round here 'cept growers. If they're honest they got nothin' to worry about."

"I guess there's no dogs allowed."

"Nope." Chuck ran a hand over a sunburned forehead. "Wanta help me water?"

"Sure."

There was a water line buried from a pond up the hill with a hose coiled at a faucet like the patches by the goat dairy. The fittings were identical since Chuck had set up Gus's system too. Chuck said the well in the middle of the patch was kept as insurance for when the pond dried up. "It's a shitload of labor but it's worth it. Last year the water was gone by August and this whole fuckin' patch died before I could dig a well."

"You lost everything?"

"Yep but I had three more. Never put all your dope in one basket. Bought a fifty-four Powerwagon last fall and had a good winter runnin' back and forth between Frisco and Portland in my VW. This year's gonna be way better if the Man don't find my patches. My old lady Sherrill is counting on it. She wants a baby." He lit a cigarette. "Live and learn, bro. The great mandala turns, and you either ride or get run over."

Paul let water soak into the ground at the base of a plant before he picked up the hose and carefully moved it to the next one. "You've got a lot invested."

"A whole year's income. You can live pretty good off the grid with no laws and no bullshit and no fuckin' taxes. I can't use my real name anyway 'cause they got a warrant for me in Virginia and one in the Virgin Islands too. It's better here anyway." Chuck grinned. "And there sure is a lotta pussy."

Paul nodded.

"And you're still with Darla after that shit came down. I didn't think a little beach bunny like her would stick to be honest. You got good karma. Most bitches skedaddle when the shit hits the fan."

"We love each other."

"That's good, but you were doin' Cindy and Rayella too right?"

"Uh, yeah."

"Fuckin' excellent."

"It just happened. It wasn't like I was planning it or anything. It was their idea."

"You're seventeen, right?"

"Yeah."

"Man you got a future. You done more shit already than a dozen of these lazy bastards who show up from the city and just hang out at the store or the swimmin' hole or rip off other peoples' shit. Punks. There's a few of 'em sleepin' in mine shafts around here you can bet. We could go in partners next year on a patch. Maybe two. It takes a lot of packin' and a strong back but I know you can handle it. Gus thinks you're pretty Skookum and he's the real deal." Chuck motioned him into the shade of the tarp and they sat on the folding chairs. He stuffed his pipe with hash and lit it. "Shit, anybody who can get down with Terry Cox and walk away from it *has* to be. That motherfucker's a killer."

"Doing some patches with you would be cool, but we need somewhere to live in the meantime."

"I know places. You can stay with me and my old lady in O'Brien if you want and I know a place that's goin' empty on Waldo Road where the people got busted for some warrant. I know the miner who owns it and he'll let somebody stay there just to keep his shit from gettin' ripped off. You never do anything there and keep it clean and just tend your patches in the woods. I'll let you dry it at my place. I got a big attic and I know you can handle a gun and hold your mud 'cause of that shit at the gypsy camp." Chuck grinned. "Hey… did you lay Fauna too?"

"Um, yeah."

"Fuckin' outstanding. I never got one word outta her myself and you laid her." Chuck produced a tiny green opium bottle sealed with a cork and filled with a thick black liquid. "My greegree."

"Rick O'Shay told me about that."

"Here, have one for your old lady too." Chuck handed him a small brown bottle along with the green one.

"Thanks."

"We're goin' partners on a patch okay?"

"Okay."

Chuck shook hands and headed up the ridge to his truck.

* * *

Paul hiked back to China Gardens dreaming of pot plants, pretty girls and lunch. He tied his shirt around his waist, stopped to pick blackberries off a tangle of vines, and sat on a log with the gun across his lap gazing at the hills. Here it was a day after disaster and they already had an opportunity for a new year. Things had come down like a hurricane to sweep up Rayella and Cindy yet had deposited him and Darla on a new shore. They were like spirits of the forest awaiting the new age. Pot should be legal in a few short years and he ought to take advantage of what was offered while he could. He should have trusted in karma.

Fauna was right. *Nothing lasts.* He didn't know how to be unattached like everybody claimed was the way to some kind of enlightenment but she sure was right about karma and trusting your hunter's spirit, and if he really *was* a mirror of the world around him, it sure paid to be living in nature. Who'd want to be a mirror of dog shit on the streets of the Haight Ashbury?

He carefully obliterated the tracks made by his shredded sneakers on any bare ground he crossed. The moccasins many of the growers wore left only soft depressions and he wanted some. Everyone said Lisa made them, who was living somewhere around here in a teepee, and he had to meet her. She was probably cute. It seemed every girl in this part of the world was. He drifted to thoughts of Darla until the sharp caw of a crow made him freeze and the hair rose on the back of his neck. Paul heard claws scampering on bark, and a vision of blood red eyes and a Cheshire grin flashed in his mind as he caressed the pistol grip of the .30-.30.

"Y'all Paul?" The voice came from a tangled mass of young maples and a figure with long auburn hair braided to his waist wearing a battered cowboy hat rose out of the bushes. He flashed a grin that exposed a hole where four top teeth were missing, uncocked a Browning lever action rifle, and tipped his hat.

"Uh, yeah."

"Ah'm Clint. Ain't good manners to scare folks but it's fun practice."

First Fauna had snuck up on him and now this guy Clint. "Yeah. Chuck mentioned you."

"Damn well better. Ah'm the one who turned him onto the seeds and this territory. Betcha he didn't tell ya that."

"He said something about seeds."

Clint bounced down the embankment on the fallen trunks of trees and was at Paul's side. "Headin' to China Gardens myself. Think them cute little veggie chicks 'ill cook us up a deer?"

"My girl eats meat."

"Good." Clint fell into step beside him with his rifle slung on his shoulder and lit up a joint as thick as his thumb. "All this heat from those killins gonna weed out the lightweights and leave things to the real growers come fall."

"Think so?"

"Know so. They're the ones easy to spot. Them fat cops like to score a few easy ones and stay away from breakin' a sweat. They're scared as shit off-road. Saw the FBI turn tail and run last week on Josephine Creek when me and Terrible Tommy stood up on a rock just to get a better view of 'em."

"Terrible Terry?"

"Tommy. Them Feds tore the oil pan outta their International Scout and had to hoof it over Tennessee Gap. We got a whole new set a' tires and some ammo off it, and a radio they took to Sebastopol Creek and hooked to the battery from Scout to listen to their conversations. Fuckin' pussies stuffed in suits." He shook his head. "Who in hell would go into the back country in a suit anyway? If they used Indian trackers or mountain folk, we'd all be fucked." He put a hand on Paul's shoulder. "Heard about you and Fauna takin' out the gypsy camp. That's some Skookum shit." Clint tipped his battered hat as he watched a pileated woodpecker hopping up a snag.

"It felt like something we had to do."

Clint nodded. "It's good to show humility. Always let other people do your braggin', 'specially 'round women." He put a hand on Paul's shoulder and gave him a gap-toothed grin. "Mystery makes 'em horny."

"Does everybody around here know about us and the gypsy camp?"

"Jus' 'bout, but that's the kinda stuff makes things easy. People talk about whatever goes on and you're gettin' a good reputation so don't worry." Clint shook his head. "'Course a couple people gettin' kilt and beheaded is big news anywhere. Sure makes the rest of us look like fuckin' maniacs. The straight folks can't tell the good from the bad as long as guys got long hair and girls don't wear bras. You seen the Oregonian? It's in the Frisco paper too. Shit, it's probably in the New York Times. People getting' beheaded gets peoples' attention but nobody who knows anything will tell the Man 'bout you. You're the good guy, and if the bums who hang around the stores say something nobody 'ill believe 'em anyway." He stroked a copper-colored mustache. "Mountain folk stick together." Clint squinted at the rocky crags overhead. "Nobody could ever control mountain folk whether it's in the Appalachians or Afghanistan. The Man should know by now but he never quits tryin'."

"Freedom pisses the Man off."

Clint scratched his beard. "Chuck invited you as a partner?"

"Yeah."

"See? You paid your dues and things are gonna get better."

"I guess so."

"There's not many places a man can live free. That's why Ah love this country. It's all hills and hollers with ol' mines for hidin' shit and good pot growin' soil, and these mines are real holes in the ground. Not like the goddamn mines where Ah'm from what tore the hell outta the mountains and just hauled 'em away. Hear of the flood last February?"

"What flood?"

"Back in West Virginia. The fuckin' Buffalo Mine dam full a' coal slurry burst and took out whole damn towns. They're still findin' bodies. Ah had cousins in West Logan downstream. Used to go to my aunt's place and climb in an ol' peach tree in her yard with my cousin Nadine. Prettiest girl you ever saw. Taught me to kiss. She had a hair up her ass to be a doctor. She fixed me up one time when I fell off a train tressel and cut my arm and we were a hell of a hike back in the hills. Goddamn angel and now she's gone. That 'ol tree's gone. The whole fuckin' town and the farm's gone and my aunt and cousins too." Clint spat through the hole in his teeth. "Goddamn coal companies treat folks like their niggers. Fuck 'em. My people got a heritage of fightin' the Man but they took the fuckin' ground right out from under 'em. Never go back to live there even if there weren't a warrant out for me although I'd sure like to see folks."

Clint sighed. "To hell with it. There's gold here, good huntin', food stamps, good eatin' from the gardens, good cookin', good pot and good women. A man can make a livin' here, love the ladies, and maybe find some gold to keep his head straight."

"I don't want to live anywhere else."

"Mountains got a spirit. The souls of medicine men are in these mountains. They been waitin' for us." Clint gazed at the treetops. "It's the natural way for a man to have some room to get his head straight. Everything else is shit. Women are here to make a man feel good and a man's here to do the same for them. That's nature's way. I seen your woman. She's good material. Great kids come outta stock like that. You knock her up yet?"

"Not that I know of."

Their footsteps sent up a covey of quail and they paused to watch them disappear in the brush.

"But I love her."

"Got a couple kids in West Virginia Ah'm sendin' money to. The fuckin' government makes it a bitch 'cause they want me for growin' pot. Shit, they wanta get ya for *not* providin' and then try and get ya when ya do. Gotta mail cash and pass it roundabouts through relatives. Got me a great lookin' daughter in Bisbee off an Apache girl. Almost got busted last time comin' back 'cross the border from Naco to see her. Got a couple kids in Oregon too."

"Five kids? How old are you?"

"Twenty-four."

"That's a lot of kids."

"Yep." Clint tipped his hat, "How old are you?"

"Seventeen."

"Y'all got time pilgrim."

* * *

Bozo bounded to greet them as they crossed the creek. Paul stripped off his pants and stepped into a pond dammed with stones from the mining heaps to wash off the sweat. He jumped out shivering to the sounds of a guitar from the bunkhouse where the women were steaming vegetables and making a big salad. Darla had her hair tied in a ponytail and dumped sliced potatoes, carrots, broccoli and onions in a big pot. She wiped a strand away from a reddened face as he entered and gave him a smile.

Paul leaned the rifle against the wall, walked around the big wood stove, and kissed her moist cheek. "You look beautiful."

"Bullshit, but thanks."

"This is Clint."

Clint tipped a battered hat and slung his rifle on a peg.

"We met. Get me that vinegar off the shelf, would you?"

Paul took down a big bottle of vinegar from amongst jars of beans and sacks of flour. He handed it to Darla and she began mixing salad dressing in a ceramic bowl. A pretty young blonde with a curly-haired baby sat next to a guy with frayed blond braids holding the guitar. "This is Jane and Gabriel, and that's Gemini Bill."

Gemini Bill nodded and went back to strumming with his eyes on Darla.

Afterward they retired to the teepee while people drank wine on the porch. Having the private space was a luxury they weren't going to waste. Darla lit a lamp and Paul lay with hands behind his head watching her drop her clothes as her shadow rippled across the teepee liner. "Chuck invited me as a partner next year."

She slid onto the bed. "Maybe it's our karma."

"Clint's from West Virginia. The dude's like an Indian. He snuck up on me."

"That Gemini Bill guy said he wanted to ball me five minutes after he got here." She rolled on her back. "We should keep looking around. Let's check out Black Michael and Danielle's place. Nobody's even looking for us I bet."

"Gus said something about the Hupa reservation."

She stared at stars beyond the smoke flaps. "I don't know. Blondes always get hassled in places like that and you'd probably get into a fight. We got invited to Josephine Creek. Chuck says there's an old man who'll give us a mining claim if we work it."

"Bob Cutler?"

"Yeah."

"I'd like to meet him. Know something?"

"What?"

"You were really cute cooking dinner, being all domestic and shit."

"Don't expect me to do that all the time." Darla grabbed one of the teepee poles behind her head, stretched and arched her back off the blanket.

Paul put a hand between her breasts. Her heartbeat made the skin jump under his palm. He spread fingers across her belly and a sudden sensation made his hand jerk away as if burned, and he let out a gasp. His fingers returned to her stomach.

Her eyes widened. "What the fuck?"

"I—"

"I *know.*" She rolled on her stomach. "A baby." Darla rose on her elbows and her eyes bored into his. She rolled over and stared up through the smoke flaps. "I felt it too. Jesus."

XXVII.
The Wages

The days slowed. People didn't do that much at China Gardens besides play music, work in the garden and have sex, which was fine with Paul and Darla. They'd seen enough excitement for a while. Darla blended seamlessly as she assumed the mantle of a vegetarian carrying on conversations about astrology, organic gardening and babies as if she were born to it while working with Laura and Sunshine in the garden or cooking dinner. One morning on the porch, she held Summer to a nipple and pretended to be nursing until the baby squalled at the dry tap and she had to hand her back. Rick O'Shay hung with the girls for hours playing his flute and in the bunkhouse at night loading his bong. Paul found the routine boring and was glad to help out in Chuck's patch with a promise of reward in the fall that would give them something to get through the winter.

One afternoon Laura had an earache and asked Rick to piss into her ear claiming it was an organic method handed down by some Swami or other. Paul and Darla laughed themselves to sleep.

He awoke on the third morning from a dream of a girl with eyes like gems. When he tried to focus she disappeared. He lay staring up through the smoke flaps trying to remember. He got up and wandered into the woods and by noon he'd discovered four good spots for growing pot with southern exposure and water. He ate a meager lunch of granola and dried fruit under the trees, put some in a day-pack with toilet paper and a canteen, and hiked up Sucker Creek to the Gold Dollar claim, where he met Gold Dollar Dave and Martha.

Dave had cut into a bank under the roots of old growth Douglas firs to work along the bedrock and was hauling buck-et-loads of gravel and rocks to a cedar plank sluice box where he shoveled black sand that had collected for a million years into the riffles. "Funny country." He adjusted his sweat-stained headband over a shock of wild blond hair. "There's igneous stuff with gold, and there's copper, chromium, platinum, nickel and lead all over these mountains but that ridge right there is all limestone from the bottom of the ocean and some has turned to marble. That's how the Oregon Caves formed." He shook his head. "These moun-tains are fuckin' amazing. Uplift twisted 'em and they rose like a corkscrew. Ever notice deer's eyes in the headlights?"

"I sure did. The bucks' eyes are like fire."

"It's from the heavy elements. It's like they're radioactive or something."

"Do the caves have any other entrances besides at the monument?"

"Sure. Even ones nobody's found I bet. The Takilma Indians used to hide out in 'em. There's one up there I found," Dave pointed to the ridge above them, "right along that creek that comes down on the left side there's a cave that connects I bet." He shrugged. "I went in about a hundred yards. There's some Indian drawings on the walls but no gold." He returned to shoveling gravel.

Martha looked like a frontier wife from the nineteenth cen-tury in her gingham dress and long hair. She offered Paul chamo-mile tea she'd brewed on a cast iron stove in the ancient cabin. He drank a cup, thanked her, and headed up the ridge.

After an hour's hike through the mossy trunks of old growth firs, he found the cave: a dark mouth birthing a little creek with the breath of night wafting from the bowels of the mountain. The purple-black trunk of an ancient yew spread its limbs around the entrance in an embrace and he examined a limb that looked like it would make a bow.

He went in until he couldn't see and lit a match. On the wall was a tall figure scratched into the limestone holding something he imagined looked like a pot plant surrounded by spirals, the outline of human hands and a circle divided into four quarters. What a place to do peyote.

* * *

He stepped out of the cave and headed up Sucker Creek toward the high country. Three hours later he reached an emerald lake, stripped off his sweat-dampened clothes, and dove in. Paul exploded to the surface with a howl and climbed out shivering to sit on a boulder and dry off. He smoked a joint while listening to the cry of a hawk amongst the crags. Paul stretched out on the rock, yawned, and closed his eyes.

* * *

He awoke when the sun dipped behind the peaks and pulled on his pants. It was a long hike back and he hurridly grabbed his things and headed down. Two hours later he was stumbling along Sucker Creek in the shadow of the mountains when he came around a copse of young willows. A black bear sow was in his path with three cubs. She stood on her hind legs and gave a snort of alarm. Their eyes met for an endless moment before she ordered her cubs into the brush and disappeared.

The gold dollar cabin had smoke rising from its stove. He crossed Sucker Creek in the near-dark and reached China Gardens as the last light touched the peak of Big Grayback.

Darla stood in front of the tipi with a tattered Pendleton blanket around her shoulders. She didn't speak as he approached but dropped the blanket and threw her bare body against him with a cry of relief. "You were gone all day."

He kissed her. "I am so hungry." He said, fighting an urge to bite her throat.

* * *

Paul spent the evening eating and wanted meat.

He acquired four peyote buttons from Gemini Bill and the next morning arose in the dark. Starting a fire to boil them into tea took too much time, so he cut the downy silver hairs off them that he'd been warned to avoid, sliced them, and forced them down with copious draughts of cold creek water while trying to stay humble as Fauna had advised so he wouldn't puke. It tasted so bad that it wasn't hard. He did a little ceremony for the spirit of a deer Fauna had taught him, checked the .30-.30, and struck out in the dark with his stomach making noises. Soon a familiar glow began to rise from the vegetation and the earth beneath his feet. The forest breathed, and he heard plants sigh as they flexed their roots in the ground. He came to a dewy meadow as the first light of dawn began to touch Big Grayback Mountain over the tops of ancient trees.

Four does stood in the grass with their coats glistening. Their heads came up as Paul stepped out of the bushes and he held his breath. The deer stared at him with dark eyes speaking of the abyss he'd peered into with the buck. Their fur bounced with the beat of their hearts. Paul raised the rifle but couldn't focus as the world swirled around him.

How does Fauna do it? She must get awfully close. He tried to set the front sight in the cradle of the rear one. A doe floated on the little dot at the end, staring back at him.

The noise of the gun deafened him and the flash seared his eyeballs.

She stared back and Paul aimed again. Heat rose from the barrel in colored filaments that made the sights dance. He fired and missed and emptied the gun as the deer fled into the trees.

"Shit!" A rush of shame roiled him and he saw the eyes of the buck in the refuge they'd shared as he reloaded. They flared brilliant red and he began to fall into them. He really shouldn't have even *tried* to shoot. He was too high.

Distant laughter made him glance around. When he glanced back across the meadow, a doe was stepping daintily through a dewy patch of ivy-like salal toward him.

Paul ran a hand over his eyes. When he took it away she was still there. He lowered the rifle and walked toward her, and they met in the center of the meadow an arm's distance away. Her skin quivered beneath her coat, making her fur dance as she lowered her head and pressed it against his thigh. He saw the other deer watching from the trees as he put a trembling hand across her forehead. Her eyelashes tickled his palm.

"Thank you." He clapped his hands. "Now... *get!*"

The doe spun in a blur, leaving colored trails in the air as she bounded away. He heard laughter and scanned the forest for the woman who had been his lover in dreams... or perhaps it was the Cheshire Cat. Paul dropped the rifle in the grass and spread his arms to the world.

* * *

On the seventh morning Darla rolled over on the bed and sighed. "I want to go to Takilma."

He stroked her cheek. "Okay."

"I miss Fauna and I promised to come see Danielle on the east fork." She watched shadows play on the canvas overhead. "And I want a teepee like this."

"Me too. I want to live in the woods forever and grow pot."

"It's so peaceful. Sunshine is nice to let us stay here."

"She gets scared at night."

"Well? She's only fourteen."

"Oh, yeah."

They hugged and kissed the denizens of China Gardens, left Bozo with them for the time being until they'd cased Takilma, and hauled their stuff to the truck. When Paul turned the key, the battery was dead. Rick jumped it from his Studebaker pickup, and the engine groaned to life with a rattle of valves and a thud to fall into rhythm one more time. Rick didn't have any oil and they drove out the gravel road hoping they'd make it to Cave Junction. Summer was past its prime and the blossoms on fruit trees had set into apples, pears and plums in the yards of cabins, houses and ranches they passed.

"Clint was right."

"Huh?"

"After busting the guys from the gypsy camp, the cops swept up a few amateurs and slacked off. He said that would happen." Paul down-shifted for a hill. "I want to mine gold like Gold Dollar Dave. He makes a living at it. You can use it anywhere in the world, and of course I want to grow a lot of pot. I want to be partners next year with Chuck."

"Where did you go the other day?"

"I found a cave and climbed to the high country. I needed the space. I want to explore more caves and mines. There's ancient Indian stuff on the walls of that one up there."

"Paul, I—" The engine made a nasty rattle and Darla frowned. "I hope it doesn't blow up."

"Me too."

"I miss Rayella and Cindy."

"I hope Cindy's not in too much shit."

"Her coach was a total dick. She told me about it. I wish she were with us."

"Here we were hanging with her when she could have been in the Olympics."

"It was karma. She could have got shot by those terrorists in Munich or something. Who knows? Maybe we saved her." Darla grinned. "Cindy's amazing. I mean, the way she can bend any which-way and stuff."

"Sure is."

"Paul?"

"Huh?"

"I missed my period."

He squeezed the big steering wheel.

"Watch the road!"

He let out his breath. "Okay. I mean we both thought we felt it, but I thought you were on BCs."

"I *am,* but I started spacing them out 'cause I couldn't get back to the clinic. That's one of the reasons I wanted to go to Takilma." She put her bare feet on the dash, wiggled her toes on the warm metal, and the glove box fell open. "Shit." She slammed it. "Could just be my body adjusting or something. They're made of hormones and stuff. I don't know how they work."

"Oh great. You and me."

"What?"

"I don't know. You and me. Like having a baby."

"Don't start."

He kissed her cheek. "Okay."

* * *

They gassed up in town, filled the engine with oil, and had a short rib dinner for $1.10 at the New Café. They bought groceries, ran into the tall blonde Paul had fantasized over, and got her to buy them a bottle of whiskey at the liquor store. The blonde who, was named Leah, said that the extra lawmen had left the valley after a few low-level arrests. They picked up a couple hitchhikers, dropped them off across from the bath house, and drove through the "Capital of the Counterculture Wracked with Gruesome Murder" as the Grants Pass Daily Courier trumpeted on its front page.

They drove up the east fork of the Illinois River and Darla

directed him across a narrow bridge with a hole under it in the near bank. "Black Michael says someone tried to blow it up with dynamite but the blast only excavated some dirt 'cause they didn't tamp the charge."

Paul laughed. "Big fucking anarchists."

A half-mile beyond was an airy little cabin made of the ubiquitous recycled gray boards with a garden watered by a black plastic pipe coming down the hill. Danielle was in the garden. She brushed hair from her eyes and waved.

The truck rattled to a stop and Darla got out. "Hi."

"You made it alive. Glad to see you guys." Danielle put down her trowel. "Michael's with the crop. Want a beer?"

Darla laughed. "You sure do."

"Damn straight."

They followed her into a house with rainbows dancing on the walls from stained glass mobiles swinging from sisal twine in the breeze. Danielle opened a big Coleman cooler on the floor, took out three cans of Pabst Blue Ribbon, and they popped the pull tabs and drank. "That's a real bummer 'bout the goat dairy," Danielle said, "and Gus is totally fucked. He got busted by the Feds and is gonna do hard time."

Paul nodded. "That sucks. We lucked out. I hope Rayella gets off."

"I heard they let her go."

"Really?"

Darla clapped her hands. "Halleluiah!"

"That's what Joyce said. Gus took the rap and said everybody else was just watching the property. The pot wasn't on it so they couldn't prove otherwise. He's got so many felonies it doesn't really matter." Danielle took a swallow of beer. "He told Joyce you can keep the rifle. He says you earned it."

Paul squeezed the empty beer can until it folded around his fingers.

"Have another."

He threw it in the trash and took a fresh one from the cooler. "That's decent of him."

"Yeah. He's a crook but a man of honor."

"Where's Rayella?"

"Dunno. I heard she headed north."

The steps creaked as Black Michael came in the door holding a wilted pot plant. He nodded at Paul and Darla as he hung it in the rafters with disgust, took a beer from the cooler, and sat on the porch. "It's not organic, but I'm thinking poison."

"Baby that's wrong."

"I know. I'm just pissed." Michael ran a hand across his forehead. "We need more peanut butter to bait those traps. The other rats ate the brains out of one that was trapped last night and they tripped a couple more traps and ate the fuckin' bait and demolished this plant anyway. I can't keep up with the little brown fuckers." He grinned at Paul. "Little brown fuckers. Does that sound racist?"

"It didn't occur to me."

"I love it here." Michael took a long drink of his beer. "When I retired from the Army and met Danielle, we took a road trip. We camped on the beach near Santa Cruz and people were totally cool with us."

Danielle sighed. "Until we went to the amusement pier."

"Yeah, at the carousel these little punks from Fort Ord started giving me shit for having a white old lady."

"And he ranked all of them."

Michael squeezed her hand. "When I was in uniform anyway. They were just green draftees who'd finished Basic and were partying before Nam," he glanced at Paul and Darla, "but the fuckers insulted Danielle and called her a nigger's slut and shit. They wanted to fight but my lady here kept me from killing their asses. We just split with them calling me nigger and went to dinner on the fishing pier."

"That's fucked."

"And when we got back—"

"They'd slashed all our tires."

Paul looked at the floor. "Bummer."

Darla hugged Michael. "That's fucked."

"Michael was freaking out. I was afraid he was gonna grab his .45 and waste 'em."

"My ol' Colt was calling to me. I was a firearms instructor for the 1911 .45 in the Army." Michael let out his breath, finished his beer, and took another from the cooler. "Thanks for being there baby. Danielle made me get rid of it when we got here."

"I didn't want you to get picked up with it by some redneck cop."

"I love you, but I still miss it."

"We've got a shotgun."

"Just a twenty gauge. Hope that's enough with creeps like those fuckers from the gypsy camp." Michael ran a hand across his balding scalp again. "Shit like that doesn't happen with truly hip people. That's why we're here. I've got a ton of white brothers and sisters and some really cool Indian ones over by Happy Camp."

Danielle hugged him. "And a white old lady from a redneck family in Oklahoma."

"There's rednecks in Cave Junction and around the valley but I don't catch much shit even in town."

"That's 'cause they think we're all crazy."

Darla grinned. "You're like the only black guy around anyway except Abdullah."

"Fuck Abdullah. His name's Tyrone and he's doing the same shit he did in Portland with chicks except he's using religion instead of dope. They're fucking slaves. He thinks Elijah Mohammed is the messiah or something and he's even worse than when he was a junkie because I think he believes in it."

"Who's Elijah Mohammed?" Paul asked.

"Some motherfucker in Chicago with stars and moons on his hat that took over from a vacuum cleaner salesman named Fard who started the Nation of Islam. You know 'em as the Black Muslims." He rubbed his brow. "I got an earful of their stuff and looked into it and even went to some of their meetings at a mosque. They say you guys were created by a mad wizard ten thousand years ago and that all white people are devils." He kissed Danielle's cheek. "Not my thing. I read up on things and found out Mohammed himself had black slaves," he put down his empty beer, "and they don't drink beer either. Anyway glad to see you're still free." He turned to Paul. "Want to see my crop?"

"Sure."

Paul and Michael hiked up the hill.

* * *

Danielle opened another beer for Darla and for herself. "This heat is kicking my ass. I've still got to finish weeding the lettuce and now I feel like taking a nap." She sighed, "It's all gonna bolt unless I screen it anyway."

"Bolt?"

"Yeah. Go to seed instead of leafing out. I'm going to shade it with some netting and see if we can get a last crop."

"I'll help."

Danielle gave Darla a clawed weeding tool and a trowel and they went to the garden. Darla took off her shirt and hung it on the fence. Her hair bleached gold from the sun glowed against her tan and Danielle had the bone-deep tan of someone who'd been outdoors all summer. They finished one row and started another. The sun cooked Darla's back and she wiped hair from a damp face.

The clatter of a truck made them shade their eyes and glance at the road. A blue International Travelall driven by a black man with his hair in cornrows wearing a shiny purple shirt appeared with two veiled women sitting on the bench seat behind him.

"Shit, fucking Abdullah." Danielle growled. "Ignore him."
She swatted at a fly and bent back to weeding the lettuce.

Darla dashed to the garden fence, grabbed her blouse, and
slipped it over her head as the truck came to a halt.

"You," a guttural voice commanded, "clothe yourselves!"

Danielle stood up. "Fuck you Abdullah. Get out of our—"

The door of the truck flew open in a squeal of metal blending
with Abdullah's cry of rage. Danielle stepped back onto the raised
bed and her feet sunk in the soft ground amongst the lettuce plants.
Darla crouched behind a pea trellis clutching the claw tool.

"Suffer the harlot!" Abdullah threw a leg over the fence and
waved a stick with some kind of writing on it.

Danielle threw up her hands. "Go away! Goddammit!"

Abdullah swung the stick and Danielle screamed as a blow
landed across her forearms. She covered her head as more blows
rained across her arms and back.

Darla sprang up from behind the trellis. "Get away! Leave her
alone motherfucker!" She charged down the row with the clawed
weeding tool in her hand, but when she got within six feet, she
stopped staring into Abdullah's yellow eyes in a face contorted with
rage. Darla stared at the tattoo of a spider on his neck as spittle
covered his thinly bearded chin and his lips curled in a snarl. "Leave
her alone!" She waved the tool. "Paul! Michael! *Help!*"

* * *

When they were halfway to Michael's pot patch, they heard a
scream.

"That's Danielle!" Michael bolted down the hill.

They heard Darla calling Paul's name when they were a
hundred yards away followed by, "Go to hell motherfucker! *Get
away!*" Paul found another gear and sprinted past the older man
as the sound of an engine roared to life over the wails of the wom-
en. He pounded around the house with Michael behind him.

Darla was on her knees hugging Danielle. Bloody welts were across Danielle's back, arms, and across her cheekbone and she had the beginning of a black eye.

"Baby!" Michael skidded to a stop, dropped to his knees, and hugged her. "Wha... *Abdullah!*"

Danielle nodded violently, gasped, and blew bloody snot from her nose.

"That guy's a *maniac!*" Darla screamed. "He started yelling at her for not having a top on and came in the garden with a big fucking stick! And those two stupid cows just sat in his truck and peeked out of their fucking veils!"

"Which way did they go?"

"Into town!"

"That's it!" Michael ran to his house and reappeared with a bolt action twenty-gauge shotgun. "Where's my slugs? All I got is birdshot!"

"I don't know!" Danielle sobbed.

Michael jumped in his old Ford pickup and the engine roared to life.

"Wait!" Paul ran to Darla's Chevy as Michael pulled out of the yard. Paul twisted the key in the ignition and stepped on the gas. The engine gave a howl, there was a loud bang, and it turned over a couple of times with a tremendous rattle and died. A cloud of white smoke billowed out from under the hood into the cab and Paul bailed out coughing. Michael was already at the road and Paul sprinted across the hillside for his truck. He leapt on the running board, tore open the door, and landed on the seat beside him. "We'll catch 'em!"

Michael's forehead was knotted in anger. "I'm gonna *get* that motherfucker! Goddamn psycho! Beating my old lady in her own garden! I don't care what he's packing! This is *it!*"

Paul glanced at the receding house and Darla's truck with his .30-30 behind the seat. "Goddamn it!"

The old Ford leapt forward as Michael stomped on the gas and they shot across the bridge and hit Takilma Road at break-neck speed. People along the road shouted at them to slow down and flashed the peace sign as Michael stared straight ahead and accelerated. When they'd reached what served for downtown Takilma, he stood on the brakes.

The Travelall was parked across from a narrow gray board edifice built along the bank of the river with a sign saying **FUNKY EGG COMPANY**, where two dozen black-and-white barred roc chickens scratched in a wire enclosure. Abdullah was talking to a bearded guy named Funky Egg Robert in front of it, who was holding a coffee can full of big brown eggs while the two women in black and white veils waited in the Travelall. The one in white glared from the cloth shrouding her. Paul recognized the blue eyes of Fatima and let out his breath wishing he had his rifle.

Michael yanked on the parking brake and stepped out with his shotgun. Paul jumped out the other side and stood behind the truck watching for weapons, which was all he could do.

A vein throbbed in Michael's forehead. "Yo, motherfucker!"

Abdullah turned from Robert with a smirk. "Your woman needs learning brother. Your ignorance is something you cling to and is of your own choosing, for you have been told. Keep such filth out of Allah's sun and no harm shall come to her."

"Ain't your motherfuckin' moon god's sun! Fuck you!"

Abdullah turned his back with a sneer and Michael held the shotgun in one hand as he approached. Abdullah spat in the road and sprinted for the Travelall, where a worn Winchester .30-.30 was now on the hood of the truck. A door slammed shut as Fatima got back in.

Abdullah laughed as he reached for the rifle. "Prepare to be judged!"

"Fuck, Abdullah… *stop!*"

Abdullah's hands closed on the rifle and Michael fired at his back. Abdullah's body bowed, his hands clawed air, and he hit the blacktop facedown. The girls in the Travelall screamed as Abdullah twitched and howled in a spreading puddle of blood. He tried to rise as Michael re-cocked the shotgun.

Fatima got out and moved toward the rifle. Paul shook off his paralysis and bolted toward the Travelall as she approached in her clumsy robes and he snatched the old Winchester off the hood. Fatima's blue eyes flared with hatred from the confines of her veil.

"Holy shit!" Funky Egg Robert said.

"Allahu Akbar!" Abdullah wailed. *"Allah!"*

Michael lowered the shotgun. "I'm sorry to bring this down Robert. He beat the shit out of my lady in her own garden and he was going for that rifle. You *saw.* Everybody saw. All I've got is birdshot in this thing and I couldn't let him get that rifle."

Someone yelled, "Julie called the cops!"

Paul laid the rifle down on the pavement and bent over Abdullah. He knew about tourniquets but Abdullah's back was peppered with little holes. He didn't know what to do. Bloody bubbles joined like clusters of little grapes as they merged and collected into foam on his purple shirt that blackened as he watched. Abdullah rolled over and gasped. Bloody foam bubbled from his lips and Paul moved away from the fine spray of blood.

Abdullah's yellow eyes found Paul's. "I don't want to die!" A trembling hand rose toward him.

Paul took it and a soul on the edge of death touched his own. "Hang on!"

Abdullah's eyes were black holes like the buck's in his refuge. Like the doe who'd offered herself as he held her with the power of his will amplified by peyote. Paul gazed into the abyss and squeezed Abdullah's hand. "Hold on."

"The cops!"

The sound of sirens came from the direction of the store.

Paul let go of Abdullah's hand, rocked on his haunches, and stared at the sky. He glanced down at the rifle lying on the road and checked for the location of Fatima. Paul took off his shirt, wiped the rifle down, and shoved it under Abdullah with his foot and Abdullah let out a faint groan. Paul stood and put his shirt on.

"Motherfucker." Black Michael dangled the shotgun in callused hands as he took in the crowd that had gathered. "Please everybody tell it like it is. Otherwise I don't stand a chance in this fucking redneck county."

"Allah…"

"Shut the fuck up."

XXVIII.
Curtains

Cops came with their sirens blaring. Michael put his shotgun down in the road and raised his hands in the air. Two sheriffs jumped out of their cars and pointed their weapons at Michael, who was handcuffed and shoved in the back of one. A trooper snatched up the rifle and a half-dozen people shouted that it belonged to Abdullah.

Medic Michael, an ex-green beret smelling of pot, examined Abdullah who shrieked, jerked, and cried to Allah. Medic Michael put a hand on Abdullah's head. "Stay the fuck still please!"

Abdullah's dilated eyes connected with Paul's before they rolled up in his head. He made a croaking sound and died.

Abdullah lay in the road for an hour before the cops let someone put a sheet over him. A big crowd had collected with people yelling it was self-defense and every emergency vehicle in southern Josephine County blocked the road.

When he was asked Paul used the I.D. for James T. Stephens as sheriffs, troopers and paramedics swarmed. Some cologne-drenched guy in a suit with dandruff-sprinkled shoulders and suspicious glances at everyone grilled him about Abdullah's Winchester five times and Paul told him five times that Fatima had placed it on the hood of Abdullah's truck. Robert agreed Abdullah was going for it. The cops ordered the girls in veils to take them off and they refused, eliciting shrieks of protest when a burley sheriff finally did it for them. They patted them down for weapons as the girls cursed in broken Arabic. Fatima had a bayonet under her robes and was as pretty as everyone said.

Danielle and Darla showed up. Darla hugged Paul. Danielle stood crying with her eyes glued to Michael in the back of a trooper car. When the car pulled away, she followed it into Grants Pass with friends.

Paul and Darla stood holding each other in the road as the day ended and the crowd thinned. He stared at the spot on the blacktop where Abdullah had died and made a fist of the hand that had held Abdullah's. He held the bloodstained hand up in front of him. "I've got to wash this off."

Darla slipped an arm around his waist, avoiding the blood on his hands. "I guess we can go to the bath house but we don't even have towels." She brushed hair from a wan complexion and glanced down the road. "We don't even have wheels. The cops are probably going through Michael and Danielle's place and our dead-ass truck is in their yard. Our packs are in it and your rifle's behind the seat."

"I wonder how long they'll believe our I.D.?"

"I don't know. I don't even know how Chuck got it. For all we know it's somebody they want someplace else," she groaned, "and you're a witness."

"Did they check yours?"

"Uh-huh. They didn't say shit."

"They said I have to be at a hearing and wanted an address for me. When I couldn't give one, the trooper said they might have to take me into protective custody to get me to show up and I promised I'd come in tomorrow. They said if I didn't they'd find me."

"Fucking great."

"Yeah," Paul held his hands up again, "I've got to wash this blood off."

She motioned to a dark-haired girl standing on the porch of a house. "Hey, excuse us, can he wash some blood off his hands?"

"Sure." Maryann invited them into one of the most modern homes in Takilma with indoor plumbing and pointed to the bathroom. "Soap, shampoo, towels, use anything you want. Take a fuckin' shower and come smoke a bowl. I saw the whole thing. It was fucked. I hope Michael's not going to get railroaded by those rednecks in Grants Pass. He's such good people. There's a new loofa in the wire basket in the shower."

"Thanks." Paul went in the bathroom.

Maryann loaded the bowl of a bong and passed it to Darla, who flopped on the couch with a groan. "Bad day, huh?"

"Fuck! We're both runaways and he's a witness to a shooting now."

"Isn't your old man the guy who burned out those assholes who killed Moses and Rainbow Bob from the gypsy camp with Fauna?"

Darla ran hands over her face. "Does everybody know that?"

Smoke oozed from Maryann's nose and she nodded. "Pretty much."

The back door opened on a balding long-haired guy with a sandy beard and a smear of dirt on his forehead. He hesitated for a moment but relaxed at the sight of Darla. "They gone?"

"Yeah, Jack."

"Shit." Jack plopped down next to Maryann and snatched the bong out of her hand. "Dammit. There's big-ass fucking spiders under the house."

"We should leave shit there overnight until things calm down."

"I hope nobody saw me. Sometimes I hate living downtown." Jack glanced at the door of the bathroom, from which the sounds of water came.

"That's her old man in the shower. He got Abdullah's blood on him so I said he could wash up."

"Oh." He passed Darla the bong. "What's your name?"

"Darla. That's Paul in the can."

Maryann put an arm around Jack. "Paul's the dude who chased the gypsy fucks off Hope Mountain with Fauna."

Jack nodded. "That was righteous. I saw him getting grilled by the cops. They'll haul him in for a witness without a doubt."

Maryann tossed hair out of her eyes. "Black Michael didn't do shit except protect himself and his old lady. It was self-defense and everybody's got to say so."

Darla rubbed her eyes. "Yeah, he only had birdshot in that shotgun and Abdullah was going for a rifle." She stared out the window at the gathering dusk. "Our truck's broke down up at Michael's and we're both runaways. I don't know what we're gonna do."

Someone knocked on the door and Jack jumped up. "Shit! I hope it's not the cops."

The shower stopped as Maryann went to the door and Jack hid the bong and tray of pot behind the couch. She opened it a crack, stepped back, and threw it wide. "Come on in!"

Fauna glided into the room in her faded hempen poncho.

Darla sprang off the couch. Fauna kissed her on the mouth and put fingers to her lips as she began to speak. Paul came out of the bathroom toweling his hair. When he saw Fauna he dropped the towel and wrapped his arms around both girls.

"God, we're so glad—" Darla began.

Fauna took their hands. "The Goddess told me where to find you. Get dressed."

* * *

Fauna drove them in somebody's truck to their own at Michael and Danielle's and they grabbed their possessions and drove to Hope Mountain. They parked and started up the path in darkness.

"Another night of freedom," Paul whispered.

At the tree house Fauna lit the lamps, hung up her pistol, and they sat on the floor.

Darla rubbed her eyes. "How did you know where we were?"

Fauna lit Mel's red stone peace pipe, offered it to the four directions, and passed it to Darla. She stared at Darla for a long time, then at Paul. "You should go into the wilderness."

Paul put a hand on Darla's stomach. "Where? How will we survive?"

Fauna shrugged. "You will if you were meant to. You're going to have a daughter who should be born free."

"How did you—"

"Let's go somewhere warm. Winter's coming." Darla stared at her toes. "How did you know I think I'm pregnant? No, I know I am."

"Because she's watching you. The Goddess lets some people know things and works through them. I've got friends in Arizona who'll put you up, peyote people with teepees in the mountains above Bisbee in this beautiful valley where Apaches hid out. It's an awesome place to have a baby."

Paul nodded. "That sounds okay."

The fine hairs on Fauna's arms made a halo in the lamplight. Paul burned the image in his mind: *Fauna,* the warrior sprite who'd appeared like a sprite of the forest to show them the way. She was an ally of the spirit who'd guided him this entire life without him knowing it. If Darla was going to have his baby, he wanted it to be a girl like Fauna.

Darla stared at the floor. "I don't know. Maybe Arizona's a good idea. I don't know anymore."

Paul kissed her. "Let's discuss it in the morning."

Darla stared out the darkened window. "You're right Fauna, about everything passing. You hold onto something you care about and it's just *gone.* I feel like I'm a thousand years old."

"You're an old soul."

Paul bit his lip.

"You're both beautiful." Darla ran a hand through windblown hair. Her fingers caught in a tangle and she yanked at it.

"Any day could be our last. We could die in the road like Abdullah, or get busted, or just be scattered to the wind and we'll never see each other again."

Paul reached into his pack and took out the bottles of Chuck's greegree. He levered the cork out of one, took a sip, made a face, and passed it to Darla. She tasted it and her face scrunched up.

Fauna laughed.

Darla passed it to Fauna, wiped her mouth, and sighed. She straightened her back and squeezed both their hands. "This could really truly be *it.*" She closed her eyes. "I'm glad it's with you guys. We'll have this to remember at least." She turned to Paul. "God, baby, don't cry."

Paul swiped at his eyes. "Sorry."

Fauna gazed at the roof. "It's time for the three of us."

* * *

In the morning Paul left his rifle for safekeeping at Fauna's and they went down the mountain. Bozo would have to stay at China Gardens until they had a place somewhere, as hitchhiking with a big dog was too hard. Paul felt guilty about it but there was nothing they could do.

They passed the clinic full of injuries, infections, pregnant girls and cases of the clap. Doc Jim was loading supplies into an ancient one-ton Chevy van with **Babymobile** painted on the side and he waved. When they got to the road, Fauna kissed them and disappeared in the forest.

Darla was the most beautiful woman in the world as the morning light spilled over the peaks and bathed her in its glow and it was the beginning of a new day. "Arizona?"

"Yeah sure. Let's see what happens."

"You never know."

Within minutes an old pickup with two girls stopped.

"Good karma!" Darla said.

They threw their packs in the back and began to jump in when the whoop of a siren made them freeze. The girl driving let out a shriek. Her passenger tossed a joint in the ditch alongside the road as a green sheriff's car pulled up behind them and two men in khaki uniforms got out.

The younger one gave them a hard look, as if he were looking down the barrel of a gun and stabbed a finger at Paul. "Let's see your identification!"

Paul dug it out and handed it to the Man.

The older heavyset cop took Darla's, held it between two fingers, and gave her a smug smile. "So... *what's* your name, young lady?"

"Susan Stevens. It's right there sir."

"You were Darla Argyle when you bought gas in Cave Junction with a credit card and you used the same I.D. when you went to the bank in Grants Pass to get money wired from your mom's account."

"I—"

The young cop waved Paul's fake I.D. "What's this one's name?"

"Don't know yet but he's a witness to that shooting. Both of 'em were staying where Gus had a marijuana garden off Reeves Creek Road with that cute little gymnast from Minnesota and the hillbilly model chick."

The young cop snorted. "What a fucking waste."

The heavyset one grinned. "Hope those guys get the reward." He turned to them. "You two are coming to Grants Pass for a talk. Turn around and put your hands behind your backs." He waved off the girls in the truck. "You can go."

"Wait," Darla blurted, "our packs are in the back."

"Okay." The young cop grabbed their packs and opened the trunk of the trooper car as the older one snapped handcuffs on Paul, took off Paul's belt and knife, and tossed them in the trunk.

The young cop threw the packs in and slammed the trunk shut. "We'll search this crap in town for dope."

"Watch out for needles Jim."

The young one nodded. "Everything these hippies own is fucking diseased."

"We don't have any needles."

"We're not junkies!"

They were shoved in the caged back of the sheriff's car.

Darla's mouth trembled and tears hovered in the corners of her eyes. Paul leaned against her damp cheek and kissed it. He wanted to escape in that instant, to rise out of the car with strides that grew longer and longer like in his dreams until they were flying into the forest and they'd get away forever.

He stared at the reddened rims of her eyes as a tear rolled down her cheek. She sniffed. "What's going to happen?"

"I don't know but it was worth it. Every bit of it. I love you forever Darla and we're going to have a baby."

She bit her lip and the tears began in earnest.

* * *

He saw her once across an office full of desks and uniforms when they were led to separate cellblocks. They locked eyes until she went behind a filing cabinet. Darla reappeared for an instant through a glass partition and was gone.

Paul spent a night in the middle bunk of a crowded six-man cell. The guy below him stunk like he hadn't bathed in a month and kept farting. They allowed Paul a shower before giving him the jail coveralls and he wondered why the bum underneath hadn't taken them up on it. He stared at the green metal bottom of the top bunk and reached out to Darla with every molecule of his spirit until his head hurt. He reached out to Fauna. He reached out to Rayella and Cindy and called with all his might to the spirit, goddess or whatever who had filled his dreams and taken his soul into her own. In the early hours of the morning he fell asleep.

He was running amongst the twisted trunks of trees with a girl whose face kept changing deep into wild mountains away from pursuers whose faces he couldn't see. She grinned like the Cheshire Cat. He knew her scent. They leapt chasms and her laughter woke flocks of bright birds whose wings beat the air like a drum. He was her lover. He was her protector and she was going to have his baby. They found refuge in an ancient mine that became a cave where ghosts whispered secrets from the bowels of the earth. Red eyes flashed in the pale face of a woman beyond beautiful, and he followed her into the labyrinth.

He was trying to light a torch when the voice of a trustee awoke him.

* * *

In the morning they filed to metal tables where watery oatmeal and white bread with a hard pat of butter awaited him next to the worst coffee he'd ever tasted and a cup of orange Tang. He ate in silence listening to inmates bragging of their exploits and the injustices that had befallen them.

A guard appeared and Paul was led to an office for questioning. He was seated at a desk where a gray-haired cop with a silver bar on his collar read paperwork. After a long pause in which Paul scanned his surroundings for some inkling of Darla's fate, the cop glanced up with obvious contempt. "Paul Aaron Hart."

Paul swallowed.

"Your identification was in the lining of your pack."

"Oh."

"You kids have been around this summer. An officer said you were with that crazy chick Fauna on Hope Mountain that runs around naked when he questioned her about those guys from the gypsy camp."

"Yeah I guess. She isn't really naked. She—"

"That's a wild one all right. We know you were at the old goat dairy on Reeves Creek with that runaway from the Olympics too." The cop shook his head. "Did you know there was a fifty-thousand dollar reward for her?"

"Uh, I…"

"What do you know about Gus?"

"Who?"

The Lieutenant chuckled. "Don't rat out your buddies even when they're hardcore criminals who steal cars and sell dope, and who knows… molest little girls?"

"I don't know a Gus, sir."

"Okay right." The cop picked up a sheet of paper and read it. He ran a hand across his face and shook his head. "You'll be glad to know a grand jury decided your buddy Michael Rogers killed that Abdullah character in self- defense anyway."

"Michael Rogers?"

"He goes by Black Michael."

"They let him *go?*"

"Yep." The cop tossed the paper at Paul. "He's a fucking redneck hero now with loggers drinking to him at the Palace Saloon. Hell, he could run for Sheriff. There's an editorial in the *Daily Courier* this morning saying he's the best citizen in Takilma, better than these white hippies who do all the crimes like cutting those poor fuckers heads off and that he's a 'model Negro.' The whole damn ball o' wax." The Lieutenant rubbed a sun-reddened forehead. "He's damn lucky he killed a nigger worse than himself by a goddamn mile. People aren't even bitching about his white girlfriend."

Paul stared at the upside-down sheet of paper. "Holy shit. That's righteous."

The cop leaned on the desk and steepled his fingers like Paul's father did. "Tell me about Chuck."

"Chuck who?"

The cop sat back in his chair with an exasperated sigh, tapped his pen on the desk and stared at the ceiling.

Paul leaned forward. "Where's Darla?"

"I wondered when you were gonna mention that little surfer brat. Too late pal. She's outta here."

"What?"

"Her mom showed up from San Diego. She flew into Medford and took a cab all the way here. Tipped the driver big too." The Lieutenant shook his head. "She's a looker and a goddamn rich one. You can bet her mom bought her something to wear on the plane so she doesn't look like homeless trash on the way back." He glanced at his watch. "They're probably landing in San Diego right now."

A roaring erupted in Paul's ears and he didn't hear the next thing the cop said.

"Hey, I said your folks are coming to pick you up. You're a minor and we don't have anything to hold you on, just a whole lot of fucking questions you're not going to answer." The cop shook his head. "You were probably too goddamn stoned to give a coherent explanation anyway." He gazed out at the hills and pinched his nose. "Jesus Christ, I cannot wait 'til retirement."

Paul stared into space, squeezed his eyes shut, opened them, and forced himself to focus. "Did... did she say anything about me?"

"I don't know pal. I'm not a fucking matron. We got a shitload of trouble from you hippies down there in the Illinois Valley, you're not giving me one *bit* of goddamn help, and I'm not passing love notes from some slutty beach bunny to another goddamn runaway." The Lieutenant grinned. "You got yourself a nice piece of ass anyway if you didn't catch something... or give something to her." He blinked at his own comment, squeezed his nose again and closed his eyes for a moment. "I have no fucking idea what you kids are living for. There's a big goddamn war on, the Weathermen are blowing people up, the niggers are running wild in the streets and you're all just floating around in LSD land with orgies and people getting their heads cut off and every other kind of unimaginable crazy shit."

The cop slapped his desk. "No fucking ambition, no morals... no fucking sense at *all!*" The Lieutenant steepled his fingers again and tried to bore a tunnel through Paul with his stare. He put palms on the desk and sighed. "Tell me kid... what the hell *is* it?"

Paul closed his eyes and Darla's hair flashed in the sun as she disappeared in the trees. He opened them and let out his breath. "It's... hard to explain officer."

XXIX.
The Break

Paul shoved the assignment across the desk and stared at a gray morning. An osprey dropped from the top of a phone pole and seemed to float motionless for a moment before it headed out to sea. Paul ran a hand through his newly shorn hair and let out his breath as part of him followed the bird.

"I expect at least five pages for credit. I want you to find a storyline that's both coherent and interesting, if that's not asking too much." Miss Lasher was saying. "You'll be graded both for punctuation and grammar, but the story itself will count for sixty-five percent of your grade. It's due Friday so I suggest that you get busy."

Susan Allen raised her hand. "What if we didn't do anything interesting this summer Miss Lasher?"

Miss Lasher turned her trademark stare upon Susan, eliciting the girl's visible retraction against the back of her chair. "Everybody did *something* Miss Allen. Since you went to Europe, I assume you're asking that to make other people feel uneasy."

The bell rang for lunch and Paul swept the paper into his notebook.

People were heading to the cafeteria. The rains of winter had begun the week before and the tables outside under an awning were empty and wet. He grabbed the lunch bag from his locker, walked outside, and the door shut on the babble behind him to be replaced by wheeling seagulls squawking in the damp breeze. He brushed off the film of water on the beige tabletop and, when it was somewhat dry, sat on top of it with his feet on the bench. Mr. Van Treska always yelled at him for sitting like that but nobody was around.

What the hell does it matter? Fuck him.

The miserable ride back to Charleston with his parents had begun a slowing of time, a cessation of motion that deepened as they approached the coast until he felt encased in cement. His mother had cried. His father had ground his teeth until the muscles stood out in his neck. His brother had sneered from behind the wheel of his new Ford pickup when he arrived at the house from a logging contract near Coquille. The fall semester had already begun and when he got to school Susan Allen acted as if she'd never even known him. She was going with a jock who looked like Terry Cox.

* * *

It took three days of begging to get his knife back. He'd lain on his bed that night turning it in his hands and staring at the blood that had seeped between the sections of the laminated leather handle.

Tweedledee or Tweedledum? Probably both.

The following night he was playing with the knife on his bed staring at the tops of fir trees on the ridge above town when he turned the sheath over and saw the number Darla had scratched on the back of it. Paul jumped up with his heart in his throat, tore apart his bedroom, and found enough change. He opened the second story window and dropped to the muddy drip-line where water always pounded the grass flat when it came off the roof. He made a wide detour around his parents' motel and ran to a phone booth by the harbor in Charleston beside a noisy fishermen's bar.

The operator waited as he thumbed in quarters, dimes and nickels, and the phone finally rang in a place called La Jolla. After four rings, someone picked it up.

The husky voice of a female who'd smoked for many years answered. "Hello?"

Paul stood at a door that had swung open a crack as a landscape of hope beckoned from the other side. "Is... is Darla there?"

"Who's this?"

"This is Paul."

"Paul?"

He held the heavy black receiver smelling of tobacco and stale beer away from his face and answered in a firm voice. "This is Paul Hart, me and Darla were together and—"

"The kid she ran off with?"

"Um, yes ma'am."

The chuckle on the other end almost sounded kind. "You got balls kid, but I expect that probably had a lot to do with it. Darla isn't here."

"Wh... where is she?"

"She's staying with her fiancée if you want to know."

"What?"

"You're the one who got her pregnant you little fucker. Who do you think you are anyway?"

His head spun as Paul leaned against the cold glass of the booth.

"She's back with her real boyfriend and she's getting *married*, Paul." Something between a growl and a sigh of resignation came from the other end of the line. "We could have done something about it but she's dead set on keeping it. Darla's a hard-headed kid as I suppose you know. Thank God that it's early enough nobody will ask questions after they're married. She says you two look alike anyway." The woman sighed again. "Look, she's my daughter and I can't blame you for liking her. I know her. Shit, she's beautiful. I was just as much a fuckup myself at that age and it was probably Darla's idea anyway at least at the start. But Darla's getting married and her past is *past.* Get it?"

"But... I, did she say anything about me?"

"Jesus, of course she did. She says you're a good kid and it's all her fault anyway, which I don't believe, but at least that says she cares about you. She's big-hearted and that's her problem but she's marrying a Scripps and she has her whole life ahead of her Paul."

"What's a Scripps?"

Her laughter was a cold tide of scorn pouring from the phone to join the damp air around him. "Darla's going to be one so maybe you'll find out someday. Look Paul, I'm sure you're a good kid. She says you have a scholarship or something so go and finish school, go to college, and maybe someday you'll deserve a girl like her too when you can afford to take care of her."

"Do you have her number?"

There was silence followed by a heavy exhalation. "You're not *listening* kid! That's the problem with all you cocky little fuckers running off to find Nirvana. It's time to get back to reality. Listen: you're not going to talk to her and she's not here anyway so don't call anymore. Have a good life and goodbye."

The dial tone roared and the operator came on asking for another seventy-five cents.

* * *

He stared at the half-eaten sandwich reliving that last conversation with the only person who might tell him anything about Darla ever again. His mom was making them extra nice since he'd gotten home but he hadn't even tasted it. It looked like corned beef. He turned it over in his hand and dropped the other half in the bag. He wanted to cry but couldn't. He wanted to feel something again, something *real,* and he really wanted to touch a girl.

Paul tossed the bag in a trashcan with four inches of rainwater in the bottom of it and headed across the half-flooded running track through the fence off the school grounds to the street as visions of liberating Darla from some tile-roofed mansion behind high walls and palm trees danced through his mind. A beat-up pickup truck cruised by and he stepped away from the curb just in time to avoid being splashed. The rain had slackened to a fine mist. He wiped water from his face and quickened his pace.

He didn't know where he was going. He was just going.

He stepped under the canopy of two big maples in the yard of an old Victorian home from the heyday of logging as the mist slackened. Something scampered along a branch and he looked up. When his gaze returned to the level, he saw a girl sitting against the trunk of the far tree. She was small and cute with shoulder-length dirty blond hair. She had her knees under her chin with her hands around her ankles and looked like Cindy.

"Hey."

The girl blinked big blue eyes and came back from wherever she'd been. She sized him up for an instant, held his gaze for another and seemed to relax. "Hey."

"What are you doing?"

"You mean not in school?"

"Yeah, I guess."

"I hate it here. My mom hauled me here from Idaho after the divorce and I hate the rain and I hate that high school. People are fucked-up." She exhaled and gazed into the mist. "I'm warning you, I'm bad luck to hang around. I don't have any friends here. Some girlfriend of yours probably hates me already and you'll probably give me bullshit too."

Paul stifled a laugh as he climbed the stone retaining wall and crossed the lawn to her. He wiped away a couple yellow maple leaves on the grass as big as his head and slid down next to her with his back against the tree. "It sucks here doesn't it?"

She brushed damp hair from her cheek. "Shit, yes. It's so *boring.* I just want to go somewhere that's away from my mom's boyfriend but I don't have any money or anything else." She stared into the branches overhead. "Life sucks."

"I know a place."

She shot him a look. "Yeah that's what you say, but I don't even know you dude."

He extended a hand. "I'm Paul."

She blinked. "I'm Paulette."

For the first time since he'd been back, Paul laughed. *"Really?"*

"Yeah, my dad's named Paul, honest. He wanted a Paul Junior."

"I had a friend named Rayella like that. Her dad wanted a Ray. That's got to be some cool karma we kinda have the same name. You believe in it?"

Her eyes flicked over his face as she licked her lips and sighed. "You're cute. Your eyes look almost golden or something with little flecks of red." She stared into his. "I've never seen eyes like that. You're a trip."

"You're cuter." Paul pressed his shoulders against the bark of the ancient maple and gazed in the canopy imagining a flash of eyes and a fleeting grin. He turned to Paulette and stared into her real blue ones. "I know an incredible place to go. Honest."

Paulette gave him a sideways glance. "Really?"

"Uh-huh. There's lots of places to stay and really cool people, and I've got a deal where I can make a lot of money too. Do you... you know..." He made a gesture of putting a joint to his lips.

"Get high?"

"Yeah."

"Yes! I'm dying for a joint! You got one?"

"No but I know where there's whole patches of pot with the coolest people in the world growing it and it's harvest time. I have friends there that will give us pot for free. There's like whole forests of it. Ever do acid?"

"No."

"Peyote's even better. There's a spirit in it that I can teach you about. I'm not lying. Really. People are following the ways of the Indians there and you can even talk to animals sometimes. I did."

Paulette's eyes were huge. "Wait… *really?*"

He felt the huge smile on his face, overjoyed to be in the first real conversation he'd had since the world had collapsed. "There's swimming holes where people go naked but you're safe and I've got this friend Fauna who runs around all summer with almost nothing on except a six-gun. She grows pot and hunts deer and knows all these Indian rituals handed down from medicine men and shamans. She's the coolest chick you'll ever meet and can talk with telepathy. She's the bravest chick I ever met too." He shook his head. "She never cries from pain when she's hurt. I think she's from a higher plane or something. I saw her sew up her own arm once when it was cut like hell I swear. We can stay at her treehouse and her friend Mel has a house built onto the tunnel of an old mine that goes into the mountains."

"A treehouse?"

"I know where we can live in a teepee too." He took a breath and scanned her face for a reaction. "And if you're like a vegetarian there's lots of people like that there too. China Gardens has lots of cool people like that."

Her eyes widened. "God… my mom will be so pissed!" She kicked at the leaves. "Fuck her. All she ever does is yell at me anyway." Suddenly Paulette sprang back against the tree. "Yuck!" She grabbed the stem of a maple leaf and poked at a huge green banana slug oozing across the damp lawn. "I wish I had some salt. I hate those things!" She turned to him. "My mom's such a bitch. A teepee… really?"

He gazed at her up-turned nose glistening in the mist. His hand closed over hers, and small strong fingers wound in his own like a flower blooming in his grasp. "You don't deserve to get yelled at. I know that."

"I hate her new boyfriend. He's a jerk. He tried to kiss me last night when he was drunk and she didn't even believe me. I really, *really* don't want to go home!" Paulette ground her feet in the grass. "Do you really know a good place, honestly, where people live in the woods and stuff and it's safe?"

"No bullshit. I swear. I just left there and I have friends that will turn us on to a place to stay. They grow this super strain of pot without seeds and a guy wants me to come in as a partner and I know where there's gold mines too, and caves..." He gazed at the fog-shrouded trees and the gray Pacific. "I can't stand it here either." He took a breath. "How old are you anyway?"

"Fifteen."

The tree against his back gave a heave and something scampered through the branches. "Cool. Ever hitchhike?"

"No."

"It's easy if you're a girl. I mean getting a ride is, and I'll protect you. My parents are at work and we can get my stuff and I have a gun to protect us when we get there."

"A gun?"

"Yeah, a .30-.30 for hunting and stuff. I left it with Fauna."

"I went hunting with my dad." Paulette's jaw tightened and she stared out to sea. "He's the coolest guy. My mom's just a bitch with an asshole boyfriend."

"I know where there's this old homestead that has nobody in it where we can live for free. I made a swimming hole there this summer with dynamite."

She put her chin on her knees. "I have to get into the apartment while my mom's working at the bar."

"What about her boyfriend?"

"He's at the mill, if he ever got his worthless ass up."

"I can break in."

She burst into giggling. "God, they'll *freak!*" She stared at Paul and he stared right back. "You look okay but can I believe you? You're not messing with me, and you're cool, swear?"

He held up his right hand. "Swear on my life."

Paulette closed her eyes and took a breath. "All right. I know where he hides his money too."

"Cool."

"And I know where he hides the keys to his other truck."

"That's bitchin'. We can drive it all the way then."

"But won't we get busted driving it around?"

"No. I know where there's an old mine shaft where we can drive it in and leave it. I can get dynamite from a friend and we can blow the tunnel up so nobody ever finds it."

Paulette's mouth dropped open and Paul stared at her lips. "Really, can I set it off?"

"Sure. I'll show you how. It's fun."

A laugh erupted from her throat and she grabbed his hand. "That'll really piss him off!" She tossed hair away from her eyes and stared into his. "You're not bullshitting me, are you?"

For an answer he kissed her.

The End

Acknowledgements

Gratefully acknowledging the yeoman's work by my editor Mara Renee Briana Hodges and the wizard of Montag Press Collective, Charlie Franco.

Bruce Lee Bond hitchhiked around the west during what was called the Summer of Love at the age of seventeen, and was in many a refuge and commune of what was called the Counter-culture through his twenties. He studied creative writing at San Francisco State College, Journalism at the University of Oregon, furthered his education at the University of Alaska and has published numerous short stories and this his fifth published novel. He has traveled the continent extensively and studied with a Lakota medicine man on the Rosebud Reservation in South Dakota at the age of twenty-two. He built cabins in the wilderness of Alaska and the pacific northwest, lived on homesteads and built a log home in the Alaskan wilderness where his children came into the world. He has lived amongst characters like those portrayed in this novel, most of whom are based on actual people. Unlike many of them he is alive at this printing.